# Two Falling Voices

## Philip Basham

| | |
|---|---|
| AUTHOR: | Philip Basham |
| COVER DESIGN: | Philip Basham |
| | H. Donald Kroitzsh |
| COVER PHOTOGRAPHY: | Lesley Soutar |
| LAYOUT: | H. Donald Kroitzsh |

Four Elms Press
FourElms@usa.net

Published by:
Four Elms Press
New York USA

Printed and Bound in Canada

Prepared by:
Five Corners Publications, Ltd.
5052 Route 100
Plymouth, Vermont 05056 USA

**Two Falling Voices**
**ISBN: 0-9705849-0-3**

For Kevin and Carrie

# Sunday

❀

My mom loved this place. Her body lies on Temple Hill, but her spirit is right here. I can place flowers on her grave and shed tears on her headstone, but I can only seek her guidance here in the Park.

I have been away for just a week and, in that time, the birches have transformed from green to yellow, the dogwoods from red to a luscious maroon and the pinnate leaves of the sumac from bronze to a deep crimson. October here never fails to dazzle, the kaleidoscopic brilliance of the fall foliage - the reds of the maples, the golds of the chestnuts, the yellows of the larches - setting the hillsides ablaze. This is a place the Seneca called Seh-ga-hun-da, the vale of the three falls. They believed that the sun hung over the Genesee River gorge so as to admire its beauty. As I stand at Inspiration Point and look down the precipitous valley, I can certainly understand their reasoning. The river's crashing descent takes it over three breathtaking waterfalls, plummeting in all almost two hundred fifty feet through a sheer-faced ravine, its walls six hundred feet high. Rainbows hover in the spray as turkey vultures circle overhead and the songs of warblers and waterthrush mingle with the music of the cascading Genesee as it traces its ancient path northwards to Lake Ontario.

My home is in Geneseo, less than thirty minutes away, so the Park has been a constant in my life, a sort of touchstone, a place where I have come in the happiest and the saddest of times. Here, I can celebrate amidst extraordinary splendor or mourn in absolute solitude. It is comforting and uplifting, peaceful and familiar.

When winter comes, the early snows paint the skeletal trees with fringes of pure white, the monochrome scene cast against a frosted earth and a solid gray sky. In the spring, flowers bloom along the thawing trails and the river runs faster and clearer, icy cold and frothing in the cataracts. By summer, many of the trails have dried and cracked, the soil compacted by a stream of visitors who come to camp out in the sylvan wilderness. It can be so very hot here in July and August, though at almost any time a sudden shower can pass through. Those downpours have magic about them, invigorating the air, energizing it. Thunder will rumble down the valley and the sun will stream in shafts through the leaden clouds. Then, just as suddenly as it arrived, it will be gone. Steam will rise from the grass as the rain evaporates and the scent of lobelia, roused and refreshed, will waft in the gentle breeze.

It is in the fall, however, that I come here most. I read somewhere that there is no biological function or significance associated with the resplendent colors of the foliage. Instead, they are merely a by-product of each tree's chemical changes as it prepares for winter dormancy. This only confirms the lack of romance in science. What I see is not the functionality of nature, but its glory.

When my mom died, I found an old Fortnum & Mason biscuit tin, full of photographs, which she kept in a drawer in the third bedroom, my sister's room, though she never slept there. Amongst those pictures were a handful taken the day after my christening in October 1960. My dad's parents had come over from England, their second trip here, the last time my dad saw his father alive. Although I had been born in May, Mom had wanted the christening in October so that my grandparents could see the fall colors. They drove up through the Park, from Portageville to Mount Morris, stopping off at the Middle Falls, where a photograph was taken of Grandma holding me in her arms, my mom looking on, her woolen cardigan buttoned to her neck and a head scarf tied about her coal black hair. There is also a picture of my dad raising me above his head, the great concrete wall of the Mount Morris Dam in the background. The faces are full of happiness, in distinct contrast to the rather somber picture taken the previous day on the steps of St. Michael's Church in Geneseo. With the christening ceremony over, the guests had gathered for a formal photograph, taken by Jimmy Randolph, a friend of Grandpa Holton. In that shot, an archetypal image of my family, my dad is staring into the distance, a questioning expression frozen on to his face. Mom cradles me lovingly, her own expression a little dreamy, a sort of dazed grin encapsulating pride and joy. John and Edith Wright, Dad's parents, seem wary and ill at ease in their aging and fashionless clothes. Grandma Holton stands shoulder-on to the camera, glowering, her white purse clenched in her bony little white-gloved hands. Beside her, Grandpa is the only one wearing a real smile, one that transcends his constant pain, the dreadful pain of his cancer which has already eaten away a third of his weight and left his face gaunt, his posture stoic, but manifestly brittle.

Grandpa Holton died just over three years later, five years before Grandma. I have no clear memory of him, just a vague awareness of his presence. He was so ill during that final winter that he was taken up to the hospital in Rochester. He had withered away to less than a hundred pounds and was unable to ingest solid foods. They hooked him up to a drip and a heart monitor, pumped him full of morphine and waited for him to die. No-one pretended that he would recover, the only hope was for a painless end. On the last day of February in 1964, Grandpa slipped into a bottomless sleep from which he never wakened, passing away in the middle of the night as snow flickered down outside the window of his room.

Along with the Fortnum & Mason tin, the drawer in the third bedroom was home to a long, shallow box. In there I found various oddments and keepsakes, including a hand-written list of the people from whom Grandma and Mom had received messages of condolence. I guess Mom had made the list so that she could send acknowledgement cards. The names were ordered in two columns on both sides of the paper, so many names, well over a hundred. They included what then remained of our family, plus Grandpa's friends, like Jimmy Randolph and Teddy Hewson and Franklyn Petersen.

Franklyn's father had been a carpenter and had worked here at the Park in the early 1900s, when the place was still owned by William Pryor Letchworth. Franklyn and Grandpa used to come here all the time back in the thirties and forties, usually with Raymond, Franklyn's son, and, of course, my mom. Between them, the two elder men seem to have instilled into their children their own sense of reverence for the Park, for its feel, for its almost religious majesty. From the time I was old enough to walk, Mom brought me here, too, the two of us picnicking up at the Tea Table or over near the Parade Grounds, while my dad sweated through another shift at the timber mill six miles away in Nunda. She used to sit with me by the river and tell me about the pioneers who settled here before the Civil War and about William Pryor Letchworth and about the native peoples, the Seneca, whose land this once was. She told me, also, of Mary Jemison and of Mon-a-sha-sha, a young Seneca bride who perished with her infant child in the falls and how legend says that their spirits live on in the park's white-tailed deer.

I used to find that story amusing, whimsical, but now I realize how people can come to think in that way. There is an atmosphere here, heavenly in its way, a sense that spirits are whispering in the leaves and singing in the falls and, yes, maybe even dancing in the effortless grace of the deer. Certainly I can feel the essence of my mom here, a feeling that has drawn me before to share with her my troubles and my pleasures. I have begged her forgiveness,

I have sought her blessing, but now I need her good sense to show what path I should take.

Yesterday's afternoon flight into JFK landed ten minutes ahead of schedule. It had departed from Heathrow on a sunny English morning and had arrived back in New York to gray skies and the threat of rain, the 747 bucking and bouncing its way through the thick, low cloud, then gliding on to the runway with hardly a bump. My friends Steve and Sally Caspar met me in the arrivals hall and drove me out to their place in Westchester, where I had left my car the previous weekend. Steve is an old colleague from The Greenleaf Corporation.

The Caspars gave me good company, hot food and a bed for the night, all of which were welcome after a week of wearing death like an old coat. My sleep, though, was shattered by vivid, fevered dreams. I woke early, dressed, found orange juice in the refrigerator, then sat in the glistening white kitchen, drinking and reading yesterday's *New York Times*, until Steve came downstairs just after eight o'clock and I was able to make my polite good-byes

I set off for Geneseo along the New York State Thruway, which is named for Thomas E. Dewey. Dewey was a man of Michigan whose career as a racket-busting US attorney won him three terms as Governor of New York. He was also the GOP's presidential candidate in 1944, when he lost to FDR, and again in '48, when Truman defeated him. These are the sort of details us would-be history graduates find so fascinating. I blame my mom.

When I was about seven years old, Mom began to teach me about the towns and cities in our corner of the state. She would lay out a big map on the table in the back room and point out names like Naples and Geneva and Warsaw and Hamburg, names from all over the world sprinkled across western New York. Belfast, she told me, takes its name from a city in Ireland, Cuba from a country in the Caribbean. Caledonia was once called Southampton, but was renamed by Scottish settlers; Dansville was named for Captain Dan Faulkner, village storekeeper in the late eighteenth century. Out east of here, beyond Conesus Lake, is Livonia, named for a province on the Baltic Sea, once conquered and converted to Christianity by the Livonian Knights. The town of Mount Morris, birthplace of Francis Bellamy, author of the Pledge Of Allegiance, and of Major John Wesley Powell, that great explorer of the Colorado River, was named for a man called Robert Morris, one time local land owner. Even the hamlet of Hunt has a story; Washington Hunt, a member of the founding family, was State Governor and his sister-in-law, Helen Hunt Jackson, is widely known for her writings on Native Americans, especially the novel *Ramona* and the non-fiction work *A Century Of Dishonor*.

As a child, I often wished for rainy days, knowing that Mom would fill the time by spreading out the map, sometimes on the table, sometimes on the floor of my bedroom. I was like a sponge, soaking up facts, absorbing names and dates, committing to memory all the legends and stories my mom had herself learned from a lifetime in this corner of the vast continent that is our nation.

Teenage years dulled the zeal with which I had once gathered such information, my mom's voyages of discovery around the, by then, ragged map seeming dreary by comparison with the lure of science class and baseball and David Bowie and, latterly, a doe-eyed Italian girl called Linda Danelli. It was a time of boundless energy and burning desire, a time when I wanted not to venerate the beautiful region of my upbringing and dwell upon its rich history, but to escape its tedium, its depressing parochialism, its far-flung detachment from an exotic world of infinite possibilities that I believed existed beyond the distant Hudson. I used to complain that living in Geneseo was like living in a museum. What delicious irony there is in that: back in 1991, the Department of the Interior designated the village as a National Historic Landmark, so now, in some ways, it actually *is* a museum.

I am reminded of this every time I drive into the village, just as I did this morning, and pass the historic marker near the Village Square Park, one of many now dotted about the quiet streets. There is one at the corner of Lima Road and Rorbach Lane, maybe two hundred yards from where my house stands, a marker recording the existence of a Civil War camp where men from the area were trained before going off to join the 104th New York Volunteer Infantry. My mom always reckoned that the back garden of the house must have once been where the camp's horses were kept, so strong and fertile is the soil. I have managed to keep alive most of the shrubs she planted, though I cannot claim to be a natural at gardening, either in aptitude or ability. My dad was much better, indeed the garden was largely his exclusive domain once Mom became too ill to tend the flowerbeds and prune the bushes. She would simply sit in a chair on the patio, usually wrapped in a blanket or thick coat, irrespective of the weather, and watch Dad weeding or mowing or dead-heading the rhododendrons and the chrysanthemums. She died sitting in that chair, slipped away while Dad watered the peonies he had planted out the previous fall. By the time the peonies flowered again,

Mom was resting on Temple Hill and Dad was back in his English homeland. He asked me to sell the house for him; I tried, half-heartedly, but soon realized I could not bear to see the place occupied by another family. That is when I decided to move back to Geneseo, to live in my parents' house, the house where I had been born and raised. I told Dad I would pay him rent, but he said that he wanted no money from me and that I might as well have my inheritance early. Now Dad is gone, too, but the peonies continue to thrive in the earth that may once have been enriched by the horses of Wadsworth's Guards.

Bobbie Petersen took care of the house while I was away at Dad's funeral and she saw me arrive back around lunchtime today. She is Franklyn Petersen's granddaughter, the daughter of Franklyn's younger son, Charlie, who lives these days down in Florida with his wife Rose. Like me, Bobbie lives in her childhood home, Charlie and Rose having signed their house over to her when they decamped to the warmth of Fort Myers. She is just a few weeks younger than I am and has a daughter called Becky, who turned nine a month ago. I would say that Bobbie is my closest friend; she knows when to call, when to drop by to talk, when to invite me over for dinner and particularly when to leave me alone. She was raking leaves in her garden when I drove past earlier; she looked up and waved, but she did not expect me to stop, was not offended that I preferred to go straight home, rather than make conversation. She knows I will go to see her when I am ready, probably tonight.

I dumped my bags in the hall, flicked through the mail that Bobbie had piled on the bureau in my study, then went to my bedroom and changed into an old pair of pants and a thick, checked shirt. Back in the car again, I drove down to Main Street, past the Geneseo Building and Village Square Park, and out of the town towards Cuylerville, where Route 37, the River Road, branches off to the Park's northern entrance. Coming in that way means passing close by the dam, then following the Park Road as it skirts the Hogs Back before crossing the Silver Lake Outlet, which carries water from the lake, four miles to the west, down to the Genesee. The sky today was mostly blue, milky clouds shrouding the sun from time to time and dappling the hillsides with light and shade. As I drove, I could see the aspens, always late to turn, still clothed in their shimmering green leaves. There, too, were scarlet oaks, passing through russet on their way to dark brown, and creamy striped maples and bright yellow hornbeam. Past St. Helena, the road sweeps right, then doubles back upon itself having crossed the

Wolf Creek. The junction with the Castile road is near Big Bend, a giant horseshoe curve that the river enters heading west and leaves heading east. Presently, one is offered the choice of bearing left to the Lower Falls or right towards Inspiration Point and the Middle Falls, close to which is the Glen Iris Inn.

Here at the Point, I can see all the way to the end of the Portage Canyon, a view that takes in the Middle and the Upper Falls, above which the Erie-Lackawanna Railroad trestle crosses the river. This is where most visitors come, the most photographed view in the Park, I would presume. Judging by the pictures that Mom kept in the Fortnum & Mason tin, it seems that everyone *she* brought here was pictured at this spot - my dad's parents, my Uncle Michael and Aunt Angela, my cousin Valerie, Kelly's folks up from Pennsylvania for our wedding. In May 1917, on the ninety-fourth anniversary of William Pryor Letchworth's birth, a bronze plaque was unveiled here. It carries the words from a poem, written in 1909 by Sara Evans, wife of one of Letchworth's nephews:

> *God wrought for us this scene beyond compare,*
> *But one man's loving hand protected it*
> *And gave it to his fellow men to share.*

Before I was twelve years old, I knew those lines by heart, just as I knew the names of all the trails and the height of the railroad trestle and the stories of the ghost towns and the canal and the Civilian Conservation Corps. I still remember everything. I sometimes wonder whether my super-retentive memory is a blessing or a curse. Even in those teenage years, when I tried so hard to wash away all trace of that historical paraphernalia and supplant it with other statistics, like RBIs and ERAs, with chemical formulae and the rules of trigonometry, with the lyrics from *Ziggy Stardust* and the names of the Apollo astronauts, even then it proved obdurate, immovable. Passing time has imbued some understanding of this, revealed, albeit gradually, the recognition that, once learned, such things are intrinsically permanent. That history, *my* history, is as much part of me as my skin and bones.

Moses Holton lived in the town of Cirencester, which is set in the heart of the English county of Gloucestershire. Much about my knowledge of Moses' life involves the word circa. He was born circa 1700, set sail for the New World circa 1735 and arrived in Savannah, Georgia circa 1738. I have no idea why it appears to have taken him three years to make his way across the Atlantic and can only assume that his route to Savannah was not entirely direct. The problem with Moses Holton is that he was not the sort of man about whom records were made, let alone kept. He was, according to family tradition, a ne'er do well, who survived more by good fortune than honest labor and who, when his luck eventually deserted him, found himself in a debtors' prison before he was even thirty years old.

Like many who encountered the same predicament, Moses was saved by the concern of James Oglethorpe. While serving as a member of the British parliament, one of Oglethorpe's duties had been to chair the committee on prison reform, experience from which had led to him persuading parliament to grant him and his associates trusteeship of the colony of Georgia. There, they had created both a refuge for debtors and religious exiles and a military presence so as to deter attacks on South Carolina by the French and the Spanish. Oglethorpe had founded Savannah in 1733 and had immediately begun to encourage the immigration of persecuted Protestants from all over Europe. Five years later, the first of my forebears to reach American soil arrived in the form of Moses Holton.

There is another circa associated with Moses, this being the year of his death, which I believe to have been around 1750. Life's toll upon Moses had been severe and that same family tradition that paints him as a rogue also tells of his never passing his own half-century. I always caution myself, however, that this tradition covers a period, now, of almost three hundred years, so it is likely to have deviated somewhat over time and its accuracy must now be doubtful.

If I accept that Moses did indeed die at the age of, say, forty-nine, I can only marvel at the resourcefulness of his wife, Ann Newbury, who was fourteen years his junior and who was widowed at a time when the oldest of her three children was only eight. Ann had married Moses when she was twenty-four and more recently arrived in Georgia even than her new husband. Evidently the two lived together a life of near poverty, as Moses drifted from job to job, the pattern of his days closely mirroring the tangled web he had woven in England. The first-born child was James, who, that dubious tradition purports, was named for General Oglethorpe, a man Moses is reckoned to have worshipped. After James came a daughter, Charlotte, then a second son, William.

The first hard evidence of this family unit appears in papers dating back to 1754, when Ann Holton moved with her children to join her cousin,

Estelle McCarthy, in the colony of Pennsylvania, making the long journey by ship. One distant branch of the McCarthy clan had money, generated by a tailoring business that supplied clothes to Philadelphia's elite. This business prospered well into the next century before it finally folded, though, amazingly, its account books and employee registers were retained by the McCarthy's descendants and are now in the possession of Robert McCarthy Sefton of Fairfax, Virginia. The registers show Estelle McCarthy working for the company for some years prior to the time Ann Holton joined the workforce. As I leafed through the pages, I soon found James, Charlotte and William Holton, each becoming an employee at the age of twelve, their dates of birth recorded by the flourishing sweeps of a practiced quill pen.

So, Ann Holton and her children went to live with her cousin Estelle and they all worked for a firm owned by kinfolk so far removed that they saw fit to grant them only the most menial of jobs. Certainly, at this earliest stage of my maternal family's presence in America, prospects were looking none too good and, rather than improving in the cradle of the Revolution, they got worse. James Holton, legendarily a fearsome youth, took up with a gang of laborers who were hired by Charles Mason and Jeremiah Dixon to help clear the path of their great line, which was intended to designate the geographical limits of Pennsylvania. In the spring of 1765, by means unknown, James Holton was poisoned. I suspect there is nothing colorful or felonious about this, especially as James's passing goes unrecorded in any of the official histories and merits only the most cursory reference in just one contemporary journal. 'Died today,' wrote Joshua Shaw, a wheelwright, 'Jas. Holton. Toxic Fever.' Most likely, I would suggest, is his having eaten wild berries or deadly fungi, or maybe, even more prosaically, a bowl of stew from one of the expedition's inevitably unhygienic chuck wagons. Whatever; James was gone, aged twenty-three, which means he survived one more year of life than his sister did.

Charlotte Holton married, a month after her eighteenth birthday, a young man called Richard Longport. I should like to think of them as besotted sweethearts, carried into wedded bliss on a tide of mutual devotion. It is an improbable image, I confess. Instead, it is prone to being a tale not of storybook love but of domestic necessity, very much in keeping with the norm for families such as the Holtons, families of borderline solvency. Charlotte would have been seen as both a liability and an asset. As a girl, she had minimal earning capability, hardly able to cover her costs. However, as a girl, she offered the opportunity of bringing much needed external capital into the family in the form of a wealthy husband. By most standards, Richard Longport was not wealthy, but by comparison with the Holtons he must have seemed like a millionaire: his father owned a barrel-making business and all four sons, of whom Richard was the youngest, had been apprenticed as coopers.

Within a year of her marriage, Charlotte was pregnant. In March 1764, she gave birth to a son, who was named Nathaniel, for Richard's father. The baby lived for just four days. Before summer had passed, Charlotte was again with child. This second baby was due the following May, one month after Charlotte's brother James was destined to lose his young life. By mid June, Charlotte still had not delivered. I try not to think of the type of treatment and support she might have received - the application of noxious liniments, the well-meaning but ignorant administration of patent tinctures, the odd, uneducated notions of the family matriarchs. Whether labor was induced by human intervention or simply by nature's course, Charlotte did at last produce a tiny baby that patently had died inside her some days earlier. Just hours after the delivery, Charlotte, too, was dead.

Only William was left of Moses and Ann Holton's children and he appears to have remained at home with his mother for some years whilst working first as a runner for one of Philadelphia's newspapers, then as an assistant to the proprietor. It was not until he was twenty-eight years old that William married. His wife was Elizabeth Wilkinson, lately arrived from England with her widower father, a tax official for the British government, which is unlikely to have endeared him greatly to the locals. Immediately they were married, William and Elizabeth gave a home to William's mother, who was, our tradition has it, still ailing from the loss of her two oldest children. This was compounded by Richard Longport taking up with another young woman and forever removing himself, along with his humble, but welcome fortune, from the lives of the Holtons.

At the same time as this was happening, the Wright family was probably scraping a living in the most diseased and neglected boroughs to the east of London. There is no absolute proof of this, for the research done by my Aunt Angela has so far uncovered the Wright lineage only as far back as the early nineteenth century. Nothing she has found, however, would suggest that the Wrights had ever occupied anywhere other than the very lowest social stratum. Two hundred years ago in England, few people ever rose above their station in life, society's immutable hierarchies constraining ambitions and maintaining a status quo that left everyone in no doubt as to where they stood and where they would remain. The Wrights were at the bottom and that is where they were predestined to stay. If the Holtons lived in near poverty, the Wrights existed deep, deep within it.

This was a pre-industrial time, a time before almost all of the inventions that we now view as the origin of our modern, technological world. It is therefore a time in which it is almost impossible to place oneself. The images we have of it are largely twentieth century creations. History books focus upon the macro level events – the Act Of Settlement, the Jacobite rebellions, the Hanoverian monarchs – whilst mostly ignoring the microcosmic lives of ordinary people. Films present a world of aristocrats and dandies, of great houses and sumptuous banquets, of wigs and duels and derring-do. If a member of the lower echelons happens to pass through a scene it is usually in the form of a ruddy-faced drunk or a toothless hag, whose role is to be run down by a coach-and-four or horsewhipped for insolence by the bad guy.

I have tried to read contemporary accounts of the period, but rarely were these written by other than the moneyed classes, who tended to dwell upon their own experiences and not upon observations of the masses. I have read, too, the finely researched viewpoints of the most scholarly historians, those who have tried to get beneath the clichéd surface of the era, but still I struggle. Ultimately, in attempting to envision the lives of the Wrights way back in the 1700s, as I can the lives of the Holtons, what I am lacking is the verbal tradition of my English family. For some reason, those who came here to America seem to have made a conscious effort to pass on their history. Maybe that was because they recognized that they had no roots in their new land, that they were, indeed, the roots from which future generations would grow. Those who continued to live in the Old World already had their roots, as well as a clear idea of their individual futures within the unofficial caste system that was English society. There was little point, therefore, in chronicling their family heritage, even if they had the literacy to do so, which they did not.

I was christened William, a name that derives from Wilhelm, a Teutonic name formed from wil, meaning will or desire, and helm, meaning helmet. Thus, my name means 'will helmet', though this is mostly interpreted as 'desiring protection', and is a handle passed down through just about every Holton generation since Moses and Ann named their second son back in the mid-eighteenth century. In these days of diminutives and over familiarity,

I am often called Bill. Our President might favor it, but I prefer my full name. Only my best friends are tolerated in their use of Will.

The christening photograph is deceptive - it makes me look tiny, even at five months. I was actually a large baby, particularly for those less well nourished times, eight pounds twelve ounces when I was born, my poor mom ripped at the seams as my head forced its way into daylight. Everyone said I took after my dad, who was six feet two and packed with muscles honed by working at the mill. It is odd, therefore, to think that Mom was always my protector, my guardian angel. When my feelings matched the meaning of my name, she would come and place herself between me and whatever danger I had to confront, be it a slavering dog that charged towards me one day on a trail near the Deh-Ga-Ya-Soh Creek or the illusory threats of night-time shadows playing on the walls of my bedroom. Dad, meanwhile, would hang back, probably sometimes wishing that she would let me learn from a little suffering.

Last year, Steve and Sally Caspar came out to stay with me for a week. Steve is tall and solid and, catching sight of him emerging from the bathroom one morning, I realized how much he resembles my dad. I dug out the Fortnum & Mason tin and found a picture taken at our Moon Landing Party in July 1969. Dad would have been thirty-five back then, just about the same age as Steve is today. The similarity between the two was obvious, especially the shock of dark hair that always fell across my dad's forehead when he played soccer with me in the back yard or chased after the raccoons that sometimes upended the trash can and strew paper and food waste all over our driveway. Steve had that same shock of hair, which I had first noticed when we used to play baseball in Central Park. I remember how Steve would smooth it back into place with an affected sweep of his hand and tuck it neatly beneath his Mets cap. My dad, on the other hand, and especially once he passed forty, would just let the thick black mass hang messily in his eyes.

On the Thursday of the week, Steve got a call from his boss at Greenleaf, Mike Grogan. Grogan wanted him back in New York City the next morning, irrespective of his vacation. Some crisis had arisen with one of Steve's clients and he needed to go meet with the guy, some semi-retired publisher out in Connecticut. Sally cursed and strutted out of the door and I watched her disappear down towards North Street. Forty minutes later, she was back, announcing that she was staying and that she would take a train back to the city at the weekend. Steve's jaw suddenly took on the appearance of a ton weight and his permanently tanned face drained of all color. Clearly, the prospect of leaving his wife alone with me for two days was not too palatable, though the defiant look on Sally's face must surely have told him that argument was futile.

I liked Sally a great deal, but until that time I had never harbored any desires for her. She has the most exquisite tone of skin, her mother having been part Italian, her father having immigrated from Jamaica. She is rummed cappuccino. Her hair is black, like my mom's, and her arms and legs have the sinewy firmness of an athlete, though both her hands and feet are incongruously large. I sat next to her in a restaurant, maybe the third or fourth time we had met, and I could hardly take my eyes off her hands, with their broad palms and long, thick fingers. Kelly noticed them too and they were the sole topic of conversation as we rode home in the cab later that evening. 'Jeez.' Kelly said. 'Thank the Lord she's a teacher, not a gynecologist.'

Once Steve had left, Sally and I went for a walk around town, then drove over to Geneva, which sits at the top of Seneca Lake, the largest of the Finger Lakes. We had dinner at Spinnaker's, a restaurant right on the water that serves great fish. By the time we got back home, the beer Sally had been drinking had re-aroused her anger at Steve. She told me he was a shit and a bastard and one or two other unflattering things, then mooched her way upstairs to bed, leaving me to reflect upon the day over a glass of wine, with re-runs of *Cheers* on the TV. Next morning, she rose before me and prepared breakfast. I found her in the kitchen wearing a kimono-like robe that flapped about her sculptured legs as she flitted from toaster to counter to oven to table. Later, she went ahead of me into the bathroom and left the place smelling of perfume, some blossomy fragrance I could not identify, but so reminiscent of the ambrosial bouquet Kelly would leave each morning in our apartment in Manhattan. I showered and shaved, lingering in the steamy solitude. When I emerged, I found her on the landing, dressed for our trip to the Park in a gray jog-bra and a pair of black cycling shorts. My eyes danced, uncertain what to gape at first: her bare midriff, her bulging breasts or her lycra-clad ass.

The route I chose that day was identical to the one I took earlier today, coming into the Park near Mount Morris and driving south, stopping off at the Big Bend so that Sally could see the canyon. It was a stiflingly hot day and the ground was dry and dusty as we set off along the portion of the Gorge Trail that loops down towards the Lower Falls. We talked about some mutual friends in New York City and about recent redundancies at The

Greenleaf Corporation, which Steve had narrowly escaped - a factor, no doubt, in the alacrity with which he had abandoned his vacation. As Sally walked ahead, I watched rivulets of perspiration trickle down her spine and swell a patch of wetness on her back. I tried to keep talking about Steve, reminding myself that this woman was the wife of one of my friends, but gradually Sally steered the topic of conversation towards me. Was I lonely? she wondered, a question I am tired of hearing. Would I not like a special someone with whom to share my lovely house? Up above, the noon sun shone from an azure blue sky, our shadows contracting until they were almost impossible to see, trampled beneath our feet. We found a picnic table near the Octagon and drank the soda I had stuffed into my backpack, then set off again, stopping for a while at the Lower Falls, before heading towards Inspiration Point. The trail is close to the river along that stretch and I managed to monopolize the conversation by pointing out birds and species of tree and identifying insects that hopped and flew and buzzed across our path. At last, we got to the Point, both physically and figuratively.

'Don't you miss sex, Will?' Sally asked, interrupting my telling her about Sara Evans Letchworth and the unveiling of the plaque in 1917.

'Woah.' I said. 'That's a little too intrusive for me.' I was not offended, but I was most assuredly not prepared to discuss the subject, particularly with Sally.

She stood, arms akimbo, not quite thrusting out her chest, but definitely accentuating her narrow and naked waist by drumming both middle fingers, thick and fleshy, against the black lycra of her shorts. Her expression seemed to ask how, if I lived alone and there was no sign of anyone on the landscape of my love life, I could possibly resist her.

After a more clumsy than awkward few moments, she exhaled loudly, then relaxed her stance and lowered her head, her hair falling about her face before she tossed it back with an artful tilt of her fine, fibrous neck. Then she smiled and declared that she was 'pooped' and could not walk another yard. It was a mile back to the car along the roadway, but I had no hesitation in volunteering to fetch it while she bathed in the searing sun.

Sally decided to cook spaghetti for our evening meal, accompanied by a tomato and basil sauce the recipe for which she claimed had been handed down through generations of her family in Modena. I called up Bobbie and asked her over, daunted at the thought of being on my own with Sally. Thankfully, Bobbie had nothing planned and brought with her both Becky and a bottle of local red wine. While the spaghetti boiled, Sally went upstairs to change, returning wearing a loose fitting summer dress and very little else. Bobbie smiled at me when she saw her, a knowing smile, the sort that ought to be accompanied by raised eyebrows and a rhythmic nodding of the head. As the evening wore on, Becky got more and more irritable, but Bobbie stuck around like a limpet, aware that I needed her support, her protection. Eventually, I carried a dozing Becky up to my bed, where she stayed for the rest of the night, undisturbed both by her mother joining her in the small hours of the morning and, simultaneously, by Sally's big feet thumping loudly and drunkenly about in the next room. I slept in the third bedroom, Jackie's room.

The next day, Sally apologized for her behavior, her manner not just penitent, but panicky. I guess she thought I might tell Steve about her performance, the object of which I still do not understand. She was unquestionably flirting with me, but was that to tease me, or test me, or was it even genuine? Did she really want me to come on to her and, if so, why? Was she planning to teach Steve a lesson by offering herself to me while he sloped off to New York City at Mike Grogan's command? Was she perhaps feeling rejected by Steve and in need of affirmation of herself as an object of desire? I am sure Kelly could come up with a hundred different explanations, but all I know is that I was pleased to see her off at the railroad station in Rochester later that afternoon.

Since that time, I have kept in touch with the Caspars by 'phone and letter; we did not see one another again until I dropped off my car in Westchester immediately prior to flying out for Dad's funeral. Sally calls me when Steve is at the squash club or working late at Greenleaf. She tells me all sorts of things about their marriage, things she seems to think it is my right to know. She still has a conscience about how she acted that day we came to the Park together, a conscience she appears to salve by sharing with me her own intimate secrets.

∼

I left the Park today around five o'clock, leaving at Portageville and making my way back up to Geneseo past the timber mill in Nunda, where my dad used to work. The house was cold, the heating having been off for a week, and it took a while for the boiler to heat and the radiators to start warming the place through. I emptied my bags and loaded the washing machine, then went into my den and took a look at the mail. It was mostly 'With Sympathy' cards from friends in Geneseo and New York City, though there was also a letter from Charlie and Rose Petersen and a brief note from Kelly's parents. Kelly too had sent me a card that said: 'I'm so sorry to hear your news. If you need me, just call.' I called and got her voice mail.

The interior layout of my house is mostly as it was when it was built back in the fifties, but I have changed the internal decoration considerably since Mom died and Dad left. I did most of it myself unlike in Manhattan where we got people in to do that sort thing. The place had become scruffy, mostly because Mom had been so ill and Dad had had more important matters to concern him than retouching chipped paint-work or replacing scuffed wallpaper. The rooms are fairly small, so I wanted lots of brightness, whites and peaches and subtle yellows, as well as a classical feel, nothing modish or ethnic or rustic. I started in the second bedroom, my old room, which acted as a sort of laboratory where I could experiment and learn. Next spring, I shall put right all my mistakes, including the pastel green color scheme, which I thought would give it a gentleness and delicacy, but which actually makes it feel soulless. I have introduced brightly patterned lampshades and curtains, which, far from adding cheer, have accentuated just how dull the rest of the décor is. My own bedroom, the largest and the only one with a view over the front garden and the street, is deliberately cocoon-like, with rugs and cushions and a deep, heavy quilt. Although the walls are plain, the fabrics are rich with autumnal brilliance, like the hillsides in the Park. I also painted the ceiling honeysuckle, another experiment, this time successful. I spent less time and substantially less effort on the third bedroom, mostly because it is big enough only for a single bed, a pedestal table and a narrow closet, all pine, all bought from a shop in North Dansville. It is a simple room, rarely used, still achingly associated with my sister.

Of all the work I did on the house, I found tiling the most relaxing and therapeutic. It felt a more creative job than either painting or paper hanging, a really tactile experience, something basic, almost alchemistic. Nothing was as satisfying as transforming the scabby walls of both the bathroom and the kitchen into gleaming plains, so polished and smooth to the touch. I toyed with opening out the kitchen into the back room, with a counter between the cooking and the eating areas, like a sit-com set. However, I quickly realized that my imagination was running way ahead of my novice abilities and decided instead to leave the partition in place. The back room now serves as a dining room, with a big oak table in its center and Grandma

Holton's old sideboard along one wall. The French windows open out on to a paved patio, beyond which the yard stretches as far as my neighbor's privet hedge, close to which mom's flower beds continue to deliver color from early spring right through to the late fall. In some ways, the appeal of sitting in the back room and watching the birds and squirrels playing on the lawn has caused the front room to become like a Victorian parlor, which is used only for Sunday best. Like last year, though, this will change in the winter, when I light a fire in the hearth and stand my Christmas tree by the window. Indeed, that front room was intended to be both the showpiece and the heart of the house. I had the old suite re-upholstered in a predominantly damson colored floral print, the fine pink of one of the flowers matched in the stripe of the wallpaper. On the shelves, I have placed framed photographs of Mom and Dad and both sets of grandparents and around the walls I have hung three of Mom's best watercolors, two painted in the Park and one at Hemlock Lake.

My study, where I sit now, is the same size as the third bedroom. Mom once had a table in here, which supported a heavy, old-fashioned sewing machine. The table is gone, replaced by my bureau, which takes up less space and at which I love to sit, usually to write. These days, that means typing into my portable computer, which I first got just over a year ago. Already it looks clunky and outdated by comparison with those I see now in the shops. I am so very lucky to be, in modest terms, financially independent. I pay nothing for the house, apart from the usual repairs and upkeep, and within a few weeks ownership will pass finally to me from Dad's estate. At Greenleaf, I earned an astronomical wage, far, far more than most folks around here could ever imagine. I also inherited Mom's portfolio of bonds and equities, which Grandpa had created from his own inheritance and had nurtured without any intention of ever enjoying the fruits of his prudent husbandry. I like to think that, having been an economist with a Wall Street investment firm, I do have some idea about how to carry on Grandpa's good work and, so far, I have not done too badly. My ego still gets a buzz from those dividend credits and bonus statements and interest checks that drop into the mailbox every month. I do not have to work, which is why I am studying, plowing through the research for the history degree I probably should have taken two decades ago, though I guess if I had done just that I would not be sitting here now writing about financial independence.

I keep some personal items in here, not private things, but objects with some sentimental or emotional significance to me. There are two more of

Mom's paintings and some more family photos, mostly taken when I was a child. There is a paperweight Becky made for my birthday, on which she has etched 'To my mommy's best friend, with love from Becky.' There is a book that belonged to Grandpa Holton, a prize he won at school back in 1918. I have a montage of pictures taken at Greenleaf events during the heady days of the mid- to late-eighties, shots from the annual conferences, of me meeting Wayne Gretsky and George Schulz and Buzz Aldrin. I used to also have here a pressed flower, a wild rose, that Mom framed with a lock of Jackie's hair, but it is the most precious possession I have and it went missing when I was fitting new bookshelves. For the first time in my life, I utterly panicked. I ran through the house gasping for breath, distraught, incapable of ordered thought. I flew up the stairs, ready to rip out all the drawers and rifle the closets, thankfully electing to begin the mayhem in my own bedroom. Just as I was about to tip over the bedside cabinet, I saw the flower, leaning against the triptych mirror on the dressing table. I had placed it there, out of harm's way, the day before and had completely forgotten about it. Suddenly, my world was total euphoria, like nothing I have ever felt. I took hold of the little silver frame and hugged it like a baby, sobbing with happiness. I have never put the flower back in the study; it is still in my bedroom, by the mirror, so that I can see it each morning when I wake and check that it is still there before I go to sleep at night.

Despite my heavy eyes and aching legs, I sense that sleep tonight will be an elusive goal. I know that no amount of physical exhaustion can compensate for the tumult in my head.

I went over to Bobbie's house after I had eaten dinner. The welcome I received was almost overwhelming, Bobbie pulling me towards her and holding me so tightly that my ribs felt crushed. Even now, I am not certain whether she was offering comfort or expressing relief. Maybe both. As we stood locked together in the hallway, Becky looked on, evidently unsure as to what exactly was happening and whether she was expected to participate in some way. I tried to make a gesture of reassurance, but I fear my expression was more a grimace than a smile, such was the oppressive grip of Bobbie's embrace.

At last the vice-like arms weakened and I was free. Bobbie's face was wet with tears, but there was no obvious indication as to whether she was weeping for me, for my Dad or for herself. Again, I suspect it was a mixture. We walked through to the kitchen, leaving Becky to follow sheepishly behind, still bearing a strange, puzzled frown.

'Come on, Becky.' Bobbie said, hurrying her daughter with her impatient tone. 'Come and get some cookies out of the cupboard. We've got Will's favorites.'

Becky lingered by the door, apparently ignoring her mother, staring instead at me.

'Come *on*.' Bobbie chivvied again, but the nine-year-old did not move.

'What's wrong, Becky?' I asked, in what I hoped was a gentle, conciliatory manner.

The child thought for a few seconds, her mouth twitching with the effort not so much of finding the words, but with working out how, perhaps whether to say them. Eventually, she looked straight at me. 'I'm sorry your daddy died.' she said.

I closed my eyes and smiled, touched. 'So am I, Becky.' I replied, a catch in my voice. 'So am I.'

She continued to stare at me, maybe thinking that, yes, it was sad that my dad had gone, but at least I had known my daddy, unlike her.

She never did get those cookies from the cupboard, those flaky, lemon-flavored cookies that have been, as Bobbie well knows, my favorites since I was in fifth grade. Instead, Becky asked her mother politely whether she could go to watch TV in her room and Bobbie, her demeanor softened by my interchange with her daughter, packed her off with a glass of milk and a Baby Ruth.

Bobbie and I sat at the kitchen counter, drank coffee and ate not cookies but the remnants of a chocolate cake Bobbie had baked yesterday. Now my parents have both gone, Bobbie is not only my closest friend, but also the closest thing I have to family. I have known her all my life. We played together, trick-or-treated together, went to High School together. Throughout those years, we both sensed an unspoken expectation that one day we would become a couple, but it never happened, even though we always cared about each other. Maybe our relationship was too sibling-like, maybe I did not find Bobbie as exciting as some of the other girls in town, especially Linda Danelli, who I dated for a short while before going off to Columbia. Linda was dark-haired and bronzed, her figure slender, her body firm, not at all unlike Sally Caspar, though Linda's hands and feet were properly in proportion. One night, we parked Dad's car in a lane near Hemlock Lake and made love in the back seat, an enjoyable encounter marred, later, by seeing Bobbie on her porch as I drove past after taking Linda home. For some reason, I had an abrupt and palpable pang of guilt, a sense that, by making out with Linda, I had been unfaithful to Bobbie.

Twenty years have passed since that night and many things have changed. Bobbie's figure is fuller, my hair is shorter, she has taken to wearing huge round spectacles and I have learned to resist Italian women, even those with half Jamaican blood. The most marked difference, though, is Becky.

We talked this evening mostly about my trip to England for Dad's funeral. I lied to Bobbie about one or two things, something I hate doing because it defiles our friendship. However, I saw no point in upsetting her unnecessarily and my untruths were of the whitest kind, intended purely to deflect the conversation away from sensitive areas that neither of us would have wanted to explore. I nevertheless felt uneasy, my discomfort almost certainly apparent to Bobbie, who reacted with her usual understanding, suggesting, a number of times, that I looked tired and that I was, quite naturally, having problems getting my head together. It was her way of creating an excuse for me and maybe also a way of bringing my visit to an early close. 'You need some sleep.' she said, as I stifled a yawn, her implication being that I should go home and go to bed. I took the hint.

Coffee tends to keep me awake, so, when I got back here to the house, I poured myself a large slug of bourbon, which I drank as I checked through my e-mail. There was nothing urgent, but I sent a brief reply to my tutor, Gary Lennart, who had been checking up on the progress of an essay that I am meant to be writing.

'Always start with your own history.' he wrote to all his students at the beginning of the course. 'Delve into your bloodlines. There is a piece of you in every second of every hour of every day this world has existed.'

He was leading up to setting our first assignment, which I should have completed last week. I pleaded extenuating circumstances and Gary granted me an extension to this coming Friday.

'Sorry to pressure you, William.' he says in his most recent message. 'I know it's a bad time for you.'

'It's OK.' I replied, having written the opening section just this afternoon.

# Monday

❀

William Holton, the son of Moses and Ann, rose above the lowly drudge of the McCarthy's clothing business and went to work instead for John Ringold, alleged friend of Benjamin Franklin and owner of a news-sheet called *The Vanguard*. Produced weekly, *The Vanguard* began by carrying tidbits cobbled together from the views and observations of a network of correspondents amongst the city's well-to-do. This was transformed by Ringold into reports bearing all the gravitas of truly serious journalism, his style being at once both solemn and loquacious. I have read analyses of Ringold's pieces which assert that many were, despite their outwardly mundane, hearthside nature, coded messages in support of American independence, though such arguments seem, to me, contrived and unconvincing. Whatever his motives, Ringold's *Vanguard* proved peculiarly successful, its content evolving from gossip to hard news, the single sheet hand-bill growing to resemble what we might today term a proper newspaper. Boys were hired, some to hawk *The Vanguard* on street corners, others as runners, ferrying messages throughout the city, flitting to-and-fro on errands for Ringold and his son, John Jr., who was to perish in the diphtheria epidemic of 1765.

William Holton was one such runner. He joined *The Vanguard* when he was fifteen years old and left only on the senior Ringold's death in 1797, when William was fifty-two. Ringold clearly favored William of all his employees, promoting the runner first to advertising salesman, then to become his own personal assistant. In reward for his service and loyalty, William was left a small bequeath in Ringold's will.

Elizabeth Wilkinson's family was from Kent, the most south easterly of the English counties. Her mother died in 1764 and, five years later, Elizabeth and her father sailed for Philadelphia, where Mr. Wilkinson was to become His Majesty's Comptroller of Taxes with Elizabeth as his private secretary. Sometime shortly after her arrival, Elizabeth must have met William Holton, who, by that time, would have been using his powers of persuasion to fill the front page of *The Vanguard* with advertisements for all manner of wares peddled by Philadelphia's growing business community. Those same powers would appear to have also worked on Elizabeth Wilkinson, for within a year of their first meeting they were married.

Elizabeth's father was recalled to England in 1774, by which time his daughter was heavily pregnant with her first child, James, who was born in July of that year and who was named for William's deceased older brother. For more than three years of marriage to have passed without the appearance of children was, at that time, most unusual, a sign that William and Elizabeth had maybe not problems, but certainly no luck when attempting to conceive. Frankly, I prefer this explanation far more than conjecturing that they *chose* to remain childless, for that would introduce to their story the grim specter of eighteenth century contraception. Whether it was by choice or through the unpredictable roll of the biological dice, William and Elizabeth's second child also took three years to arrive; this time it was a girl, who they named Caroline.

William's work with *The Vanguard*, combined with the closeness of his relationship with John Ringold, brought him acquaintance with a great many people, from entrepreneurs to politicians, from writers to soldiers. He appears to have cultivated one such contact more than any other, this being Jacob Fulmer, head of the Fulmer family that, through a labyrinth of marriages that yielded few legitimate heirs, allegedly had rights to land in the north of England. What is more, the affluence Jacob Fulmer had achieved in America had been based principally upon those rights, against which he borrowed heavily. It was not until after his death that those rights were discovered to be complete illusion, maybe even *de*lusion on the part the Fulmers, who had either been the victims of misunderstanding and poor legal advice or, I fear, the willing accomplices in and beneficiaries of a clever transatlantic scam. They claimed the former, of course, but I have always tended toward believing the latter. Ultimately, the explanation is irrelevant, for the product was the ruination of the Fulmers and, almost, of the Holtons.

Jacob Fulmer had three daughters, Virginia, Jessica and Rebecca. Virginia was much the same age as Caroline Holton and the two girls became close friends, even though Virginia attended one of the most select and expensive schools in Philadelphia, whilst Caroline's education came courtesy of an altogether less grand institution that was funded by charitable donations. The friendship between the two girls brought Virginia into regular contact with Caroline's brother James, who, after completing his own studies, found employment with the fledgling state government. The relationship between James and Virginia must have been a slow burning fuse, for it was not until

1801, when he was twenty-seven and she was twenty-four, that the two became engaged.

Two years previously, tragedy had struck the Holtons with the death of Caroline, who was said to have always been a sickly child and who was, during the harsh winter of 1799, fatally struck down by what was probably influenza that turned first to pleurisy, then to pneumonia. This woeful turn of events may well have contributed to the protracted courtship of James and Virginia, both of whom were greatly affected by Caroline's loss. James, indeed, paid for an elaborately chiseled headstone, the inscription on which was taken from Romans 14:8 and reads 'For whether we live, we live unto the Lord; and whether we die, we die unto the Lord.' Now worn by the passing of two centuries, the words have almost disappeared, but Caroline's grave remains as the oldest of all Holton resting places still marked in the USA.

Buried close by is Caroline's father William who, at fifty-seven years old, died in the spring of 1802. *The Vanguard* had folded on the death of John Ringold and, despite his small inheritance from his former employer, William had been forced to find work with another of Philadelphia's proliferating newspapers, *The Daily Advertiser*. Sometime in late 1801, an accident had occurred in which the horses hitched to one of the company's delivery wagons had been harried by a barking dog and had reared up, pushing the wagon backwards and knocking down William, who just happened to be passing by at the time. The horses then bolted forward and a wheel ran over William's left ankle. My guess is that the ankle was broken, for William never walked again without the aid of a crutch. His general health also deteriorated, maybe a sign of some untreated complication, his steady decline reaching its conclusion the following April.

That summer at last saw the wedding of James Holton and Virginia Fulmer. James was doing well in his job with the state government, working chiefly on land registration. Virginia, meanwhile, was a lady of leisure, freed from the obligation to earn a living by her family's fictitious rights to prime English real estate. The couple bought a home in central Philadelphia and settled down to what most would have predicted would be a comfortable life. Possessions were accumulated – paintings, ornaments, furnishings – paid for both from James's wages and an allowance that Virginia's father continued to provide, despite such benefaction usually ceasing once a daughter had married and had become the responsibility of her husband. In retrospect, it appears that Jacob Fulmer was maybe spreading his risk.

Material effects abounded, then, but children did not. This time, it was not a matter of choice on the part of the couple, or of bad luck. Instead, the barren marriage resulted from illness. Virginia, it would seem, suffered from a condition that turned menstruation into torture. Back in the first decade of the nineteenth century, it would not have been diagnosed as an illness, of course. Indeed, it is hardly likely to have been discussed. Most other women and absolutely all doctors would have viewed it as simply severe period pains, part of a woman's lot, something to be endured, stop complaining. In Virginia's case, she shared her distress only with her sisters, which is why, thanks to her sister Rebecca's longevity and lucidity, I am now aware of Virginia's dreadful plight. I can also account for her shockingly premature death.

Rebecca recalled how, one afternoon in the early fall of 1806, Virginia had retired to bed with what, by then, she knew was the beginning of her monthly onslaught. It soon became apparent, however, that this month was different. The atrocious pain was accompanied by profuse bleeding, so bad that by the following morning, the bedclothes had turned completely from white to red. James had Jessica and Rebecca summoned from the Fulmer house half a mile away, then left for work. Horrified by the sight that greeted her, Jessica sent a maid to fetch the doctor, who arrived within the hour. By then, Virginia had lost so much blood that she was becoming drowsy and disorientated. The doctor's problem was that the bleeding emanated from inside Virginia and there was no way he could get to the source. Nothing he could do would stifle the flow and, as time ticked by, Virginia Holton fell into unconsciousness. When James returned home around lunchtime, his young wife was dead and her two anguished sisters were being comforted by their mother.

When Rebecca Fulmer related this story to her great-great-nephew Thomas Holton, it was 1890 and Rebecca was a hundred years old. She made it clear to Thomas that James Holton, Thomas's great-grandfather, was not uncaring, that his going off to work on a morning when his wife was so evidently and dreadfully unwell was not the action of an inconsiderate man. He was simply, she contended, a man of his time. Knowing what I now know, I believe she was making excuses for James.

The Fulmer sisters were all, it was said, highly intelligent and divertingly pretty, an opinion certainly held by James Holton. Wasting little time after Virginia's death, he began a relationship with Jessica, who moved into his house and became his 'consort'. This is a genteel way of saying that they lived together outside of wedlock, lived in sin, as it was termed until so very recently. The euphemism was no doubt necessary in order for James and the Fulmer family to maintain propriety, though the Fulmers' propriety was soon to be shot to pieces.

In 1809, Jacob Fulmer dropped dead. Literally. He was walking down the street when suddenly he collapsed and was dead before his head hit the ground. I guess the cause was a stroke or a huge heart attack. If the loss of the family's patriarch was not bad enough, the questions then asked by the Fulmers' creditors about their ability to repay their debts soon began to pick at the legitimacy of the land rights that had always formed the basis of their collateral. Without Jacob around to cajole and bluster his way past awkward inquiries, it was discovered that the family had, for years, been securing loans on rights that were not worth the paper on which they were written.

Everything was reclaimed. Jacob's wife was left homeless and relied on the kindness of friends, who paid her passage to England, where she went to live with a relative. James Holton's house was gutted, all the finery removed to repay his father-in-law's debts, yet still the ravenous creditors were not satiated. Eventually, the house itself had to be sold. James was shattered. He rented a tiny house in one of the poorer parts of the city and set up home there with Jessica and Rebecca, both of whom he had to maintain on his government worker's pay. What was more, he and the two young women now carried a stigma, the mark not just of failure, but of fraud. He needed to rebuild, he knew, to start over, preferably in a place far distant from Philadelphia.

The Empire State Transportation Board had just been established in Albany, the capital of New York, to advise upon and oversee the development of the state's transport infrastructure. At that time, the Board's interests lay solely in the movement of cargoes and people by water and land, the former by means of rivers and canals, the latter through use of mostly undeveloped and unpaved public roads and turnpikes. Through contacts in New York, one of the friends who had helped Jacob's wife return to England became aware of a vacant position at the Board that seemed to suit James Holton's experience and abilities. The man alerted James to the job and made personal representations so as to assist James's application. In September 1811, James moved, with Jessica and Rebecca, to Albany.

Within a month of their arrival, James and Jessica were married. Work was still anathema to Jessica, who had been raised in the expectation of being kept for the whole of her life. Rebecca, though, had fewer affectations and took a job as a ledger clerk for the new Hudson Colonial Bank. The domestic arrangements were ostensibly clear, James being the head of the household, Jessica being his wife and Rebecca being their lodger. Things were not quite as they seemed, however. The reality was that James Holton was having an affair with Rebecca Fulmer. It was an affair that resulted in James impregnating Rebecca while his wife was still suffering from morning sickness as her body nurtured the embryo of their first child. It was a child that Jessica would soon miscarry, due maybe to the shock of discovering her sister's pregnancy.

Rebecca gave birth in October 1814, by which time she had left the house of her sister and brother-in-law and was living in a home for young women run by nuns. The child was named Peter and lived until he was five months old, when his little body at last gave up a struggle for life that had begun the moment he had left his mother's womb. The nuns placed him in an unmarked grave in the corner of the nearby Roman Catholic churchyard and registered his death in the same mammoth tome as they had recorded his birth. Rebecca named the father as James William Holton.

There never was a rapprochement between Jessica and Rebecca, the younger sister eventually leaving the home and moving to New York City, where she worked for the Catholic church, having converted from the Anglican faith whilst living with the nuns. She never married. Meanwhile, the relationship between James and Jessica survived intact and, in 1815, they produced a son, who was named John, in honor, perhaps, of John Ringold.


Kelly called me this morning, just before ten thirty, when I was still in my bed, not quite asleep, but drifting in the no-man's-land of semi-consciousness. The ringing of the 'phone mingled with a dream out of which I was trying to rouse myself.

'Hello.' I croaked, still a little uncertain that the ringing was indeed reality.

'Hi there.' Kelly said. 'I woke you, didn't I?'

'Yep.' Now we are divorced, we no longer lie to one another.

'Sorry.' she said. 'I thought you'd be up and about by now. I wanted to say I was sorry about not being here when you called yesterday.' What is this? I thought, two apologies in one sentence, not to mention the 'Sorry' she had written on the condolence card, though that was in a different context. 'I was working.' she explained. 'Over in Brooklyn. This kid had pushed his baby sister in front of a truck. They were just strolling together along Schermerhorn, when -'.

'Spare me the details.' I interrupted, knowing I was about to get the full gory account.

'It was pretty bad.' she offered, thankfully summarizing. 'Anyway, it was good to hear from you. How are you, Will?'

'Bushed. I haven't slept properly for a week. I feel like staying here in bed for the rest of the day.'

'What's stopping you?'

'Nothing, I guess. Just me. I promised myself I'd do a few things this week. Get a few things in order.'

'Sounds serious, Will. Can I help?'

'Maybe. I don't want to talk about it right now, I need to wake up and blow some clean air through my brain. I'm going to write you a letter.'

'You haven't written me a letter since those days when I used to spend Christmas with my folks.'

'I know, but when people live together there doesn't seem to be that much need for written correspondence.' I chose not to say that, in fact, I *had* written her letters since that time, but that they had been returned, unopened, by her lawyer. Just as divorce has freed us from the necessity of untruths, so it has relieved us of the burden of baiting each other.

'Well,' Kelly said. 'I'm looking forward to getting your letter and I promise I'll write back to you.'

'Sure.'

There was a brief, tricky silence before she said: 'OK, then. I'll let you get moving with your day. If you need me, you know where I am.'

'I sure do, Kelly. Thanks.'

'Bye Will'

'Yeah. Bye Kelly. Thanks for calling.'

I hung up the 'phone and clambered out of bed. It was a clear, sunny day beyond the scarlet and gold patterned curtains, which I pulled back to let the light into the room. I looked across at the mirror, against which leaned the framed wild rose, with that gossamer fine lock of Jackie's hair. My reflection revealed a man in an old gray T-shirt and a pair of boxer shorts, the way I usually dress for bed, a disheveled man, his thick black hair standing to attention, as if he had been zapped by a bolt of lightning. My eyes squinted in the brightness, their lids appearing red and sore. I looked a mess.

Once I had showered and breakfasted on yogurt and cereal, which Bobbie had bought and placed in my kitchen cupboard on Saturday, I felt re-humanized. I quickly scanned the sports page of the newspaper for the details on the American League Championship Series, this year between the Yankees and the Red Sox, then filled up a small backpack and drove off to the Park.

As I did yesterday, I drove past the Mount Morris Dam, round the Hogs Back, then motored south, beyond Gardeau to the picnic area at St. Helena. I was not hungry, but I drank some of Bobbie's lemonade, which had been kept ice cool by an insulated bottle she bought me last Christmas. One day she will surely run out of ideas when it comes to presents. I have already exhausted my own imagination, so Bobbie now looks forward to her regular gift of perfume, although I do try to buy a different brand each time.

For a while, I was the only person at the old ghost town. I sat and drafted my letter to Kelly, which I have since rewritten on to some watermarked blue paper that I keep for the increasingly rare occasions when I write letters by hand. Like most people, I tend these days to take the lazy approach and type them on my computer.

Around two o'clock, a couple from across the border in Ontario rumbled into the parking lot in their RV, a monstrous contraption the size of a bus, with a satellite dish pointing skywards from its roof. They set up a small table on the grass and laid out a salad lunch, tomatoes and lettuce leaves and what looked like chicken legs fried in breadcrumbs. Soon after, they were joined by another couple in a car with Virginia plates, though they turned out to be German, their stiff and forceful mother tongue so familiar to me from my days at Columbia. One of my classmates, Dieter Buchmann, was from Cologne and when he called home each weekend it always sounded like he was having an argument with his father. Today, the Germans disappeared along the trail towards the Tea Table, from whence emerged, minutes later, three young women, college students I would guess, each toting camping gear. By the look of them, they had just hiked all the way from Texas. Sweat stained their armpits and their hair was mangled far worse than mine had been when I checked the mirror this morning. Their legs were tanned but scratched by thickets and brambles, their faces were flushed and their pendulous breasts swayed heavily in cheap underwear beneath regulation gray T-shirts.

'This St. Helena?' one of the girls asked me as she scanned the area, presumably having expected there to be more to the place.

'This is it.' I said, gesturing with a sweeping arm.

The girl looked deflated. All that effort and this is what you get?

From St. Helena, I drove down past the Big Bend to the Visitor Center. One of the ladies who works there lives in Geneseo, though I only know her by sight and by the name on her badge: Hillary, like our First Lady, who may, next year, become our Senator. I bought two postcards, then walked back to the Middle Falls. One card was for Aunt Angela, thanking her for being so kind to me at my dad's funeral and inviting her over here next summer. The other card was for my cousin Valerie, who I hope will be having one of her good days when she receives it.

The cool breeze was brewing into cold gusts that scattered the leaves about my feet. I walked briskly back to the car and headed out of the Park at Portageville, then took the road up through Nunda, Mount Morris and Cuylerville before reaching Geneseo. My first task once back here at the house was to rewrite my letter to Kelly, which I did using not just the smart blue paper, but also my underused fountain pen. I sealed the completed letter in a matching, lined envelope, then, preferring not to leave it in my own mailbox for collection tomorrow, I wandered down to the Post Office, a pleasant walk by way of Highland Road and Center Street. I bought stamps, deposited both the letter and the two postcards in the collection box, then set off for home again. It must have been the gentle incline up to Temple Hill that rekindled my tiredness. I am fighting sleep, desperately trying to save it for the proper time, but I fear it may get the better of me.


The first photographic evidence of my being at the Park is from my Christening, though I find it difficult to believe that I had not been taken there before that time. Grandpa and Grandma Wright are in those pictures, visiting from England, an occasion certain to have involved one of Mom's special 'Holton Tours' of the area. They drove up through the Park, south to north, that day. I would guess therefore that they would have taken one of Mom's favorite routes, heading out first to Conesus Lake, then on to Livonia and probably all the way down through Sparta and North Dansville before turning west to Ossian, Nunda and thence to the Park. This was a circuit she especially enjoyed in the fall, when the conflagration of the foliage would have reflected faultlessly in the mirror-like lake, when the road-side orchards would have been brimming with apples, when the air would have had the same sharp clarity as it had this morning.

On the regular visits we made to the Park when I was a child, Mom usually took a more direct route, straight to Mount Morris and along the Park Road. We would picnic at one of our regular spots, or sometimes, mostly in the summer months, set off along the Hemlock Trail, across the Deh-Ga-Ya-Soh Creek and right round to the museum. It was here where Mom had herself learned so much about the Seneca and where she tried to stir my own interest. The collection in the museum is made up of hundreds of items gathered by William Pryor Letchworth from the 1870s onwards. Originally, he housed it in a smaller building, known as the Genesee Valley Museum, but it was swelled so much by further acquisitions and donations that it soon needed bigger premises. The present museum was opened in 1913 and is home not only to native artifacts, such as stone tools and pottery, but also to Letchworth's personal library. Mom would stand with me by the display cases and read the typed descriptions, embellishing them with snippets gleaned from books and from the talks given at the Historical Society. I admit I was not always an attentive student, my childhood fascination being fired more by the museum's mastodon remains, found near the village of Pike in 1876. It was my first exposure to pre-history, if one discounts *The Flintstones*, and, as with most children, the idea of gigantic animals once roaming the vicinity seemed infinitely more exciting than a bunch of natives with puny stone implements.

The Seneca were the most populous of the nations that formed the Iroquois Confederacy. Within the Confederacy, they were known as the Keepers of the Western Door. The Iroquois lived in long-houses, a number of families to each dwelling, and they envisioned their Confederacy as one great long-house in which lived all the peoples of the five nations. Indeed, they referred to themselves as haudenosaunee, meaning 'the people of the long-house'. Being the westernmost, the Seneca nation would protect the western door of the long-house, while the Mohawks defended the eastern door. Between them lived the Oneida, the Cayuga and the Onondaga.

As far as I can fathom from all the books I have read on the subject, no-one knows for certain when the Iroquois Confederacy was founded. Some say it existed long before the arrival of Columbus, others date its inception very specifically in the 1530s. What does seem clear is the reason for its existence and the manner in which it was created. For generations, the Iroquois tribes had fought not only with adversaries like the Algonquin, but also amongst themselves. With relations between the tribes at their lowest ebb, there came a holy man named Deganawida, who is reputed to have had a vision of peace, a vision received from the Creator. Visions were one thing, but convincing the tribal chiefs of the merits of mutual trust and co-operation was something else entirely. To help him in his quest, Deganawida won the backing of Hiawatha, a Mohawk chief of Onondaga lineage. The two men traveled all over the Iroquois homelands in New York, ultimately persuading the tribes to join together in what became known as the 'Great Peace'.

It was a great peace for the Iroquois. For many other tribes, it brought about nothing but war. With the combined might of the five nations, the Confederacy was a huge and ferocious military power. Through that power, various other tribes were first vanquished then adopted, none of them being admitted as members of the Confederacy, but all falling under the auspices of its laws. Iroquoian influence extended across an immense swathe of territory, west into Michigan, east as far as the Connecticut River, north into Ontario and Quebec and south to the Chesapeake.

Military strength was coupled with wily diplomacy, something that enabled the Iroquois to deal on equal terms with European powers. The council of chiefs negotiated complex alliances, ostensibly for trade purposes, but often to allow the Iroquois to gain advantage over their traditional native enemies by using European firearms. The French, the Dutch, the Swedes and the British all became embroiled with the Confederacy, as either allies or enemies, throughout a period stretching from the early seventeenth century right up to the beginning of the Revolutionary War.

William Johnson, an Irishman by birth, had immigrated to New York in the 1730s. He became a fur trader in the Mohawk Valley and took a Mohawk wife called Molly Brant. He also learned the Mohawk language and the nation's customs and rituals, impressing the natives with his willingness to understand their culture and with his forthright honesty. As a consequence, the Mohawk listened to and trusted Johnson, who, in 1755, emerged in control of British policy toward the natives. With war between the British and the American colonists becoming inevitable, Johnson attempted to convince the Mohawk to side with the British. Whilst making an emotional speech to that effect, he was struck down by a stroke from which he died some days later. His son-in-law Guy Johnson replaced him as British Indian commissioner, but the greatest influence over the Mohawk was now Joseph Brant, Molly Brant's brother, who William Johnson had treated as a son, paying for his education at an English school. In 1775, Brant had been commissioned as a captain in the British army and later took part in the Battle of Long Island.

That same year, 1776, the council of the Iroquois Confederacy recognized the new United States, but chose to remain neutral in the war. Joseph Brant, who had risen to become a Mohawk sachem, was certain that the Americans, if victorious, would take away Iroquois lands. In defiance of the council, Brant took his warriors north, during the winter of 1776-77, in an effort to prevent the Americans capturing Canada. The council had, for some time, found itself unable to control the adopted tribes in the far reaches of its widespread empire, but now one of its founding members was dissenting. Worse still, the Oneida were diametrically opposed to the Mohawk move, their belief being that they should ally with the Americans. The Great Peace came to an end in August 1777 at the Battle of Oriskany, where Mohawks and Senecas fighting with the British came into direct military conflict with the Oneida, who fought alongside the American army.

The British were defeated at Oriskany and Brant's warriors fell back into their homelands, from where they continued, in concert with British Tories, to launch raids along what was then the American frontier. It was a bloody, guerrilla-like war, a war during which Brant was labeled 'Monster Brant' for the savagery of the attacks. In the summer of 1779, General George Washington ordered three armies, under the command of Generals John Sullivan, George Clinton and Daniel Brodhead, to converge upon western New York and destroy the Iroquois lands. Again with the help of the Oneida, the Americans captured the Confederacy's capital, the Onondaga village of Kanadaseagea. They then set about burning Cayuga and Seneca settlements and driving the people westwards.

One of those settlements was Kanaghsaws, which is now the town of Conesus. Two days after Kanaghsaws' destruction, an American scouting party, which included an Oneida guide, was ambushed by a group of Indians and Tories at what we know today as Groveland. During the skirmish, Lieutenant Thomas Boyd and Sergeant Michael Parker were captured by the Seneca chief Hiokatoo. The two young soldiers were taken to Little Beard's Town, close to modern day Cuylerville, just two miles outside of Geneseo. There, Joseph Brant, who had led the Indians at the ambush, is said to have assured the captives of mercy. However, for some reason Brant was summoned elsewhere, leaving British Major John Butler in charge.

Butler's previous record of brutality had shocked even 'Monster Brant', so the events that followed were totally in character. Lieutenant Boyd was subjected to the most gruesome torture, a whole series of atrocities that culminated in his being beheaded. His comrade, Parker, met the same fate, though the young sergeant was apparently spared the pre-execution torture.

Eventually, Sullivan's forces reached Little Beard's Town, known to the Seneca as Deonundaga, and razed it to the ground. It was the limit of the American expedition into the Iroquois homelands. The job had been completed; the Iroquois were in flight, many of them heading for the British Fort Niagara, where they were to suffer from freezing cold and near starvation during the following winter.

The Iroquois Confederacy was in tatters, the Great Peace nothing but a memory. Inspired purely by revenge, Joseph Brant raised a war party at Fort Niagara and moved against the Oneida. Villages were obliterated and hundreds were killed as the one-time allies fought out a bloody internecine war. Brant later led two thousand followers into Canada, where they settled in southern Ontario.

When the Revolutionary War ended, the Treaty of Paris included transfer to the United States of all Indian territory bounded by the Mississippi, the Great Lakes and the St. Lawrence River. In 1784, a further treaty, formulated at Fort Stanwix, saw what was left of the Iroquois in the USA restrained within their traditional lands in New York State. Within a short period of time, however, the natives found themselves being squeezed out by white settlers, who monopolized the natural resources and left the Iroquois only the option of selling their dwindling lands in order simply to subsist.

Two of the new United States, New York and the Commonwealth of Massachusetts, had disputed ownership of the Seneca land. It was determined by the courts that although the land belonged to New York, Massachusetts had the right to buy it from the Senecas. As it turned out, Massachusetts decided to sell its right to Oliver Phelps and Nathaniel Gorham. Phelps had been born in Connecticut in 1749, but had settled in Massachusetts. He had served as a member of the Constitutional Convention, then as a state senator and would go on to be elected to the US Congress. Nathaniel Gorham, eleven years Phelps' senior, had also been a member of the state Constitutional Convention and the Massachusetts State Senate. He had signed the US Constitution on behalf of his state and had acted as President of the Continental Congress.

At a meeting at Buffalo Creek in 1788, these two illustrious men negotiated the purchase of more than two and a half million acres of land, stretching south from Lake Ontario to the Pennsylvania border and east from the Genesee River to the Preemption Line. In exchange for their land, the Seneca received a cash sum of five thousand dollars, plus a perpetual annuity of five hundred dollars.

The following year, Phelps and Gorham began selling the land to settlers and speculators, one major purchaser being Colonel Jeremiah Wadsworth of Durham, Connecticut. Although destined to be known as a businessman and politician, Wadsworth had gone to sea in 1761 and had risen to the rank of first mate, then master. Later, during the Revolutionary War, he had served as a deputy and commissary general, then had become a member of both the Continental Congress and the US Congress. In 1790, two of the colonel's nephews, William and James Wadsworth, bought from their uncle part of what was known as the Big Tree tract. They then made their way to the Genesee Valley both to settle their own newly acquired land and to act as agents for the sale of the tract's remaining four thousand acres.

Opinions are divided on how the Wadsworths' tract came to be called Big Tree. Some people believe it took its name from the Seneca chief Go-on-dah-go-wah, who lived in Kanaghsaws at the time of its destruction by John Sullivan's army and whose name means 'Big Tree'. The claims of this viewpoint are strengthened by Chief Big Tree's participation in the Treaty of Buffalo Creek, at which Phelps and Gorham purchased the land from the Senecas. The most popular theory as to the origin of the name derives, however, from an enormous white oak tree that once grew on the east bank of the Genesee River. Certainly the tree, which had a circumference of twenty-eight feet, did stand on the tract bought by the Wadsworths, but its adoption as the origin of the settlement's name may well have more to do with romantic legend than with fact.

It was William Wadsworth who was mostly responsible for the development of the settlement at Big Tree. Of the two brothers, he was the more practical, the less scholarly. James Wadsworth spent many of the early months back in Connecticut, where he endeavored to sell land contracts. Later, he was to travel on a similar mission to Europe. He also procured more land for his family, Wadsworth holdings eventually covering almost thirty-five thousand acres. Meanwhile, William was left to enlarge the settlement, through rental to tenants, and to extend the Wadsworths' farming and milling operations, something he achieved with the constant help of a slave girl called Jenny.

Massachusetts had also been granted the right to buy Seneca land to the west of the Genesee River. Again, the state sold that right, this time to a man called Robert Morris, who had helped bankroll the Revolutionary War. Morris subsequently sold these four million acres to the Holland Land Company. Part of the deal was that he would extinguish the claims of the Seneca to the lands, but this proved more difficult than he maybe had imagined. The Dutch withheld payment in full until the natives' claims were dealt with and Morris found himself deep in debt. In desperation, he arranged for a meeting to be held at Big Tree between the Seneca chiefs and Morris's agents. Acting as commissioner on behalf of the United States was Colonel Jeremiah Wadsworth.

It was a meeting marked by constant wrangling between the parties, by fine oratory and blatant bribes and, particularly on the part of the Seneca, by much diplomacy of the brinkmanship variety. In the end, the Big Tree Treaty was agreed, the terms of which provided for Morris to pay for the clearance of the Seneca claim to the lands, whilst setting aside eleven reservations on which the natives would be allowed to remain.

One of these reservations was at the Gardeau flats on the western bank of the Genesee, which had become the home of Mary Jemison. Mary had been born on board a ship bringing her family to Philadelphia in 1742. While in her early teens, she was taken captive during an Indian raid on her home near Gettysburg, Pennsylvania. First adopted by Senecas, then married to a Delaware called Sheninjee, she was soon producing the first of her many children, Thomas. Not too long afterwards, Mary, together with her son and two Indian 'brothers', set off on the six hundred mile trek to visit her husband's relatives in the township of Genishau, which is also documented as Chenussio and Connecchio and which seems to have been located south-west of present-day Geneseo, near the confluence of the Genesee River and the Canaseraga Creek. Meanwhile, Sheninjee decided to transport some furs and hides to Wiishto, then join Mary at Genishau the following spring. With her two brothers, Mary picked her way through the wilderness, carrying her baby on her back. Utterly exhausted, she at last reached Genishau, where she was enthusiastically welcomed by her husband's family, who provided for her food and accommodation.

Winter passed and spring came, but Sheninjee did not appear. Eventually, word reached Mary of her husband's fate. He had fallen ill on his journey to

Wiishto and had died. Yet again, and certainly not for the last time, Mary was forced to rebuild her life, settling in nearby Little Beard's Town and, after a while, marrying Chief Hiokatoo, the man who went on to capture Boyd and Parker and who reputedly took part in their ruthless torture. With Hiokatoo, Mary had six more children, five of whom she took with her when she fled, in late 1779, ahead of the advancing American army. She laid low in the surrounding countryside until Sullivan's men had completed their mission and had started back east again. She then returned to find Little Beard's Town completely burned out. Once more she headed off, again with her children, this time to the Gardeau flats, where, at first, she struggled to survive. In time, she was able to build a house and settled down to what she hoped would be a peaceful existence.

Although born a European, Mary had become a Seneca. She spurned the opportunity to return to her own people and instead became a respected and influential figure in the Seneca nation. She was given the name Deh-Ge-Wa-Nus, 'two falling voices', though most of the books about her refer to her as the 'White Woman of the Genesee.'

This course I am taking will, one day, bring me a degree. Sometimes I wonder why I am studying so hard for something that will never be of any practical use to me. The reality is that I am not doing it for the qualification. I am doing it so as to keep myself focused, disciplined. It brings structure to my life, in much the same way as my job once did. I guess it also brings purpose, but admitting to that is tantamount to saying that, without it, my life would drift aimlessly. I should like to think that would not be so. Throughout my childhood, my mom tried to instill in me a sense of direction, a sense of value and worth. This often seemed to me an anachronistic attitude, something that should be condemned to the past along with so many other manifestations of outmoded, all-American wholesomeness. Late in my fourth decade on this earth, I am at last beginning to see my mom's great wisdom.

Liberation from the shackles of Cow Town, USA – that is what I craved as a teenager. When that liberation came, however, the change was practically seismic.

After graduating from High School, I was accepted at the Columbia Business School. Suddenly, my world inverted. From the sleepy security of small town Geneseo, I found myself in the urban maelstrom of New York City, a place of clamoring, non-stop energy. As an occasional and transient visitor, the place had seemed alive and exciting, but actually living there made me realize what a hick kid I was. During my first week on campus, three people were murdered in a nearby neighborhood and one of the sophomore students at the Med. School was raped by a gang of three black kids, who then beat her senseless. The next week, some self-styled white vigilante randomly selected a fifteen-year-old black boy and blew off his balls with a handgun.

If I thought that the ambience of imminent physical harm was bad enough, my life was further complicated by the discovery that, although I had been one of the brightest kids in my hometown, I was no more than an average student at Columbia. Moreover, the expectations of my tutors at the university were much different from those of my schoolteachers. Whilst Economics demands the retention of many facts and formulae, it also requires its academic apprentices to explore more philosophical and esoteric ground. The combination of my High School teachers and my mom had prepared me well for the facts and formulae, but the only philosophy to which I had been exposed had been of the humdrum, homespun variety. One specific teacher always springs to mind, a middle-aged lady who taught me in the seventh grade and who I only ever recall speaking in axioms. She would tell us frequently that we should do unto others as we would wish others to do unto us. 'Stupid is the fish who drinks the pool.' she would say and 'The devil makes work for idle hands.' One of her favorite insights was that the biggest fool is the one who only fools himself. Little wonder that, at Columbia, I found Adam Smith and Milton Friedman just a little more challenging.

I think my eventual degree says more for the brilliance of Columbia's teaching than for the innate talent of this particular student. Contingent upon my graduating was a job with The Greenleaf Corporation, an ethical investment firm headquartered in Lower Manhattan, who had sent their Employee Relations people up to Columbia during a recruitment fair the previous February. I know Mom was disappointed that I accepted the offer from Greenleaf, rather than returning west and maybe finding a job in Rochester or Buffalo. I had, however, grown to like New York City, not for its intrinsic quality of life, but for its pervasive culture of ambition. Heading back upstate would have meant returning to the backwoods from which I had wanted so much to escape. It would also have meant turning my back on the chance to make something of myself, to aspire, to make piles of money in the heat of the world's financial cauldron.

My Columbia classmate, Dieter Buchmann, decided to stay at the university and do post-graduate research into the implications of chaos theory upon the world economy, or some such obscure use of his rich father's wealth. Every fortnight or so I would meet up with Dieter, sometimes at the apartment I had taken in an ugly and low rent block way out near the East River, other times at his rooms on campus. One particular Saturday in late January, I found myself sitting opposite Dieter in one of the university's dining halls, where we had gone to grab lunch before heading off to meet some other friends at the Museum of Modern Art. As we ate, there appeared beyond Dieter's right ear, a face of unbelievable innocence amidst the usual mass of prematurely weathered and earnest expressions. Dieter could see me gazing past him and turned to see what was stealing my attention away from some story he was telling about one of the professors, who had been arrested for snipping small clumps of hair from women on the subway. He was a wearisome narrator and well used to losing his audience mid-anecdote. Yet, even Dieter could tell there was something different about this instance. As he turned, the young woman looked up and must have seen him staring straight at her from behind his little round spectacles, his head obscuring me from her perspective.

'Yes.' he said, returning his gaze to me. 'I see now.'

'She is beautiful.' I drooled.

'Maybe.'

Dieter scooped up a spoonful of ice cream and fed it into his tight European mouth.

'What do you mean: "Maybe"?' I asked.

'Maybe she is beautiful, maybe she is not. It depends upon who is doing the looking. You find her beautiful, I find her interesting, intriguing.'

I frowned. 'What?'

'Her name is Kelly Samuels. She comes from Hershey, Pennsylvania, where they make the chocolate. She's a psychology major. Fresh faced, but very together, very much in control.'

'How do you know all this?'

'My neighbor also studies psychology. She has visited him two, maybe three times.'

'Is she dating your neighbor?'

'No. She dates no-one.'

Dieter's precise diction, coupled with the idiosyncrasies of his English, often left me wondering his exact meaning. 'You mean she hasn't got a boyfriend at the moment?' I sought to clarify.

'No.' he said firmly. 'I mean she dates no-one. She does not date. She wishes to have no date.'

I looked across at Kelly again. She was sipping at a cup of tea, staring at the person facing her, listening with a look of great concentration. Kelly Samuels, I thought. Hershey, where they make the chocolate. Psychology. I realize now I was searching for an angle, looking for some line of attack.

Dieter returned to his ice cream, the separate colors of which had melted into one another to form a gray-brown sludge. Thankfully, he seemed to have given up on his story concerning the hair-clipping professor and chose instead to finish his meal in silence, as I continued to take surreptitious glances at my future ex-wife. How I agonized, wanting to go talk to her but scared of making a fool of myself in such a public place. Eventually, as Dieter drank from a huge beaker of coffee, Kelly began to gather her books into a cavernous shoulder bag. She was about to leave.

My movement was so impulsive that I cannot remember walking across to where Kelly was sitting. What I do recall are her mannerisms, her posture, the way she held herself completely still and drilled straight into me with those cold, probing eyes that seemed so incongruous, set in a face so round and amiable and unsophisticated.

'My friend tells me that you don't date.' I said. 'I am hear to cure you of that affliction.'

'I see.' she responded, analyzing me in a way with which I would become very familiar over the next few years. 'And how do you propose to do that?'

'By taking you on a carriage ride around Central Park.'

'Don't you know that's cruel to the horses?'

'Who said anything about horses? I shall personally be pulling the carriage.'

One of her friends snorted coffee through her nose as she tried in vain to suppress a giggle. 'Oh. I see.' Kelly continued, without averting her eyes from me for a moment. 'And when will this be?'

'Tomorrow evening at seven thirty.' I told her. 'Meet me by the Sherman statue opposite the Plaza Hotel.'

'I'll think about it.'

That, I was sure, would be the last time I would speak with her. There was no way she was going to show up for our date and, after that, I would be way too embarrassed to ask again. That is if I even saw her again.

The next evening, I waited in the gloom, pigeons pecking at the ground around my feet, an especially scruffy specimen acting as sentinel up on the head of Sherman's horse. The chill wind rasped against my face. I touched my tongue against the tip of my nose – it was icily cold. All around me the city was operating at its usual frenetic pace, buses and yellow cabs plowing up and down Fifth Avenue, pedestrians side-stepping through the traffic and scurrying busily along the sidewalks. I was, it occurred to me, the only person standing still. I felt rather forlorn, not to say hopelessly conspicuous. Where *was* she?

One thing I was to learn about Kelly is that she is always punctual. Of course, I had been waiting since seven fifteen; Kelly arrived on the stroke of half past, wrapped warm against the cold wind in a black, calf length coat.

'You came.' I said.

'I came.' she said. 'Does that mean I'm cured?'

Not entirely was probably the answer to that question because, even though we began to see each other regularly, there was always an aloofness about her, as though there was an invisible moat keeping her just out of reach with no sign of a drawbridge. She did not come to my apartment, nor was I invited to her room. We kissed in a tight-lipped way that was at the other end of the spectrum completely from the serpent tongued Linda Danelli. She did not snuggle close to me, or place her arm around my waist as we walked, or rest her head on my shoulder while we waited on a subway platform. I sensed that she did not want me to become a distraction, someone who would divert her attention from her prime objective, which was to complete her degree, then to build a career. I wondered if, in fact, I was part of the means to that end, an experiment, a case study. Kelly did not so much have conversations with me as conduct interviews. She constantly asked how I felt about things, anything, from Sino-US relations to the merits of vegetarianism. Never once, though, did she ask how I felt about her. Had she done so, I could only have said that I was falling in love with her, even if she did treat me like a rat in a lab.

I guess it is not surprising that Kelly took it upon herself to analyze the reasons why I had experienced such feelings for her at that time. I recall we were at a friend's apartment one Sunday afternoon, a group of us, maybe seven or eight people. We had all just been to see *When Harry Met Sally*, which places it in 1989. With heart-sinking predictability, the discussion got round to the nature of relationships between men and women and Kelly led the way with a dissection of our first year together. My adoration of her, she said, had been fueled by a series of challenges, each of which I had needed to overcome in order to satisfy the male imperative of competitive success. The first had been at the very outset, when Dieter Buchmann had told me that Kelly did not date. I had wanted both to prove him wrong and therefore assert my superiority over him and to prove my powers of persuasion were stronger than Kelly's determination to remain uninvolved with a man. She had, she admitted, acted in a rather cold way towards me in those early days, holding back from great displays of affection, maintaining a distance between us. This had had the effect of heightening my desire still further as it challenged my innate compulsion to break down such barriers and demonstrate my might. Like all men, I had also entertained the egotistical belief that I could not possibly be rejected. Kelly's announcement, a month or so into our relationship, that she was a virgin and intended to stay that way until her wedding night had thrown yet more fuel onto the smoldering fires of my passion. It had introduced the greatest challenge of them all. I had wanted not just to subjugate her through sexual conquest, but also to prove myself worthy of being the first man to do so. It had been a potent mix, which simply could not have failed.

What still bothers me about this explanation is that it was largely correct, though I had certainly considered, indeed expected rejection and I do not believe that subjugation was ever an objective. No matter. Kelly's analysis had, in the main, rationalized my ostensibly *ir*rational act of *falling in love* with this person who had been behaving in such an indifferent manner. Maybe the more difficult it is to achieve something, the more intense we feel about it. Maybe the more we strive to crack an enigma, the more it captivates us, the more we fall under its spell.

The first Christmas after we had started dating, I came home to Geneseo, while Kelly went out to Hershey to be with her folks. She was never enthusiastic about trips back to Pennsylvania and, when I spoke to her on the 'phone, she sounded unusually subdued. On New Year's Day, she called me and we talked for over an hour. She was so down, so despondent, I wanted to hold her, to wrap her up in my arms and tell her how much I loved her and that this would be the last time we would be apart. When we got back to New York, though, nothing had changed; she was still as tantalizingly remote, still as frustratingly cool.

As the months passed, she became more and more involved with work for the student journal and then with the university's radio station. This meant that we would meet perhaps only twice a week, when we would go to a movie or a coffeehouse or maybe stroll around Central Park. When we walked, we talked solely about Kelly's studies or how my job at Greenleaf was progressing. What I craved, though, was some intimacy, the type I saw so many of my friends enjoying with their partners.

The next Christmas, 1984, Kelly came here to Geneseo and discovered that all I had been telling her about my mom was true. Kelly adored her, reacting in a quite uncharacteristic way, embracing her in thanks for her present, linking arms with her as they walked down Main Street looking at the colored lights on all the buildings. Meanwhile, Dad and I walked behind, talking about nothing in particular. I know now that it was that Christmas when I decided I wanted to marry Kelly Samuels. She had bonded, as she would herself say, with the most important person in my life.

I proposed on Kelly's birthday, June 22nd. She accepted straight away. She then went to the telephone and called my mom. I believe the news reached her own parents later in the week. Engagement had no effect on Kelly's views regarding our living arrangements, however. She remained in her cramped student room until she graduated in the summer, then found a slightly larger place out on East 23rd Street. Our apartments were three blocks apart, close enough for pedestrian convenience, distant enough for Kelly to enjoy a sense of separation and independence.

One Saturday night, after we had been out to a jazz club down in the Village, she asked me not only to walk her home, but also to stay over. Her apartment had three rooms, one for sleeping, one for bathing and one for everything else. We sat at the kitchen counter and drank coffee, then talked for a while, Kelly sitting cross-legged on the floor, me nestled back in an old sofa - which is also where I slept. Coffee and conversation drained, Kelly went to her bedroom, brought out a blanket and handed it to me matter-of-factly, as though I could not have been expecting anything different. It was a pattern that continued for a long, long time, no matter whether we spent the night together at Kelly's apartment or at my own. She always got the comfortable bed, I always got the lumpy sofa and the itchy blanket.

Charlie Petersen just called.

'Hello there.' he said. 'How are you, William?'

'Fine.' I told him. 'Thanks for the letter you sent. I really appreciate it.'

'No thanks necessary. It's the very least we could do. Is it insensitive to ask how the funeral went?'

'Of course it's not insensitive, Charlie. I guess everything went as well as it could have done. There weren't that many people at the church and even fewer at the cemetery, so it was really quite a small affair.'

'And you, Will. How are you holding up?'

'Pretty well, I think.'

'You're like your dad. You wouldn't say even if you *were* having problems.'

'You underestimate me Charlie. I do open up every now and again. Anyway, everyone's been really kind. My aunt let me stay at her place when I was over in England, my friends down in Westchester took care of me the night I got back, Bobbie looked after things here while I was away......'

'She's a good kid.'

'Yes, she is Charlie.'

'Has she mentioned Christmas to you?'

Indeed, Bobbie had mentioned Christmas. A couple days before I left for England she told me that Charlie and Rose wanted me to go with her to Florida for the holidays. All I told her was that I would think about it. Apart from now not knowing quite what direction my life is about to take, I also have to admit that the prospect of spending a week in Fort Myers fills me with nothing but dread. I love Charlie and Rose, but I loathe Florida. As Bobbie refuses to fly, I would have to drive all the way down there. I would then be subjected to the company of mosquitoes the size of mules, not to mention those pesky little bastards they call no-see-ums that like nothing more than to feast on the blood of sallow, half-English northerners.

'Yes, she has.' I said in response to Charlie's question. 'I'm not sure what I'm going to be doing right now.' I tried to sound upbeat. 'I will come down and see you, though, even if I don't make it at Christmas. Maybe we can do something early in the New Year. I think a little sun might do me some good by then.'

'Anytime you want, William. Just remember to bring your DEET.'

'Don't worry, Charlie, I will. Those insects aren't going to make a meal out of me again.'

Some weeks back, Charlie telephoned to ask whether I might be interested in creating a library of old films shot around here. He has about forty reels, some dating back as far as the 1940s. They are nothing more than home movies, but it had occurred to Charlie that they not only gave a picture of his family's life, but also provided a unique historical record of the area. I thought it was a great idea and suggested it to the County Historian. She liked the concept and even discussed with me ways in which we could get more films from other local people and thereby add to Charlie's collection. Just when I thought her enthusiasm was going to result in some action, the bright light of practicality lit up in her mind. Her office has so little space, tucked away at the back of the Livingston County Museum on Center Street. Any library would require storage capacity and a place for people to view the films. New equipment would have to be bought and, to preserve the original film, it would probably be necessary to transfer them all on to videotape. It would all require money and she is strapped for that even more than she is for space. Because I had been called away so suddenly, I had not had a chance to tell Charlie all this.

'I went to the County Historian.' I now told him, guiding the subject away from the thorny question of a Christmas trip to Florida.

'Oh yeah?'

I told him the story.

'That's too bad.' Charlie said. 'I thought we could call it the Holton-Petersen Memorial Archive.'

I laughed, thinking he was joking, but he had obviously been giving it some thought. 'Why should the Wadsworths keep getting all the glory?' he asked. 'Other families have lived in the valley, too.'

'That's true.' I replied. 'But the Wadsworths had a lot more money to spend on benevolent works and memorializing themselves.'

'Do you think we could get private funding?'

'Yeah, maybe. I need to think about it some more.'

'Will you do that?'

'Of course I will, Charlie.'

'Thanks, William. I guess I'd better be getting off the line. Rosie keeps telling me how these long-distance calls cost a fortune.'

'You should get e-mail. You can have as long a conversation as you like pretty much for free.'

'I know, but I'm too old to learn about computers. I'll stick with the old dog and bone, as your dad used to call it.'

'OK Charlie, you take care now.'

'I will, William. See you soon.'

With a click, Charlie was gone and I left my study and came here to the front room. Outside, I can hear my neighbor's children, who have been placing jack-o-lanterns along their porch, decorating the house for Halloween. They bring to mind one of the films I know Charlie has, shot sometime in the mid-sixties and showing Bobbie and some friends dressed as ghosts. It is one of the few films in which Grandma Holton appears, albeit fleetingly. As the little girls dance ghoulishly about the Petersens' yard, the camera focuses on the gaggle of on-looking adults. My mom is there, standing alongside Olive Petersen, Charlie's mother. There too is my dad, holding a can of beer. Everything is very casual, very relaxed. Then Grandma comes into view. She stands detached from the others, arms folded as if freezing cold, expression set as if she were sucking on a particularly sour lemon. Poor Grandma; I cannot recall her ever smiling. In fact, that pursed, testy look seemed to be permanently etched on to her face. The only other one of Charlie's films that I have seen provides further evidence. It was taken at our Moon Landing Party and shows bright sunshine interspersed by moments of deep shade as someone, Charlie I assume, given his absence from the pictures, pans the camera along the line of people – relatives, friends and neighbors - waiting by a smoking barbecue. Grandma is not in the line, however. She is sitting primly on a wooden seat, leaning forward on to her walking stick and glaring disapprovingly at the children, many of whom, including myself, are dressed as astronauts, with plastic helmets and pieces of old hose pipe masquerading as oxygen lines. I remember my dad calling me 'Colonel Buzz'. Twenty years later, I shook the hand of Buzz himself.

Charlie has told me that there are films shot over at the Park, 8mm movies of his father, Franklyn, and Grandpa Holton and some also of Raymond Petersen and of my mom. The four of them used to drive off in Grandpa's old Ford, usually on some roundabout route that gave Grandpa the opportunity to relate facts and anecdotes about the places through which they passed. In fact, it was Franklyn who coined the phrase 'Holton Tours' to describe these excursions. When Grandpa died, Mom took over the role of tour guide, delighting in telling visitors all about Geneseo and the surrounding towns. She would take them up to the Groveland Ambuscade to show them where Boyd and Parker had been captured, or to Long Point

Park on the shores of Conesus Lake, or sometimes to the Clara Barton House down in Dansville, or to the Gaslight Village across the county line in Wyoming. Just as Mom used to sit in the back of Grandpa's car and listen to his commentary, so I sat, as a child, in Mom's car and let what were probably the same stories infuse themselves in my memory. What is so sad is that Grandma never came with us. She never told us stories, she never shared her experiences or told us about her childhood or her parents or her two brothers. I know, now that I am older and have delved into our family history, that Grandma was, not to put too fine a point upon it, ashamed. She was embarrassed about her parents, about their constant need to strive so hard simply to put a roof over their heads and bring food to the table. She feared humiliation should people learn about her brothers' dubious antics. She had, in effect, reinvented herself when she met and married Jack Holton, but reinvention is merely re-packaging, re-labeling, it does not change the person beneath. Grandma's fight to keep the mask in place became a struggle against the world. Maybe if she had been prepared to let the mask slip now and again she would have been more content and those films would have shown her enjoying the Halloween fancy dress and the children playing as astronauts.

I have a great deal of respect for James Holton, for his ability and character in recovering from financial disaster. In his personal affairs, he was not, it is clear, an entirely honorable man, but the unreconstructed side of me harbors a sly admiration for any man who can bed three beautiful sisters. Way to go, James.

In the same year as James moved to Albany, De Witt Clinton was elected for his third term as mayor of New York City. Six years later, he became Governor of the state, already the most prominent supporter of the proposed Erie Canal, for which he had acted as commissioner, determining the route the great waterway should take as it linked the Hudson River with Lake Erie. The whole scheme was considered by many to be ridiculous; when first suggested by Geneva miller Jesse Hawley, the then President Jefferson described it as being little short of madness. However, with Clinton installed as Governor, the great project was begun, even if opponents did continue to call it 'Clinton's Folly' and 'Clinton's Big Ditch'. When opened in October 1825, the canal was over three hundred sixty miles long, was forty feet wide and four feet deep. Despite there being more than eighty locks, travel time between the east coast and the Great Lakes was reduced substantially, as were shipping costs which were reckoned to be only a tenth of the cost of similar journeys by the former land routes. The canal brought great wealth to many of the communities on its course: New York City became the principal port in the country; Buffalo developed into a major commercial hub; Albany profited handsomely from controlling traffic on the canal, and Rochester was transformed into a boomtown. As well as goods and cargoes, the canal brought immigrants to the region, many making their way to the new territories of the Mid West.

As the building of the canal progressed, James Holton at the Empire State Transportation Board found himself involved with the numerous petitions, received from across the state, for the creation of lateral canals which would act, so to speak, as tributaries to the Erie Canal. One such petition came in 1823 from the people of Livingston, Genesee, Monroe, Cattaraugus and Allegany counties, who wanted the state legislature to provide money for a link between the Genesee and Allegheny Rivers at Olean. This would then form an unimpaired waterway connection between the region and the valleys of the great rivers to the west, including the Mississippi and the Missouri. The Board's role was to take a sort of bird's eye view of the state's transportation system, then offer expert guidance to the legislators who would ultimately decide upon which schemes should and should not proceed.

In early 1824, James traveled out to the Genesee Valley and took a look for himself at the route for the proposed new canal. It was a low-key visit by an Albany bureaucrat and appears to have passed without most locals even knowing of James's presence. It is unclear how instrumental that visit was in delaying any decision as to whether building should go ahead, but certainly many months went by before any positive action was taken. Ultimately, it was Governor De Witt Clinton himself who fired up the legislators and recommended a full investigation of the proposed plan by 'able engineers.'

Although of the opinion that the canal was practicable, James was not at all certain about its commercial viability. Once again, though, he set off for the Genesee region, this time in the company of both engineers and representatives of the canal commissioners. His reservations about the canal were rooted in a belief he had formed that *all* canals would be a short-lived success. He had been reading about the prospect of railroads, a prospect that seemed to offer far greater benefit, both in the cost of construction and in the speed of travel. It would be almost two years before the first passenger railroad in the United States would be chartered, but James Holton could already envision a time when they would make canals redundant.

On his second visit to the valley, James intended to keep his views on railroads to himself, though he had already shared them with his young son John, who was wide-eyed with excitement at the great, smoke-billowing locomotives his father described. James roomed in Mount Morris while on that second visit and wrote home to his wife and son, describing the splendor of the area, most especially the giant gorge of the Genesee River and the three beautiful waterfalls. He also wrote of a man called Micah Brooks, who was one of the most enthusiastic supporters of the Genesee Valley Canal. It seems that James found in Brooks a man who was open-minded enough to listen to his concerns about the canal and the coming of the railroads. Brooks may have listened, but he was seemingly unconvinced. He recognized in James, however, a man who was prepared to offer a well-considered argument contrary to the prevailing wisdom. Brooks respected this and the two men struck up a friendship that was to last until James's death. In truth, it was much more than a friendship, for Brooks offered James a job, a position helping to manage the extensive lands he had acquired, including six thousand acres on the Gardeau flats purchased from Mary Jemison.

So, in the late summer of 1825, James, Jessica and John Holton moved from Albany to Mount Morris, where they lodged at Micah Brooks' expense until their new house was built.

The Holtons had arrived in Livingston County.

# Tuesday

❀

When Kelly stayed here over the Christmas holidays in 1984, she slept in Jackie's room, which I remember having to be cleared of Mom's painting equipment before Kelly arrived. I had come on ahead, leaving Kelly to go down to Hershey for a week or so. Mom and I used the time to prepare the room for her, removing the easel and all the paint pots and a whole array of Mom's early pictures, placing everything carefully in the garage, from which the car, a brown Mercury, was to be displaced during Kelly's stay. On Christmas Eve, Kelly arrived by train in Rochester, from where I collected her and drove her down to Geneseo. Mom met her on the doorstep, while Dad, as usual, hovered in the background, his innate English reserve keeping him from participating in the show of emotion about to be played out right before him. I watched Mom closely: she studied Kelly as she approached, wondering what sort of girl I was bringing home for her to meet. Then, as she realized how beautiful Kelly was, Mom seemed to gulp, to swallow a lump that had formed in her throat. I do believe she cried a little, but she hid it deftly, composing herself as they separated from their introductory embrace. Dad looked bemused and searched for ways to be useful, grabbing Kelly's bags from me and taking them upstairs. 'She's very nice.' he said to me, as I caught up with him on the landing, an observation that was about as effusive as my dad could get.

I cannot remember whether anyone from outside the family had ever slept in that room before. I know my dad had spent some nights in there, mostly when either he or Mom was unwell and did not want to disturb the other with coughing or sneezing or trips to the bathroom. There were times, also, when they slept apart for reasons I did not, as a child, understand, though doubtless they were no different from any other married couple in having intermittent fallings out. Always it was Dad who went to sleep in Jackie's room. Mom could not bear to be alone in there in the darkness.

'I'm so glad you brought her home.' Mom said to me that Christmas Eve night, kissing me on the head as she prepared to follow Kelly up to bed. 'That room needs a young woman to bring it back to life.' Kelly, my mom's adopted daughter, was sleeping in a room still decorated for her real daughter.

This place – this house, this town - always seemed to draw out a sweeter, kinder, more easy-going version of Kelly. It is only in the last year or so that I have discovered that, hidden beneath the hard shell she has formed around herself, that same, infinitely more appealing version does still exist. When she graduated, she found a job with KWZA, a small radio station with tiny offices in Queens. Her forté there was filling sixty-second slots with human interest stories, lending to them her psychological insight. Soon, she had her own thirty minute show each afternoon, addressing issues that effect women in the modern city, an eclectic mix ranging from prostitution to the price of cosmetics.

'These things need exposure.' she told me one evening as we ate in some Midtown pizzeria. We had been discussing that day's show, the subject of which had been the plight of some immigrant Asian girls, whose fathers would not allow them to attend school and who were then married off as little more than domestic slaves. I had agreed completely with everything Kelly had said both in the show and during our conversation. Her tone, though, suggested I had been arguing.

'These are people who have no voice.' she went on, her clenched fist annihilating a slice of pepperoni pizza. 'They *need* someone to stand up for them, to tell their story to the world.'

This was not a unique exchange between us, but it was the first time I appreciated the sheer intensity of Kelly's belief, the belief that she was performing a service far more important than simply broadcasting an informative afternoon diversion for middle class housewives.

At the end of that meal, she realized how much tomato sauce had got beneath her fingernails and, worse still, how much had dried in the setting of the engagement ring I had bought her. The ring was made of eighteen-carat gold and had a single diamond set between two rubies. Engraved on the inside were our first initials, K and W, so small that they were hardly visible without a magnifying glass.

'Jeez.' Kelly exclaimed, as she tried to clean the ring with her napkin. 'Why didn't you tell me about this mess?'

'I did.' I told her honestly. 'But you didn't hear me. You were so wound up.'

'Oh.' she replied, sheepishly

Summer passed and fall brought grubby golds and browns to the city parks, the drab colors soon replaced by the cold bareness of winter. We spent

Christmas again in Geneseo, which was when I first had a hunch that all was not as it should be with Mom. Her complexion was dry and her eyes looked heavy-lidded, as if she were constantly dozing off. Dad told me she had been to the family doctor, who had prescribed penicillin, reckoning she had an infection. His face, like his words, was vague. Some weeks later, still in pain, Mom again went to the doctor, who sent her to a gynecologist, who altered the diagnosis to an ovarian cyst. The operation was straightforward, but the lump the surgeon removed was not a cyst. The subsequent biopsy revealed that it was malignant and an oncologist recommended a full hysterectomy. By this time, another three months had passed and our wedding plans were well advanced. Kelly went to Geneseo, ostensibly to meet with the caterers, though we had agreed that she would also make an assessment of Mom's condition. Mom opened up to Kelly more than she did to either my dad or myself, as though Kelly were indeed her own grown-up daughter. She told her just how weak she really was, two weeks after having had much of her insides removed, and just how frightened she was at the prospect of discovering, from further tissue sample tests, whether the cancer had spread beyond her pelvic organs. Kelly wanted to postpone the wedding, but Mom was insistent to the point of belligerence.

Kelly returned to New York City and the wedding countdown resumed. One morning before she went off to do her show at KWZA, she got a call from Mom, who told her, elatedly, that the doctors had found no further trace of cancerous cells in the samples they had taken. Kelly, too, was thrilled and 'phoned me at Greenleaf both to pass on the news and to suggest a quiet celebration that evening. We agreed to meet at her apartment, then go on to a restaurant, but when I arrived she told me that she had changed her mind and that she had cooked a meal instead. This was quite a moment. Kelly's previous attempts at cooking had resulted in nothing more ambitious than a pot of fearsomely spicy chili con carné and, on another occasion, a disastrous pair of stuffed eggplants, the recipe for which she had mistranslated from European metric measures.

Wisely dispensing with the stress of preparing an appetizer, she had concentrated on making a rich, creamy sauce to accompany pan-fried pork escalopes that she had cooked perfectly. The vegetables had all been placed in a casserole dish, drizzled with olive oil and sprinkled with herbs, then baked in the oven. She evidently had no idea that different vegetables require different cooking times, so, for instance, the finely sliced carrots were more like chips, whilst the chunky potatoes were still hard in the center. I uttered not one word of criticism however, knowing that Kelly had gone to a lot of trouble for me and that I could certainly have done no better myself.

'They don't teach kids to cook in Hershey.' Kelly said, noticing me deliberate over a dried-up shallot. 'Not unless the recipe involves chocolate.'

'This is fine.' I told her, trying to be reassuring.

'No it's not.' she insisted.

'It is.' I said, equally adamant. 'The meat was fantastic and I really liked that sauce.'

Kelly smiled apologetically. 'Thanks.' she said. 'I guess I just need to listen more carefully when Claude our radio chef does his next show on vegetables.'

Dessert was a tangy lemon cheesecake that came from a deli close to the KWZA studios in Queens. It was a good choice, the citrus flavor having the effect of neutralizing the lingering woody taste of undercooked potatoes.

'Your mom's amazing.' Kelly said, as I licked the last smear of cheesecake from my spoon.

'I know.' I said, downing the spoon, then draining a few lingering drops of convenience store Merlot into my glass.

'She just wasn't going to let her illness get in the way of our wedding.' Kelly continued. 'It was as though she felt that, if we delayed it, she might never see her son get married. She might not survive that long.'

'It's not surprising that having cancer gives you a sense of your own mortality.' I said.

'I think it also makes you realize how important *today* is, don't you agree?'

'I guess so.'

Kelly sighed in mild frustration. 'Today *is* important, isn't it Will?'

'Sure.' I replied, wondering why the conversation had switched so completely from good-natured ribbing about Kelly's cooking to something much more serious. 'Every day is important.'

'You miss my point.' Kelly said. 'What I mean is that we ought to ensure we do the things we really want to do because there's no guarantee that there will be a tomorrow, or that, if there is, we'll be fit and able to do those things.'

'Absolutely.' I agreed with obvious lack of conviction.

She huffed. 'Will. Help me here. I'm trying to rationalize.'

'Sorry. I don't understand.'

'I'm trying to justify what I'm about to do. Justify it to myself.'

'And what are you about to do?'

There was a second or two of silence, during which Kelly stared down at her engagement ring.

'What I'm about to do,' she began again, her eyes lifting to meet mine with their familiar piercing gaze, 'is ask you to sleep with me tonight.'

I gulped on my last mouthful of wine. 'Oh.'

Although Kelly's convictions about pre-marital virginity had hitherto been expressed in terms more befitting some religious fundamentalist, the underlying truth was that she had been in constant conflict with her natural instinct. She had for some time, in fact, been wanting to begin our sexual relationship, but had steadfastly stood by her beliefs, something I have always found to be both touching and laudable. It had nothing at all to do with denying me the opportunity to subjugate her, however. As I would later find, it was more a matter of not allowing the genie out of the bottle. Now, she had figured a way of legitimizing our sharing a bed, her reasoning based upon my mom's apparent newfound 'live for today' philosophy. It seemed a rather lightweight argument to have had the effect of tipping the scales in such an absolutely opposite direction and, of course, it was. In reality, the balance had been moving, slowly but inexorably, for some time. Ever since Kelly had realized that I was, most definitely, the person with whom she wished to share the rest of her life.

That first time was not the stuff of steamy fiction or soft focus scenes in romantic movies. It passed quickly, nervously and very, very gently and afterwards there was a sense of release, of having cast out some demon. I remember looking at Kelly in the dim light of the next morning's early dawn. She was naked, her body hardly moving as she breathed, her eyes closed in contented sleep. She was perfect, completely unblemished, almost as though she had just been born. So this, I thought, is what she had been keeping from me for so long. I was glad she had.

Over the following couple months, I stayed at her apartment most weekends. Our lovemaking became more competent and gradually more ambitious, Kelly revealing an adventurousness as thrilling as it was startling for one so inexperienced.

'I knew it would be like this.' she said to me one Sunday afternoon.

'Like what?' I asked.

'Like……. *this.*' She motioned with her arm, its sweep encompassing the bed, the disheveled sheets and our unclothed bodies. 'I knew that once I started making love, I wouldn't be able to stop. I could *sense* it. You might not believe me but I've known how highly sexed I am ever since I was young, fourteen, fifteen, maybe. I just knew that, if I started having sex with a boyfriend, I'd enjoy it so much and want it so much that I'd end up sleeping with every guy I dated. So I didn't date. I didn't risk temptation. I wanted to save all that pent-up desire for one special person.'

'So I'm special, am I?'

'I dated you, didn't I?'

'I know, but why?'

'Because I liked you. I liked the way you looked, the way you moved, the way you talked. You have a beautiful voice, Will Wright. A holy voice.' I cuddled her close to me, so that I could feel her breasts press against my skin. 'I liked your sense of humor, too. You made me laugh when you first asked me out.'

Our last weekend together as an unmarried couple was spent up in the Catskills, where I had booked a hotel near Phoenicia. I left the office at lunchtime on the Friday and made my way to Kelly's apartment, where we were going to meet before heading off in a rental car. I rang the bell, but she was not at home, so I let myself in with the key she had given me. I made coffee and sat down on the sofa to read a newspaper I had bought earlier that morning. Piled on the floor beside me were about a dozen books, all but two about psychology. One of the misfits was a paperback novel, a real drugstore type with a wilting yellow rose pictured on the cover. The other book, of which I could see only the spine, was entitled *Step By Step To Great Sex*. I picked it out of the pile and thumbed through the first few pages. I skipped over the description of male and female genitalia, lured by the illustrations of lovemaking positions and diagrams showing exactly how each partner should stimulate the other. As I turned the pages, I mentally ticked them off. Yes, I thought, we have done that. And that. And that. Suddenly, I realized that not only had we done these things, but that we had done them in the same order in which they were covered in the book.

'How did you feel about that?' Kelly asked later that evening, after we had returned to our room from a gigantic dinner in the hotel's restaurant.

'Mmm.' I scratched my chin as if to summon a response. The wine we had been drinking, together with a large brandy, had muddled my mind. She had picked a perfect time to ask. 'Well.' I began, cutting a way through the mental fog. 'I respect you for going to the lengths of reading up on the subject.' This was a poor choice of words, making it sound as though she had been researching the history of the Erie Canal or something. 'I'm flattered, also, because you obviously want to make sure I get as much pleasure from sex as you.'

'And do you?'

'I don't know. How much pleasure do *you* get?'

'The best feelings I've ever experienced.'

'Well, then, yes. I do get as much pleasure as you.'

'Good.' At this point she stepped towards me, slipping off her shoes as she did so, and placed a hand on my pants, squeezing softly. 'Is it coming out to play?' she asked, affecting a lascivious smile.

The answer was yes and it played for most of the night.


Apart from spending an hour at the supermarket up on Lakeville Road this morning, I have passed much of the day by reading through my ancestor Thomas Holton's notes, made after his meeting with Rebecca Fulmer in 1890. 'Her memory is rich and vivid.' Thomas writes. 'She speaks strongly and fluently, her recollection and delivery rarely betraying her grand age.'

Thomas also writes of a time seventy years before that meeting when, he says, the economy here in the Genesee Valley was flourishing. Despite this, the state government had continually denied banking charters to towns in the area. Only when six counties filed a joint petition did the government relent and in April 1830, the Livingston County Bank was founded. Confidence in the new bank was so high that the entire $100,000 capital stock was raised in three days.

One of the biggest investors was Allen Ayrault, who became the bank's first president, opening the business on the second floor of what is these days a funeral home. In June 1830, work began on a new, two-story brick building at 38 Main Street, Geneseo, right next door to which Ayrault subsequently had built his own home, the Big Tree Lodge.

James Holton, Thomas's great-grandfather, knew Allen Ayrault through discussions they had had with regard to Micah Brooks' land dealings. This, I am sure, was a working relationship as opposed to a friendship, but it was close enough for James to suggest his son John for the position of messenger boy with the Livingston County Bank. John was fifteen years old, a chirpy, gregarious youth, who never grew taller than five feet three inches. He had a sharp wit and evident intelligence, but he was not a scholarly boy. He much preferred the outdoor life, fishing in the creeks, trapping rabbits and squirrels with tensioned wire snares that had the propensity not just to kill the unfortunate beasts, but to rip their heads clean off. He could perform a great repertoire of bird songs and imitate the calls of wolves and deer. He kept newts and spiders and stick insects for pets, collected arrowheads and axe-blades fashioned by Senecas and found, at that time, throughout the nearby woodlands. Whatever made James think that his son would be ideal as a bank worker is a mystery to me, though John did have one skill that would be of obvious use - he could ride a horse, which was a big advantage for a messenger with the only bank in six counties.

James and Jessica Holton returned to Philadelphia for the first time in over twenty years when James's mother, Elizabeth, died during the winter of 1833. John, who had never met his grandmother, did not attend the funeral. Instead, he continued with his duties at the bank, duties that required him to spend more and more time within the bank's offices on Main Street. He was taught how to keep accounts, how to maintain the heavy ledger books, how to count, with the fleetest of fingers, the bank's specially printed bills, which ranged in denomination from one dollar to twenty dollars. So sound were the bank's reserves that it backed its own money, with no involvement from either the state or the federal government.

By the time John met Catherine Greeley of Center Street, Geneseo, he was twenty-one years old and was acting as an assistant to the bank's chief cashier. Catherine was an orphan, raised by her aunt and uncle after her parents had died in a hotel fire in Boston when Catherine was eleven. Her aunt, Clarissa Van Oost, was her mother's sister; her uncle, Benjamin, was a half-Dutch, half-English land agent, recently retired to Geneseo from the firm of Van Oost and Sprague in Rochester. Although John had matured considerably since his squirrel-trapping, newt-collecting days, his lack of height and his freckled face made him look much younger than he was. Benjamin Van Oost was not impressed and discouraged the relationship. His wife, however, was more amenable, swayed, maybe, by John's infectious charm and by reasoning that anyone employed by that fine Mr. Ayrault must have something about him. Perhaps that quality was persistence, which John is said to have possessed in abundance, as evidenced by his gradual, but tenacious turning of Van Oost's opinion. When John and Catherine married, in May 1839, it was with Benjamin Van Oost's unqualified approval.

For a while, John and Catherine lived with the Van Oosts on Center Street, where their first child was born in 1841. The child was named William and emerged from his mother's womb already crowned with a head of thick black hair, a genetic legacy from Catherine's father. The delivery of a baby into his hitherto peaceful retirement swiftly convinced Benjamin Van Oost of the need for his niece and her family to have their own home. Geneseo was growing quickly and there were new houses being built all the time. By chance, a new house on Second Street had been abandoned with only the first floor completed after the owner had lost money in a collapsed business venture. The man was delighted to allow Van Oost to purchase the half-finished house and thereby clear some of his debt. Van Oost then contracted a builder to add the second floor and a pitched roof, the ultimate design being not quite as grand as the original owner had envisioned, or as opulent as most of the neighboring residences, but perfectly good enough for the young Holtons.

The second Holton child was Joseph, born in December 1843 and immediately recognizable as his father's son, being small, blond and with a face covered with freckles. Despite his age, James Holton would drive in his carriage up from Mount Morris every Sunday afternoon, undeterred by the frostily cold months of January and February 1844. He doted on his grandchildren, bringing them gifts and even opening an account for each of them with the Livingston County Bank. It was on his way home from one of his weekend visits that James was taken ill, complaining of chest pains when he arrived back in Mount Morris. Jessica sent for the doctor, who gave James some sort of powdered medication that did nothing for the pain, but caused James's saliva to turn yellow. Night had fallen when a neighbor rode off to Geneseo to fetch John, who left for his parents' house immediately and spent much of the night sitting silently by his father's bedside as the old man slowly yielded to the call of death.

James Holton's grave is in the Oak Hill Cemetery in Mount Morris, just about the only reminder left in the town of the Holtons' presence. Their house, which Jessica sold before moving to Geneseo to live with John and

Catherine, was demolished back in the 1920s, the old wooden structure replaced by one built of red brick.

The third and last of John and Catherine's children arrived with the first blossoms of spring in 1847. They named their new daughter Margaret, for Catherine's mother, though, as with their first-born, the new baby bore all the hallmarks of a Greeley, with its mahogany eyes and raven hair. Each child in turn went off to the little cobblestone schoolhouse on Center Street. William was a thoughtful, earnest boy, softly spoken and with none of the charisma the young John had possessed. Joseph was starkly different, both in size and disposition, though he too was more bookish than his father had ever been. He displayed an interest in science and engineering, often retreating to a workshop in the cellar where he would build model boats that he sailed on the nearby creeks and carefully crafted box kites that he and John would fly up on Groveland Hill. Meanwhile, Margaret would play with her wooden dolls, her dark hair tied back from her face in long plats patiently woven by Catherine, who worried about her daughter's solitary nature and saturnine manner.

As the children grew, great changes occurred in the lives of John and Catherine. In July 1855, the Livingston County Bank closed down, its twenty-five year charter having expired. John had been with the bank from the earliest days of its existence and had become a well-recognized figure in Geneseo, most of the townsfolk being familiar with his ever-smiling face. He was forty years old when the bank closed and he had the opportunity to move, as did the extant accounts, to the Genesee Valley Bank, which had opened its doors for business in 1851 and is actually still around, nowadays in the guise of Key Bank. John, however, had been offered a position by one of his regular customers, County Treasurer John White Jr., who wanted him to join his team at the County Courthouse. The pay was not quite as good as was on offer at the Genesee Valley Bank, but that no longer mattered to John Holton. Three years after the birth of his daughter Margaret, John had sat by another old man's bedside and watched him die, this time Benjamin Van Oost, who left half of his not inconsiderable estate to Catherine, the other half going to his wife Clarissa. Within a year, Clarissa too was dead, said to have died of a broken heart. Now Catherine had all of the Van Oost's fortune, including the house on Center Street, into which she and John moved, along with their children and Jessica Holton, allowing them to sell their home on Second Street to a man named Theodore Kent.

William Holton was nineteen and his brother Joseph was seventeen when Abraham Lincoln was elected to succeed James Buchanan as President of the United States. Thankfully, their grandmother Jessica did not live to see in the year of 1861. She died on the day of South Carolina's secession from the Union, December 20th 1860, and was buried, in accordance with her own instructions, in the Temple Hill cemetery. She had long before decided that, in death, she would have no desire to lay beside her husband or with her father Jacob Fulmer and her older sister Virginia in Philadelphia. Amongst her effects, John found a bundle of letters from her other sister Rebecca, all written from New York City and all, according to what Rebecca told Thomas Holton in 1890, unanswered. Jessica was, in Rebecca's words, a hard-hearted, resentful woman, who never forgave her husband for his infidelity and who made the poor man suffer for it until his dying day. These are strangely un-Christian things for a woman so devoted to the church to say, but, then, Jessica did marry the only man Rebecca ever loved.

Our wedding was held in Geneseo entirely because of the setting, which Kelly thought more photogenic than anywhere, absolutely anywhere in Pennsylvania. Mom invited Charlie and Rose, Teddy Hewson and his wife, Jimmy Randolph and a host of neighbors, some of whom I hardly knew. My aunt and uncle flew in with their daughters from England and members of Kelly's family arrived from various points in the Rust Belt. Even Great Aunt Clara was there, eighty-two years old and utterly cogent.

Holton Tours went into overdrive in the days leading up to the ceremony. Aunt Angela and Uncle Michael came to Geneseo a few days beforehand, combining the wedding with a long-awaited holiday, neither of them having ever before left England. With them were my cousins Valerie, who was twenty-four, and Anna, who was still only nineteen. Angela and Michael stayed over at my parents' house, taking my old room, while Valerie and Anna were billeted with the Petersens.

From the moment she arrived, Angela was brim full of energy, supercharged it seemed to me, jabbering incessantly with Mom and Dad, badgering her brother to take her out in his car and show her around. 'Come on Eddie.' she kept saying. 'I want to see *everything*.'

Considering it had been eleven years since Dad had last seen Angela, his reaction was ludicrously cool. 'Fay can show you round.' he said. 'She was born here. She knows the place a lot better than I do.'

'Yes.' Mom agreed, her eagerness only just masking her disappointment at Dad's lack of enthusiasm. 'I'd love to.'

'Me too.' I said, as much to shame Dad as to offer my assistance.

If I am to be honest, I was motivated also by wanting to be with Anna. Dad had collected his English family from Rochester airport and had delivered them to our door late the previous afternoon. While my aunt and uncle had settled into their new surroundings, I had driven my cousins to the Petersens' house. It had been a short journey, but, throughout, I had been unable to take my eyes off the rear view mirror, in which I could see Anna gazing back at me. She was stunning. Her skin was rich ochre, her dark brown hair shone with vigor and health, her arms and legs had the solidity and smoothness of youth. It was her face, though, that was so extraordinary. She had the face of an angel.

Charlie and Rose had brought my cousins back to our house later in the evening and had then stayed with us for dinner. I had tried to position myself opposite Anna, but Mom had foiled the plan by rearranging the seating so as to enforce some sort of male-female symmetry around the big old table. After dinner, Anna's attention had been cornered by Charlie, who I am sure had been as smitten by her as I had, then by Bobbie. I had been left with my aunt and uncle to talk through, for the umpteenth time, the wedding arrangements.

Now, by volunteering to co-host a Holton Tour, the opportunity had arisen to once more have Anna in my close company. Mom took Angela and Michael in her car, while I followed behind in the Chevy Monte Carlo I had hired when I too had arrived at Rochester airport three days previously. With me were Valerie, who, through her seniority, sat in the front passenger seat, and her ravishing sister, who sat in the back, bobbing from side to side, window to window, so as to see the sights on which I was providing commentary.

We went first to what is now Vitale Park in Lakeville, which is right at the top of Conesus Lake. Pockets of wildfowl dotted the shoreline, as warm sunlight shimmered off the rippling waters and cast tangled shadows across the face of the lush, verdant forest. We walked to a small inlet where two boys were fishing, both naked to the waist, their young, immaculate bodies perfectly tanned. From the lake we drove to Avon, where I showed my cousins the five arch bridge, then to pretty Caledonia, where they pottered about in the shops with Angela, while Mom, Michael and I sat in the little square and drank ice cold Cokes. Next, we took Route 36, down through York and Leicester, the names of which Valerie found amusing, being so obviously English. Near Perry, we pulled up at a farm shop and bought a pannier of strawberries, then, between the three of us, ate the lot even before we reached Silver Lake. There, apart from a few humans lounging on the decks of their waterside houses, hardly a living thing was in sight, the animal life having hidden itself away from the afternoon heat. Only the butterflies were in evidence: Swallowtails, Harvesters, Checkerspots.

Presently, we came to Castile and from there we headed into the Letchworth Park. I showed my cousins the Glen Iris Inn and the Middle Falls and the view from Inspiration Point. It suddenly occurred to all of us that Aunt Angela had stopped talking, that actually she was silent, her excited chatter subdued by the place. We went next to see the Lower Falls and the view across the river to Lees Landing and the great horseshoe of the gorge, the strata in its cliffs caught clearly by the sun. Then we drove north, along Park Road, over the Silver Lake Creek, round the Hogs Back, arriving finally at the dam, where Michael leaned on the rail, staring blankly at the immense gray wall, while Mom told Angela and Valerie and Anna about Hurricane Agnes.

On the drive back to Geneseo, Valerie talked almost as breathlessly as her mother had earlier in the day. Meanwhile, Anna sat gazing impassively at the passing countryside. I sensed some problem, perhaps between the two young women, perhaps between Anna and myself, but I had no idea what it might be, other than Anna maybe having spotted me watching her in the mirror.

The following day, Kelly's folks arrived. They wanted to help Mom and Dad with the final arrangements for the wedding, but there was very little left to do. Jimmy Randolph, whose wife Kathleen had passed away the previous fall, gave the Samuels lodging. Jimmy could hardly keep himself fed, let alone two guests, so I knew the throng around our dinner table would be swelled even further by the presence of Al and Laurel. Still with the ulterior motive of being in Anna's company for a while, I asked my two cousins whether they would like to eat out that evening, then maybe go to the Park to see the Middle Falls floodlit after dark. To my joy, they both agreed.

During the afternoon, my parents, the Samuels and I went over to the Glen Iris Inn to take a look at where the reception was going to be held. This gave Mom the chance to show her guests more of the Park, including the Council Grounds, up to which she struggled on foot, grimacing from time to time with the pain in her abdomen. She held Laurel's arm and showed her Mary Jemison's grave and the bronze statue. She showed her also the cabin that William Pryor Letchworth had moved there from the Gardeau flats, the cabin Mary had built for her daughter Nancy. I followed behind with Al, who had difficulty hiding his absolute lack of interest in all of the Iroquois stuff, Al being one of those men whose idea of Indians had been formed by John Wayne movies. He did his best, shaking his head in feigned wonderment at the story of how the Council House had been transported from Caneadea, but I could see he would rather be back at home, drinking beer and watching ESPN.

From the Council Grounds we drove to the Lower Falls, then arced around the Big Bend and made for the Mount Morris Dam, which Al evidently found much more to his liking. He hung out over the same railing against which Uncle Michael had leaned the day before. 'Quite a chunk of concrete.' I heard him say to my dad. I did not hear Dad's reply, which was drowned out by Mom animatedly telling Laurel about, yes, Hurricane Agnes.

There was a message from Kelly when we got back home. She had left New York City with Steve and Sally Caspar and was en route to Geneva, where they would be staying in a hotel prior to the day of the wedding. I had considered asking Dieter Buchmann to be my Best Man, but Dieter was back in Germany. Anyway, Steve was a far better choice. He was humorous and sociable and people tended to stay awake when he was speaking.

I went to collect Valerie and Anna from the Petersens' house around seven o'clock. When I arrived, Anna was sitting in the back yard with Charlie and Rose, but there was no sign of Valerie. Anna explained that Valerie had decided not to go out to eat with us and had instead gone with Bobbie to The Idle Hour for a drink. I was so delighted at the prospect of being alone with Anna that I did not stop for even a second and consider just how contrived this situation was.

Earlier in the day, while I had been at the Park, Valerie and Anna had both been with Bobbie to one of the new malls on the southern edge of Rochester. Both my cousins had bought clothes, Valerie a skirt, Anna a blue dress with big white dots, not exactly classy, but, on Anna that evening, sensational. I took her to The Leaning Tower in Mount Morris, where we ate pizza and watched through the window as the light of the long day gradually began to decline. We then drove into the Park and headed south, the sun slowly waning and casting long shadows across the road. When we reached Inspiration Point, the sky beyond the great railroad trestle above the Upper Falls seemed surreal, like a vast golden dome decorated here and there with streaks of blue-gray cloud. We sat on the wall and watched as the gold turned to a fiery orange, then to an oddly placid crimson.

'Isn't this beautiful?' I said to Anna.

'Mmmm.' she replied, in much the same manner as when she had first tasted one of those strawberries the previous day. 'It's romantic.'

'Do you like romance, then, Anna?'

'Of course I do. Don't all women?'

'I guess so.'

She turned away from the setting sun and looked instead at me. 'You're a romantic.' she said. 'Aren't you, Will?'

'No.' I told her, trying to be droll. 'I'm an Economist.'

'I mean under*neath*.' Anna persisted. 'Under those smart clothes and that big city ego, you're a dreamer. I can tell by your voice, especially yesterday when you were telling us about this place. I bet you don't talk like that back in New York, do you? I bet you've never told any of your city friends about that Indian girl who threw herself and her little baby into the waterfall.'

'No, I haven't.' I confessed, startled at the perceptiveness of this nineteen-year-old.

'You pretend to be something you aren't and one day it'll harm you.'

'How do you know that?'

'I just do. We are what we are, Will. No matter how much we pretend, we can't change what's in our genes, in our hearts.'

I do not mind admitting that I was a little spooked by this. It was not just what this young woman was saying, but the way in which she was saying it. She was calm, her tone so assured, so authoritative.

'What about you, then, Anna?' I asked, attempting to turn the conversation around. 'What are you really like?'

'Oh, I'm exactly as you see me.' she replied. 'Exactly as you see me in the mirror while you're driving.'

So she had caught me spying on her. 'Sorry.' I said, more embarrassed than apologetic.

'You've no need to be.' Anna half smiled, her face in the dimming light a myriad of unfathomable suggestions. 'As I said, we are what we are. You are attracted to me and I am attracted to you.'

'Yes.' I said. 'And your mother is my father's sister. We're cousins.'

'You still want me, though. Don't you Will?'

Aware we were on treacherous emotional ground, I stood up and walked away, heading purposefully back along the path towards the parking lot. When I reached the Inspiration Creek, I looked back, expecting Anna to be following behind. She was nowhere to be seen. I waited for a minute or two, but still she did not emerge from the quickly gathering dusk. Irked, I trudged back up to the overlook. She was still sitting on the wall, looking utterly serene.

I stood directly in front of her. 'Anna -' I began, but she interrupted me.

'Kiss me.' she said.

'Anna, this is ridiculous.' I told her. 'It's late and it's getting very dark. It's time we went home.'

'Kiss me.' she repeated.

'No.'

She raised herself slowly from the wall and stepped toward me. She then placed her arms around my neck and looked at me with eyes that were both doleful and determined. 'Stop pretending, William.' she said. 'We both want the same thing. Kiss me.'

'I'm not pretending.' I replied, though which one of us I was trying to convince remains a moot point.

'You are.' she maintained, her breath now warm against my face in the cool, gentle breeze of the late evening.

God forgive me for what I did next.


While I was in England last week, Aunt Angela gave me a copy of the Wright family tree. She has been researching it now for two years, but has managed, so far, to get no further back than her great-great-grandfather. Thus, the earliest date on the tree is 1825. My own name appears along the bottom, where I share the same generational echelon as my sister Jacqueline and my cousins Valerie and Anna.

We are all descended from Henry Robert Wright, who was born in London in September 1825. At some point, Henry married Beatrice Chandler, though Angela has found no record of the marriage. All she knows is that Henry and Beatrice lived together in the Borough of Stepney and that, in 1849, they produced a son who they named Arthur. The census returns for 1851, the first in which he appears, indicate that Henry was a 'journeyman', which is not too enlightening, and that Beatrice was a 'presser'. The following year, aged just twenty-seven, Henry was dead. He is recorded as having drowned, but we have no idea how.

At the age of twelve, Arthur Wright began work as a warp winder at a textile mill. This tedious job involved winding all the yarn on to the warping frames for the looms. Being a warp winder was typically a first step on what might loosely be termed a career ladder and certainly, by the time of the census in 1871, Arthur had moved on from loading the looms to helping to operate one of the steam-driven behemoths. His occupation is recorded at that time as a 'cotton and textile machine hand'. He is also shown to be a married man, his young wife being Katherine Leader, formerly of Bromley-by-Bow.

In 1877, Arthur and Katherine had a son, George, who lived for only a week. Two years later, a second child arrived, a daughter who they christened Gertrude. She was joined by a brother, John, in 1880 and a sister, Julia, in 1889. Poor Julia, who suffered from epilepsy, died in 1893.

Gertrude, known to the family for some reason as Gin, left school at thirteen and went to work in the same mill as her father. By all accounts she was a melancholy girl, a characteristic that stayed with her all of her life. She lived with and nursed her parents throughout their old age and never married, her interest in men having evaporated along with a young Welshman, to whom she was engaged for a while, but who disappeared one morning from his lodgings, never to be seen again. Gin's already gloomy demeanor darkened still further. By contrast, her brother John was a bold, squarely built young man, well suited to the job he took as a porter at the Smithfield meat market. His conversation was said to have been peppered with profanities, while his behavioral habits were disgusting and his personal grooming repulsive. When, in 1899, he met Maud West, a girl renowned for her fishwife's vocabulary, the two seemed perfectly suited. Strangely, each had a moderating effect upon the other. In John's case, the vulgarity was toned down, the spitting, belching, farting and nose-picking became more covert and there were even reported sightings of him having a bath.

Such were my English ancestors.

After our wedding ceremony at St. Michael's, Steve Caspar came over to me and asked what I had been thinking whilst standing at the altar. 'You went incredibly pale.' he laughed.

'I was thinking about my grandparents.' I told him.

'Oh.' he said, abruptly deflated.

I have never felt so guilty as when I stood in church that day. How in hell the minister chose the subject for his reading, I have no idea. 'You have heard that it was said, "Do not commit adultery".' he read, raiding Matthew Chapter 5 as part of a sermon on fidelity and the sanctity of marriage. 'But I tell you that anyone who looks at a woman lustfully has already committed adultery with her in his heart.' He omitted the bit about gouging out and throwing away your right eye if it causes you to sin, but he did extend his theme into 1 Corinthians 6:12. 'The body is not meant for sexual immorality, but for the Lord.' he said.

Silence hung heavily on our family and friends, who had come to join us in celebration and who found themselves being treated to a lecture. After a few moments of uncomfortable reflection, the minister spoke again. 'Please stand.' he said quietly. 'So we can all say together the Lord's Prayer.' I stopped at "Lead us not into temptation." I could say no more.

'You were *so* nervous.' Kelly said to me later. 'I thought you were going to lose your voice before we got to the end of the vows.'

'Sorry.' I said.

'That's OK.' my new wife assured me. 'It's nice that you were so moved by it all.'

The reception was held in the restaurant at the Glen Iris Inn. Steve made a fine and funny speech and even Al Samuels raised a laugh or two when he remembered Kelly's childhood and how she had once told him, at the age of maybe twelve or thirteen, that she would never, ever, ever, get married. It made me think about how even our strongest convictions are gradually eroded through maturity and realism. We made the usual toasts, cut the three-tier cake, led the dancing to what sounded suspiciously like the music from *The Godfather* and, finally, after a long, long day, escaped to the solitude of the Cherry Suite. We walked out on to the tiny balcony and looked across at the Middle Falls, illuminated in the darkness just as they would have been three nights previously, when Anna and I should have been standing down there by the wall.

Our honeymoon was in Bermuda, at the Hamilton Princess. We stayed for ten days, then flew back up to New York where we took up residence in our first, and only, marital home. We had each moved out of our rented places shortly before going to Geneseo for the wedding; now we had an apartment up on West 61st that somehow we had managed to buy. It was almost impossible to find *any* property to purchase in Manhattan. That we found somewhere we could *afford* was unbelievable. I was, it is fair to say, enjoying the most stupendous level of income, thanks to Greenleaf's ability to ride the crest of what was the tidal wave of 1980s prosperity. My bonuses alone were more than my dad earned in a whole year. Even then, we were fortunate to find a place that the owner needed urgently to sell, due to some trail of events that did not sound too dissimilar from those that had befallen my forebear James Holton on the death of Jacob Fulmer.

Although safely distanced from the really unsavory elements of the city, the apartment was in a building with three entry security systems. There was also a full-time concierge, who studied the comings and goings of the residents on a bank of closed-circuit television screens as he sat behind a bulletproof glass window in the lobby. We needed to remember one four-digit code number to gain access to the building from the street, another to operate the elevator and another to enter our apartment on the fourth floor. I had, by this time, been away from Geneseo for so long that such precautionary measures seemed routine. Once inside the apartment, one found a narrow entrance hall, off which there were doors to the two bedrooms, the bathroom and the main living area, which comprised a big sitting room with a screened dining area and a recently refurbished, sparkling white kitchen.

Kelly immediately set about furnishing the place, though she soon found her attention diverted by an approach from one of the local TV companies, WONM – 24 Seven News, whose executives liked her show on KWZA and, perhaps more importantly, coveted her telegenic good looks. Meetings were arranged, an agent was appointed, screen tests were held and all the time the value of the potential contract kept getting higher, especially when another company made a rival bid. For a while, Kelly could think or talk about nothing else except her move into television. I could have felt sidelined by this, but instead I was deeply grateful. It stopped her thinking too much about the problem with which I was about to be faced.

One Friday evening, when Kelly was having dinner with WONM's Managing Editor, I arrived home from work to find a message on our answering machine from Anna. She sounded tired. Her voice was lifeless and I thought I could detect the chafe of soreness in her throat. She wanted me to call her back, but it was after seven o'clock in New York and therefore past midnight in England. I decided to leave the return call until the following morning.

Kelly arrived home around eleven. Her drawn face would have been an appropriate accompaniment to Anna's jaded voice. She told me briefly about her dinner and about the specific job WONM had in mind for her, but the day had obviously drained her and it was not long before we were in bed and asleep.

I woke late on the Saturday, which was unusual because I normally roused at exactly the same time every day, six-thirty, a habit formed by needing to get to work by eight o'clock each weekday morning. I guess it must have been early afternoon in England when I finally got around to calling Anna.

Angela answered the 'phone.

'Hello, William.' she said, sounding surprised. 'Nice to hear from you.'

'Yeah, good to hear you too Aunt Angela.' I replied. 'I was actually calling for Anna. Is she there?'

'I think so.' Angela told me, a little vaguely. 'I think she's in her room.'

I heard her shout for Anna to come to the 'phone and, presently, my cousin's voice came warily down the line.

'Anna.' I said. 'It's William. You called me.'

'I can't talk now, Will.' she whispered. 'I'll call you in five minutes.'

She hung up.

It was nearer ten minutes later when the 'phone rang and the operator asked me if I would accept a collect call from England.

'What's going on, Anna?' I asked, when we were at last connected.

There was sniffling at the other end of the line. 'I *need* you William. I need you so much.' Anna sobbed, her voice echoing around what was obviously one of those English telephone boxes.

'*What?*' I exclaimed.

'Please don't be angry.' she pleaded. 'I don't want you to be angry with me.'

'I'm not angry, Anna.' I said, trying to be composed. 'I'm just taken aback. What's brought all this on?'

'You know what's brought it on. I told you how I feel about you.'

'Anna, look. I really don't want to have this conversation.'

I was now scared to death at the possibility of Kelly hearing what I was saying. I had left her asleep and there was still no noise from the bedroom, but that did not mean she was not now awake and listening.

'It doesn't matter what you say.' Anna continued. 'I love you William.'

'Sweet Jesus, Anna.' I said, exasperated. 'You've got to stop this.'

'But I can't.' she insisted. 'I need you more than ever.'

'Anna, you have got to get a grip -'

'I can't get a grip. I need you to help me. Please help me.'

She was now horribly distressed.

'Anna. Anna.' I said, striving to calm her. 'What do you want me to help you with?'

There was no coherent response, just the agonizing sound of my cousin crying so much that it made her choke.

'Anna.' I said once again, but listening to her gasping and reaching was unbearable. Shame on me, but I put down the 'phone, determined not to accept another collect call should it come through. I felt wretched, but I did not know what else to do.

Kelly emerged about half an hour later and found me sitting at the dining table, my eyes scanning the *New York Times*, but my brain registering not one word of what I was supposedly reading.

'Who were you talking to?' she asked.

'Anna.' I told her.

'Sounded serious.' she said. So Kelly *had* heard the conversation. Now I felt not just wretched but petrified. What the hell had I said?

'She's just a bit confused.' I said as casually as I could.

Kelly let out a hollow laugh. 'She's more than just confused, William. She's one real cooky kid.'

'What do you mean?' I asked.

'Oh come on, Will.' Kelly responded. 'You must have seen the way she behaves. It's like her mind and her body have been grafted together from two different people. She looks like a normal kid, but when she opens her mouth it's as though someone else is talking. I wondered, at first, whether she was on some sort of medication.'

'Do you think she is?'

'No. There's something more to it. Something to do with the way she's been brought up. I'd say she feels unloved.'

'Oh come on, that's ridiculous. You couldn't find more loving parents than Angela and Michael.'

'That's not the point, Will. Parents might be loving, but children don't always see it that way. They can view that love as being smothering, or interfering, or even as a means of control and manipulation. Most people think of parental love as being simple because it's instinctive and natural, but it's very, very complex and its effect is far more profound than just about any other type of love, like that between a husband and wife.'

Suddenly, the telephone rang with all the force of a hand grenade exploding. I moved to answer it, but Kelly was much closer and got to the receiver ahead of me. To my relief, the caller was Alex Wardell, one of Kelly's friends from Columbia, who was 'phoning to confirm a lunch date they had made for later in the week. I tried again to read the newspaper, but still it was impossible, though I found a crumb of comfort in the knowledge that, while Kelly and Alex were talking, Anna would not be able to call.

I was in two minds about resuming the conversation once Kelly had finished her call. Part of me wanted never to think again about Anna, whilst another part was keen to hear Kelly's opinion.

'So.' I said, resuming, 'How does a perceived lack of love turn a young woman into such a scary person?'

'Scary?' Kelly mused. 'Yes. That's a good word. Anna *is* scary. Or maybe dangerous is a better description because she's a danger to herself and to the people around her.'

'I don't understand.'

'Because she thinks she isn't getting any, she's tried to kid herself that she doesn't *need* love. She puts on an act of self-confidence. She's perfected a pretence of maturity, partly through being innately intelligent and observant, but mostly through practicing that pretence with men, who are, one, far less intuitive than women and therefore not so likely to see through the smokescreen and, two, prone to transferring their brains to their dicks when in the company of attractive young women.'

'That doesn't sound too scientific, Kelly.'

'I disagree. Such an observation is maybe crudely stated, but it is scientific by virtue of it being the truth. I watched her at the wedding reception. She works the room like a politician, moving from person to person, but only lingering in the company of men. She flirts mercilessly, but always in a different way with each man, seeking out each individual's On button. When she was with older men, like Charlie and that old guy who was a Sheriff -'

'Teddy Hewson.'

'Yeah, him. When she was with them, she played up like little orphan Annie. Then when she turned her eye to Steve Caspar, she came on like a hooker, all wild and dirty.'

I tried frantically to suppress a rage of jealousy. My cousin Anna had been flirting with Steve Caspar? Yuck!

'One good thing, though, Will.' Kelly continued. 'She seemed to keep well clear of you. Probably because you're family.'

'True.' I said, the jealousy partially assuaged by relief. Indeed, Anna had said very little to me at the reception, mostly through my ensuring I stayed surrounded by other people at all times.

'Anyway.' Kelly said in the manner of someone wanting to bring the discussion to a close. 'Flirting gives the lie to this notion she has of not needing love, because, in her case, it's a means by which she can make people love her. Or so she thinks. Unfortunately, what she interprets as being signs of love are no more than the manifestations of basic lust. She's the kind of girl who could end up sleeping with legions of men, each time thinking she's found the Holy Grail when all she really has is a paper cup.'

Nice analogy, I thought, just the sort Kelly would deploy during her radio show, the demise of which was soon to be announced. As I reflected on that, I realized this conversation about Anna was the longest we had had in a month about any subject other than Kelly's impending move to WONM.

'Don't worry about her, Will.' Kelly said. 'She's not your responsibility. She probably just called to get a bit of attention. If she calls again, I'll talk to her.'

'OK.' I replied, a cold sweat forming at the prospect. 'Thanks.'

'No problem. Now, I'm going to take a shower.'

She turned away toward the hall, but something was still nagging at me.

'Kelly.' I said.

'Yeah?'

'If Anna *had* tried flirting with me, how do you think she'd have gone about it? How would she have found *my* On button?'

Kelly smiled. 'Easy.' she said. 'She would have appealed to your mind. She would have figured that physical attraction might fail because of the mental barrier created by your being cousins. So, she would have tried to appear knowing, as if she could see into you. You like insightful people. That's why you like me.'

We went shopping that afternoon and met up with the Di Napolis in the evening. Freddie Di Napoli is one of the most unassuming people I know. I met him a short while after I joined Greenleaf, when I was sent on a training course held up in Boston. We were seated next to each other on the plane and soon discovered that we were attending the same course. He looked to me like a downtown guy wearing a downtown copy of an uptown suit, which turned out to be a pretty accurate assessment. Freddie's father was a street vendor, selling hot dogs and pretzels in Battery Park. His mother worked in a laundry and his grandmother, who lived with them in their Bronx half-house, was a retired seamstress who still worked on consignment at home for some of the smaller fashion houses. The Di Napolis were poor, but they were determined that Freddie would get the best possible shot at escaping their hitherto parlous existence. Through much graft and sacrifice, he had managed to get to university, then find a job with a Wall Street brokerage. Like me, he began to earn colossal sums of money, all of which went towards getting his family out of the Bronx and across the river into a pleasant part of Brooklyn. He married his childhood sweetheart, Maria, and they have recently moved out of New York and settled near Greenwich, Connecticut. Not once, however, has he forgotten his background. He still makes fantastic money, but there is no ostentation about him. The wealth has not spoiled him in any way.

The Di Napolis had introduced us to a terrific Italian restaurant on West 42$^{nd}$, which, in a way, had become *our* restaurant. Kelly and I ate there two or three times a month, lured back time after time by the freshest pasta and the most fragrant sauces in town. On the evening after Anna's call, it was so heartening to walk into that place with Freddie and Maria, so soothing to eat such great food and wash it down with three bottles of full-blooded Barolo.

When I awoke the next morning, my head seemed to have trebled in weight. My temples throbbed and my neck felt swollen into paralysis. I needed water to revive my parched mouth, so I delicately made to get out of bed. Beside me, Kelly lay apparently comatose. She had drunk at least as much wine as me and had sunk a large Armagnac while Freddie, Maria and I had shared a titanic zabaglione. She looked so inert that I pulled back the covers slightly to check whether she was still breathing. She was, so I continued on my way to the kitchen.

At that moment, the last thing I needed was another call from Anna.

'I have a collect call from England.' the Operator said, as I grabbed the receiver off the kitchen wall. 'Will you accept?'

'No.' I thought, but I said, 'Yes.'

'Will?' the next voice on the line inquired.

'Yes, Anna.' I replied. 'It's me. What do you want?'

'I want to talk to you.'

'That's fine, Anna, but you'd better make a bit more sense than you did yesterday.'

'I was making sense, but you didn't want to help me.'

'Anna, I'm not sure I'm the best person to give you help. I've been talking to Kelly about it -'

'*Aaaargh!*' The scream was otherworldly, a guttural howl, induced simply by the mention of my wife's name, that cut through my aching head like a flying machete. 'Don't talk to me about that woman.' Anna yelled.

'OK, OK.' I endeavored to pacify her. 'Don't get so hysterical.'

'*Hysterical?* Who in hell wouldn't be hysterical in my situation?'

'Look, Anna -'

'No, *you* look, William.' She sounded angry now, spitting out her words through clenched teeth. 'I've told you how I feel about you. I've opened up my heart to you. I love you, Will. I love you and I need you.'

'Neither of those things is true, Anna.' I said, fighting back.

'*Yes.*' she insisted. 'Yes they are. I have never needed anyone like I need you now.'

'Stop it, Anna. Stop this crazy -'

Before I could finish the sentence, she was screaming at me again.

'*William.*' she hollered. 'I'm *preg*nant.'

'What?'

'I'm pregnant. Having a baby.'

'I know what it means. How the......? Who have you told?'

'No-one. I can't tell anyone.'

'Not even a doctor?'

'No. I did my own test. It's positive, Will. I did two. They were both positive.'

I tried again to soothe her, without suggesting I might be able to do anything to help her. After all, what could I do? I was on the other side of the Atlantic Ocean. She needed to confide in someone closer to hand. Her sister Valerie seemed an obvious choice, but Anna seemed only to want me. I managed to mollify her long enough for her to tell me what had happened, when she had first suspected something was amiss, how long ago she had done the tests, but before long she was crying again.

'I can't face this without you.' she said. 'You can take care of me.'

'I can't, Anna.' I maintained. 'You know I can't.'

'How can you do this, William?' she begged. 'How can you do it?'

I felt desperately sorry for her, but my patience was frayed to breaking point. 'Look, Anna.' I said, firmly. 'You have *got* to resolve this for yourself. You have got to find someone to help you.'

'I've told you.' she wept 'I want *you* to help me.'

'I can't, Anna.' I told her again. 'And you know I can't.'

'If I can't have you with me, William,' she bawled, 'then I don't want to live.'

'Anna.' I said. 'I'm going.'

~

Bobbie and I share a similar attitude towards Geneseo, though we have reached the same position from different directions. She has lived here all her life and, until her parents moved to Fort Myers, vacationed no further afield than the Jersey Shore. She cannot comprehend why anyone would want to leave the place, though certainly she understands why those who do stray, like me, would wish to return. Like Bobbie, I love the Genesee Valley, but I accept that there is a world beyond it that is not all bad. Unlike Bobbie, I have the personal experience - through my years in Manhattan, through my vacations both in the USA and abroad - to place my home in context.

Around four-thirty this afternoon, I abandoned my essay and went for a drive to Conesus Lake, deliberately timing my return to Geneseo to coincide with Bobbie finishing work at the former Arcade Gallery. The gallery used to be owned by a local artist, who befriended my Mom back in the seventies and encouraged her to go to painting classes out at the Community College. At the busiest times, Mom would help out behind the counter, though busy times became less and less common and eventually the gallery was sold to new owners, who marginalized the paintings and concentrated instead on craft type gifts. The Arcade Gallery became known by the name of some ancient Peruvian deity, which I can neither spell nor pronounce.

Bobbie trained as a secretary after leaving school, but hated working in an office because she saw the same people day after day. She lasted out until she got pregnant, but decided that, once Becky was at school, she would take a job that enabled her to meet a greater variety of people. Her part-time job at the old gallery seems perfectly suited.

'*Will.*' she said with surprised delight as I walked into the store just before five-thirty. 'What are you doing here?'

'I was passing by and thought you might like a ride home.'

'Sure. That'd be great. Give me a couple minutes and I'll be right with you.'

She locked the till with a key she had dangling on a chain around her neck, then disappeared out back. I leaned against the counter, watching through the big windows as spots of rain began to spatter the sidewalk. Inside the store there was a pervasive smell of scented candles mingled with incense. All around me were islands of shelves, loaded with wooden and glass trinkets, recipe books and greeting cards with messages garnered from spiritual poetry. The walls were covered with what looked like native artifacts – masks, shields, elaborately painted spears.

'OK, let's be getting along.' Bobbie said, re-emerging with her coat draped around her shoulders. Outside, she pulled it up over her head for the short walk to my car. 'This is so kind of you Will.' she said as I started the engine. 'I'd have got soaked if I'd walked.'

Our first stop was at the house on Prospect belonging to Jenny Kefnik, who takes care of Becky when she finishes school. The rain was now streaming down, so I was pleased to see that I could park the car on Jenny's driveway, making the dash to the house only a short one. Even so, water ran off the brim of my baseball cap as I stood on the porch and waited for someone to answer my knock on the door. That someone was Melissa, Jenny's daughter, who is the same age as Becky.

'Hello Melissa.' I said, but the child just ran from the door, as though scared out of her mind. Seconds later, Jenny came hurrying down the stairs.

'William.' she said, identifying me with some relief. 'We weren't expecting you.'

'Sorry.' I said. 'Did I frighten Lissa?'

'Just a little.' Jenny smiled. 'We all thought it would be Bobbie. Still, no harm done.'

Along the hallway, I could see Becky donning her coat and hitching her school bag on to her back. Jenny pulled up the coat hood and told her to be careful out on the slippery path, but Becky seemed to pay no heed and sprinted out to the car, where her mother was waiting behind steamed up windows.

'Thanks Jenny.' I said, as I too took my leave.

'No problem, William.' Jenny smiled. 'It's nice to see you. I'm sorry about your dad.'

'That's kind of you to say.' I replied, then quickly waved to Melissa and headed for the car before any awkward silence could form, the type of silence that seems so often to follow such an exchange.

Back at Bobbie's house, we hung our wet coats in the hall and went through to the kitchen, where Bobbie made coffee and Becky constructed a sandwich from some cured ham, a big tomato and some mustard flavored mayonnaise. She then went up to her bedroom, where, she said, she was going to watch TV.

'Do you think Becky would like to stay over at Jenny's on Friday night?' I asked Bobbie, once I could hear the TV had been switched on in Becky's room.

'I guess so.' Bobbie said, a questioning look on her face.

'I thought you might like to go out for dinner. Just the two of us.'

'Yeah. That'd be great.'

Bobbie frowned, wondering *why* I wanted to take her out. When we ate together, it was usually at one of our houses and just as usually with Becky in attendance. Why did I want to get her alone?

'Is there some special occasion?' she asked.

'No.' I said. 'I just thought it would be good to spend a little time together.'

'Where are we going, then?'

'I'll book us a table at the Big Tree. I figure we could walk down into town, then go back to my house after dinner.'

'You want me to stay over?' Bobbie's voice sounded breathy - not excited, more anxious, I would say.

'You don't want to?' I asked.

'Of course.' She seemed at pains to correct the earlier impression she had given. 'I'd love to stay over. Maybe I can drop by tomorrow and leave an overnight bag with you.'

'Sure. No problem. Come over after you've finished at the store. You and Becky can stay for something to eat.'

'Thanks, Will. We might just do that.'

As a place to dine, the Big Tree Inn is a little obvious, but Geneseo is not blessed with many fine restaurants. In Manhattan, Kelly and I would simply walk to the curb, hail a cab and, within ten minutes, find ourselves in one of any number of bistros and trattorias and princely palaces of delicious ethnic food. Here, to borrow Bobbie's words, eating out - certainly at places like the Big Tree - is usually reserved for a special occasion, rather than being a matter of every day course.

'What sort of food is Becky into these days?' I asked, remembering a recent picky period brought on by believing her legs were too fat.

'Anything!' Bobbie cheerfully replied. 'Didn't you see the sandwich she took upstairs. She seems to have forgotten all about this weight thing.'

'Good. The last thing you need is a kid with an eating disorder.'

'Too true. Thankfully, she seems to have been jolted by some class at school about anorexia and kids having to go into special hospitals to be cured.'

I shook my head, incredulous at the idea of Geneseo children being taught about such things, as well as drugs, no doubt, and AIDS and safe sex and substance abuse. Maybe there is no need to leave the area so as to experience the world; maybe gradually, insidiously, the world will come to us.

'I'll make a risotto.' I said.

'And I'll bring a big apple pie.' Bobbie rejoined.

'Great idea.' I told her.

'And,' she continued, placing her hand on my arm, 'we'll have a good time on Friday night.'

'I'm sure we will.' I said. 'We've got some catching up to do.'

Bobbie looked into my eyes and squinted suspiciously.


Kelly's first day with WONM was also the first day of November. It would be a week or two before she would be seen on TV screens across New York City, but already she was being groomed for that first appearance. 'Work' at the station in those early weeks consisted of visits to beauticians, manicurists, fashion consultants and a plethora of other practitioners and advisers, all of whom were concerned with just one thing: image. True, she was trained how to use a teleprompter and even how to hold a microphone, but it was clear from the start that presentation was going to be at least the equal of content.

Her first broadcast report was pre-recorded, so I had the strange experience of watching my wife speaking on television while she was sitting by my side, herself viewing the pictures with her hand slapped across her mouth in horror. Her voice, she said, was awful, her hair was a mess and her on-camera technique was downright amateur. I admit I had seen better, but I had also seen experienced reporters do far worse jobs.

We went out to eat that evening, choosing our favorite French-style brasserie for a modest celebration meal. I think both of us expected Kelly to be recognized everywhere she went, but, of course, no-one had a clue who she was. It had been a five-minute report buried at the back end of the six o'clock news hour, not exactly prime time for most people in Manhattan.

We were in bed long before midnight and gently made love before going to sleep, our bodies still partly entwined. I remember waking in the small hours and hearing police sirens wailing in the street below, not an infrequent occurrence, but, on that occasion, particularly loud. I lay there for a while, an uneasy feeling keeping me awake. It was a sense of foreboding, about what I cannot recall, though I think I half expected the police to knock at our door and deliver some dreadful news, or maybe arrest me for some crime I had not committed. In the dead of night, irrationality has a habit of seizing control of even the most logical of minds.

In time, I got back to sleep and did not wake again until the alarm went off at six-thirty. I clambered out of bed and went through to the bathroom, where the bright light and the shower's hot water immediately dissipated any lingering nocturnal fears. Having washed and shaved, I dressed in the spare bedroom so as not to disturb Kelly, then went to the kitchen for my usual breakfast of cereal, yogurt and orange juice. I had just finished eating and was preparing to rinse the dishes in the sink when the telephone shattered what had been an agreeable silence.

'Hello.' I said.

'William.' the caller replied, deliberately pronouncing each syllable of my name. 'It's Mom.'

I knew from her tone that something very bad had happened.

Mom came straight to the point. Aunt Angela had called her in the middle of the night. It was awful. Anna was dead. My beautiful cousin had been a passenger on a motorbike that had slid off the road. It had been raining; the road had been greasy and had turned sharply. The young man driving the motorbike had been drunk. The road had turned, but he had not. Both he and Anna had died at the scene, the driver from multiple injuries and massive internal bleeding, Anna from a broken neck.

I slumped against the kitchen wall, then slid down to the cold, tiled floor, with Mom still on the other end of the line. I cried uncontrollably. Kelly, who had been roused by the ring of the telephone, came through from the bedroom to find me curled up like a baby, rocking to-and-fro, still cradling the receiver in my hand. She prized it from me, spoke to Mom for a minute or so, then gathered me in her arms and hugged me until I could cry no more.

'It's not your fault.' she kept repeating. 'It's not your fault.'

# Wednesday

❀

I wanted this room, my study, to serve as an office, but not to feel merely functional. The walls are hung with patterned wallpaper, silver leaves intertwined with golden tendrils, all on an undulating white background. My bureau dates back to the 1920s and is made of yew, which has darkened over the years, but is still rich in grain and luster. It has a drop front that opens to reveal my carefully ordered papers and notebooks, as well as little drawers filled with envelopes and staples and paper clips and such like. Beneath are more drawers and a cupboard with doors that press against my knees when I sit here and write letters or type on my computer. On the top of the bureau is Becky's paperweight, along with a Seneca ornament, a reading lamp and a photograph of my mom taken in New York City on her sixty-second birthday. Next to the bureau is a stand on which rests my laser jet printer and beside that is a low table, atop of which I have my telephone and answering machine, a few books, mostly those I am in the process of reading, and a Perspex display case. Inside the case is my grandpa's book, *Sing All Of Four Seasons*. Above the table I have hung Mom's paintings, whilst behind the door, my photomontage adorns the wall, with a trestle table beneath it, covered with family photos in wooden frames. The bookshelves, which now cover one whole wall, are home to my library, a collection I have built since leaving Columbia. It began with textbooks and tracts on things like deficit financing and monetarism. Dotted amongst these were baseball almanacs and accounts of the Apollo missions. Over time, the academic stuff has been subsumed by history books and reference works. Now there is also a growing number of novels, classics mostly, Dickens, Austen, Hardy, Twain, predominantly English and American, but extending to *War and Peace* and *Les Miserables*.

It has been another warm, sunny day, last evening's freak rainstorm having seemingly drained the clouds from the sky. I slept sporadically again throughout the night and although I can blame the weekend's transatlantic flight, or even the rogue rumbles of thunder that continued to groan in the distance until the small hours, I know that the real reason is Anna. As the years have passed, I have trained myself not to think of her, but standing over Dad's grave last week, knowing that Anna lay only yards away in the same cemetery, the old feelings of remorse were revived. I should have been there when they buried her.

I crawled from my bed at around eight o'clock, the restless night having left me just as weary as one without any sleep at all. After breakfast, I should have worked on my essay, but I knew I would be unable to concentrate. I needed to get out of the house, to get outside and into that blessed sunshine. So, foregoing a shower, I dressed in some old clothes, then went to the kitchen, where I made up sandwiches and placed them in my small backpack, along with a waterproof jacket and some apples. I then pulled on my boots and set off for the Park, driving via Nunda so as to come in by the Parade Grounds and sweep round the southern side of the river to Lees Landing, where I left the car and set out along the Dishmill Creek Trail. The creek itself flows mostly northwards, spilling into the Genesee near St. Helena; the trail named for the sparkling stream follows a similar, but rarely parallel path, crossing the creek before it reaches the river, then merging with the Trillium Trail and the Big Bend Road. The loop I like to take is about four miles long, an undulating hike through, today, dazzling red maples and fiery white ash, interspersed with lofty pines and firs. With a stop for a late lunch and numerous halts to admire the incredible scenery, it took me over two hours.

I last walked the Dishmill Creek Trail back in July. It was, or would have been, Mom's sixty-sixth birthday and Bobbie, Becky, Melissa Kefnik and I had been planning to go to the Yard Of Ale, a family-friendly restaurant in Piffard. We never got there. Bobbie, whose idea it had been to commemorate Mom's birthday, had called me while I was sweating my way through the baked woodland and had left a message on my answering machine to inform me that Becky had broken her arm. She had fallen from a playground climbing frame and had needed the fracture setting at the Noyes Hospital in Dansville.

So, I stayed at home that evening, sitting out on the patio, reading a book and drinking beer. Dad called around seven o'clock, which would have been midnight over in England, and we had an odd conversation during which I knew he wanted to say how much he missed Mom, if only he could find the words to articulate the feeling. He asked whether I was keeping well, when I would be leaving for a planned trip to Georgia, whether there were any problems with the house, whether I had spoken to Kelly recently, all sorts of things apart from what really mattered. The only emotion in his voice came when I told him about Becky's accident, but even then it was expressed with his usual English restraint.

After I had spoken to Dad, I went to find the photographs I had taken four years earlier, when he and Mom and Bobbie had come to New York City to celebrate Mom's sixty-second birthday. I had been concerned that Mom, even if not too weak to travel, would be unable to keep up with the pace of Manhattan. The evidence of a visit I had made to Geneseo the previous spring, when, after very little exercise, she had needed a sleep each afternoon, suggested that I ought not to plan anything at all strenuous. By July, however, she seemed to have entered a period of remission.

It was only a month after my divorce from Kelly had been finalized. Aware of this and still, I believe, with the notion of a Geneseo-home-town-dream-team pairing, Mom called me a week before she and Dad were due to arrive and told me she had invited Bobbie along too. She needed a break, Mom said, and Charlie and Rose would be happy to take care of Becky for three days. I confess I was unsure about this arrangement right up until the point when they stepped off the train at Grand Central Station. Then I saw how much it meant to Mom, how much pleasure it gave her to bring Bobbie away from Geneseo so that she could, for the first time in her life, see the great city, that frenzied microcosm of the nation's diversity. It was, most assuredly, a different world altogether from the Genesee Valley.

That first evening we took a carriage ride around Central Park, then picked up some Chinese food and took it back to my apartment. I had been living there since the beginning of the year, Kelly and I having sold the place we had owned while we were married. This new apartment was rented and was much smaller. Now, with my parents, Bobbie and three sets of luggage, it felt confining and airless. I had given Mom and Dad my bedroom and had planned to sleep in the single bed in the spare room, but that was given over to Bobbie. I slept on the sofa. There was no itchy blanket, just a thin summer quilt, yet still it felt like those old days of courtship with my ex-wife.

The next day we took the ferry across to Liberty Island, where Mom and Dad sat on the grass and ate ice creams while Bobbie and I climbed to the crown of the statue. We then hopped aboard the ferry again and took a look at Ellis Island, where my parents found, in the computerized files, dozens of Holtons and Staffords and Wrights, who had come to America from Britain. They had passed through the echoing immigration hall on their way to what all of them must have expected would be a better life. Bobbie looked up Petersen and up came a list of Scandinavians, with forenames like Per and Ulf and Björn.

We landed back at Battery Park and took a stroll up to the financial district, where the traders stood around, on street corners, on the steps of the old Federal Hall, some eating sandwiches, others smoking cigarettes, their multicolored jackets strewn on the ground or thrown casually over their shoulders. I led the way along Wall Street, then into the canyons of Madison and Jefferson. At the Filmore Building, we walked in through the chrome-rimmed glass doors and made for the elevators, passing the security guard, who checked my ID and took a look inside Bobbie's shoulder bag and Mom's purse. We then rode up twenty-two floors, where the elevator doors slid open and we stepped out into the reception area of The Greenleaf Corporation. Beyond another set of doors, the main office area spread endlessly, a mass of desks and computer screens and well-dressed young people talking into telephones. Mom was appalled, partly by the hubbub, but mostly by the amount of money I told her was traded each day. Dad looked indifferent, as ever. Bobbie simply could not, and still cannot, understand.

Dinner that evening was at a Tex-Mex cantina, where Mom proved a revelation by tackling fajitas, while Dad and Bobbie opted for burgers and fries. Replete, we walked three blocks to Fifth Avenue and took another elevator ride, this time to the top of the Empire State Building, where we watched the sun set gloriously over Jersey City. I saw Dad reach for Mom's hand and the two of them stood completely still, gazing at the sky as it transformed from yellow, through a flaming amber to a hazy, polluted purple. I felt Bobbie take my arm, snuggling close to me, her head on my shoulder.

After Mom and Dad had gone to bed that night, Bobbie and I stayed up talking until half past two. It was childhood recollections, mostly, remembering our school days, how we used to do our homework together, how Mom would sometimes help us with our history or geography assignments, how our teachers would impart their simplistic wisdom, how the biggest fool is the one who only fools himself. She laughed at how a kid called Martin Bartlmens had built a rocket in his garden and had tried to organize us into an astronaut crew, with Martin as Neil Armstrong, naturally, me as Colonel Buzz and Bobbie as Mike Collins. The rocket had been constructed from a wooden frame, the planks taken from the Bartlmens' garage, and three full rolls of kitchen foil. When Martin's mother discovered this, she stormed into the garden, grabbed the world's first moon-walker by the scruff of his neck and sent him to his room.

Aided perhaps by a little too much beer, Bobbie and I agreed that we would take Mom and Dad up in a helicopter the next day, Mom's birthday. I called first thing next morning to book the flight, then took Dad to breakfast while Mom and Bobbie went shopping. We met up again at the Rockefeller Center and took a cab out to the East River, where the helipads are located. Mom had no idea what we had planned and when told that the little blue and white craft, with the flimsy-looking rotors and a big goldfish bowl for a front window, would shortly be taking her aloft, her expression oscillated for a few seconds between girlish exhilaration and utter fear.

This was the second time I had taken one of those flights; Kelly and I had decided to take one after Greenleaf had paid my half-year bonus in 1988. Since that time, the city government had decided, for safety and environmental reasons, that the helicopters should not fly directly over Manhattan. This meant that Mom's birthday trip consisted of a steeped arc out across the bay and a pattern of sweeps up and down the Hudson and East Rivers, which were punctuated by the helicopter hovering above the Brooklyn Bridge, Staten Island and the old dockyards. From these points, the guide talked us through the major landmarks. Mom was obviously thrilled and even Dad's face betrayed a degree of awe, though Bobbie looked terrified throughout, despite her previous experience as pilot of the Apollo 11 command module.

For dinner that evening, I took them all to the Italian place on West 42nd Street. I had arranged for a birthday cake to be brought to the table, complete with candles, once we had finished our meals. When the moment arrived, the lights were lowered and the intricately decorated cake was paraded to our table accompanied by a choir of waiters who sang *Happy Birthday*. Mom's lip quivered and she wiped her moistening eyes with her napkin. Dad, meanwhile, looked edgy and embarrassed, Bobbie smiled fixedly and I just sat and watched it all happening, realizing that, despite her tears, I had made Mom happy, which was precisely my objective.

My three visitors left the next morning. Mom's remission lasted only a few more months, then the road was all down hill. She was too ill even to get out of bed on her next birthday and, by the time she would have turned sixty-four, she was gone.

During the first decade of the nineteenth century, a gentle trickle of white settlers arrived in the Genesee region. Under the guidance of the Wadsworth brothers, the village of Geneseo grew both in size and importance, the hub of the settlement being an area of some fifteen acres set aside by the Wadsworths so as to emulate a typical New England village square. Here, there was space for military drills and traveling shows, as well as a town house for meetings of Geneseo's inhabitants. Opposite the square, James Wadsworth had built The Homestead, a simple but elegant home with a west facing porch that enabled him and his new wife, Naomi Wolcott, to look out across the glorious valley.

While Americans like the Wadsworths had been pushing back the boundaries of their new republic, the British had been struggling to come to terms with the loss of their colonies. They still had a military presence at Fort Niagara and were known to be inciting native tribes to attack frontier communities. The British navy, as part of its war against Napoleonic France, was blockading US shipping. It was also arresting American ships on the high seas, seizing their cargoes and impressing the crews. President Jefferson had sought to avoid war by introducing an embargo on foreign trade, but this proved more hurtful to the US than it did to the British. Congressional elections in 1810 brought more right-wing Republicans into the House, where these so called War Hawks exerted substantial influence. They asserted that maritime seizure and impressment was an act of outrage against American national rights and demanded military action to destroy the native menace and to invade and conquer British Canada. Ultimately, diplomatic attempts to defuse the crisis failed and, in June 1812, President Madison's declaration of war was ratified by Congress.

William Wadsworth, as leader of the local militia, offered his services and was made a Major-General. He was seriously wounded at the Battle Of Queenston Heights, but fought on with immense courage until he was taken prisoner by the British. At that time, and indeed during the Civil War, captured men were often sent home on parole, banned from fighting until they had been nominally exchanged with a prisoner taken from the opposing side. In William Wadsworth's case, this meant returning to Geneseo, where he was to become increasingly worried about his health. Many returning volunteers had been infected by typhoid pneumonia, often known at the time as 'cold plague'. This shocking disease, which had spread from the British army in Canada through to American soldiers on the Niagara frontier, reached epidemic proportions across Western New York. Little wonder, then, that William Wadsworth feared the disease might account for him too.

The War of 1812 has been referred to as a forgotten war, something that strikes me as odd. True, there was, before a shot had been fired, mixed enthusiasm for conflict amongst many Americans. True, some of the early battles, not least Queenston Heights, resulted in ignominious defeat for the US forces. There were other setbacks too, such as the burning of Buffalo by the British and, even worse, the capture of Washington DC and the incineration of the Capitol and the White House. Yet, the Americans also had their successes, notably naval Captain Thomas Macdonough's victory on Lake Champlain, which greatly influenced the Ghent peace negotiations.

Ironically, the Americans' finest land victory came at the Battle of New Orleans in January 1815, two weeks after the Ghent peace treaty had been signed. It may have had no effect on the outcome of the war, but it did make a national hero of Andrew Jackson. It also helped restore a good deal of national pride, which was crucial as the war had cost many lives without producing a conclusive result. The peace treaty provided for the return of all territory to its pre-war ownership, though the US did keep West Florida, which it had won from the Spanish. The treaty also established a commission to settle, once and for all, the northeastern boundary between the USA and Canada. The core issues of the dispute, such as maritime seizure and impressment, were not addressed, however. Maybe, then, it is not so surprising that it has become a forgotten war. Apart from galvanizing the young nation and instilling that sense of pride, it achieved very little.

After the war, the speed of settlement in the Genesee Valley quickly increased. With enlargement of the population came an additional burden upon those charged with local government and the administration of justice. Since 1802, the whole of Western New York had been divided into just two counties, Ontario and Genesee. With the number of people living in the area growing so rapidly, it was recognized that further division would be necessary. Thus, in February 1821, Livingston County was formed, with Geneseo as its shire town.

The county was named for the first Chancellor of the State of New York, Robert R. Livingston, who, in 1789, had undertaken the duty of administering the oath of office to George Washington. The Livingston family had originated in Scotland: James Livingston had acted as regent for King James I; Lord Livingston had been hereditary governor of Linlithgow Castle, birthplace of Mary, Queen of Scots. Although defeated by Thomas Jay in the gubernatorial election of 1798, Robert R. Livingston was appointed, two years later, as Jefferson's minister to France. There, he successfully negotiated the Louisiana Purchase. He also financed steamboat experiments conducted on the River Seine by his compatriot Robert Fulton, his involvement in that new technology continuing after his return to the United States. He secured, with Fulton, the monopoly on steam navigation on the Hudson. Indeed, the first paddle-wheeler to ply the route from New York City to Albany was named by Fulton for Livingston's Columbia County estate, 'Clermont'.

The choice of Geneseo as the Livingston county seat was due in no small way to the Wadsworth brothers making a gift of land for the courthouse and jail. William, recovered from his illness, became a town assessor and a county supervisor. Back then, Geneseo was home to around sixteen hundred people, roughly a quarter of whom were involved in farming and therefore living, not in the village itself, but in the surrounding countryside. Even so, the need for housing had increased significantly, a state of affairs that led to the development of Center and Second Streets. The townsfolk's spiritual welfare was also of vital concern. There had been a Presbyterian Church since 1795 and the Congregationalists had established their own place of worship in 1810. It was not until 1823, though, that the first Episcopalian church, St. Michael's, was organized.

Also in 1823, Micah Brooks profited from a classic piece of self-serving politics. Nine years earlier, he had been elected as a Republican Congressman to represent the whole of New York State west of Cayuga Lake. Like William Wadsworth, he had already seen active service during the War Of 1812 and was well known locally as a major landowner. For a long time, he had coveted the land at Gardeau granted to Mary Jemison under the Big Tree Treaty. Unfortunately for Brooks, Mary was not a US citizen, but a ward of the government and therefore unable to enter into any contract of sale. While in Congress, Brooks introduced the necessary legislation to give Mary citizenship. By 1823, that legislation had been passed and Mary had leased to Brooks all but four thousand acres of her reservation. In September of that year, a council was convened, attended by representatives of the United States and by a number of native chiefs, in order to assent to Brooks' purchase of those same lands. Brooks and his associates paid Mary fifty cents an acre. It was a steal.

As well as being a substantial landlord, Brooks was, of course, a powerful proponent of the Genesee Valley Canal. Among many others who worked hard for its construction was Allen Ayrault, who first came to Geneseo in 1814, at the age of twenty-one. He had been born in Sandisfield,

Massachusetts and had, like so many other New Englanders, worked his way west. In Geneseo, he was employed at the Spencers' store overlooking the village square, but he left the town after a short while and moved to Mount Morris, where he started his own business. Later, he moved to Leicester, known then as Moscow, where he became a successful cattle dealer and where he also served as Town Supervisor. In 1830, however, he returned to Geneseo, having been elected as the first president of the Livingston County Bank.

More and more men of influence, like Allen Ayrault, were beginning to emerge, yet in Geneseo the Wadsworths were still the dominant family, even after the death of William Wadsworth in March 1833. William had never married, but his brother James had ensured continuation of the Wadsworth dynasty. In May 1834, his eldest son, James Samuel Wadsworth, who had been educated at both Harvard and Yale, married Mary Craig Wharton. It was a moment of happiness following after the death not just of William, but also of Naomi Wadsworth, who had passed away in 1831.

Naomi's death had left her youngest daughter, Elizabeth, as mistress of The Homestead. When she was twenty, her father received a visit from the Honorable Charles Augustus Murray, a Scottish aristocrat. Evidently, Elizabeth and Charles fell in love and wanted to marry, but James Wadsworth refused to allow it. Murray headed out west, returning a year later to find James, initially at least, in a more accommodating mood. At first James agreed to the engagement, but then changed his mind again and forbade Elizabeth from having any further contact with Murray. The relationship was apparently over.

After a long illness, James Wadsworth died in June 1844, by which time the settlement he and his brother had founded could boast a population of around twenty-nine hundred. Having been incorporated in 1832, the village of Geneseo had developed steadily throughout the 1830s, with further housing added along every street and new businesses arriving to create both wealth and employment. One distinguished addition was at the north end of Main Street, where James S. Wadsworth and his wife Mary had built Hartford House. Whilst honeymooning in Europe, they had met the Marquis of Hertford, who owned a sumptuous villa in London's Regent's Park. The young couple had been so enchanted by the house that they had obtained a copy of the plans and had determined to replicate it in Geneseo.

In the same year as James and Mary first moved into Hartford House, 1837, another of Livingston County's prominent men, Dr. Daniel Fitzhugh, had sold nearly seventeen hundred acres of land at Groveland to the United Society Of Believers In Christ's Second Appearing. This religious sect, better known as Shakers, had originated as an offshoot of the Quakers in mid eighteenth century England. In 1770, 'Mother Ann' Lee had become the sect's head and, four years later, she had led a number of members to America. By 1822, the Shakers had established eighteen communities across New England, New York, Ohio, Kentucky and Indiana. The nineteenth community had been founded at Sodus, New York, in 1826, but, ten years later, plans had been put forward for the construction of a canal that would cut right through the Shakers' land. Thus, they had decided to decamp and set up a new community in Groveland.

Following the death of James Wadsworth senior, contact between Charles Murray and Elizabeth Wadsworth was re-established and, once again, Murray proposed. This time Elizabeth refused, supposedly because she thought he was simply taking pity on a twenty-eight-year-old spinster. Instead of marriage, she settled down to a solitary life at The Homestead. Meanwhile, her brother James Samuel had inherited the Wadsworth estates. 'Samuel' proved to be a prudent and considerate landlord, as well as a lavish host to the many friends who visited him at Hartford House. That same generosity also manifested itself in other ways. In 1847, he gave a whole ship-full of grain for victims of the famine in Ireland. He also gave land and a five hundred dollar loan for the building of Geneseo's St. Mary's Roman Catholic Church, as well as funding various town improvement projects.

Like so many men of wealth and standing, James S. Wadsworth held a keen interest in politics. He was certainly a principled man, as shown by his substantial donations to charity and by his munificent works locally. Those principles extended much further, though. He was a strong believer in education for young women, which was something of a rarity in the middle of the eighteenth century. He was also a committed Abolitionist. Twice he was urged to run for the state governorship and twice he declined in favor of other candidates.

In 1850, James Samuel's sister, Elizabeth, left The Homestead to travel with friends to England. By the most unlikely of coincidences, she was sitting in a railroad carriage one day when in walked Charles Augustus Murray. The meeting instantly re-ignited their feelings for one another and, within a week, they were engaged. The wedding took place six months later, after which they went to the Egyptian capital, Cairo, where Murray was the British Consul General and where Elizabeth soon fell pregnant. In a final and tragic twist to the couple's story, the beautiful Elizabeth died during the delivery of their baby son, Charles James.

With Elizabeth gone, James and Naomi Wadsworth's second son, William Wolcott Wadsworth, who, in 1846, had married Emmeline Austin of Boston, occupied The Homestead. In 1852, however, William Wolcott died suddenly and his widow and three sons subsequently made use of The Homestead for only a small part of each year, spending the remainder in Emmeline's home city. At that time, Geneseo's population was nearing three thousand and more land was being used for residential development, such as that along Elm Street. Another bank had been established, the Genesee Valley Bank, whose first president was James S. Wadsworth. There was even the hope of the railroad coming through the town.

For more than two decades, construction had been in progress on the Genesee Valley Canal. The first stretch had come into service in September 1840, running between Mount Morris and the intersection with the Erie Canal at Rochester. By the fall of 1841, a second section had been opened, linking Mount Morris with a junction at the Shaker community in Groveland. Having moved from Sodus to escape the building of a canal that never actually materialized, the Shakers had arrived at their new home to be almost immediately disturbed by digging work for another man-made waterway.

Soon, the canal had been branched from Groveland to Dansville and thence to the Genesee River. For reasons partly to do with engineering, but mostly concerning politics and finance, the next major opening had not occurred until spring 1851, when the main canal had been completed between the Shaker community and the village of Rounesville. From that time, work had moved apace, but the whole project was still some way from completion. Meanwhile, much greater progress had been made on the canal's land-bound nemesis.

By the late 1850s, the Genesee Valley Railroad, a branch of the Erie Railroad, was already in operation between Rochester and Avon. The Erie, which spanned the distance from the Hudson to Lake Erie, had come about thanks in significant part to a speech delivered to a convention of railroad men by one Micah Brooks, formerly a dedicated supporter of canals. Maybe the views of a certain forebear of mine had had some effect upon the man?

There had been some early talk of the Genesee Valley Railroad being extended all the way to Pittsburg, but it was struggling to get much beyond the northern part of Livingston County. After much protestation by the residents of Geneseo and Mount Morris, the railroad company relinquished all rights to the line south of Avon. In its place, a new company was created with, among its first directors, James S. Wadsworth and Allen Ayrault. Like Micah Brooks, both these men had been advocates of the canal, but had soon seen the greater advantages of railroads. So too, it seems, had many others, for stock in the new company sold rapidly and, by October 1856, construction work on the line was underway. It was supposed to be finished within a year, but work had to be halted during a nation wide financial panic in 1857. Early the next year, building resumed and, on New Year's Day in 1859, the first train rolled into Geneseo. In April, the service commenced to Mount Morris, but one well-known local was not there to see it. Micah Brooks had died two years before.

The Greenleaf Corporation was founded in 1977 by three Wall Street securities traders who recognized the potential of discretionary investments and who had the contacts, the reputation and the financial muscle to exploit it. Such investments are made in companies not engaged in what investors consider unethical activities, such as manufacturing armaments or tobacco products. Alternatively, investments could be made in companies of which investors approve, again on grounds of ethics, maybe because they have good employment records or are involved in sound environmental projects, like developing sustainable energy sources. The term 'discretionary' evolved first to 'socially responsible', then simply to 'ethical', with its attractive overtones of idealism and integrity.

The company's name comes from one of America's greatest poets. John Greenleaf Whittier was born near Haverhill, Massachusetts, in 1807. He read avidly, his early writings being greatly influenced by the work of the Scottish poet Robert Burns. He became a journalist, editing newspapers in Haverhill, Boston and Hartford, then emerged as one of the most prominent writers of the Abolitionist movement. He was renowned as an advocate of justice and liberal humanitarianism and, as his poetry matured, he became as famous and as well regarded as Longfellow.

I look back with mixed feelings on my time at Greenleaf. It was an enjoyable place to work. The founders and the senior management were, on the whole, straightforward guys, who treated the staff well and who were always accessible. I also had some good friends there, not least Steve Caspar. At its core, though, Greenleaf is a money making machine. Worse, it is a machine making money for people who already have more money than they could ever need. We described them as having high net worth, which is jargon for being inconceivably rich. It was noticeable how that reality took about a year to penetrate the minds of those idealists who had once queued to join us, and how quickly after that they became disenchanted.

I joined Greenleaf under no such delusions. I wanted a job, I wanted one in New York City and I wanted one that paid well. I thought ethical investments were a nice idea, but I soon grasped the fact that most clients were investing in funds that brought the best returns and Greenleaf's investment managers were, for a while, almost peerless. In the early nineties, when one or two of the funds began sliding, clients soon amended their portfolios, often moving to offerings from other firms managing non-ethical funds. Ethical or non-ethical, it mattered little. They just wanted the highest yield.

I am sure my working for Greenleaf had a positive influence on the earliest days of my relationship with Kelly. When I explained what the company did, she thought *I* was one of those idealists. I think the truth did slowly dawn upon her, but, by that time, any disappointment was fully allayed by the lifestyle my job enabled us to afford.

I guess the apex of our hedonism came in the summer of 1988. Greenleaf's half-year figures had shown extraordinary increases in fund values and in the value of assets under management. The staff bonuses reflected this, unprecedented sums finding their way into our bank accounts at the end of July. In one morning, Kelly and I spent five thousand dollars on clothes. We then went to Tiffany's, where I bought her the most exquisite diamond eternity ring. Later, we took a sunset helicopter flight up and down the great avenues, then concluded our day with dinner at our own apartment, cooked by a Vietnamese master chef who I had hired for the evening.

I shudder now when I think of such extravagance. It is a measure of how I viewed it, even back then, that I never told my parents about it. Instead, our regular calls covered more mundane ground, such as tittle-tattle from Geneseo and updates on how Kelly was doing in her job at WONM. There was even one occasion when Mom called, panting with excitement at having seen one of Kelly's reports on WONM's affiliate station in Rochester. By then, though, a year had passed since my wife had moved into TV and the novelty, for me, was beginning to diminish.

Kelly's working hours went from inconsistent to preposterous, despite a supposedly rigid shift system agreed with the broadcast unions. This system utterly disintegrated when a story was unfolding in what Kelly called real time, meaning that she was tracking events and reporting them live, as they developed. On these occasions it was often impossible to supplant one reporter with another, so the original reporter would have to stay with it, no matter how long it lasted. Our situation was exacerbated when I was asked to instigate what were amusingly termed flexible working hours at Greenleaf. The idea was to ensure that a core group of staff was in the office throughout the period during which the European markets were open. This meant having staff in place from three o'clock in the morning. On the weeks when I was one of those staff, I saw more of Kelly on the television than I did in our apartment.

Such antisocial working arrangements did have some compensation. With some planning and careful manipulation of colleagues' shifts, we were able to take three-, sometimes four-day breaks, most of which we spent away from the city. We often drove out to the Hamptons, or up to Connecticut, or into the White Mountains of New Hampshire. We passed one rainy weekend tucked up in a cottage on Martha's Vineyard and another, sun-filled mid-week furlough tramping the Cape Cod seashore.

Although Kelly and I had made a habit of spending each Christmas in Geneseo, there was some debate before we decided to come here in 1989. One of the senior guys who worked with me at Greenleaf had resigned in late summer and, while we sought a replacement I had volunteered to cover his workload by working a number of double shifts. My time account showed that I was owed seven days in lieu, days I intended taking over the Christmas holidays. I suggested to Kelly that we go down to Mexico, or maybe the Caribbean, but she was unhappy about taking a lengthy break away from WONM. This was despite her already long hours, coupled with my extended days at Greenleaf, having considerably restricted the amount of time we had together. In the end, we compromised, agreeing to spend Christmas with my parents, then to head back to New York City for the New Year celebrations, which Kelly would be covering as a roving reporter in Times Square.

This scheme had been devised in ignorance of my mom's state of health. When we reached Geneseo on Christmas Eve, we found her looking cadaverous, her skin gray, her eyes lachrymose and inflamed, her hair thin, her limbs creaking with every movement. This was a complete shock to us. I had seen her the previous fall, knowing that she had been unwell during the summer, but unaware that the illness was so serious. Certainly her appearance at that time had given no clues as to the gravity of her condition. She knew the cancer had returned, but she had told no-one other than my dad, placing her trust in a course of medication prescribed by her doctors in

Rochester. Now, the effects of the drugs were more pitifully manifest than the illness had ever been. She looked like she was a hundred years old. I really thought she was about to die.

On the day after Christmas, Kelly and I went to the Park and took a short walk by the Middle Falls. Suddenly my legs gave way, as though every muscle had momentarily dissolved. I staggered, preventing myself from falling only by grabbing on to Kelly's arm. She shepherded me to a low wall where I sat down, realizing that I was scared stupid. Kelly hugged me, rubbing my back to rekindle the warmth that had drained from my whole body. I was shivering, I was crying and I could nothing about it.

Later that day, we concluded that it would be best if I stayed in Geneseo for a few more days. Kelly would return to the city as planned and I would fly back from Rochester on New Year's Day. Both of us wondered whether this might be the last chance I would get to spend time with my mom.

Once Kelly had left, the atmosphere became increasingly subdued. I wanted to talk with Mom, but she was so tired that she could hardly finish a sentence without her words fading into a mumbling slur. Dad, who was never the most garrulous of individuals, withdrew even deeper into himself. Gaping chasms of silence opened up, as each of us stared at one another, Mom unable to speak, Dad unwilling and me caught uncertainly in the vacuum.

To escape, I left the house one afternoon and went out for a wander around the town, along North and Second and Center Streets, then down Main, taking a look in some of the shop windows, which were decorated with snowmen and Santa Clauses and red nosed reindeer. The place was eerily deserted, but near Village Square Park I saw a young woman dressed in a brown coat, its fur rimmed hood hiding her face. Even so, I knew that it was Bobbie.

'Hello Will.' she said, sounding oddly alarmed. 'What are you doing here?'

'I needed some air.' I told her.

'Me too.' Bobbie half smiled, an obvious device to hide the fact that she was upset.

I offered her my hand. 'Walk with me?' I asked.

'I'd love to.' she said and we set off back up Main Street, Bobbie with her arm looped through mine.

We talked mostly about Mom, who she had last seen the day before Kelly and I had arrived. Mom and Dad had gone with the Petersens to see Teddy Hewson and his wife, who had had their sons staying with them for the holidays. Mom had struggled valiantly against the lethargy and incoherence brought on by the drugs, but had finally had to succumb. Bobbie had also felt tired, not to mention a little bored, as the conversation had revolved almost exclusively around the feats of the Hewson boys, now both in their fifties and both unmarried. As Dad had readied Mom for the short drive home, Bobbie had asked if he could drop her at the Petersens' place, leaving Charlie and Rose to chat into the early hours with their hosts and their hosts' peculiar sons.

'Your mom looked beat.' Bobbie told me. 'As soon as she got in the car, she fell asleep.'

'You must come to the house and see her.' I said, an inference of urgency in my voice that betrayed my increasing belief that Mom did not have long to live. Bobbie agreed that she would stop by in the next day or so, but was reluctant to be specific.

Via a round about route, we eventually wound up back at the Petersens' house. I expected Bobbie to say goodbye and head inside out of the cold early evening, but instead she suggested I join her for coffee and a piece of Rose's Christmas cake. Having been obviously seeking solitude when I met her at Village Square Park, she now seemed anxious for company. We went indoors and through to the kitchen, where she boiled a kettle, spooned some roasted brown granules into a cup and poured over the steaming water to make a dun colored concoction that I guess bore some resemblance to the promised beverage. She then cut me a piece of the rich, moist fruit cake, baked from a recipe Rose had been given by my mom, who had been given it years before by Grandma Wright.

Bobbie led the way upstairs to her room, voices from the television filtering from the lounge, where Charlie and Rose were entertaining their neighbors, the Meads. We sat on Bobbie's venerable sofa, a relic from her grandparents' house into which we sank so low it was clearly going to require a big effort to get to our feet again. I recall having to balance the coffee cup on my knee so that I could avoid the need to bend double to retrieve it from the floor. The cake, though, made up for all the discomfort. It was boozily succulent, the mixture having been steeped in rum before being cooked on a low heat for more than four hours. It transported me back to my childhood, back to when Mom had made the cake each year and I had been allowed the annual treat of licking clean the mixing bowl.

'Good?' Bobbie asked.

'*Fantastic!*' I said.

Two months later, indeed on the last day of February, the anniversary of Grandpa Holton's death, Mom called me at Greenleaf, a unique incident in itself. I had spoken to her only the previous evening, when she had told me how much better she was feeling since her doctors had modified the drug cocktail. Now she was 'phoning me at the office, which had to mean bad news. As it turned out, the news was more dramatic than bad: Bobbie was pregnant.

I have never thought of my mom as being devious, but I cannot deny my suspicion that she called me at work that day so as to catch me off-guard. Would I be stunned, or flustered, or outraged, or evasive? Would I expose the fact that I was responsible for Bobbie's condition? In the event, my being in an open office, with colleagues clustered at their desks all around me, forced me to maintain my composure.

Mom never asked me directly about my role in the pregnancy, but she, like others in Geneseo, could do the math. Bobbie was two months expectant and was that not Fay Holton's son who was here without his wife at Christmas? Some people had seen Bobbie and I walking, arm in arm, around the town, checking out the festive shop window displays like a pair of young lovers. Reports of those sightings oiled the wheels of the rumor machine still further and I know that even today, almost a decade later, certain individuals take an abnormal interest whenever they see Bobbie and I together. They continue to look for signs.

Becky was born in September 1990, a strong, vigorous baby, blessed with rude health and lungs so powerful that she could holler all night without a break. Charlie now jokes that it was during that first year of Becky's life that he and Rose took their decision to move to Florida. They figured that, if Bobbie ever had another child, then they would prefer to be fifteen hundred miles away.

Just three weeks after Becky's arrival, Kelly and I had a visitor from England, my cousin Valerie. I had been dreading the day I would have to go to collect her from JFK. How much did she know about what had happened between her poor, dead sister and myself? Indeed, had she been involved, as

I by then suspected, in engineering that evening, more than four years before, so that I could be alone with Anna while Valerie and Bobbie hung out at The Idle Hour? My biggest fear was not the prospect of Valerie confronting *me* with any of this. It was that she would, maybe for some vindictive or vengeful reason, reveal the damaging truth to Kelly.

My fears, I was relieved to discover, had been utterly misplaced. Valerie hardly spoke of Anna the whole time she was with us. She had no need to. She had transformed herself into an almost exact replica of her sister. She had grown her dark hair long, taken to wearing the same type of jeans, the same style of dresses, perfected a verbal intonation identical to Anna's. She even seemed to have darkened her eyes and made up her face in such a way that it carried the same beatific appearance. The effect was, simultaneously, disturbing and alluring.

'That family is *weird*.' Kelly said to me as we settled into bed after taking Valerie on a nighttime tour around Midtown Manhattan.

I could do nothing but agree. 'I wonder if weird is the right word?' I replied, meaning that maybe something stronger would be more accurate. *Crazy*, for instance.

'Probably not,' Kelly conceded, missing my gist, 'but I'm too tired to invent some sort of rationalization.'

'Invent?'

'Sorry, another wrong word. Like I said, I'm tired. Ask me again in the morning.'

I did just that.

Kelly had two potential diagnoses. It was possible that Valerie was trying to look and behave exactly like Anna in some sort of effort to actually replace her dead sister. This may have been because she felt some blame for Anna's death and was attempting to soothe her conscience by assuming Anna's role, Anna's identity. Alternatively, Valerie may have simply been expressing her grief by paying homage to her sister, in a similar way to those people who turn up at the graves of dead pop stars dressed in the same way as their idols. In essence, they are demonstrating that, through them, the spirit of the deceased lives on.

Valerie stayed with us in New York City for four days, then we all drove out to Geneseo. The foliage was at its zenith and the hillsides sparkled with implausible combinations of color. Valerie seemed awe struck. She gaped,

wide-eyed at the spectacle, sometimes gasping with amazement, constantly asking me to pull over, as we drove along the Livingston County by-roads, so that she could snap countless photographs. I remember her at the Park, standing by the Middle Falls, a film of water droplets blown onto her face by a soft breeze, her eyes closed as she listened to the tumbling Genesee. I remember, too, sitting opposite her later that day at the Big Tree Inn, constantly aware of her staring at me with those dusky eyes.

It was during Valerie's visit that Kelly and I first saw Becky. Mom had warned us of the child's strident crying and of the exhausting effect her sleepless hyperactivity was having on Bobbie. Even so, nothing prepared us for what we encountered as soon as Charlie greeted us at the Petersens' door. The whole house seemed to be alive with noise, a high-pitched din that made both Kelly and I cringe. Bobbie looked like the undead, slouching in one of the armchairs in the living room and eyeing us as though gazing into oblivion. Only when Rose appeared with a bottle of milk for Becky did Bobbie seem to realize who we were. The infant's voracious appetite was soon apparent from the way she almost sucked the teat from the bottle. It was no wonder that she had proved too demanding for poor Bobbie to breast-feed her. The impromptu meal did at least silence the screaming, though once the milk was consumed and Becky was laid in her crib, the irritable whining began again, rising through a demonic wailing to a crescendo of indescribable screeches. Bobbie hauled the baby from the crib and propped it on her shoulder, rubbing its back gently to bring up what was apparently non-existent gas. For some reason, Bobbie must have assumed at that point that Kelly, in keeping with most female visitors, would be hankering to hold the child. Much to my wife's surprise, Bobbie placed Becky on her lap, inducing Kelly to cradle the baby awkwardly in her arms. Kelly was most definitely not accustomed to nursing. She seemed to have not even a clue as to how babies should be held. I can still picture her face, a cross between disbelief and panic, to which was soon added disgust as the elusive gas at last surfaced, bringing with it a stream of puke that trickled colloidally down Kelly's new cashmere jacket, bought a week before at Macy's.

By the middle of 1861, the men of Livingston County had already responded to the call-to-arms in sufficient numbers to supply at least one full regiment. However, it was apparent to James S. Wadsworth, who had been commissioned as Major-General of the state's volunteer force, that the war of rebellion would not be over as quickly as some had predicted and that even more men needed to be prepared for action. General Wadsworth approached Colonel John Rorbach, who lived in Geneseo, and persuaded the Colonel to launch a further attempt to recruit men from the locality. In order to have a place to quarter and train the new enlistees, he established Camp Union at the top of North Street. Here, over seven hundred men were readied for war. They were known as Wadsworth's Guards and, at the end of February 1862, they marched with great ceremony - band playing, banners waving – to the railroad station at the foot of Court Street, from where they were transported away to become Companies A to G of the 104th New York Volunteers.

Among those men were William and Joseph Holton, attired in their smart blue uniforms, their departure witnessed by their parents John and Catherine and their sister Margaret, all of whom must have been filled with a mixture of pride and fear. From Geneseo, the two brothers and their comrades were taken first to Albany, where they were prepared for field duty, then south to Washington DC. As a Private in Company D, William was paid fifteen dollars per month, while Joseph, although of the same rank, received only thirteen dollars due to his being two years younger. There was also the promise of a one hundred dollar 'bounty' at the end of the war or at the time of their discharge, though only one of them would live to collect it.

In August of that year, Robert E. Lee achieved his magnificent victory at Manassas. His Army of Northern Virginia then marched into Maryland, followed by General George B. McClellan's Federal Army of the Potomac. On September 15th, the two sides established battle lines along the opposite banks of Antietam Creek, near Sharpsburg. The following day, Lee's troops were bolstered by the arrival at Sharpsburg of Stonewall Jackson and his men, who were returning to Lee after capturing Harper's Ferry. At dawn on September 17th, the battle began as Federal artillery pounded Jackson's positions. Hours of savage fighting ensued, at the end of which more men had been killed or wounded than on any other single day of the war, over twenty thousand in all. Neither side could truly claim victory, though Lee was forced to withdraw his army back across the Potomac River and accept the failure of his first attempt to carry the war into the North.

The Second Division of McClellan's army was under the command of Brigadier General James B. Ricketts, whose First Brigade consisted of the 97th, 104th, 105th and 107th New York Volunteer Infantry. Fighting with the 104th, which was led by Major Lewis C. Skinner, were the Holton brothers, William having recently been promoted to Corporal. Such is the nature of battle and so many were the casualties at Antietam that there is no record of exactly how Joseph was killed. Most assuredly William did not see the fatal moment, for he was lying, his right knee shattered by a bullet, amidst a mass of bloodstained young men wailing with the agony of their injuries. Years later, he told his son Thomas that Joseph had been the lucky one, lucky because he had not lived to witness the scene at the end of that day, when so many bodies littered the battlefield. No matter whether they wore the blue or the gray, he said, their blood ran red.

William was treated at a field hospital, then evacuated to a sanatorium north of Washington DC. His leg healed slowly and it was some months before he could hobble along on crutches. Nevertheless, that degree of mobility made him well enough to return to Geneseo, where, in October 1863, he received formal notification of his honorable discharge from the United States Army. The hundred dollar 'bounty' took a while longer to arrive.

Through his father, William was offered a job at the County Treasurer's office, where John was still employed. Meanwhile, Margaret Holton, now seventeen, was working at the huge American Hotel, which stood on the corner of Main Street and North Center Street, now Ward Place. Still sullen of appearance and somber of attitude, Margaret had, on the news of Joseph's death, turned suddenly and surprisingly to God. In a manner more associated with our modern teenagers, she had previously expressed only cynicism when it came to religion, grudgingly accompanying her parents to the old St. Michael's Church each Sunday, then sitting sulkily throughout the sermon and refusing to join in the hymns. Since she had lost her brother, though, she had been going to pray in the church every day and had taken to reading the Bible every night before she went to sleep.

In the fall of 1867, the Chapman family passed through Geneseo en route from Rochester to Bath, where Adolphus Chapman, a hirsute mountain of a man, was to become manager of his uncle's foundry. Since the late 1850s, the railroad had greatly reduced the volume of wagon traffic through the town, but Chapman was an unconventional, maybe even eccentric individual, who had, only the previous year, moved his family across from Connecticut aboard his own hand-built carriage. He had never traveled by railroad, never would, and could not understand what was wrong with a good rig and a pair of decent horses. Little wonder that, within months of his taking over the foundry, it went bankrupt.

While Chapman and his wife slept comfortably in the American Hotel, their two sons, both in their early teens, were detailed to guard the wagon, which was loaded with the family's rather meager belongings. The boys' sister, Alice, was spared this task, though she was expected, early each morning, to feed and groom the horses, each of which always sported a plume of white feathers in its headpiece. It was whilst Alice was about this chore that she first met Margaret Holton, who was arriving at work after her daily prayers, which, while the new St. Michael's was being constructed, meant her going to the Session Room of the Presbyterian Church on Second Street. Evidently, the cheerless Margaret and the put-upon, but good-natured Alice quickly struck up a friendship, so much so that Alice was invited for supper at the Holtons' house. There, she met William, almost eight years her senior, and a similar friendship developed.

After the Chapmans moved on, William and Margaret kept in contact with Alice by letter. The following summer, Alice came to visit, originally for two weeks, but it turned out to be for the rest of her life. She shared the same room with Margaret that William had once shared with Joseph, while William took over Margaret's room at the back of the house. William recalled the companionship between the two young women as being 'rum', which is an intriguing description. Margaret never showed any interest in men, living all her life as a spinster and not once, to anyone's recollection, 'stepping out' with a gentleman. As she grew older, her stature thickened and her countenance hardened, her appearance made all the more masculine by her hair being swept back combatively from her forehead. All interest in girlish things has gone - she abhorred the memory of those plats her mother had once woven and had long ago consigned unsentimentally to the fire her wooden dolls. Alice, on the other hand, was a paradigm of femininity, which is probably why she preferred to stay in Geneseo than go back to mucking out horses for her father. Her friendship with William developed steadily into courtship and then to engagement, but throughout that time, and throughout their subsequent marriage, she remained enigmatically ambiguous about her feelings for and relationship with Margaret Holton.

The wedding between William and Alice took place at the newly built St. Michael's Church in July 1870. They continued to live with William's parents until a new house had been built for them on North Street. There, in February 1873, was born their first child, Thomas, my great-grandfather. Less than two years later, another William Holton was born, followed in 1876 by a daughter, Miriam, and, in 1879, another girl, who was named

Sarah in memory of Alice's mother, who had died two months previously. Margaret was Godmother to all four of them.

It is said that William Pryor Letchworth first visited the Genesee Valley in the spring of 1858. Six years prior to that, the North Western Division of the Erie Railroad, between Hornellsville and Buffalo, had been opened. The railroad crossed the Genesee River at Portage, where a great wooden bridge had been constructed, eight hundred feet long, over two hundred thirty feet high, the longest and highest in the United States. The bridge towered above the Upper Falls, lending magnificent views to passengers as their trains slowed and they pressed their faces against the carriage windows. On that morning in 1858, Letchworth was returning to Buffalo from a business trip to New York City. Apparently, he decided on impulse to dismount his train at Portage - not the sort of action one would have associated with this sober, thoughtful man.

At that time, the debris of pioneer life would still have been scattered across the landscape, yet the inherent beauty of the place must have struck Letchworth immediately. Half a mile from the Portage Bridge, the Middle Falls would have sung with the same captivating melody as they do today. The forest-clad hills would have been rich with the density of life reawakened after the harsh winter. The great gorge would have seemed, to this deeply religious man, like tangible confirmation of God's touch.

William Pryor Letchworth's great-great-grandfather, John Letchworth, had brought his family from London to Philadelphia in 1766. The Letchworths were of old English stock, one of their forebears, Baron Letchworth, having perished in 1066 whilst fighting for King Harold. The Norman invaders took possession of the baron's estate, near the village of Hitchin in the county of Hertfordshire, and the family dispersed, some to northern England, others to the southeast. Records have been found of one Urban de Lecheworth living in the county of Essex and it is from this branch of the family that John Letchworth himself is likely to have descended.

Quakerism was a major force in the lives of the Letchworths, one of George Fox's first converts being Robert Letchworth, who was consequently excommunicated from the Church of England in the mid seventeenth century. John Letchworth's eldest son, John Jr., became a noted preacher, traveling widely to spread the faith. Meanwhile, his younger brother William remained in Philadelphia, where he fathered eight children, the oldest, a son, named Josiah.

Born in Brownville, New York, in 1823, William Pryor Letchworth was the son of Josiah and his wife Ann Hance, his middle name taken from his paternal grandmother, Mary Pryor. At the age of fifteen, he left his home in Sherwood, over in Cayuga County, in order to become an apprentice with Hayden & Holmes in Auburn. Later, he worked in New York City, then returned upstate to become a partner in the old Buffalo firm of Pratt & Company. There, he worked assiduously, rarely taking leave and having almost no social life. Eventually the strain began to effect his health. In 1854, he took a winter break in Florida, during which time his brother Josiah joined the company and started to take over much of the more taxing work. At last William had the opportunity to grow beyond the boundaries of his career, traveling more and cultivating an interest in art and literature. He had wondered about having a weekend haven somewhere near Buffalo, perhaps in the Niagara area, but once he discovered the wonders of the Genesee Valley, his mind was made up.

The settlers who had come to the valley in the early years of the nineteenth century had endeavored to make a living by harnessing its resources. In the area that became the Letchworth Park, those pioneers had created lumbering settlements like St. Helena and Gibsonville, where mills and factories had been built to process the timber taken from the hillsides. The future Park had also seen great activity during the building of the Genesee Valley Canal. To the south of Mount Morris, a mile long cut had been made through a hillside to accommodate the route of the waterway. It had then been extended all the way to the banks of the river, where a thousand-foot tunnel had been planned between the Middle and Upper Falls. The construction had proved far too hazardous, however, and the scheme had been abandoned, though not before a number of men had lost their lives.

William Pryor Letchworth purchased the first parcel of the Glen Iris Estate in 1859. It was a time of burgeoning industry, soon fueled by the northern states' military needs, then by national rebuilding in the wake of the Civil War. The Genesee Valley had so much to offer, so many natural assets: a seemingly boundless supply of timber; medina sandstone, used to pave the streets of the growing cities; the charging river, its potency soon to be coveted by the power companies. Natural beauty had few champions back then, the ambitions of the industrialists unfettered by conservation laws. However, using his own personal wealth, Letchworth set about preserving the Genesee Valley, protecting its inherent splendor and the legacy of its native peoples, the Seneca.

In 1871, Letchworth visited Caneadea, so as to see there a Seneca Council House, which was at least a century old. The house had once been the scene of great native gatherings, but was now in a very dilapidated state. Letchworth immediately decided to purchase the house, then arranged for it to be transported to Glen Iris. It was a painstaking process, each log being marked as it was removed, then drawn by teams of workmen and horses to the Genesee Valley Canal, along which they were carried by scows, flat canal boats, until they reached what is now Letchworth Park.

The reconstruction and restoration was carried out on a high plateau that became known as the Council Grounds. One year after he had first seen the house in Caneadea, Letchworth invited descendants of many famous Iroquois to hold one more council. The War of 1812 had brought about a schism in the relationship between the Seneca and Mohawk nations. From the outset, the Mohawks had sided with their Revolutionary War allies, the British. Meanwhile, Seneca chiefs, like Red Jacket and Cornplanter, had ensured that their people remained uninvolved in the conflict. That was until the British had attacked and occupied Grand Island in the Niagara River, which was land claimed by the Seneca. The nation's neutrality had come to a sudden end and Seneca warriors had taken up arms alongside their former American enemies. It had not been long before Mohawks and Seneca met on the battlefield. Since then, bad blood had simmered through the generations, but somehow Letchworth managed to convince them to come together again. Colonel W. J. Simcoe Kerr attended, the colonel being the principal chief of all Mohawks and the grandson of Joseph Brant. Also there were 'Buffalo Tom' Jemison and James Shongo, both grandsons of Mary Jemison, and John Jacket, grandson of Red Jacket, and Solomon O'Bail, grandson of Cornplanter. They were joined at the council by other native descendants, plus white men like the poet Henry Howland and former US President Millard Filmore, a personal friend of William Pryor Letchworth. They all sat and talked, recalling bygone times. Speeches were made, pipes were smoked and, eventually, after many hours, Kerr and O'Bail, Mohawk and Seneca, clasped hands in brotherhood over the council fire.

Two years later, Letchworth had the body of Mary Jemison re-interred on the Council Grounds. Mary had lived for many years on the Gardeau flats, which were situated just north of Letchworth's Glen Iris Estate. Having been granted the land at the Big Tree Treaty, Mary had hoped that she could live out a peaceful life there with her family. That peace had been shattered, however, when her son John killed his brother Thomas at the culmination of what had been a long-running feud. Tribal chiefs had subsequently cleared John of murder, finding that Thomas, under the influence of intoxicating liquor, had been the aggressor. Later in the same year, Mary had lost her husband, Hiokatoo, who had lived to the age of one hundred and three. Widowed and elderly, Mary had needed then to rely upon her children, especially the youngest, Jesse. Once again, though, tragedy struck and once again it was due to John. In yet another argument fueled by whisky, the two brothers had begun to fight, the brawl ending with Jesse lying fatally wounded from the blade of John's knife. Five more years had passed, then, in 1817, John, too, had been murdered, his death the result of a drunken pact between two Indians from the Squawkie Hill reservation.

If Mary's family misfortunes had not been enough, she had also been duped by a man claiming to be her cousin and cheated of the true value of her land by Micah Brooks and his associates. Throughout all this, she had continued to live as a native, shying away from rejoining her own people, even though there had now been white settlers all around her. Eventually, in 1830, she had left the flats and moved to the Seneca reservation at Buffalo Creek, which is where she had died, three years later, at the age of ninety, and where she had first been buried. In 1874, William Pryor Letchworth became aware of the damage that had been done to Mary's headstone by souvenir hunters and of a plan to build a road through the reservation that would completely destroy the grave. This greatly troubled him, for he had long taken an interest in Mary's astonishing story. He decided that she should be re-buried by the Genesee River, close to where she had lived most of her life.

Having discovered the wonder of the Glen Iris Estate, Letchworth was determined from the outset that it not be simply a weekend retreat, but also a place in which he could settle once his business career ended. Not that genteel retirement was ever on his agenda; Letchworth had far too much energy for that, which was just as well, because protecting the valley in the way he did required great vigor, especially when the Genesee River Company wanted to build a dam or reservoir near Portageville. The company's pretext was the avoidance of flooding and the improvement of sanitary conditions in the valley, but its charter also claimed the right to use the river to generate electricity. The potential repercussions were horrifying, with the beauty of the whole area threatened by development. To thwart the River Company's ambitions, Letchworth set about acquiring land on both sides of the river, buying it lot by lot from the various owners. He also placed the whole estate under the supervision of the American Scenic and Historic Preservation Society, a move designed to further deny the power companies, though Letchworth still had to battle with them right up to the time of his death.

Notwithstanding the effort he put into Glen Iris, coupled with continuing business interests, William Pryor Letchworth managed to find the time and energy to devote to a string of civic and philanthropic activities, becoming a tireless advocate of the underprivileged in New York State. In 1873, he was appointed as State Commissioner of Charities, though he took no salary during the twenty-four years he served. Neither did he charge any expenses, despite traveling regularly to view the poorhouses, reform homes, asylums and other charitable institutions throughout the state. He even went to Europe so as to learn how the mentally ill were housed and treated there. His reports and papers pulled no punches and often his proposals provoked substantial opposition. Not that he was fazed by that. He guided through numerous changes that helped alleviate suffering, changes that enabled the poor to have hope, and the disabled and the sick to have some degree of comfort and dignity in their lives.

One group of people was of particular concern to Letchworth: epileptics. The only places available for the shelter and treatment of these people were either the madhouses or the poorhouses, which Letchworth knew to be completely inappropriate. Aware of work done in Ohio to create a separate institution for epileptics, Letchworth pushed for a similar facility in New York. As a result, he was appointed to a committee, chaired by Oscar Craig, which was charged with selecting a site for a specialized colony, where epileptics could be cared for, educated and employed. The location chosen was the site of the Shaker community at Groveland. Due to their practice of celibacy, the Shakers' numbers were dwindling and they were keen to sell their Groveland property so that the remaining members could join another group at Watervliet. Before the property could be converted to use for housing epileptics, Oscar Craig died. Letchworth asked that the new institution be named in his former colleague's honor and thus the Craig Colony opened its doors in 1896.

In his later years, Letchworth spent more and more time at Glen Iris, finally enjoying the relaxation he unquestionably deserved. It was then that he really indulged his love of the arts and literature, inviting writers, poets, painters and sculptors to share with him the idyllic setting on the banks of the Genesee River.

One of the last things he did at Glen Iris again concerned Mary Jemison. Mary's grave on the Council Grounds had been marked originally by a marble monument, but, in 1910, Letchworth had this replaced with a beautiful bronze statue. The statue depicts Deh-ge-wa-nus en route through the wilderness to Genishau, her baby swaddled in a cradleboard. These boards, carried on the backs of nursing mothers, were carved and painted by the Seneca to show a mother bird feeding her brood in the branches of a flowering tree, a tree believed to exist in the Sky World, home of the Creator. Sadly, failing health kept William Pryor Letchworth away from the unveiling of the statue, which he had himself commissioned. Just ten weeks later, he was dead, taken to meet his own creator, the last days of his life having been spent dispatching a new edition of Mary Jemison's biography.

When he died, Letchworth's body was taken from Glen Iris to Buffalo where it lies in the Quaker cemetery beneath a simple stone, cut from the Genesee river bed, bearing just his name and the dates of his birth and death. There are no statues, no columns, no obelisks, which is doubtless how he would have wanted it. Never in his lifetime had he sought honors or courted celebrity or chased personal glory. He was content to allow the fruits of his labors to be his monument.

The Seneca, though, ensured that within their own culture Letchworth was not forgotten. In 1872, once the final council meeting at Glen Iris was over, the Wolf Clan of the Senecas had adopted William Pryor Letchworth. They had given him the name Hai-wa-ye-is-tah, which means 'The man who always does right'.

It was a Thursday afternoon in March 1991 and I had been in a meeting for most of the day. I kept looking out the window, up there on the twenty-second floor of the Filmore Building, watching the storm clouds converge upon the city. Our discussions paused around three o'clock for what Mike Grogan always described as a comfort break. Marcia, Grogan's PA, had placed messages, scrawled on bits of yellow paper, on the table just outside the meeting room door, so, after returning from the restroom, I checked to see whether there was anything for me. Only one, I was initially pleased to note. 'William.' it read. 'Call Doctor Lazerno.'

Doctor Lazerno worked in the ER at the North Central Hospital. Miss Samuels, he told me, had been admitted three hours ago with lacerations to her head, face and arms.

Kelly had been out with her crew at a community center in the Bronx, recently opened and already the scene of three burglaries and an arson attack. While setting up the equipment prior to an interview with the center's manager, Kelly had been kneeling to help with a sound check. As she had risen to her feet, she had been shoved, accidentally, by one of her colleagues, who had been reeling out cable to the gaudily painted WONM van parked outside.

'Dear God.' I gasped when I first saw her lying in the stark hospital bed, her face bruised, her head bandaged. I had dashed across town, by cab and on foot, through thunder, lightning and a tumultuous downpour, and my shoes squelched on the tiled floor.

'It's okay.' she said calmly. 'My face is fine, just minor cuts. I'll still be pretty.'

She collapsed into tears and I held her as tightly as I dared.

'You're wet.' I heard her mumble into my jacket.

'I'm soaked.' I corrected her.

'I'm sorry.' she wept. 'I'm really sorry, Will.'

Caught off balance by her colleague's inadvertent push, she had tumbled towards a closed glass door. All she could recall was seeing the glass coming towards her and the reflex of lowering her head and raising her arms to protect her face. As a result, Kelly's arms were a mess of cuts and there was one deep gash on her head that had required five stitches. To clean the wound and insert the sutures, the ER staff had cut, then shaved away an unfeasibly large patch of hair.

Even before Kelly had been discharged from the hospital, WONM executives were meeting with their lawyers to work out who could sue whom. Writs were served on the city government for failing to install the proper grade of glass and then by the city government on the glass manufacturers for making misleading safety claims. The upshot was an out of court settlement, from which WONM financed its legal expenses, the payment of Kelly's medical accounts and her full salary throughout the eight weeks she was away from work. I consulted one of the lawyers on the Greenleaf payroll and he told me that we should sue the city government, the glass manufacturers *and* WONM, but by then it had all got way out of hand. I decided we should try to put it behind us and move on.

During the time Kelly was on sick leave, her disposition fluctuated between grumpy and downright antagonistic. To begin with, I thought that this was the product of being cooped up in the apartment for extended periods. However, it soon became apparent that she was depressed at being unable to work, that being forcibly kept from doing her job was little short of torture. She was suffering withdrawal symptoms; she was like a drug addict going cold turkey.

In May, we decided to go back to Bermuda, partly to celebrate Kelly's recovery, partly to breathe fresh life into our relationship after two months of Kelly's barely tolerable mood swings. Returning to the Hamilton Princess, where we had taken our honeymoon, seemed like a good idea, but the whole island, not just the hotel, proved too claustrophobic for Kelly. After seven days, I was pleased to be back on the plane to New York.

Once Kelly resumed her work at WONM, things seemed to return to what we laughably defined as normal. Without either of us noticing, we had become a quintessential Manhattan couple, focused upon our jobs, leaving the city only for prearranged weekends, mixing solely with other people in the same circumstances. We became insular, endlessly analytical about ourselves, seeking out stresses where there were none, creating friction when all around us should have been so smooth. We were financially secure, had a superb standard of living and a decent band of intelligent friends - like the Caspars and the Wardells and the Di Napolis - who we entertained at our elegant apartment, upon which Kelly spent much of her creative talent and a good deal of her income. She even went out one day and bought Shaker furniture, which she told me was highly fashionable, but which seemed to me rather primitive.

There was a tendency for us to compare diaries at the beginning of each month and arrange social events to fit around our work commitments. Cinema and theater visits were planned well in advance, as were restaurants, although that was primarily because the ones for which we had acquired a liking – the modish new places serving French cuisine – had styled themselves on exclusivity. They maintained strict control over reservations, even when minor television celebrities, as Kelly was becoming, called to book a table.

As the months passed, we left the city less and less. Kelly was so passionate about her work that three or four days were not enough for her to switch off and wind down. She would sit silent in the car as I drove, behave like a zombie over dinner, even become distracted during foreplay, which I found infuriating.

One weekend in August 1992, we did contrive to organize our schedules not just so that both Kelly and I had four consecutive days off work, but that the Caspars were free also. We decided to go again to Martha's Vineyard, to the same cottage where Kelly and I had watched the rain running down our bedroom window. For that whole weekend, only three years previously, neither of us had cared one bit about the weather, content to stay in bed until the nearby restaurant opened and we could dash there and back beneath my big golf umbrella bearing Greenleaf's name and logo. The four days with Steve and Sally were much different. The cool Atlantic breeze tempered the blazing sun as we strolled along the beach, Steve holding Sally's huge hand, Kelly kicking sand truculently, refusing to walk next to me. Back at the cottage, the atmosphere was electric. Steve beckoned me on to the veranda and whispered that he and Sally would go out on their own that evening, leaving Kelly and I alone to resolve our problems. I told him that I did not know exactly what those problems were, as Kelly had declined to inform me what was so troubling her. Steve shrugged his shoulders and smiled sympathetically. 'Just keep on asking her.' was his advice.

I did keep on asking her and eventually, after numerous denials that there was anything at all on her mind, we reached flash point. It was the worst such argument we had had, less an argument, in fact, than a tirade of abuse hurled in my direction. I had apparently insisted upon this ludicrous break, when I knew that Kelly was deeply involved in a major new story that could substantially enhance her career. I had also insisted that we spend the time with Steve, who was two-faced and detestably insincere, and Sally, who was a nonentity. Add to this my mistake in returning to this puny little island and my culpability for this disaster was signed and sealed.

It felt as though I had been run down by a train. I was livid, speechless with anger at this patent injustice. Unaccountably, I was convinced by a voice within me not to rise to this bait, to instead be conciliatory. I have concluded since that it was the voice of my levelheaded English ancestors. I actually told her I was sorry, apologizing for a crime I had not committed so as simply to calm her down and return to some semblance of sanity. I offered to take her back to New York the following day, but she told me the damage had been done and would not be undone by her early return. Further irritated that she was still needling me when I was trying to resolve the situation, I once again chose penitence, offering yet more apologies and telling her I would ensure the same problem did not occur again.

I was certainly correct about that. Never again did I suggest we take a break from New York, never again did I allow *anything* to interfere with Kelly's work. It had become obvious that the main motivator in her life, indeed its epicenter, was her career and that I was going to have to mould my own life around that constant. In retrospect, I am not sure it had ever been any other way, right from the very start of our relationship, though the degree to which her career had dominance over all other things unquestionably increased as our marriage progressed. I know now that we had grown apart considerably even before that explosive moment at the Vineyard. How this could have happened when analysis of our relationship had superseded and replaced conversation, I cannot properly explain, other than to observe that analysis is sometimes a deception. It gives the appearance of being enlightening when it is actually delusional.

That fair-minded Englishman within compels me to also look at myself, at the way *I* had evolved since leaving Columbia. I had fallen into the same trap as Steve Caspar and all those others, the snare that is advancement – advancement of career, of social status, of material wealth. It seemed natural, it fitted like a glove, but, in the end, it was not what I was about. It was a different set of values from those of my upbringing, from those of my hometown, Cow Town USA, from those of Jack Holton and Franklyn Petersen and my poor, dear mom. My life in Manhattan was a mirage, an act, the same as Mary Stafford affecting airs and graces to conceal the realities of her family's past. What is now clear is that I knew all along that it was unreal, that it had no substance, no root deep inside me. I was merely playing along with a charade and the more Kelly accepted that charade as her reality, the more I saw it for what it was.

At the very time Kelly and I were on Martha's Vineyard, Mom was going back to the hospital in Rochester to see the oncologist. She had survived more than two and a half years beyond the time when I feared she was about to die, a testimony to the medication she had been given. Now though, the limits of that medication had been reached. The cancer, whose slow, merciless spread had been checked by the drug, had seemingly discovered a way to outsmart it.

Over the ensuing months, Mom was subjected to an imaginative, sometimes terrifying array of treatment. Always that treatment was one step behind the disease. As each new outbreak was identified, the offending tissue was removed or zapped with invisible rays or attacked by pharmaceuticals with grotesque side effects. By the end of 1992, when Kelly and I made our last Christmas visit together to Geneseo, the doctors thought they had the situation under control, though all that really meant was that they had smoothed the path of her decline.

That Christmas was Becky's third and I remember her assaulting Kelly's silk stockings with the stick from a plastic xylophone. It left a slit in the left leg six inches long. Kelly stared thunderously at the child, fuming behind an expression so murderous that it may well have required a license. She stalked off to our room, with Bobbie in apologetic pursuit, though my Mom stood up, almost bald, a sackful of bones, and halted Bobbie before she could get to the stairs. It was Mom who went to talk with Kelly, to pacify her. They were up in that room for almost an hour, their low voices, behind the closed door, interwoven with occasional sobs. When Kelly returned downstairs, she came to find me in the back room, where I was leaning against Grandma Holton's old sideboard, alone, gazing at the debris of the Christmas lunch on the dining table. She stood before me and leaned forward, her head resting on my chest, a weary gesture that said she knew that our marriage, like my mom, was ebbing away.

Becky brought me a picture this evening, one she had painted at school, a cacophony of color, of rich yellows and cherry reds and shades of brown from chestnut through to deep mahogany. There was violence in the scene, great splodges of paint merging and mingling as if thrown on to the paper with no predetermination, no vision in the mind's eye of the finished product. She called it 'Fall' and it had won her a gold star from her teacher.

'Will you put it in a frame?' she asked me. 'Like the ones your mommy did?'

'I shall.' I promised her. 'Then I'll hang it in my study so that I can look at it while I'm working.'

'Show me where you mean.' Becky said. 'Show me the wall.'

I took her hand and we went through to the study, where my part-written essay lay on the opened bureau. 'Up there.' I said, pointing to an empty piece of wall near the door. 'It's just the right size for your painting. I'll take it to be framed tomorrow and, when it comes back, we can have an unveiling ceremony. I'll make a speech and you can pull the cord.'

Becky chuckled. 'Just like Queen Elizabeth.' she said.

The child's eyes are the same color as her mother's, tortoiseshell, green and fawn fusing like the splodges on the painting. Her hair is auburn, Rose's coloring, with a hint of red that catches the light when she turns. Judging by how much risotto she ate this evening, her concerns about her weight have disappeared completely, which is perfectly right given that her build is as lean as I recall Bobbie's being when she was Becky's age. Becky even has the same type of legs as the young Bobbie, slim, but with muscular calves that may easily have stoked her anxieties about them being fat.

Long ago, on high summer visits to the Park, Mom used to take Bobbie and I swimming in the pools near the Parade Grounds. I remember watching Bobbie evolve from a child into a teenager, noticing, as the months and years went by, how her breasts grew from almost indiscernible bumps to plump round ridges, how her whole body became longer and more slender. After my engagement to Kelly in 1985, my parents held a small party in Geneseo, to which they invited the Hewsons, the Petersens and a handful of Mom's friends, mostly from the painting class at the college. It was the first time I realized how much Bobbie and I had grown in different directions. Her hair was still girlishly long and her clothes were style-less, hometown – long denim skirt, plain T-shirt and underwear so lacking in support that those once plump ridges hung hefty and limp. By contrast Kelly seemed so incredibly sophisticated in her tailored two-piece and subtle pearl earrings. Bobbie still dresses in that same old way and, since Becky was born, her figure has swelled noticeably. For the last fortnight her elderly Buick has been in the shop for life-saving repairs, so she has had to walk to and from work each day. I do believe I can see the change in her already. She seems to have more energy, less sloth, more zest. She has lost a pound or two, I would guess, particularly from her hips. Those pneumatic calves have also deflated and now I can see again the old Bobbie beneath, the nicely contoured, unpretentious teenager, the person into whom I can imagine Becky evolving.

Maybe I should take Becky to the Park more often. Maybe I should take her swimming. Maybe I should encourage her to go hiking with me. I think I would start her on a simple trail, around the Big Bend, say, with its regular river views. I could show her the differences between the leaves of the birch and the larch, between the texture of bark on an oak and that on an elm. I could give her my spare binoculars, the ones my mom once used, and we could watch the swallows and the snipe and even perhaps spot a kestrel soaring high above the canyon. I could do all these things, and so much more, just as Grandpa Holton did for my mom, his daughter, just as Mom did for me, her son. I could be Becky's father.

Before I left the Park this afternoon, I went to the Visitor Center, where Hillary was serving at the counter.

'Thank-you, sir.' she said as I handed her a postcard I had selected from the nearby rack. 'You're Mr. Wright, aren't you?'

'Yes.' I replied, surprised that she knew my name.

'My friend at the County Historian's Office was talking to me about you just this lunch time.' she explained. 'She says you want to create a home movie library.'

'That's right. Do you have any?'

'Only recent videos, I'm afraid. It sounds a wonderful idea, though.'

'Thanks. I just wish I could get funding from somewhere. We need premises and equipment.'

'I'm sure there must be someone who can help.'

'I hope so. We've already got access to about forty films, but we'll want to get as many as we can.'

'Well, when you're ready, have some posters printed and I'll put one on the notice board in the lobby. People come back year after year. I'm sure some of them have shot film around here.'

This was something I had not considered. I had expected to source the archive from local people, but visitors are just as likely to have used movie cameras in the area.

'That's a great thought.' I said, taking my change and resolving to give a lot more thought to how we can make the idea become a reality.

I went back to the car and wrote Jimmy Randolph a message of good wishes on the postcard, then drove back to Geneseo via Mount Morris, where I dropped the card in the mailbox.

My essay awaited me on my return home, but tiredness soon overcame inspiration. Having given up on the composition, I went to lie down for a while on my bed, only to be woken, around six o'clock, by Bobbie and Becky knocking at my door. I ran downstairs, aware of the fact that I had not showered this morning and that I had since been on a long hike in the Park. If I smelled, then both my guests were too polite to comment. Instead, after I had been presented with Becky's picture, we all sat in the back room and enjoyed a hastily prepared dinner.

Alone again now that my guests have left, I sit here in my study and wonder at the infinity of consequences awaiting the events of the next few days. Earlier, when up on the low ridge close to the where the Dishmill Creek Trail dips down to cross the stream, I once again could feel my mom's presence. For a moment, everything seemed clear. Having been guided by what I sensed at Inspiration Point last Sunday, I now felt her reassuring me of the outcome. Tonight, however, the questions and doubts have returned, especially after having Bobbie and Becky sit and eat with me at the big table, just like a proper family.

When I looked at Becky earlier this evening, I thought about that Christmas in 1992, about the Wrights and the Petersens sitting around that same table. I wondered if Becky remembers Kelly's stockings; indeed, I wondered if she remembers Kelly at all. She was only two years old when she caused havoc with that xylophone stick. When Kelly was here last, on the day of Mom's funeral, Becky was at school. If she looked carefully tonight she will have seen a photograph of Kelly that I keep *inside* my bureau, visible only when the top is open, but I am not altogether sure she would have realized that the smiling, wavy-haired blonde and I were once married.

# Thursday

❀

Kelly moved out of our fortress on West 61$^{st}$ in September 1993. 'I don't want the place.' she told me. 'Sell it. You have my permission.'

'Sure.' I said. 'But what about *until* I sell it? Are you going to pay half of the mortgage?'

'Why should I do that if I'm not living there? Anyway, I have to rent a new place, I can't afford to give you money.'

'But it's a joint responsibility. We both signed the papers. You're obligated to pay your share.'

'Not according to my attorney.'

This was nine days after her departure and already she had an attorney. Dieter Buchmann had been so right: Kelly was very together.

Her reputation as a news reporter had been growing steadily, despite my idiocy in tearing her away the previous summer to go to Martha's Vineyard with the Caspars. During her time with WONM, she had developed from a generalist covering all manner of stories, into much more of a specialist, focusing on stories about women, her preference, if that is the right word, being for victims of violence that usually took place in the home. Kelly had been riding the trend of depicting men as ogres, mindless aggressors who saw women as punch bags. She had added to her reports a psychological undertone, cherry-picking snippets of wisdom, frequently taken out of context, to imbue the stories with tones of academia. She had even been interviewed on an afternoon talk show, where she had been presented as some sort of expert, despite the fact that she had learned everything from books and had not a single day's field practice to her name. What she was able to do, however, was instantly access a reservoir of psycho-babble sound bites, always finding one to both suit the circumstances and confirm the prejudices of her audience.

I had developed a fervent dislike for this approach, which was fast becoming the *modus operandi* for all such reporters. I had also begun to dislike the image Kelly portrayed, the visage she presented to the camera, the character she played. With the passage of time, I could hardly tell the character from the actor. Worse still, I had realized that they were becoming one and the same.

Kelly's range of stories had recently broadened to include children, usually girls, who had been beaten or sexually abused or both by fathers, step-fathers, uncles, friends of fathers, friends of step-fathers, you name it. Men. She had received invitations to awards dinners, where I was merely an appendage, referred to commonly as Mr. Samuels, Kelly having determinedly retained her maiden name after our marriage. So far, the closest she had come to taking home one of those fake gold statuettes had been a nomination in some obscure news gathering category, but she was getting closer, she had told me, getting constantly closer.

On our last night of married life together, she had arrived home late, past midnight, her head still full of a case she and her crew had been following. Some guy had held up a liquor store, then hijacked a passing car to make his get away. The car had been driven by a young woman and in the back had been her two-year-old son, strapped into a child seat. Forced to a stop in a tailback at a red light, the woman had opened the car door and fled. This had left the hijacker, brandishing a handgun of such mammoth size that it had appeared to me quite impractical as a weapon of urban crime, alone in the car with the child. The news crews had arrived only seconds after the cops and I had had my evening repose disturbed by Kelly's voice delivering, in her so obviously false tone of earnestness, a full commentary on the unfolding events. The kid had been held hostage for more than two hours as a police negotiator slowly calmed the guy, then won his confidence and finally persuaded him to give himself up. While all this went on, the news channels had beamed live interviews with the kid's grandparents, his mother's neighbors and a clutch of professionals, all supposedly expert in various aspects of hostage situations. We had been informed about police negotiation procedure, about the motives of such young criminals, the way their minds work, about the way in which trauma counselors would be essential if both mother and child were not to be irreparably damaged by the experience. I had switched off for a while, going back to the story just as the guy got out of the car and a squad of uniformed men suddenly appeared from nowhere. The men had floored him, three of them pointing guns at his head while the others trussed up his wrists and ankles with what looked like bailing wire.

With the hijacker safely in police custody, I had returned to the second bedroom, where I had been lining the rosewood shelves with some newly acquired books on British history. My aim had been to get some use out of the room, ideally as a study, rather than reserving it solely for the increasingly rare occasions when we had people stay over. As I sat arranging the books, I heard the beep of the security keypad out on the landing, then the turn of Kelly's key in the lock. There were clicking, high-heeled footsteps in the hall, then the light went on in the kitchen and there was a clink of wineglasses. Moments later, Kelly appeared in the doorway of the bedroom.

'Drink?' she inquired, gesturing towards me with the wine bottle, whilst simultaneously kicking off her shoes.

'No thanks.' I said. She poured herself a glass of the Ontario Sauvignon Blanc, which the Wardells had bought us as their idea of a joke. *Canadian wine?!*

'Did you see it?' Kelly asked.

'Did I see what?' I was trying to get the books into chronological order.

'Jeez.' she exclaimed. 'The show, of course. Did you see the show?'

'Yes, I saw the show. Pity you can't find a better word to describe it.'

She huffed and turned away, leaving me to my sorting. Minutes later, she returned, her legs now devoid of pantyhose, her jacket removed, no sign of the wine. Again she stood in the doorway, her posture at once both threatening and vulnerable, her face set ready for either rage or tears, presumably depending upon which would be the response most likely to give her victory in the ensuing battle. Clever girl.

'You hate what I do, don't you?'

I sat on the floor, my back propped against the shelves. 'No.' I said. 'I don't hate it. I just question the method and its validity as entertainment.'

That prompted an outburst of accusations about people like me, whoever they are, who want to censor what the public sees so as to portray a society that is fantasy, not reality. Apparently, those people wanted to gag the media, to suppress the truth, to sweep evil under the carpet and pretend it does not exist, to have us all think that the world is more Disney than Tarantino. The hidden motive of this being, she said, to cover up their own evil and allow them to carry on practicing their own vices and depravities without fear of rightful exposure. This all sounded like the rantings of a particularly rabid tabloid editor trying to justify his use of sex and violence to sell his newspaper.

'I'm not trying to censor anything.' I told her. 'I have nothing against reality, but why does a kid being held hostage by some crazy guy with an elephant gun have to be put out in the middle of the evening? That guy could have blown the kid's head off, with close ups transmitted into every home in New York City. Maybe that's what the networks want so they can then fill up the schedules with days of analysis and weirdoes on *Oprah* and court cases brought by people claiming compensation for illnesses caused by the distress of seeing a little boy's brains explode on prime time TV.'

'But people want this sort of story. The ratings go through the roof when we run one of those real time pieces.'

'Yes, I know. But they aren't watching it as news any more, they're watching it as entertainment, like they watch *Cheers* or *Monday Night Football.*'

For a psychologist, Kelly had a strange inability to differentiate debate from personal attack. If ever I questioned the values of the medium in which she worked, I was deemed, in her mind, to be denouncing her, Kelly Samuels, and rubbishing all that she believed in. I was being unsupportive and undermining; I was feeding the fire of her deep insecurity and demeaning her worth as a woman. This was complete nonsense. Kelly was insecure to order, using a great range of body language and facial cast to manipulate her audience, whether it be thousands beyond the lens of a TV camera or one man, her husband, staring up at her from the bedroom floor. If arguments were not going her way, her bottom lip would quiver, then she would shudder, as though great terror had awoken within her. So often I had fallen for it, gathered her in my arms and let her sob into my shoulder, tears conjured with the deftness of a Bacall or a Streep. Far from devaluing her womanhood, I had become increasingly impressed by the way in which she used it to exploit every possible situation, from the eye-glinting suggestion of untold pleasures in return for buying her an eternity ring, right through to the tough cookie sarcasm when ambushing a police captain on his doorstep in Harlem one morning. That luckless schmuck had so obviously wanted to tell her to shut her smart-ass mouth and get her goddam microphone out of his face, but he had been compelled by his office to bite his lip. Once he had bustled past, Kelly had turned to the camera and gloated, as if having achieved some great triumph. All she had done, of course, was force a man into glowering silence, rather than telling her what he really felt about a detective who had accidentally shot a pregnant woman during a bank robbery.

'People know the difference between fact and fiction.' she asserted.

'Kelly.' I said, with a smile. '*You* can't tell the difference.'

The smile had been intended to defuse the increasing hostility, but she interpreted it as my mocking her. 'Why do you do this to me?' she asked. 'I do a job and I do it damn well. I give people what they need, a chance to see what really happens in the world, a shot at understanding the reasons why the world is so screwed up. I've put in almost eighteen hours today, worked my butt off and all you can do is ridicule me.'

'One, I'm not ridiculing you and, two, you haven't been at work for eighteen hours. Even from here I can smell cigarette smoke on your clothes and beer on your breath.'

Kelly and her crew often went to a bar nearby the TV company offices, particularly after a tense and technically difficult story. Though she had no need to justify herself to me, she had always chosen to do so, giving me some psycho jive about the importance of transitioning through shared expression. What it boiled down to was that she liked to relax over a beer with the guys at the end of a hard day, which was fine with me, no problem.

'You poor repressed bastard.' she sneered. 'You can't bear the thought of a woman with a career and an independent mind. You want me chained in the kitchen all day, cooking you meals and washing your clothes. Well, let me tell you, brother, you're living in the past, in all those books you read these days about dead people and meaningless events.'

I found myself contrasting the tone of voice she was using now with the poised, neutral, accent-less delivery she used on TV. With me, there were hints of Harlem and the Bronx, absorbed from too many interviews with housing project widows; with her public it was the educated Central Pennsylvanian, as dependably consistent as Mr. Hershey's chocolate.

'Go get your wine and calm down.' I said, hauling myself to my feet.

'Oh yeah. So you can call me a drunk?

'Kelly, don't be so crazy.' I started towards her, but she turned away and headed for our bedroom. 'Kelly.' I called out, probably a little sharper than I intended. She slammed the bedroom door behind her.

It was not a bad argument, nowhere nearly as bad as some we had had, and that single bitter exchange was not why Kelly left me the next morning. It was, instead, the cumulative effect of the many altercations over the past year or more, themselves the result of the ever-widening breach between us. We had, for a while, grown in parallel, developing in the same direction, our objectives identical, our paths joint and synchronized. One of us, Kelly, had not strayed from those objectives or deviated from that path. It was me, me who had blinked, me who had begun to suspect that the goal we sought was an illusion, unreachable. I had caused our paths to diverge because I had begun to want something different, something simpler, and that desire had made me challenge what we were doing and in so doing alienate Kelly and drive her away. I know I was right, but that is scant comfort.

She kept her key and emptied the apartment of her things, with visits while I was at work. She called me up one evening to tell me she wanted her old trunk, a repository for all her college textbooks and three shoeboxes full of keepsakes. The conversation was businesslike and not unpleasant, until we got to the part about the mortgage payments and the attorney.

Gary Lennart, my tutor, called me this morning, inquiring tactfully about my emotional state, but wanting really to know whether he would, as I had promised, see my essay by the end of the week. Just as on Sunday, I tried to reassure him.

'I'm making progress.' I said. 'My family's always been diligent about recording its history, so I've got more than enough research papers.'

'That's good, William.' Gary told me in his Carolinian drawl, which seems undiluted by his years of teaching at Ohio State, and by the cosmopolitan mix of his now entirely remote student body. He will only meet us all for the first time next July, when we go to summer school near Columbus.

Once my conversation with Gary was over, I pulled on my oldest pair of training shoes and headed off to the framing shop with Becky's painting. My walk took me along Lima Road, past the site of the old Camp Union, where William and Joseph Holton were trained for service in the federal army. All the way down North Street, the chestnuts were in fine color, their golden leaves carpeting the sidewalks and verges. At the foot of the hill, I stopped at the Civil War Memorial, a granite cenotaph placed, in 1915, on a small island that is bounded by North Street, Church Street and Avon Road. It is a beautiful spot, especially when, like today, the vivid foliage is ignited by bright sunshine. I often stop to read the inscription on the monument, to somehow reach across more than a hundred thirty years and sense that young man, Joseph Holton, who left Geneseo to go to war at the same age as I left to go to Columbia.

The most prominent Geneseoan to perish in that bloody conflict was James S. Wadsworth, whose home, Hartford House, is over on the opposite side of Avon Road, hidden these days by a fence and a screen of mature trees. Anyone who fights in a war is a hero, but Wadsworth had courage that went way beyond the norm and may even have touched upon recklessness. In early 1861, with Washington almost entirely cut off by enemy forces, he chartered, at his own cost, a ship in New York and sent it, laden with supplies, to the Union troops at Annapolis. Following that feat, he advised on the defense of the capital and was then commissioned as a Major General by the Governor of New York. He fought at Bull Run, where he had a horse shot from beneath him, as well as a number of other engagements, including the battles of Chancellorsville and Gettysburg. It was at the Battle of the Wilderness, in May 1864, that he bravely, but rather inevitably met his end, this time having two horses shot beneath him in one morning and another that same afternoon. Wadsworth himself was shot in the head and, although taken by Confederate soldiers to a nearby hospital, he passed away two days later.

James Wolcott Wadsworth, son of James Samuel and Mary Wadsworth, inherited Hartford House on his mother's death in 1874. After marrying Maria Louise Travers in 1876, he and his new wife instigated a number of changes to the place, including replacement of the gateway and the installation of iron fencing. I have seen early pictures of the house, painted prior to the Civil War, that show the place surrounded by open countryside, like some great English estate. Once James Wolcott took possession, it became a far more private place and I guess today's seclusion is an extension of that.

Leaving the memorial, I set off again, heading south along Main Street. I crossed the road by the old Wadsworth Land Office, then passed the former Kelsey house and the old Brodie House, which later became the Coddington House and is now an elegant bed and breakfast. I passed also, on the opposite side of the street, St. Michael's Church, where the bell has recently fallen and become awkwardly lodged in the tower. Not so many yards beyond the church, is the site where the American Hotel stood until it burned down in 1885. The old Livingston County Bank building still exists however, having been sold to James W. Wadsworth in the same year as the fire at the hotel, then converted for use as the town's Post Office. I know some people in Geneseo who consider it to be a rather fine-looking building, though, to me, it is precisely what it was designed to be, a simple, prosaic place of commerce, made marginally more glamorous this morning by the bright sunshine invigorating its whitewashed walls.

At the Bronze Bear Café, I bought myself a breakfast of hazelnut coffee and a deliciously moist muffin, then sat by the window, looking out at the bronze bear itself, which sits atop a column in the center of the Wadsworth Memorial Fountain. Erected in 1888, the fountain was the idea of Herbert and William Austin Wadsworth, who wanted to commemorate their mother Emmeline. Its base of red granite was quarried in Maine and transported from there, all fifteen tons of it, by railroad. It was then moved from the depot at the foot of Court Street and placed in the middle of Main Street, where the water supply was connected and that bronze bear was put into place. The bear is now very much the symbol of the town.

On leaving the café, I went a few doors down the street and dropped Becky's picture into B&D. At Lily's, where the window is decorated for Halloween with a pumpkin-headed witch, I bought flowers to place on the Holton graves. I then wandered down to Village Square Park.

The original town house was moved from the Village Square in 1805 and placed on what became known as Meeting House Hill, adjacent to the burial ground. Over the following years, the square saw much use, but gradually fell into neglect. In 1845, Elizabeth Wadsworth wanted to enlarge the grounds of The Homestead and asked that the line of South Street be altered. As a condition of the authorities' approval, Elizabeth was requested to make improvements to the square, which she seems to have done with some gusto, planting a whole range of trees, graveling the footpaths and enclosing the square with fine railings. Another makeover was required in 1865, when the iron fence was replaced with one of oak picket, and again in 1879, when the fence was removed completely. In 1895, a log cabin was built on the square as the first home of the Livingston County Historical Society. Five years later, further alterations were made, when the square was re-landscaped. Added at that time were a croquet lawn, tennis court and bowling green, as well as a stone wall along the eastern side, bordering Main Street.

The old log cabin still stands, though it is now locked up and empty, and there are no longer any sporting facilities. The grass today was thick and lush, still damp from the overnight dew. On warmer days, especially in early summer, the square is used, for sunbathing and reading, by students from SUNY, the State University of New York, which has its Arts and Sciences campus on the site of what was known as the Geneseo Normal School. The school opened in 1871, offering curricula in both elementary and advanced English, as well as the Classics. These days, the range of courses is mind-boggling, attracting over five thousand students from all over the state, though enjoying the experience is not compulsory. Two young women passed me by in the square, one of whom, not a month past Homecoming, was telling her friend that she could not wait to get out of this God-forsaken dump.

I smiled at the thought of how I, too, had wanted to break away from this place when I was just a little younger than them. Now, I cannot imagine wanting to live anywhere else.

I walked almost to the end of Main Street, to its junction with South Street, which was, at Elizabeth Wadsworth's request, re-routed to give The Homestead more land. Once Elizabeth had died in childbirth and her brother William Wolcott's widow, Emmeline, had inherited the place, its infrequent occupation left it in need of much restoration. Craig Wadsworth, son of James Samuel, bought the house from his aunt in the late 1860s and made the necessary repairs, though he passed away in 1872 and the young William Austin Wadsworth, son of Emmeline and future co-donor of the Memorial Fountain, took possession. He lived in the house with his mother, who had previously shown about as much enthusiasm for Geneseo as that student I overheard at Village Square Park. Once back as a permanent resident, however, Emmeline threw herself into improving the old house, first having it moved three hundred fifty yards further back from the road, then making extensive alterations to both the exterior appearance and the interior layout and decoration. By the time she died in 1886, The Homestead must have been unrecognizable from the house James Wadsworth had built eighty-five years earlier.

Heading back along the opposite side of Main Street, I passed the Geneseo Building and the shops that once were the Farmers' Exchange. I then turned into Center Street, passed the disused and crumbling Riviera Theater and made for the Wadsworth Library, noticing that, by the clock on the Baptist Church opposite – the official town clock, no less – it was almost eleven o'clock.

The library began life in 1843 when James Wadsworth, just a year before his death, gave land for the building of an Atheneum Library, which was to house thousands of books, available for any county resident to borrow free of charge. When James S. Wadsworth was killed, his will made provision for a new library to be constructed on the plot beside the original. Three years later, the present building was opened. It is an imposing structure, built in an Italianate style and having the same dimensions as those of the Parthenon in Athens. Inside, it still has the darkness and hush of a bygone era, though the assistants are always helpful, especially when, like today, I want copies of things normally kept in storage. I asked one of the ladies for back copies of the *Livingston County News*, which she happily dug out for me from one of the archives. I wanted to remind myself of how Charlie and Rose had announced the birth of their first and so far only grandchild. 'Petersen, Rebecca.' the announcement read. 'Born September 10th 1990 to Roberta, daughter of Charles and Rosemary Petersen of Geneseo.' Yes, I thought, remembering as I read it, how very formal.

Back out in the sunshine, I continued past the Cobblestone Schoolhouse, built in 1838 as a gift of the Wadsworths and now the home of the Livingston County Museum and the County Historian's office. As I always do, I stopped at the junction with Elm Street and looked through the trees towards the house where Jimmy Randolph and his wife Kathleen once lived. I recall so clearly from my childhood the visits I used to make there with my mom, when Kathleen, a gentle and kindly spoken lady, would offer me her wonderful home made cookies. Now Jimmy lives in a retirement home in West Virginia, close to his son and daughter-in-law.

On the corner of Center Street and Temple Hill is a trough from which the townsfolk once watered their horses. It dates back to the same time as the Memorial Fountain and once made use of the same water supply. This time of year it is usually smothered with fallen leaves, but someone must have cleared them away yesterday, possibly the same person who had so conscientiously tidied the grass verges on the way up to the cemetery. Maybe, a century-and-a-half ago, young Chet Arthur kicked his way through the leaves at that same spot. Chet is reckoned to have been a student at the Temple Hill Academy, formerly the Livingston County High School, which had been founded in 1826, thanks to yet another donation of land by the Wadsworth brothers. Alumni included the man who taught Mark Twain to be a Mississippi riverboat pilot, New York State Governor Washington Hunt and the man who wrote the first history of Livingston County and to whom all local historians are indebted, Lockwood L. Doty. Chet Arthur went on to be admitted to the New York bar, then served as quartermaster general of New York during the Civil War. President Grant appointed him Collector of the Port of New York and he was James Garfield's running mate in the presidential election of 1880. When Garfield was assassinated in July of the following year, Chet Arthur, purported one time student at Temple Hill Academy, became the twenty-first President of the United States.

Just about the whole of my family is buried up on Temple Hill, as is much of the Wadsworth dynasty, including the pioneers William and James, James' wife Naomi and most of their children. Unlike the Wadsworths, the Holtons have no specially enclosed area of the cemetery, though the plot is not insubstantial, tucked over near the southwestern corner. I took the flowers I had bought at Lily's and placed them, one by one, on the graves, leaving Mom's until last. There, I laid two white roses against the headstone, just beneath my own name. 'Faith Mary Wright.' the inscription reads. 'Daughter of John and Mary Holton, wife of Edward Wright, devoted mother of William.'

I talked to Mom for a while, telling her about Bobbie and Becky, about Kelly and about Dad, who I asked her to care for now that he has joined her in spirit, even if his body is an ocean away. I was completely alone, for once able to speak aloud without that feeling of English self-consciousness that I inherited from my dad. I think I could have stayed there all day, but I could sense Mom telling me to get home, to get back to my studies, just as she had when I was at school. I could almost hear her saying that, yes, it was nice to talk, but that I ought not to be squandering my time with her when there were more important things to do.

So, I left the cemetery and set off back along Temple Hill and into Highland Road, which was once known as Temple Hill Street, then as Mill Street. Half way down is the entrance to Highland Park, on to which backed my grandparents' house, and where once I used to go to play baseball with my school friends. It was, this morning, almost as deserted as the cemetery, just a handful of people walking dogs or jogging. I took a look at the old railroad depot building, which was moved to the park from Court Street in the 1970s, three decades after the last train had stopped at Geneseo and the tracks of the old Genesee Valley Railroad had been removed. Its present color, an odd drab green, is quite hideous, but local preservationists insist it is authentic.

It was now early afternoon and I knew I should hurry home and get on with my essay. I exited the park, back out on to Highland Road, and walked down the hill, past Oak Street, which is where Franklyn and Olive Petersen once lived, and then across North Street and homeward along Lima Road.

When William Holton retired from the County Treasurer's Office in 1901, he was presented with a silver fob watch, which, along with his Civil War campaign medals, was buried with him when he died in 1921. He also took to his grave on Temple Hill a small photograph, taken that same year of his retirement, in which his son Thomas and Thomas's wife, Louisa, are shown holding their month old baby who they had named William. Four months after they had posed for that photograph, little William was dead, the victim of scarlet fever.

Of all the children of William and Alice Holton, Thomas was the most like his father. He grew to be a few inches taller, but his facial features were almost identical and he had about him the same bearing William had had before he had been wounded at Antietam. Thomas also had a similar unobtrusive manner, along with a keen intelligence that saw him excel in school. His younger brother, William Jr., was the complete antithesis, a stubby, rebellious little boy, who carried the same characteristics through his teenage years and into his brief adulthood. He ruthlessly tormented his sister Mim, who had inherited all of Alice Holton's femininity and had developed it to the point of punctilious delicacy. Poor Mim would often be found by her mother, sobbing in the arms of her younger sister Sarah, who had been blessed with Thomas's dark good looks and, perhaps more importantly, her Aunt Margaret's solid physique. Many was the time that William Jr. and Sarah would settle an argument by scrapping on the floor of the Holton's drawing room, while Mim stood tearfully on the sidelines, pleading with them to stop.

In 1890, aged just seventeen, Thomas made his own way to New York City and sought out Rebecca Fulmer. Thomas had learned of his great-great-aunt from his parents, the boy having shown an unusual interest, for one so young, in the history of his family. Indeed, throughout his life, he pieced together as much as he possibly could about his forebears, a story that has been augmented and updated by every successive generation of Holtons. In his papers, he describes the centenarian Rebecca as being white-haired, slightly built, with a kind face and tiny hands that she waved about continuously as she talked, maybe a habit formed from having worked for the church with so many Italian immigrants.

Back in Geneseo, Thomas completed his studies at the Normal School and was then taken on by the Rochester firm of Cordle & Company where he was trained as a surveyor. At the end of each week, he would travel back down to Geneseo, where he was carefully nurturing a relationship with Louisa Kent. Louisa, who is said to have been one of the most beautiful young women in the town, was the granddaughter of Theodore Kent, to whom

Thomas's grandparents, John and Catherine Holton, had sold their house on Second Street.

The marriage of Thomas and Louisa took place at St. Michael's Church in 1899. The two of them went to live in Rochester, which is where their first child William was born and where that photograph of the three of them was taken. William's death, however, appears to have made Thomas, in particular, re-evaluate his life and his ambitions.

Since moving to Rochester, Thomas had become friendly with a man called Robert Langman, who was twelve years his senior and who had been an architect, first for the city government, then for a private firm part-owned by Barnabus Sprague, who was the grandson of Benjamin Van Oost's former partner. Originally a native of Livonia, Langman had often talked of returning to his hometown and establishing his own business. Coming from a poor family, Langman had never had the financial resources to realize this aspiration. Thomas Holton, on the other hand, was the eldest son of a family that, through hard work and the good fortune of one forebear in marrying the ward of the wealthy Van Oosts, had achieved a decent measure of prosperity. This, combined with the longing of Louisa to return, after the loss of her son, to the bosom of her family and the familiar streets of Geneseo, decided Thomas to suggest a partnership with Langman. The two of them would found their own firm, intending to profit from the ever expanding development of the area, on the demand for new housing, for schools and offices and factories, for buildings of almost every conceivable type.

The two men re-established themselves in Livingston County, Langman back in Livonia and Thomas Holton in Geneseo, where he had a house built, to Langman's design, on the recently opened Oak Street. As well as being a fine home, the house proved to be a great advertisement for the new firm, with its elegant neo-classical façade that immediately caught the eye of passers-by. Inside, it was filled by Thomas with all sorts of features, from a dumb waiter modeled on one he had seen down at the Brodie House on Main Street, to a kitchen fitted with all the most modern laborsaving contrivances, to a hidden spiral staircase rising to attic rooms lit by sunshine streaming through roof windows that were completely invisible from the outside. Countless prospective customers were treated to a tour of the house, so many in fact that Louisa, who was, between 1904 and 1916, rarely without a suckling child to nurse, eventually put a stop to it. By then, though, the reputation of Holton & Langman was well known and the need had passed for Thomas to impress with tours around his own home.

In 1902, Thomas's sister, Miriam, married Arthur Spink of Buffalo. Spink was a shy, rather effete man, three years younger than Mim, but, it was thought, a good match for his ostensibly fragile and vulnerable new wife. As a teenager, Mim had suffered from what sounds to me, from the entries in Thomas's journal, like the Victorian equivalent of ME. It had laid her low for almost three years, during which time her already slender frame had become terribly frail. She had met Spink on a train as she was traveling with her mother to a hospital in Buffalo to see yet another doctor. Spink himself never looked the picture of vitality, his skeletal face seeming always sad and lugubrious with its thin, droopy moustache and vacantly gazing eyes. Once married, his physical state deteriorated still further and no-one was surprised when, in 1914, aged just thirty-five, he went to sleep one night and never woke up. It left Mim a widow for almost forty years, her longevity considered nothing less than a miracle by all who knew her.

Mim even outlived her younger sister, who no-one could recall ever suffering from anything more serious than the cuts and bruises she sustained in childhood fights with her brother William. Sarah married, in 1903, a man called Richard Weber, who was descended from a German family that had settled in the area almost a hundred years before. Oddly, Weber bore a resemblance to Arthur Spink. Both had the same long, thin face, both had sunken eyes and both had a gaunt, frangible stature. For Weber, whose personality matched his appearance, to have married a woman like Sarah seems, to me, an act of either great courage or simple masochism. She became an aggressive, domineering wife, who forced him to hand over every cent he earned and who then drip-fed him pocket money. She particularly enjoyed the times when he needed, for instance, a new shirt or a pair of boots, and he had to beg her for the cash. It is a character trait that found its way into both her children - Phyllis, who I never met, but of whom I have heard many tales, and Harriet, known to all as Aunt Hatty, who, when I was a child, sometimes came from her home in Syracuse to visit my mom, visits during which Dad and I tried to find urgent business elsewhere.

Sarah was sixty when she died in 1939, ten years after her browbeaten husband. Mim survived until 1953, when at seventy-seven, she had a fall that broke her pelvis and caused multiple complications from which she had no hope of recovery. Both sisters lived many years beyond the death of their brother William, however.

William left Geneseo when he was sixteen and took work first on a farm near Batavia, then in a number of factories in Rochester. He was constantly in trouble, his problems stemming from what was reportedly an uncontrollable temper. At the least provocation, he would fly into fits of rage that, as time passed, became increasingly violent. He was sent to prison for two months in 1902 for his part in a fracas at Rochester's main railroad station, then went back to the pen for a further five months after a bare knuckle fight in a dockside bar. Greatly concerned, his mother Alice visited him in jail and persuaded him to return home once he was released. In Geneseo, Thomas, more out of kindness than good judgement, gave him a job and, for a short while, William appeared to have mended his ways. That was until a rain-sodden afternoon in January 1904, when a debate about continuing work on a new house in Avon led to William, soaked through from fixing roof slates all morning, suddenly swinging a rock-like fist at the foreman and laying the man out cold. Thomas was left with no choice but to fire his own brother.

Within days, William left the family home in North Street and was not heard of again for over a year. Then, astonishingly, a letter was received from him, addressed to his Aunt Margaret, who was still living in the old Van Oost house. In the letter, William pleaded with Margaret to pray for him, to beg God to forgive him for his past behavior, for the crimes he had committed and for the hurt he had caused his family. Maybe William, like Margaret before him, had found religion? I think not. From everything I have heard and read about William, I am compelled to conclude that the poor man was unstable, that his condition was the result of some mental illness. It is a view reinforced by the manner of his death, which came in New York City in 1908. He had taken up with a woman, Felicia Garrett, who kept a menagerie of stray dogs, feral cats and captured wild birds in and around her apartment in Hell's Kitchen. She claimed to be the divine messenger of St. Francis of Assisi and would wander through the neighborhood reciting aloud passages from the Bible. Most people thought she was a crank and ignored her, but some of the youngsters would tease her and up-end the old wagon she used to pull along, often with a sleeping, flea-ridden cat nestling inside. On one such occasion, William Holton saw a boy not just spill a cat from the wagon, but kick it as it scampered away. In a flash, William grabbed the child, who was twelve years old, and began pumping his face against a railing. Felicia Garrett, screaming, attempted to intervene, but quickly found herself the target of William's fists. With both the boy and Felicia lying bloodied on the sidewalk, William fled, winding up at a disused warehouse, a place he had used for shelter when he had first arrived in the city. There, the following day, he was found, hanging from an iron beam, suspended by a length of grimy rope wound about his neck.

William's parents arranged for his body to be brought back to Geneseo. The funeral took place at St. Michael's and the burial at Temple Hill cemetery, where William was placed in the family plot, close by his great-grandmother Jessica and his grandparents John and Catherine, who had died within a year of each other back in 1877 and 1878. Also buried there was another William, his nephew, the infant son of Thomas and Louisa.

For my eighth birthday, Grandma Wright sent me an atlas of the world, an English version with the British Isles at the front, then Europe and Africa and Asia. Only Australia and New Zealand came after the Americas. I asked Mom to show me where Grandma lived and she pointed out a small circle on the map, an inch or so above London. Then she told me about Grandma's family and how it came from what she called East Anglia, that bulbous protrusion where England thrusts its rump in the direction of the Low Countries. It was, Mom said, an expanse of flatlands dotted with tranquil villages, with thatched cottages and stone-built churches dating back to Norman times, with windmills and placid rivers and wide, reed fringed lakes, called broads, that formed when ancient peat workings flooded. Life there, she said, was gentle and uncomplicated and the people of East Anglia reflected that.

Aunt Angela has traced her mother's family to the town of Kings Lynn in the county of Norfolk. There, around 1811, was born Edward Chapel, who later married Mary Cox and fathered two children. For some reason the children were registered at birth with different surnames, Lydia Chapel, the first born, and Frederick Chapple, her younger brother. Angela tells me this was a not uncommon occurrence, especially in rural communities, where levels of literacy were low and where the lives of the laboring classes did not command, in local officials, any great attention to detail.

Frederick followed his father into farming, while Lydia moved away from Kings Lynn and became a maidservant in a large house in the cathedral city of Ely. She remained there, in the employ of the same family, until she died in 1893, by which time she had become the housekeeper, responsible for all the domestic staff. Frederick, meanwhile, had married Victoria Goodwin. Victoria's father worked in the fens, a great area of marshes kept drained by wind pumps and crisscrossed by a lattice of dykes. It was a solitary existence, checking the water levels, operating the sluice gates, often seeing no-one else all day. By comparison, Kings Lynn, a lively market town with busy quays on the Great Ouse and Purfleet rivers, must have seemed to Victoria like a seething metropolis, maybe in a similar way to how New York City appeared to me when I went to Columbia.

The Chapples' first child was Walter, a spindly boy, prone to illness, who, it was evident from an early age, would be unlikely to emulate his father as a rugged farm hand. Three years after Walter's birth, in 1878, his sister Emma was born and she too possessed the same physique and vulnerability. Emma's life was punctuated by constant poor health, which is actually how she came to meet her husband, Hugh Bletchley. As an itinerant showman, Bletchley had only a brightly-painted, horse-drawn trailer, or caravan, as a home. During the winter, he would find a farm and offer his services in exchange for food and drink and for being allowed to pitch his trailer in one of the farmer's pastures. In November 1906, he appeared at the farm where Frederick Chapple worked. Emma, twenty-eight years old by that time, was passing through another poorly phase. When Frederick mentioned his daughter's health to Bletchley, the showman produced a bottle of foul smelling liquid which the label declared was a specially prepared blend of oils and herbs that had a curative effect upon 'all known maladies'. This was quite a claim and one the desperate Frederick was not going to ignore.

The following summer, Bletchley returned to the area as part of a traveling fair. To his amazement, he was approached by an attractive, if rather thin woman who appeared to know him, but who he could not recognize at all. It was Emma Chapple, who had recovered so quickly after using Bletchley's cure and who now wanted to confer her grateful thanks. Bletchley, of course, was delighted and invited Emma to become part of his show so as to testify to the efficacy of his preparation. Emma agreed, but only on the condition that he married her first, for it would be completely inappropriate for the two of them to share, as single people, such intimate living space as was afforded by his trailer.

Hugh and Emma Bletchley remained on the road for the remainder of Emma's short life. She died in 1918, aged just thirty-nine. Hugh lived on until he was seventy-six, always a colorful character, always a showman. When Aunt Angela was maybe nine or ten, he told her the story of how he and Emma had met. Even then, forty years afterwards, he found the story hilarious. Emma, he told Angela, had misunderstood how to use the cure he had concocted. He had intended it to be used on a poultice, which would then be applied to the effected area of the body. Emma, however, had *drunk* the stuff, which, knowing what was in it, Hugh found quite unbelievable.

Walter Chapple's life, by comparison, was utterly banal. At the age of twelve, he was taken on by his Aunt Lydia's employers in Ely, where he eventually became a footman. In 1906, he married Rose Spicer, a pixie-like woman, who Angela vaguely recalls as being bug-eyed and almost bald, this by the time she was in her late fifties, and, as such, a frightening sight for four-year-old Angela, Rose's grand-daughter. Nonetheless, Walter must have once found her appealing, though his having waited to marry until he was thirty-one, combined with what Angela has learned of his rather timid demeanor, does suggest that the female of the species was rather a stranger to him. Even the interest of a bug-eyed pixie may well have been a blessing.

The couple's only child arrived in 1908. They named her Edith, for no obvious reason, and she proved to be, despite her parentage, a dark-haired beauty, reminiscent, it was said, of her Great Aunt Lydia. With a child to care for, Walter and Rose moved to Madingley, a village just outside Cambridge, where they became two of the live-in servants at Madingley Hall, which had been built by Sir John Hynde in 1543 and was still home to his descendants. Once Edith was old enough, she too helped out around the grand Tudor house.

Down in the grubby depths of London's East End, the Wright family was still eking out an existence on the breadline. John and Maud, who had married in 1902 and were living with John's dying father and liquor-loving mother, had produced two children, Percy, born in 1904, and John, who had arrived two years later. As a result, there were six people living in a house with two rooms on each of its two stories. Even so, such arrangements contrasted favorably against the predicament of many neighbors who commonly had ten or more people in their identically proportioned houses. Both Wright boys received a basic education at a nearby school and each left before he reached thirteen. Percy worked first in a factory, but had always intended to join the Merchant Navy, an ambition he duly achieved once he turned sixteen. John also had a hankering for travel, though his aim was to work on the railways, preferably as either a driver or engineer, which would enable him to see more of the country whilst also earning some independence from his squalid home. As it transpired, he had to settle for something less

room and Kelly and I drove to the stores to buy her some underwear and toiletries. The earlier remoteness had returned, as though she felt the need to stress her point that her decision to stay over should not be misinterpreted. She scarcely spoke. Instead, she just stared out the window, looking at the illuminated houses along Center Street and the garish store signs and fast-food courts on Lakeville Road. She went into Wal-Mart alone, came out with her purchases in a plastic bag, then held them tightly on her lap as I drove home again, past those same signs, past those same houses.

She went to bed within half an hour of our arrival back at the house, sleeping overnight in Jackie's room. With Angela in my old room, I was once more consigned to a sofa, though not before Dad and I had shared a beer together.

'I'm going home.' he said, quite suddenly, after a long silence.

'To England?' I asked, knowing the answer already.

He nodded.

'Why?'

'There's nothing for me here now.'

'*I'm* here.'

'I know, but you've got your own life, William.'

'Do I, Dad?'

He looked at me curiously.

'We've both lost the women who were the centers of our lives.' I explained.

'Oh.' he said with a peculiar finality. He had spotted the danger of the conversation exposing our deeper feelings.

'When are you planning to leave?' I asked.

'Soon.' he replied. 'In the next two or three weeks.'

I sat up in the armchair, shocked. '*Really?* Don't you have things to clear up here?'

'Nothing that can't be done by letter and telephone.'

'What about the house?'

'I was hoping you'd deal with that for me.'

I guess I knew that was coming, that this was all leading up to something.

'Will you sell it for me?' Dad asked, perhaps a little imploringly.

'OK.' I agreed with a resigned sigh. 'I'll do what I can.'

We finished our beer without another word on the subject.

I had a restless night's sleep, as did Dad, whose tossing and turning made the old bed in the room above me creek and moan. I must have fallen into my deepest sleep around three in the morning. Even so, I was awake again at seven o'clock. I was dry and thirsty, in need of a drink, so I got up and made for the kitchen. It was then that I found that Kelly had already departed. There, on the hall table, was a neatly written note: 'Will, I've gone back to NYC – working this p.m. Love to your Dad. Kelly.' I took the note with me to the kitchen, where I poured myself a glass of water, then trudged slowly up the stairs to Jackie's room. There, the sheets had been taken from the bed, folded and piled tidily on the adjacent chest of drawers. I set the glass on the floor, placed the note on top of the bedclothes, then lay down and buried my face in the pillow, trying to divine some essence of Kelly, whose head had rested there only an hour before. There was nothing, not even the faintest hint of her perfume or a single strand of her blonde hair.


Sally called tonight. Steve was at some function at The Lincoln Center, she told me. She did not expect him home until past midnight. As usual, this was the cue for one of Sally's confessionals. She told me about the latest argument she and Steve have had and about some guy who teaches at the same school as her and who has twice now taken her out to dinner. Is she seeking my sympathy, I wonder, or maybe my approval? I try to remain dispassionate, to listen rather than comment, but when I do speak I often hear my own voice, unruffled, apparently imperturbable and so much like my dad.

'And how are *you*, Will?' Sally eventually asked.

'Just fine, Sally.' I replied. 'It's beautiful out here at the moment. The foliage is just great.'

I knew Sally had not the slightest interest in the colors of the leaves. 'Great,' she said, 'but don't you feel more isolated now that your dad has gone, more abandoned?'

I groaned. 'You still don't get it, do you Sally?'

'No, Will. I don't.

When I first got my apartment in Manhattan following my separation from Kelly, I found myself hounded, through gentle inquiries and innuendo, by people who seemed to see it as their duty to cheer me out of my sad and lonely existence. 'Why don't you come spend the weekend with us?' I would be asked, the intonation one of pity. I would try to decline such invitations politely, yet there were times when civility needed to be supported by solid determination. I would detect, in a facial expression or a faint gasp down a telephone line, that my firmness had caused some minor affront, though in no way was that my intention. My friends simply had to learn that I had *opted* to live alone and that I was not the victim of cruel circumstance.

The passage of time, as well as my moving back here to Geneseo, has changed many attitudes. In fact, the tables have turned almost completely and I now get people telling me how much they envy my situation, the freedom and the absence of accountability. When I go to New York City and meet up with my old colleagues from Greenleaf, I see them constantly checking their watches, anxious not to be out too late for fear of a partner's disapproval. I have no such concerns. I can stay out as late as I like, I can do what I like and with whom I like. When I am at home, I enjoy the solitude, the knowledge that no-one is watching over me, analyzing every move I make, every cough, every sneeze, every fart. I live alone, but I am not lonely and most certainly I do not feel abandoned.

'Just stop bothering yourself about me.' I told Sally. 'I enjoy the way I live. Anyway, I think your energies should go into sorting out your life with Steve. You guys sound like you're heading for a fall.'

'I know.' Sally sighed. 'I just don't know how to fix it. Steve spends so much time at work that he has nothing left for me. I want some attention.'

'That's obvious.' I said. 'But seeking that attention from another man can only hurt your marriage more.'

'I haven't slept with this other guy.'

'I didn't say you have.'

'I know you didn't. But I want to, Will. He's fun to be with. He *talks* to me. He cares.'

'You know, Sally, I bet Steve cares, too. I bet he cares a great deal.'

'I guess so. But he doesn't show it.'

'His mind's elsewhere. You need to do something to make him take notice of you again.'

I realized that I had now moved away from my usual fence-sitting, that my practiced non-alignment had vanished. This was because, a little to my surprise, I really did feel strongly about the state of my friends' marriage.

'What should I do then, Will?' Sally asked. 'Should I go out and buy some new clothes, maybe some sexy underwear or something?'

'Sure.' I said, still not returning to neutrality. 'That could be a good idea, but don't think it's just a matter of sex, Sally. Fixing that for a night, or even for a week, won't fix the underlying problem.'

'What if it *is* the underlying problem?'

'I doubt that it is.'

'You don't know when we last made love, Will. Three weeks ago. That's how long it's been and it was at least the same before that. He just doesn't seem interested any more. Maybe I should buy us a sex manual.'

My mind instantly switched back to when I discovered that Kelly had bought *Step By Step To Great Sex*. It undeniably did a lot for the fledgling intimacy of our relationship, but, with Kelly following the instructions so dogmatically, taking those steps one by one and in the exact order they were presented, I could not avoid the feeling that I was still part of one of her experiments, still a rat in a lab.

'Sally.' I said firmly. 'I really don't think sex is the problem. What you do in bed is just an extension of your broader relationship. If you haven't slept together for three weeks, it doesn't mean that the problem is sexual. It's more likely to mean that other parts of your marriage are broken or unsteady. Let's face it, you're not really taking an interest in this other guy purely to get laid. You're doing it because he fills a gap in your relationship with Steve.'

'For Chrissakes.' Sally laughed. 'You sound just like Kelly.'

'It's osmosis.' I told her. 'You soak it up if you're around it long enough.' I paused for a moment, then continued, my voice lower. 'Look.' I said. 'You need to talk with Steve, not me, not this guy at school. Talk with your husband and find some resolution. If you both want it enough, you'll find a way.'

'I know, Will. I know. You're a good friend, you know? You've got such good sense.'

'No, Sally, it's just *common* sense.'

'Well, whatever it is, you've got it. From what I remember of her, you're just like your mom in that respect. And just as big a hunk as your dad.'

'I don't think I want to go there, Sally.'

'Sorry, Will. That was tactless.'

'It's OK. I'm not offended, but I do feel we should draw a close to this now, Sally. I'm tired and you've got some thinking to do.'

'You're right again. I'll call you next week and let you know how things are.'

'You do that. Goodnight now.'

'Bye Will.'

I was pleased to get Sally off the 'phone. I could feel her edging towards a line I have no wish to reach, let alone cross, a line I draw to mark where my personal space begins. Another few minutes and Sally would have been asking me how long it is since *I* last had sex and my honest answer would have opened up a whole new realm of conversation.

I believe Sally thinks that I have been celibate since the moment Kelly walked out on me. It is true that I have chosen to pursue platonic relationships with most of the women I have known, chiefly because I have had no desire to get mixed up in the sort of heavy, emotion-laden relationships that tend to result from sexual involvement. However, this has not always been the case. In May of last year, while vacationing up in Manitoba, I met a group of Canadian students who were canoeing around the lakes, camping out each night rather than finding, like me, a proper roof and a comfortable bed in which to rest their weary limbs. Leading the group was a young teacher, Sarah Weston, who shared with me the distinction of being half English. Having chatted briefly with her one afternoon, we met again, by coincidence, a couple days later when I arrived in Grand Rapids to find Sarah and her group stocking up on provisions at a convenience store. By the time they departed, we had exchanged telephone numbers.

We subsequently met up half a dozen times, twice when I drove round Lake Ontario to the outskirts of Toronto, where she had made her home, and four times in Geneseo, when she came down here to visit me. We slept together on every occasion and I felt myself yielding to the temptation to fall in love with her, a temptation I had schooled myself to resist, not just with Sarah, but with any woman. My divorce from Kelly had resolved me never to allow my heart to be broken again. As it turned out, Sarah called to end our relationship a few days after her fourth visit here, citing as her reason the geographical distance between us, combined with increased responsibilities at her school that would mean her having less time to see me at weekends. Although sad at this turn of events, I also had a sense of having been saved from tumbling into a familiar, but frighteningly deep chasm, extrication from which involves substantial volumes of hurt. Sarah and I still write to one another and we arranged a reunion back in June when we spent two days in Quebec City, where she was attending a conference. It was a walking-the-walls, sharing-the-check, separate-rooms type of reunion, the propriety aided by an engagement ring that had materialized on her left hand with no prior warning in her letters. His name is Jacques and, as far as I am aware, the wedding is planned for next Spring. I doubt I shall be invited.

So, a few weeks after Sarah's cooling off call, when Sally asked whether I missed sex, I would, if inclined to reply, have had to say that yes, I did, but not as much as I missed the *company* of a woman, female companionship. Indeed, spending time with Sally – at the Park, in Geneseo, out at Seneca Lake – reminded me just how enjoyable it is to share the beauty of my surroundings with an intelligent, articulate and attractive woman, a delight somehow quite different from the pleasure of similar visits by male friends. It brought to mind the same feelings I had had when Sarah spent time with me here, when we had also hiked along the Gorge Trail and dined by the water at Spinnakers.

Thinking this way makes me realize that, between returning home this afternoon from my walk around the village and receiving Sally's call late this evening, I did not speak with another person. I sang along a few times with the radio as I cooked dinner and I laughed aloud once or twice as Tim Allen and Patricia Richardson exchanged cute one-liners on *Home Improvement*, but my voice was not used to communicate with a single fellow human being. I had no 'phone calls, no visitors, just a junk e-mail offering airfare discounts and two bills delivered by the mailman. Nothing necessitated my speaking. This, I know, would unnerve some people, maybe even instill come sense of having been deserted. Yet, days like these can be so agreeable. I could be impulsive. I could secret myself away and plow through my essay, I could finish my working day at six-thirty, eat exactly what I wanted and at the time I wanted it, read in peace, think in silence, pour myself a beer and watch inane sitcoms. At no time was I obliged to make conversation, compelled to communicate solely to let someone else know that they were not being ignored or shut out. At no time was anyone there to demand my attention, to pester me, albeit caringly, with offers of help or advice or coffee and cookies. I could have worked all evening had I wished, stayed up into the small hours in front of that screen. I could, alternatively, have taken a walk down to the Vital or gone to see a movie at the multiplex on Lakeville or retired to bed at seven thirty and let the radio play me to sleep. I could, indeed, have done anything I wanted to do, for I am absolutely independent. Free.

The trick I now need to pull off is to convince myself that I am prepared to give up that freedom, to exchange its pleasures for those of a committed relationship. Not that the two could or should be incompatible. I believe successful relationships allow each partner a degree of independence, the magnitude of that degree calibrated to suit the individuals involved. What I find strange now is to reflect upon my feelings when my marriage had evolved into little more than a series of meetings during which Kelly and I synchronized our personal organizers. Our degree of independence had become so great that, in effect, we lived separate lives, coming together only for well planned occasions, maybe something like the Caspars are experiencing. Like Sally now, I hated that period. I saw no point in us having a relationship if we were unable to benefit from *shared* spontaneity, from *joint* autonomy. This gives me cause for optimism; I feel I can differentiate between the expectations I have whilst living alone and those I would have as one half of a couple.

# Friday

❀

Grandpa Holton was born in July 1906 and, although christened John, he was known from birth as Jack. The third child of Thomas and Louisa Holton, Jack arrived five years after their first-born, William, who survived only a few months, and two years after their second child, Clara. After Jack came his brothers Lester, born in 1909, and Philip, whose delivery took place at the home of his grandparents, William and Alice Holton, in the spring of 1911. It appears that Thomas was having some alterations made to the Oak Street house and that Louisa had withdrawn to the home of her parents-in-law for her confinement, this despite Alice having been poorly for some months.

Dear Alice, whose illness was never diagnosed, died when her heart failed on a bitterly cold winter's day in 1912. Thomas, in his journal, wrote eloquently of his mother and hoped that the next child he and Louisa produced would be a girl, so that she could be named Alice. I presume Louisa was of the same mind, not so much about honoring Thomas's mother in this way, but about having another baby. She was already raising her four surviving children in a house that was more like a public exhibit, so regularly did Thomas conduct a potential customer around the place, pointing out the finely carved newels and the cleverly disguised dumb waiter and the state-of-the-art water heating system. In the event, the number of such tours, perhaps indeed the original Holton Tours, reduced considerably, possibly as a result of Louisa's sixth pregnancy, for, in March 1915, my great uncle Hartley was born. It was evident from the beginning that Hartley was not the brightest or most responsive child. Thought maybe to be deaf, he was, in fact, retarded, not so much that it was life threatening, but enough for him to have to spend most of his existence in institutions. Maybe Thomas and Louisa should have heeded the warning. Intent on trying one more time for another daughter, Louisa became pregnant again in early 1916, but this time the child was stillborn. Nevertheless, she was named Alice Chapman Holton and is buried right beside her grandmother on Temple Hill. At forty-one, Louisa's childbearing days were over.

I am pleased to say that the First World War had little impact upon the Holton family. Thomas Holton was far too old to fight and not one of his boys had even reached his teens when the USA joined the war in April 1917. The outbreak of hostilities did coincide, however, with a perceptible change in Margaret Holton. To begin with, this change revealed itself in her failing to finish sentences, or re-starting conversations that had ended minutes, sometimes hours before. Her forgetfulness increased, even to the extent of not attending church each morning. Concerned friends would go to her house and find the drapes closed and no apparent sign of life. After much calling and knocking at the door, Margaret would appear at an upstairs window, utterly bemused, wondering why she was being disturbed in the middle of the night – this despite it being unmistakably mid-morning. Her brother William, now a widower, suggested she move in with him, but Margaret insisted there was nothing wrong with her and continued to live alone at the old Van Oost house on Center Street. As time passed, she became more and more solitary, reverting to her childhood disposition, though now her manner was not just sullen, but mournful. No-one seems to have noticed or commented at the time, but it seems obvious to me that the trigger for Margaret's decline into senility was the death of her closest friend, Alice Holton.

The end came for Margaret in February 1919, when her body was discovered by her great-nephew Jack, who had, at his grandfather's instigation, shinnied up a drainpipe and forced his way into Margaret's house through a partly opened window. The rotund old woman was lying on the floor of her bedroom, still in her nightgown. Jack shook her, but she was cold and stiff and there was a smell about her, a dull, septic odor, that he later described to my mom as the smell of death.

It was a huge funeral, held at St. Michael's, which was so full that latecomers had to stand in the side aisles. Afterwards, four horses pulled the gleaming black hearse, bedecked with flowers, up the incline of Center Street, past the house where Margaret had lived all her adult life, and eventually to Temple Hill, where another Holton was placed in the family plot.

The Van Oost house stood empty for more than two years as William, suffering from creeping infirmity, wrestled with what to do with the old place. He never did decide. On a hot summer's day in 1921, William Holton, my great-great-grandfather, passed away as he took a late morning nap, just like my mom. Six days later, the same scenes were repeated as had unfolded at his sister's funeral two years previously – the packed out church, the flower draped hearse, the solemn cortege making its way up Center Street. Now Thomas was left to dispose of both the Van Oost house and the place on

North Street where he had been born and where his parents had made their home since the early 1870s. Both houses needed a good deal of restoration, something which Thomas, through his successful partnership with Robert Langman, had all the facilities to do. He wrote in his journal of the terrible dilemma he faced – should he sell these two symbols of his heritage or should he modernize them and rent them out, retaining them in his family's ownership? It was not, of course, entirely his decision to make, for his two sisters, Mim and Sarah, had each been left a one third share in each house. Uncharacteristically equivocal, Thomas appears to have allowed himself, maybe through the same good nature that had once convinced him to employ his wayward brother, to be swayed first by the imperious Sarah, then by meek little Mim, who was no doubt under her sister's broad thumb.

Thus the houses were sold and Thomas settled back into his roles as husband, father and businessman. Clara Holton left school and took two jobs, one as secretary to her father, the other as a sometime assistant at the Geneseo Candy Kitchen on Main Street. This latter job was really more of a favor to Peter Bondi, who owned and ran the Candy Kitchen and whose stepfather, Francis Scoville, had been a friend of Clara's grandfather. She appears, both from the early extraction and replacement of all her teeth and from the amplitude of her figure, to have been paid by Bondi more in candy than in money.

Meanwhile, Jack Holton had grown into a laddishly handsome young man, from whom charm oozed as easily as it had from his like-named great-grandfather. Also like the senior John, he enjoyed the outdoor life, but his interest was not in hunting or trapping animals, but in studying them and understanding their behavior. His favorite haunt, at that time, was Conesus Lake, to the east of Geneseo, where great flocks of waterfowl would gather, particularly during the winter. Joining him, on occasion, would be his brothers, Lester and Philip, both of whom wanted to join the army, much against their mother Louisa's wishes. It was not a life that appealed to Jack. While he admired his brothers' spirit and patriotism and had, through their long hikes around Conesus Lake, learned to respect their strength and unshakable determination, Jack remembered the stories he had been told by his grandfather, stories about the Civil War, about Antietam, about his great uncle Joseph.

Affable, smiling Jack Holton found his own niche in the ultra-low risk world of insurance, initially as an apprentice with First Provident in Rochester, then as the company's agent in Livingston and Wyoming counties. Which is how he came to meet Mary Stafford.

The Stafford family, in the muscular form of Jacob Stafford, arrived in this area sometime around 1853. The family's history prior to that time is an impenetrable maze of dead ends due mostly to there being no record of Jacob Stafford's birth, leaving this particular researcher grasping at possibilities rather than certainties. He possibly came across from New England, where there are a number of old Stafford families. My mom had always thought he hailed from New York City, but she could not recall how this belief had become lodged in her mind and readily accepted that she may have just imagined it. All that I can say with any degree of confidence is that, way back before Jacob, the Staffords probably originated from in or around the English town of the same name.

What brought Jacob to western New York was the Genesee Valley Canal, on which there was work for almost any man who could wield an ax or a hammer. At first, Jacob lived in the workers' camps. At some point, though, he met a woman called Anne Radley and soon settled into her cabin near Nunda. There is no evidence that these two ever married, but they did produce a son, John, who was born in 1855, just months before his father was killed.

As with Jacob's birth, little is recorded of his death. Many men lost their lives building the Genesee Valley Canal and Jacob Stafford must have been one of the last, but so inconsequential were the construction workers that their deaths merited little attention. All I have discovered is that Jacob perished near Olean and that his body was brought up to Nunda and buried in the Oakwood cemetery. He is mentioned in the burial records, but the site of his grave is unmarked and may even have been re-used.

Anne Radley, who registered her baby's surname as Stafford, lived in her cabin until 1897, scratching a living from farm work. Her son John lived with her for some years, even after he had finished his schooling and had also begun working on the nearby farms. He moved eventually to Mount Morris, where he married Emily Francis, who was five years older than John and already pregnant with their first child, Charles, who was born in 1884. Another son, Frederick, arrived in 1888 and a daughter, Faith, in 1890.

The Staffords of Mount Morris would never have moved in the same social circles as the Holtons. While the Holtons mixed with the Micah Brooks and Allen Ayraults of the area, the Staffords' only connection with such people would have been as the humblest of employees. John was a farmhand from the moment he started working at the age of twelve until the day he died in 1925, aged sixty-nine. Emily, too, knew nothing but hard, poorly paid toil, her work being more seasonal than her husband's – helping with the harvest of the fields in late summer and of the orchards in the fall.

Charles Stafford married Molly Horner of Castile in 1902 and they produced, over the next six years, three children: Bertram, Harold and Mary. Charles was a self-taught carpenter, not of the craftsman variety, the type who would have carved Thomas Holton's ornate newels, but the sort of tradesman who tackled less glamorous jobs, like laying floorboards and fixing gateposts and hanging doors. He knew he would never get rich, but at least he had a skill, coupled with the necessity-driven willingness to do anything, anytime, anywhere. After living first with Molly's parents, the couple rented a house close to Perry, which is where the children were all born and raised and where, on a May evening in 1929, Jack Holton first met Mary Stafford.

Jack had been visiting a client in Castile and was making his way, on his new motorcycle, back to Geneseo. Passing by the Stafford's house, he spotted Mary sitting primly on the porch, enjoying the warmth of the late evening sun. Jack waved, but Mary did not acknowledge him. In typical Jack Holton fashion, he turned his motorcycle around and rode back to the house, pulling up at the side of the road and, this time, calling a greeting to the pretty young woman. She responded with a crisp 'Good evening' then returned to the book she had been reading. Jack made some general comment about the weather, about the glowing sunset that was forming slowly in the western sky. Again, Mary's response was brief and wary. She shuffled in her seat, trying to straighten her back, trying to appear now not just prim but positively regal. Jack smiled to himself, for he could easily recognize someone putting on an act. What he was intrigued to know was whether this act was Mary's usual way with strangers or whether it was especially for him.

He bade her a polite, but smiling farewell, telling her that he often passed that way, which was stretching the truth somewhat, and that he hoped to see her again. Two evenings later, he did indeed pass by again, but not because of any business he might have had nearby.

The courtship lasted for over a year before the two of them became engaged on Christmas Day in 1930. Six months later, they were married at St. Michael's Church in Geneseo. In came the troops, as my mom always used to say of her family on such occasions: Jack's parents, Thomas and Louisa; Jack's rotund older sister Clara, who held poor Hartley Holton's hand throughout the ceremony and in all the photographs; Jack's brothers Lester and Philip, each in the dress uniform of the US Army; Auntie Mim across from Buffalo; Aunt Sarah, recently widowed, down from Syracuse with her daughters Phyllis and Hatty. The central aisle of the old church acted that day as a sort of social divide, with the Holtons in their finery on one side and the Stafford clan, dressed with the usual incongruity of working-class smartness, billeted restlessly on the other. There was Mary's mother and father and her brothers, Harry, who, despite continuing Prohibition, had about him the constant aroma of liquor, and Bert, who never looked anything but shifty. There, too, was Uncle Fred, owner of a brutal, ruddy face, evidently the sort of man who could take care of himself and who many times had done so. Beside Fred stood his wife Eliza and their two teenage children, James and Ann. Absent, however, was Mary's Aunt Fay, who had always been so kind to her, but who had been felled by tuberculosis in 1923 and who had died that year on All Saints' Day.

Thomas Holton's wedding gift was a house on Highland Road, to where the young couple returned after a honeymoon at Niagara Falls. In his journal, Thomas disclosed his frustration at having sold both the Van Oost house and his parents' former home on North Street. For the first time, he confided his annoyance at his sister Sarah, who, he wrote, 'has no feeling for our past.' By that time, his partnership with Robert Langman had been dissolved following Langman's retirement in 1926. Thomas, at fifty-eight, was himself semi-retired, his only income being from small pieces of private work, most of which involved him providing reassuring second opinions on the proposals of the younger generation of surveyors, architects and builders who now had the town's development in their hands. He did this not for the money, his inheritances and his lifetime's work having already brought him ample wealth, but to keep his mind occupied. The house he gave to his son and daughter-in-law had taxed him a little more than he would have preferred, however, the builder he originally hired going broke with the job not even half complete. 'One would believe,' Thomas wrote in his journal, 'that the experience of so many years would have taught me to inquire not only of a tradesman's ability, but also of his liquidity. There is, indeed, no fool like an old fool.' Another firm took over the work, but delays caused by the late delivery of some materials and fittings caused Thomas yet more anxiety. 'I am thankful to Jack,' he commented at the end of a weary catalogue of another day's setbacks, 'for agreeing to extend his stay with Mary at Niagara. I fear we shall need every available minute so as to have the house fit for their return.'

In the year 1330, Queen Phillipa of England gave birth to a son, Edward, who later became known as the Black Prince. At the time of the birth, the queen was at Woodstock, in the county of Oxfordshire, while the king, Edward III, was hunting near Stevenage, some fifty miles away, in the county of Hertfordshire. With the birth of a son and heir, it was imperative that the news be relayed to the sovereign. Staying also at Woodstock was a Hertfordshire man, Thomas Priour, who was commissioned to ride off at speed to the king and deliver word of the new arrival. In reward for his service, the king granted Priour all the land he could see from the top of the church tower in the nearby town of Baldock.

The story of how Thomas Priour came into possession of his estate is probably no more than a myth, but what is sure is that Priour and his descendants were land owners in Hertfordshire for many centuries. Over the years, the spelling of the name evolved to Pryor and evidently at least one branch of the family found its way to America, for it is from this same line that Mary Pryor was descended. This is the Mary Pryor who was William Pryor Letchworth's paternal grandmother, the Pryor from whom his middle name is taken.

The Pryors' lands bordered the ancient Manor of Letchworth, which long pre-dated the Domesday Book of 1086, where it is recorded as being owned by Robert Gernon. Over subsequent centuries, the manor, centered on Letchworth Hall, was passed to various owners, including the Knights Templar, the Knights Hospitallers and the Lytton family who lived at Knebworth House, close to Stevenage. By the second half of the nineteenth century, however, the manor had faded into obscurity.

In 1898, Ebenezer Howard published a book entitled *Tomorrow: A Peaceful Path to Real Reform*, in which he advocated the creation of Garden Cities, towns carefully designed to offer decent housing in a clean, rural setting, with residential areas kept separate from industrial zones. Garden Citizens, through mutual ownership, would have influence over and would benefit from their town's development. Although educated in both Suffolk and Hertfordshire, Howard had, through his London upbringing, gained first-hand experience of the squalor and poverty of inner city living. At the age of twenty-one, he had emigrated to the USA, settling first in Nebraska, then heading back east to Chicago, known at that time as the Garden City of the Mid West. There, Howard had taken particular interest in the work of Frederick Law Olmstead, who, as well as planning the Riverside development in Chicago, had more famously laid out Central Park in New York City. After his return to England in 1876, Howard had begun to formulate his Garden City ideas, taking particular account of a book by

Edward Bellamy, published in 1888, that foresaw the future development of Boston, Massachusetts with open spaces, well planted parks and a population enjoying a healthy, unpolluted environment. Howard's own book was met with mixed views, but he was a great evangelist and gradually interested more and more people in his proposals, including a number of respected public figures. He formed the Garden City Association, the aim of which was not just to promote his ideas, but to bring about a practical plan to realize them.

Howard's book was republished in 1902 as *Garden Cities of Tomorrow*. In the same year, the Association established the Garden City Pioneer Company, which began the search for the ideal site on which to construct the first Garden City. Having considered locations in various parts of England, it was decided that the town should be built on land that formed the Manor of Letchworth. The manor alone, though, would not be big enough, so as well as purchasing the manor from its last owners, the Alington family, the company began acquiring adjacent land, including a substantial parcel owned by the Pryors. The total estate amounted to almost four thousand acres and was bisected by the Cambridge branch of the Great Northern Railway and by the road that connected the historic towns of Hitchin and Baldock. Flowing through the estate was the Pix Brook, which rose from springs close to what is now called Letchworth Gate. The brook wended its way through a marshy area known as Pix Moor, then through what is now Norton Common and eventually joined the River Hiz.

The men chosen to take Howard's ideas and turn them into a real Garden City at Letchworth were Barry Parker and Raymond Unwin. The two architects had worked together since 1896, though they had known each other for much longer - three years before, Unwin had married Parker's sister. Their company had been involved in designing a number of middle-class homes around the English midlands, their work becoming increasingly influenced by the Arts and Crafts style, which was itself derived from the work of men like William Morris and his Pre-Raphaelite associates. Gradually, Parker and Unwin's efforts became more ambitious, embracing ideas similar to Howard's with regard to urban planning. They were concerned with the type and quality of living accommodation, with the provision of communal amenities, with sunlight and space and with the participative management of environmental development. Both had been associated with the Garden City Pioneer Company and when its successor, the First Garden City Limited, had sought a firm to undertake the layout of the town, it was Parker and Unwin who had won the contract.

In *Garden Cities of Tomorrow*, Ebenezer Howard had included a number of diagrams depicting his view of how a town should be laid out. These were little more than concepts, but were naturally influential when Parker and Unwin sketched their first designs for Letchworth. Building began in 1904 and moved apace throughout the early years. Always, though, the town's growth was carefully controlled, ensuring that each street was planted with grass verges and trees, that all houses had gardens and were designed in sympathy with their surroundings, that there were ample parks and recreational areas. Norton Common was set aside, protected from development, a lung for the townsfolk, as if they needed it, just like Olmstead's Central Park is for New Yorkers.

Having been founded upon ideals, the town attracted more than its share of idealists. George Orwell, in his book *The Road To Wigan Pier*, described the Garden City as home to 'every fruit juice drinker, nudist, sandal wearer, sex-maniac, Quaker, nature cure quack, pacifist and feminist in England.' Few lampooned the place better than the great English poet Sir John Betjamin. In his collection *Old Lights For New Candles*, Betjamin's *Group Life: Letchworth* comments upon the self-centered behavior of children reputedly dedicated to work for the welfare of all. Later, in *Huxley Hall*, he wrote of 'the Garden City café' where he ate his 'vegetarian dinner' and drank 'lime-juice minus gin.'

For a man already enamored of good ale and porter, Letchworth would not seem the most obvious place to set up a new home. Yet, that is what John Wright did in 1930. Letchworth was a growing town, attracting major companies and workers from all over the country. Jobs were in ready supply and the new housing meant modern homes in large plots, each with enough land for a garden and a vegetable patch. Unfortunately, for men like John, the town was completely temperance, an alcohol-free zone. To get their fix of liquor, the Garden Citizens had to make their way to nearby villages or, like John, head for the Two Chimneys or, later, the Wilbury Hotel, both of which were located just yards across the town's eastern boundary line in otherwise open country.

John took a job as a delivery driver with an agricultural merchant, whose main offices were in Hitchin, five miles away, but who also had a shop and a small depot in Letchworth. Edith, meanwhile, found work at what was commonly known as Castle Corset, a great factory built near the town center to manufacture ladies' corsetry. The company, which had been founded by an American named William W. Kincaid, used a spiral wound spring in its corsets in place of the traditional whalebone and was therefore called The Spirella Company. Distinct from many employers, it preferred to recruit married women, like Edith, as they needed less training than younger girls. What training they did give to Edith, though, was of only limited value. Before the end of 1931, she had fallen pregnant.

Edward William Wright was born in July 1932 and his sister Angela arrived two and a half years later. Their father, John, continued to ply his regular routes around the North Hertfordshire villages and between the depot in Letchworth, another in Baldock and the warehouses in Hitchin. He continued also to walk, across a style and a cow pasture, to the Two Chimneys, twice, often three times a week, returning cloaked with the aroma of strong tobacco smoke and with a bottle of stout for Edith. She, too, had developed a taste for beer, dark beer with a creamy head. Edith's taste, though, was much more advanced than John's; the flavor mattered little to him, for it was the feeling he enjoyed, along with the exclusively male domain of the pub's tap room and the avuncular banter of landlord Jack Woods. He would work all day to earn the money his family needed; he would tend to the fabric of their home and grow them vegetables in the patch of ground at the foot of their back garden. He would also protect them, act as judge and jury in family disputes, discipline his son with clouts from his belt and rebuke his daughter with threats of punishment that he rarely carried through. He loved them, but it was not his job to cook and wash and clean the house, to iron the shirts and feed the children, to change their dirty diapers when they were babies or mend their ripped and worn clothes as they grew. No, that was a wife's place and that was that, no room for debate. Why should he feel guilty about his yielding to the lure of the tavern? After all, the cirrhosis that would eventually kill him was years away and did he not always take a present home for Edith?

John was, as Rebecca Fulmer had once said of James Holton, a man of his time.

By the close of the nineteenth century, Geneseo's population was around thirty-six hundred, the most significant increase having come in the period since 1870, during which the number of residents had risen by a fifth. The now familiar layout of streets had been established at the town's heart and most of the buildings that exist in today's Historic Landmark area had been erected. Geneseo had cemented its place as the center of local government and justice. The railroad was in operation, there was a small, but thriving

commercial community, the various churches each had sizeable congregations and a host of institutes and societies had been formed to occupy and educate the townsfolk. What is more, the years since the town's inception had also seen the seeding of any community's backbone, its customs and traditions, the most notable of which, and certainly the most conspicuous, was the Genesee Valley Hunt.

It has always amused me how, having fought so hard for independence from colonial government, the landed echelons of American society have constantly endeavored to emulate the manners and ways of the English nobility. James S. Wadsworth was a prime example, building, as his home, a copy of an English aristocrat's residence and creating about it a typically English landscape. In 1876, William Austin Wadsworth perpetuated this trait by founding a foxhunt, complete with hounds and all the other quintessentially English accessories.

William Austin Wadsworth is said to have been a direct, authoritarian figure, a man of great presence and no little arrogance, who was used to getting his own way. Born in 1847, he moved, at the age of twenty-five, into The Homestead with his mother Emmeline. Four years later, he formed what was then called the Livingston County Hunt, setting himself up as Master Of Foxhounds. Within five years, what had become the Genesee Valley Hunt had developed into the premier such group in the country. It was very much William's 'baby' and he oversaw every aspect of the organization, as well bankrolling all expenses. He was, at heart, a lover of country life and, most ardently, of horses. Hunting was his way of indulging that passion. After his mother died in 1882 and he became sole occupier of The Homestead, he took his indulgence still further by instituting equestrian games, played in The Homestead's grounds each Independence Day, where riders proved their skills in a series of exercises.

In 1898, William went off to fight in the Spanish-American War, leaving his cousin Jim Sam Wadsworth in charge of the hunt. William returned the following year, however, and resumed as Master, though very soon another interest was vying for his attention, this in the form of Miss Elizabeth Perkins, who, in 1901, married the fifty-four-year-old former army major. Immediately, the new Mrs. Wadsworth began transforming The Homestead, which for almost twenty years had been William's bachelor home, into a graceful and stylish marital residence befitting one of the area's most important figures.

There is little evidence that marriage, or even fatherhood, which came in 1906, had any mellowing influence upon William's autocratic manner. He still retained his iron grip on the Genesee Valley Hunt and proved a resolute negotiator whenever local causes were seeking benefaction. Not that he had ever failed to uphold the Wadsworth tradition of munificence. The fountain in Main Street is the most obvious illustration of his gifts to the town, but he also donated the watering trough on Temple Hill, another example of his equine interest, and, in 1900, paid for substantial improvements to Village Square Park.

The early years of the new century also saw other changes in the town. The County Courthouse had already been rebuilt after the old structure had been condemned as unsafe. Nearby, the original Catholic church was renovated and converted to act as St. Mary's parish center. At St. Michael's, even more dramatic repairs were required when, early one Sunday morning in 1902, lightning struck the spire. More destruction occurred on Main Street in 1904, when two stores, a legal practice, an insurance office and the Town Hall were all gutted by fire. On the opposite side of the street, down beyond the fountain, the Geneseo Building was erected and opened in 1908, providing accommodation for the town's fire fighters and their equipment, as well as a banqueting suite and a theater.

Since 1876, James Wolcott Wadsworth and his wife Maria had been in residence at Hartford House. James appears to have been a more low-key personality than his cousin William Austin, but he still made his mark on the town, contributing generously to St. Michael's as well as serving a number of other worthy causes. He had been Town Supervisor during the 1870s and had later served as a member of the New York State Assembly. In 1881, he had been elected as a Republican to the US Congress, this first term ending in 1885. Six years later, he had again won a congressional seat and was to serve there until 1907. One of the many appointments he took up after leaving Congress was the presidency of the Genesee Valley National Bank.

For all of James's achievements, accounts of his family's history seem always to find him eclipsed by his son. James Wolcott Wadsworth Jr. was born at Hartford House in 1877. He graduated from Yale in 1898 and, in that same year, served in the Puerto Rican campaign of the Spanish-American War, not as an officer, like his uncle William, but as a private soldier. Following his father's lead, he entered politics, becoming, in 1905, a State Assemblyman. Then, in 1914, he was elected to the US Senate. By that time, of course, the attention of the country's political leaders was being drawn to events across the Atlantic.

The First World War claimed the lives of eight men from Geneseo, among them mariners and infantrymen. The town also played its part in the formation of the valley's cavalry troop, which sprang from the area's renown as an equestrian center. It was formed in 1914, with Captain Nathan Shiverick in command and Senator James W. Wadsworth Jr. as First Lieutenant. During the unrest along the Mexican border in 1915, the troop was sent to help thwart the activities of the bandit Pancho Villa. It returned home in March 1917 and three months later was mobilized for action in Europe. Once the war was over, it was reorganized, with Jim Sam Wadsworth as its new commanding officer and with the Bailey Farm, on the edge of Geneseo, as its new HQ.

William Austin Wadsworth died in 1918, leaving his widow and young son, William Perkins Wadsworth, in residence at The Homestead. 'W.P.', as he became known, was given the task of exercising the hounds of the Genesee Valley Hunt, experience that no doubt stood him in good stead when he became Master of Foxhounds in the early 1930s. Before then, though, he had married local girl Martha Scofield and the two of them settled at Cornerways, which today is one of my favorite homes in Geneseo, standing in all its Federal-style glory at the corner of Center Street and Highland Road.

There were, indeed, a number of fine houses built in the town during the 1920s, including the one purchased by Thomas Holton for his son and daughter-in-law. Developments were also taking place in Geneseo's commercial hub, with a Ford Motor Company dealership thriving after its opening in 1915 and another automobile showroom emerging from the remodeling of the old public concert hall, which had been built as a gift of James S. Wadsworth way back in 1851. The hall had hosted numerous entertainments over the years, including the Genesee Valley Hunt's annual ball, but had fallen into decline after alternative facilities had become available at the Normal School and the Geneseo Building. New businesses were springing up, new stores, new workshops, new cafés and restaurants, even a new hotel.

The year of 1930 saw the death of Jim Sam Wadsworth, who, for the previous four years, had been joint master of the hunt, having relinquished command of the cavalry troop but having never faded as one of the area's brightest characters. The following year, James Wolcott Wadsworth Jr. inherited Hartford House on the death of his mother, his eminent father having passed away in 1926. The younger James had, in 1902, married

Alice Hay, daughter of US Secretary of State John Hay, and the couple had made their home at the Hampton estate in Groveland. Their plan on taking possession of Hartford House was to make wide-ranging renovations, during which they would remain at Hampton. However, in 1932, Hampton was burned down and the Wadsworths were forced to live at Hartford House while the renovations took place around them. None of this impinged upon James's political career, though. Having lost his Senate seat in the 1926 elections, he returned to Washington as a Representative in 1933 and retained his place in Congress until his retirement nineteen years later.

With Jim Sam gone, the time came for W.P. Wadsworth to take over the Genesee Valley Hunt, a position he held until his death in 1982. I remember him clearly, a strangely ordinary-looking man for someone with such distinguished lineage. When the hunt gathered, as it still does, on the last Saturday of each September, W.P. would lead the riders out from The Homestead and parade along Main Street. I guess he was an old man by then, so maybe the years had withered his posture. Even so, I was always surprised that, despite the polished livery and the handsome navy blue riding coat, there was nothing explicitly *special* about him. He was, unlike his lordly father, an unassuming man, attentive in conversation, thoughtful and quietly spoken. Decent. Likeable.

Another Wadsworth, James Jeremiah, the son of James Wolcott Wadsworth Jr. and always known as Jerry, had, in 1931 become a State Assemblyman. In 1932, he came to the aid of the local cavalry troop by persuading the state to build it a new stable complex. Later, he is believed to have influenced the decision to retain the troop as a cavalry unit whilst other such troops in New York were being assigned to new purposes. This would have pleased W.P., who served for a time in the thirties as the troop's First Lieutenant.

Despite this reprieve, the military career of the horse was fast coming to an end for all but ceremonial duties. The story was the same on the farms, where horses had been replaced by tractors, and, of course, on the roads, where cars and trucks now reigned. This was reflected clearly on the streets of Geneseo, where the old livery stables had all disappeared. In their place were not only those early car dealerships, but also the new gas stations, the most prominent of which was the Standard Oil property on the corner of Main and Park Streets. Elsewhere, other signs of progress were apparent, not least on the site of the old Candy Kitchen, where Clara Holton had once helped out. In the early 1930s the site was redeveloped as the Palace Theater, competing with the Riviera, which had opened on Center Street way back in 1915, as a venue for the town's moviegoers.

In the face of all these modern advances, though, there was a strong local movement in favor of recognizing and preserving the area's past. The county's historical society had been in existence for more than half a century, its headquarters, since 1895, being the log cabin in Village Square Park. In 1932, it moved to the former cobblestone schoolhouse on Center Street, which today its excellent museum shares with the County Historian's office, though there is sadly too little space for a home movie archive. That same year, 1932, saw fire damage the Palace Theater. Four years later, it happened again, leading owner Peter Bondi to convert it, in 1938, into a bowling alley. Around the same time, Main Street also saw the opening of the exotically named Spanish Lantern Restaurant.

At the very end of that fourth decade of this century, the town witnessed the final act in the internal combustion engine's rise to supremacy. Just as the railroad had superseded the canal, so did road transport supplant the railroad. In 1940, in a scene that has been repeated in small towns across the nation, the Geneseo depot was closed down.


Franklyn and Olive Petersen moved to Geneseo in March 1933, taking up residence on Oak Street, no more than a hundred yards away from the house of Thomas and Louisa Holton. They had lived previously in Rochester, where Franklyn had trained in dentistry, then in Warsaw, where he had worked at a clinic on North Main Street and where their first son, Raymond, had been born the previous year. Now Franklyn, at twenty-eight, was to become a partner in a practice on Geneseo's Main Street, close to Village Square Park.

As usual, Jack Holton knew all about the newcomers even before they had arrived. The practice's senior partner was one of his clients and had suggested that Jack might want to pay Franklyn a visit once he got settled. This Jack duly did, but instead of gaining another client, Jack gained a fine friend whose family would become inextricably linked with the Holtons.

In July of that year, Jack and Mary were delivered of their first and only child, a daughter, who they named Faith in honor of Mary's long dead aunt. Meanwhile, Thomas Holton was planning a vacation for himself and his wife, part in celebration of their granddaughter's birth, part to mark, at last, Thomas's official retirement. What little remained of Thomas's business affairs were being handled entirely by his daughter Clara, who had moved to Sonyea to be closer to the Craig Colony, where Hartley was being cared for.

Two days after little Faith's christening on the last Sunday in June, Thomas and Louisa set off for New York City, their journey beginning at the railroad depot on Court Street. From there, they would travel first to Rochester, then to New York City via Albany. They would be staying for a week at the Waldorf Astoria Hotel.

The following Thursday, Clara came across from Sonyea to check her parents' mail. There was a handful of letters, nothing of any importance, so she left them lying on the hall table, locked up the house and went to visit her new niece up on Highland Road. She stayed until early evening, when Jack returned home from a visit to a new mill down in Nunda, where the owner had bought insurance for all the machinery he had just installed. Jack was, as ever, full of talk, telling his wife and his sister about the mill and about how much he admired the owner, who seemed to have such good business sense. Time wore on. Clara helped Mary as she bedded down Faith for the night, then the three adults ate supper at the kitchen table. Around nine o'clock, Clara said she should make her way home. Like Jack, she had recently acquired her first motor car, but unlike Jack she was not the most confident of drivers. The journey back to Sonyea in the dark was not a prospect she relished. Nevertheless, she put on her coat and headed off in her black Ford.

Later that night, Jack and Mary were asleep when there was an almighty banging at their front door. Jack dragged himself out of bed, worried more that the hammering would wake Faith than that it might herald bad news. He scrambled downstairs and opened the door to find Officer Theodore Hewson standing on his porch. Jack knew Teddy Hewson well, the two of them having been in the same class at High School, and that familiarity must have comforted Jack for he seemed, to Teddy, amazingly unconcerned at having a Sheriff's officer so noisily come to visit in the small hours of the morning. The news Teddy quickly delivered soon changed Jack's mood however. Fire trucks were, as they spoke, in attendance at Jack's parents' house.

Jack dashed back upstairs to get dressed, then he and Teddy ran the short distance to Oak Street, where they found the town's fire brigade battling to control flames that were, by then, spurting through windows already broken by the heat inside the house. Teddy called to one of the firemen and told him that Jack was the son of the owner. To Jack's surprise, the fireman said that a woman, presumably Jack's mother, had already been rescued from the house, but that there was, so far, no sign of Jack's father. This was the point at which dread surged into Jack's eyes. Had his father's vacation plans been no more than a ruse to give he and Louisa some romantic solitude in their own home? Had they maybe had to return early, perhaps because Louisa's recent bronchitis had flared up again? Jack grabbed at the fireman, who was about to walk away to join his comrades at their hoses. Where was his mother? Jack wanted to know. Being tended by Doctor Bull he was told.

Jack and Teddy raced down the hill to the doctor's house, in which all the lights were shining. Teddy rapped at the door in his heavy-handed, law officer's way and was greeted, presently, by the fretful face of Mrs. Bull. Having maybe feared the arrival of another casualty, the woman's expression turned instantly to one of relief when she saw the two men. She opened the door wide and led them inside, jabbering so much that Jack did not immediately discern that the woman being treated by the gruff Dr Bull was not actually Louisa Holton, but her daughter, Clara. Indeed he only fully realized this when he at last saw his sister sitting in the doctor's consulting room.

After a tearful conversation during which Clara explained about deciding to stop over at her parents' empty house, rather than return home so late to Sonyea, Teddy Hewson departed and made his way back to the burning house, where he assured the firemen that there was no-one else inside. The firemen already knew, in fact, that there was no-one left *alive* in the house, such was the intensity of the heat.

The next day, Teddy arranged for someone from the New York Police Department to go to the Waldorf Astoria and inform Thomas and Louisa of the fire. The following afternoon, they arrived back in Geneseo to find their house no more than a shell. Everything was gone, all the fine furnishings, all their clothes, all their personal effects. All, except the contents of the heavy metal safe in the basement, in which Thomas kept jewelry, money and all his important papers, including his notes on the Holton family history and his journals dating back to when he was a teenager. Until the day he died, he contended that God had specifically preserved those things.

No-one knows what caused the fire, but Clara blamed herself. She may, inadvertently, have been responsible, perhaps dropping a still burning cigarette as she dozed in one of the armchairs. If forgiveness was necessary, it came unreservedly from her parents, who, although shocked and deeply upset, showed fortitude that I know was inherited by both my grandpa and my mom. They salvaged a few scorched items, then moved in to live with Jack and Mary, while Jack oversaw their insurance claim with First Provident.

Living with their son and his wife was, for Thomas and Louisa, intended to be a temporary measure while they sought a new home in Geneseo. Over the following year, however, Louisa's health again took a downturn and she was admitted to hospital for a while. She had, in the pollen rich days of spring 1934, suffered horribly from hay fever, which, combined with a chest infection, developed into a terrifying period during which she had struggled desperately to breath. At the hospital, she was placed in an oxygen tent and given drugs to kill the infection, treatment that, after a week, remedied her breathing problem, but left her weak and, for some time, susceptible to every cough and chill she came anywhere near.

It was another year before Jack and Mary were once again left to live alone in their home with their growing daughter Faith. Thomas and Louisa found a small house on Second Street that suited them, in their dotage, just fine and, as the next few years passed they gradually replaced many of the items that had been destroyed in the fire. Then, as the threat of war loomed disquietingly in Europe, the Holton family moved into a period when all they seemed to do was attend funerals. In 1937, Mary Holton's father, Charles Stafford, died in his sleep at his home in Castile. Seventeen months later, Sarah Weber, sister to Thomas, aunt to Jack, collapsed while waiting for a bus in Syracuse and was dead before the ambulance got her to the hospital. Franklyn Petersen's father was the next to pass away, the victim of a heart attack, and once more the Holton's donned their black coats and veils and paid their last respects at the Presbyterian Church in Perry. As the new decade began, news of her brother Bert's death reached Mary. Bert had long ago fled to the Mid West, reportedly with a debt collector on his tail, and no-one in the family knew precisely where he was. It emerged that he had been living rough in Chicago, which is where he died, of cold and starvation, in a boarded up tenement in the poorest part of the city. His mother Molly could not afford to have his body returned home, but Jack and Mary Holton gave her the money and paid also for the funeral in Castile.

Throughout this time, Jack's brothers, Lester and Philip, had been serving officers in the United States Army. Sometimes they had taken leave together in Geneseo, times when they would join in passionate debate with their father about America's isolationist attitude to the growing tensions in Europe. When war came in 1939, Lester could see no good in America becoming involved, viewing the conflict as some sort of mediaeval confrontation between Old World powers and therefore not something with which the New World should sully its hands. Philip, who, like his father, would sit thoughtfully and listen to his older brother's powerful, often emotional and sometimes narrow and naïve views, did, on reflection, agree that America would be better off on the sidelines, preferably as a broker of peace. This was not a position with which Thomas could concur. His views were vehement, more so than either brother had ever before heard from his father. Americans should remember their heritage, Thomas told his sons. The Holton family, he reminded them, had immigrated to the USA from England. There were people in Lester's Old World who were Holton descendants. Where English blood was being shed, *Holton* blood was being shed. What was more, the Holtons had enjoyed, through their many generations, the fruits of this New World, its freedom and its democracy. How could America stand idly by and allow some mustachioed, goose-stepping dictator to deny, with military force, those same fruits to the people of Europe? Where was America's conscience? he asked.

I wonder now how Thomas would have felt had he known that, when America was at last driven into the war, not by its conscience, but by the Japanese attack on Pearl Harbor, both Lester and Philip would be killed upon and be buried beneath European soil. Perhaps he would still have felt the same, that heritage and liberty and the facing down of tyranny were worth the sacrifice even of his own dear sons. Perhaps not. In the event, Thomas did not live to see his boys go off to war. In July 1941, he was sitting on a bench in Village Square Park, reading a newspaper in the midday sun. Jack and Franklyn sat by his side, both taking a break from their work. As he exhaled the smoke from his second lunchtime cigarette, Jack noticed that his father was rubbing his forehead. There was also a strained expression on Thomas's face, the look of someone puzzled by having forgotten what he was saying. No. Worse. The look of someone who has forgotten where he is, *who* he is. Jack tried to speak to his father, but Thomas only mumbled an incoherent reply. It was obvious that something serious was wrong. Franklyn sprang into action, loosening Thomas's clothing, laying him out flat on the bench and checking his pulse and his breathing. He then told Jack to go get an ambulance, as well as to summon Doctor Crowley from his nearby surgery.

My mom, who went to visit her grandfather in hospital the following day, told me that, overnight, Thomas had transformed. Gone was his distinguished bearing, gone too was his fine head of dark hair. Instead, he looked emaciated, his skin milky, almost transparent, his hair completely white. The stroke had paralyzed the left side of his body; his arm lay inanimate on the bedclothes, his mouth was crooked, his eye was barely open. Before she left, her father lifted her so that she could kiss Thomas on the cheek. The old man smiled lopsidedly and raised his good hand to brush her hair. She never saw him again. By midnight, he was dead.

'The troops' once more came to Geneseo, but even eight-year-old Faith Holton could see that there were less than before. Clara brought Hartley and the two of them cried throughout the service at St. Michael's and the burial on Temple Hill. Philip and Lester arrived in their uniforms and together escorted their mother and their Auntie Mim, who always looked so elegant in black. Their Aunt Sarah's daughters arrived late and bickered with one another all day, Hatty's husband, Richard Cope, trying valiantly to prevent the argument, the cause of which no-one else could fathom, from escalating into an unseemly confrontation between the two solidly built sisters. Mary Holton's mother attended, but not, to Mary's relief, her brother Harry, who had long been a slave to the whiskey bottle.

Then there were the friends and neighbors: the Langman family, Franklyn and Olive Petersen; the Butterworths and the Dwyers from Oak Street; the Carsons from North Street; the Randolphs and the Hewsons; Doctor Crowley and his wife, and even Alice Hay Wadsworth.

Louisa Holton survived her husband by nine years, passing away in her sleep in May 1950.


In an hour or so, I shall be leaving to take Bobbie to the Big Tree Inn. Since mid-morning, I have been working on my essay, but I am still not finished. Gary Lennart's patience is failing, though he hides it politely behind his gracious Southern inflection. I have forty-eight more hours. Period.

I have already showered and have decided what to wear - a navy blue jacket, one I bought in New York City last year, a pale mauve shirt and some gray pants that came from a factory outlet I found when down in Georgia during the summer. My aim is to look smart without seeming formal, which is pretty much the Big Tree's style. I enjoy eating there, though I seldom do so, even though it is maybe the best restaurant in the county and only a ten-minute walk from my house. Since moving back here to Geneseo, I know I have become more casual or, as Sally Caspar observed last weekend, less tight-assed.

'You live at your own pace.' she said, as she, Steve and I ate supper after they had collected me from JFK.

'It's easier away from the city.' I told her. 'In Manhattan it's perpetual motion, everyone trying to keep up with everyone else.'

'Or have someone behind them, keeping them moving, dancing to the corporate tune.'

After last night's 'phone call, I realize that comment was a gibe at Steve, though he dealt with it impassively. Perhaps they exchanged harsh words once they were in the privacy of their bedroom, but I did not hear them. By that time, I was asleep, albeit restlessly, my body still on English time and exhausted by the journey and by the constant, nagging apprehension about what is now my imminent discussion with Bobbie.

The Petersen family came to the Genesee Valley in 1903, when Franklyn's father was employed as a carpenter at the Park. They made their home initially in Portageville, but moved to Perry once the job at the Park was completed. From that point, Franklyn's father found ample work with local construction firms. I have tried to find out whether he ever worked on a building designed by Holton & Langman, but few records of such detail survive.

Franklyn's mother was a nurse, which accounts for a boyhood interest in medicine. This developed throughout his adolescence and resulted in his going to a Rochester teaching hospital to study dentistry. The partnership in Geneseo came at an unusually early age but Franklyn soon became one of the most popular dentists in the town, especially with children, which is quite an accolade. My mom described him as the kindest, most gentle man she had ever met and often recalled how he once pulled one of her milk teeth without her even knowing. I always suspected this was a slight exaggeration, perhaps to help me past my own fear of dentists, but I got the drift.

Franklyn's love of the Letchworth Park came from his boyhood, when his father, who adored the Glen Iris Estate from the moment he first laid eyes on it, would take him there in his little horse-drawn buggy. For some reason, Jack Holton had always been attracted more to the Finger Lakes than to the Genesee River gorge, so when Franklyn suggested Jack join him and his infant son Raymond on a visit to the Park, he had no idea that he was in for a life-changing experience.

Maybe like William Pryor Letchworth before him, Grandpa was struck instantly by the sense of proximity to a divine creator. Surely something so beautiful could not have occurred by chance. He was also carried along on the tide of stories Franklyn had to tell, stories of the last Seneca Council Meeting, of the demise of Mon-a-sha-sha, of the ill-fated canal. Rarely did a weekend pass, after their first visit together, when Franklyn and Grandpa did not find their way out to the Park. When Mom was old enough, she too went along, discovering in Raymond what a joy it would have been to have had an elder brother. Perhaps to balance the wealth of tales Franklyn told about the Park, Grandpa would take them there on round-about routes so that he could relate his own stories about the area, things he had learned whilst traveling on his rounds for First Provident. So were born what Franklyn christened 'Holton Tours'.

To imagine the Park at that time as being anything like it is today would be to create a wholly inaccurate picture. Certainly the place was very different from when William Pryor Letchworth had first acquired his estate. The disfigurement caused by the defunct canal was mostly healed; the canal's aqueduct close by the Middle Falls was gone, and the great wooden railroad bridge had been replaced, after a huge and destructive fire, by the iron trestle that remains today. Nevertheless, planned development was slow after Letchworth's death in 1910.

By the early 1930s there was depression throughout the country, the effects of which Grandpa witnessed at first hand as many of his clients, especially farmers and small business men, struggled to survive, often dispensing with what they saw as the luxury of insurance. Grandpa's own income dipped considerably and, for the first time in his adult life, he was forced to rely on the Holton family's not insubstantial savings. He was lucky; most people did not have that safety net. Bankruptcies soared, poverty became a way of life and more than fifteen million were standing in unemployment lines.

At Letchworth Park, the authorities ran out of funds. The moribund development program was saved, however, by a government initiative that many people now view as one of FDR's greatest achievements. In March 1933, he signed into law the creation of the Civilian Conservation Corps. The Corps was to be constituted from unemployed young men, aged seventeen to twenty-five, who would be organized to undertake conservation projects throughout the country. Sixty-seven CCC camps were established in New York, four of which were in the Letchworth Park, at Big Bend,

Gibsonville, St. Helena and the Lower Falls. Almost eight hundred young men were garrisoned at these camps and, over a period of seven years, they utterly transformed the Park. They built roads, picnic sites and parking lots, cleared woodlands to reduce the risk of fire and blazed miles of hiking trails. They constructed the footbridge across the Genesee by the Lower Falls. They erected walls and laid walkways, installed drainage, electricity and telephone lines and expertly landscaped many of the public areas. It was an astounding exercise, undertaken with vigor and pride, and one that resulted in what is often considered to be the jewel of the State Parks system.

Having been established to provide healthy and meaningful employment to young men who could so easily, in those times of depression, have drifted into delinquency and crime, it is a sad irony that the CCC prepared many of them not for useful roles in a recovered economy, but for service in a world war. The skills they had learned and the disciplines they had encountered served them all too well in the military.

Like countless others who had reservations about American involvement in the war, the views of Lester and Philip Holton were changed completely by Pearl Harbor. As America entered the war, they were among the first to be shipped to Europe, Lester as a colonel, Philip as a major. Their older brother Jack, who had worn spectacles since just before his daughter's birth in 1933, was deemed to have eyesight too poor for military service and remained in Geneseo, doing his best to support the war effort by organizing car clubs, promoting Victory bonds and even volunteering as an air raid warden. In early 1942, Jimmy Randolph, who Grandpa had known since Jimmy had moved to Geneseo a decade earlier, took over the real estate agency where he had worked for seven years as a salesman. One of the first things he did as owner of the business was to form an alliance with the First Provident Insurance Company of Rochester, enabling Grandpa to work from the agency's Main Street offices and offer land, buildings and household policies to Jimmy's customers. It was to be a busy year for Grandpa, with numerous insurance claims arising from severe flooding in the Genesee Valley. It was also to be a tragic year, for one morning, while Grandpa was sitting at his desk, chatting with Jimmy, he learned of his brother Philip's death. His mother had received a telegram and had asked a neighbor to go fetch Jack from the real estate office.

Philip had been killed, not in action, but in an accident at an army base in Suffolk, England. Somehow an ammunition store had gone up in flames and Philip, along with three other soldiers, had been caught in a colossal firestorm. All of them had died instantly. My mom recalled that it was the first time she had seen her father truly angry. Having returned home from his mother's house, he sat in the kitchen and stared fixedly at a knot in the grain of the wooden table. After a while, he began to shake with rage and his face turned a hideous red. He slammed his fist down on the table, clenching his teeth and appearing to be on the verge of exploding. Shocked and scared by this site, Mom ran out of the room, then out on to the street, heading for the Petersens' house, where she knew Raymond would protect her, although, as she later understood, she really had no need to fear. Jack Holton had just been so furious that his brother had died in such a pointless way.

Lester's death, in April 1944, came as less of a shock. He had written home a number of times to prepare his family for the dangers he and his men were likely to face as they formed the vanguard of the invasion of central Italy. Even though they were obtusely phrased so as to content the military censors, the warnings in the letters were clear. The first news of Lester once the invasion began was that he had been wounded and evacuated to an army hospital near Anzio. There was no indication as to the severity of his injuries, but Louisa primed herself for the worst. She stayed indoors for almost three weeks, waiting for the telegram and, when it finally arrived, she conducted herself with what Mom described to me as the most heart-rending calmness and dignity.

Lester was buried in Italy and not one of the family has ever visited his grave. Philip was buried in the vast American cemetery at Madingley, near Cambridge in England and I am honored to have stood by his headstone just last week. The army sent the Holton brothers' personal effects to Louisa. In 1966, twenty-five years after America entered the war, Mom donated her uncles' medals, on permanent loan, to the Livingston County Museum.

With news of casualties arriving at homes across the USA and a steady stream of crippled and traumatized men returning from the many fronts, the war touched every community in the country. In 1944, the people of the Genesee Valley were brought into even closer contact with the conflict when hundreds of German prisoners of war came to the area. During the previous year, POWs had begun arriving at Fort Niagara, the headquarters for such operations in Western New York. The shortage of labor caused by so many American men having been enlisted had soon decided the authorities to set up further camps so that the Germans could be put to useful work. The old Civilian Conservation Corps buildings at the Letchworth State Park were among the first to be employed, with around two hundred prisoners detained there and made available to local farmers to help tend the land and gather the harvest. Later, a crew from the Park came to Geneseo and built another camp near the Birdseye-Snider canning factory close by what is now Route 63, where the Germans worked alongside local people in what my mom always depicted as a peaceable, respectful, but rather detached relationship.

With the end of the war, the Germans went home and Geneseo families saw the slow return of their own men from both Europe and the Pacific. Louisa, Clara and Jack Holton had a stone laid in the family burial plot on Temple Hill to commemorate Lester and Philip. The Petersens, whose sons had been too young to go to war, helped found a short-lived group to provide support and solace to bereaved families over the first post-war Christmas. The world had changed. FDR was gone, the Bomb had arrived, the Iron Curtain had descended and Communism had been elevated to the status of global evil. From depression in the early 1930s, the United States had emerged into prosperity. Out of war, it was now about to emerge as a superpower and the most prominent influence on world culture for the rest of the twentieth century.

Raymond Petersen left school when he turned sixteen and became an apprentice with a printing firm in Batavia, Marden & Sons. Meanwhile, Mom completed her education at the High School and found a clerical job at the college. Not surprisingly, no-one can quite pinpoint when the friendship between the two teenagers developed into anything more profound, though Ray's increasing absence from Geneseo whilst working for the Mardens appears to have strengthened their feelings for one another. By the time Mom reached eighteen, the childhood friendship had blossomed into romance and, on her nineteenth birthday, in July 1952, the two of them became engaged. In celebration, Jack and Mary Holton hosted a small gathering of friends, who, according to Charlie, all tiptoed about the house in fear of disturbing the flawless frigidity of Grandma's regal residence.

Among the photographs I found in Mom's Fortnum & Mason tin was one of her and Raymond together a month or so after their engagement. The Holtons had taken their week-long summer vacation near Blue Mountain Lake, up in the Adirondacks, and had invited Ray along too. The photograph shows the young couple standing in the doorway of a log cabin, set amongst the pine trees, a thin plume of smoke spiraling from the chimney pipe. The blackness of mom's hair is what startled me most, its thickness, its strange, heavy styling. Her clothes, too, look odd: a plain blouse accentuating her fearsomely upholstered figure, a flower-patterned skirt reaching way below her knees, a clumpy pair of sandals. It was a mom I never knew, a different person, Faith Holton, soon to be Mrs. Petersen. I studied her eyes, like polished nuggets of coal, shining out through the crevices of her broad smile. It was an uncanny feeling, as though someone else was in there, someone to whom I owed my own existence, but who, at that moment in time, had yet to emerge.

Since Louisa Holton's death, the house she and Thomas had bought on Second Street had been rented, through Jimmy Randolph's agency, to a lecturer at SUNY. However, at the end of the fall semester in 1952, the man decided to move on. Jack Holton immediately offered the place to his daughter and her fiancé, who would be married the following spring. The house, which was substantially smaller than Thomas and Louisa's original Geneseo home on Oak Street, needed rejuvenating after seeing Louisa through her old age and the lecturer through his brief and, it was said, unhappy time in the town. Jack had it in mind to hire a decorator, but Ray was keen to tackle the job himself. Thus, in early January 1953, Ray moved into the house and began sprucing it up with fresh paint, new wallpaper and modern fittings.

The wedding invitations were sent out at the beginning of March, a day Ray marked by buying Mom a bouquet of flowers. Two days later, Harold Marden, owner of the Batavia printing firm, asked Ray to go down to Cleveland to visit a prospective customer. Marden & Sons specialized in making boxes and Ray had become expert in calculating the most efficient means of cutting and scoring the card for each new job and in estimating the cost of production and printing. He had journeyed all over New York on the company's behalf, often with Cal, Harold Marden's youngest son, who was the same age as Ray and who was learning the business from the bottom up. Cal would now accompany Ray on the trip to Cleveland.

They set off at dawn on a sunny Wednesday morning, heading out first to Dunkirk, then along the lakeshore into Ohio. They reached Cleveland in early afternoon and spent the rest of their working day debating with their potential new customer how they should design the packaging for a line of auto parts. It was after six o'clock when they at last set off for home and neither of them had eaten since breakfast time. Near Conneaut, they decided to stop at a roadside diner, where they appear to have stayed until well into the evening. They were probably both tired and maybe a little drowsy after their meal, but it was not a long journey by today's standards, the weather was fine, the traffic was sparse and the car's big round headlamps illuminated a swathe of road up ahead. By midnight, though, Raymond was dead and Cal Marden was on the operating table of a hospital in Erie.

The accident was caused by a kid in a heavily laden farm truck. He claimed, when questioned by the police, that he had lost control during an attack of sneezing. The hulk had then careered across the road and driven Cal's car into a ditch. Raymond's neck was broken, snapped by the whiplash jerk of his head. Cal's body was crushed by the steering wheel and he had to be freed by rescuers, who also doused spilled diesel from the farm truck. The kid, incredibly, walked away unscathed.

On duty that night at the Livingston County Sheriff's Office was Teddy Hewson, who took the call from the police department in Conneaut. Teddy sat down and stared blankly at the wall, wondering how, in God's name, he was going to break the news to Mom, not to mention Franklyn and Olive, people he knew so well. It was late, almost one-thirty, so first Teddy had a colleague 'phone Franklyn and ask him if he could come to the dental practice. Believing, as Teddy had hoped, that there had been a burglary, Franklyn quickly dressed and headed outside to get his car. On the porch stood an ashen-faced Teddy, his breath hanging in clouds as he waited nervously in the cool night air. The Deputy told Franklyn straight, told him about the accident, told him that his son was dead. He then told him how sorry he was to have to bring such news. Franklyn nodded in acknowledgement, but could not bring himself to say anything. Teddy offered him a cigarette, which he readily accepted, and the two of them stood out on that porch, without another word spoken between them, until their cigarettes had burned down to their fingers and Franklyn knew it was time to go and tell Olive.

As he drove up to Highland Road, Teddy passed the site of the house where Thomas and Louisa had once lived, the house that had burned down in 1933. He remembered clearly how he had raced up the hill and had summoned Jack Holton from his bed by hammering on his front door. Now he was about to do the same thing again.

Grandpa, too, instantly recalled that night, almost twenty years before, as soon as he heard the banging and looked out the bedroom window to see his uniformed and plainly apprehensive friend. Unlike Franklyn, Grandpa did not dress before he went downstairs and opened the door. This meant that Teddy delivered his news to a man wearing a bottle green robe over striped pajamas. He offered to speak with Mom too, but Grandpa told him he would take care of that. Teddy smiled momentarily, an involuntary reaction of relief, he told me once.

Back inside the house, Grandma was awake and testy. When Grandpa returned to the bedroom, she was huffing and snorting with displeasure at having been disturbed not just by Teddy's pounding at the door, but now also by Grandpa switching on the light. Her face a-glower, she sat up in bed, as Grandpa propped himself on the edge of an old wooden chair. 'Ray's dead.' was all he could say, an understandably direct statement about which Grandma complained for years to come, condemning its lack of preamble or corner-rounding embellishment. '"Ray's dead."' she would say, raising her eyebrows. 'That's what he said and nothing else, just "Ray's dead."'

Tutting and puffing affectedly, Grandma hauled her skinny frame out of the bedclothes and donned a robe and slippers. She then went with Grandpa into Mom's room, where they found their daughter in a deep sleep, from which it took some time to awaken her.

Distraught would seem to be a hopelessly inadequate word to describe Mom's reaction to the news. No matter what Grandpa said, no matter how much love he showed her, nothing could stop the howls of despair that echoed around the house. It was the same howling I would one day hear when Mom lost Jackie. The doctor came on the Sunday morning and gave Mom something to soothe her, but the grief fought so hard against the tranquilizer that it was well into the afternoon before she cried herself into a twitchy, bedeviled sleep. While she slept, Grandpa walked to the Petersen's house, where he found Franklyn and Olive sitting in a darkened front room, with Charlie and his girlfriend, Rosemary Coates, perching wordlessly on the arms of the old easy chairs. As Grandpa entered, Franklyn released his grip on Olive's pale, dumpling-like hand and stood to embrace his friend.

'She'll always be our daughter.' Franklyn said, referring to my mom. 'You tell her that, Jack.'

'I'll tell her.' Jack Holton replied.

Cal Marden never fully recovered and lived out the remaining six years of his life in a succession of hospitals and convalescent homes. He died in 1960, the day after I was born. The kid in the farm truck stuck by his sneezing story and never even went to court; I have no idea what became of him.

Last year, returning home from my second trip to see Sarah Weston, I decided to head east from Toronto, along the north shore of Lake Ontario, past the Thousand Islands and on up to Prescott, where I stopped off for the night. The following day, I crossed the St. Lawrence River, back into the USA, and took a leisurely drive through the Adirondack Park, all the way to Blue Mountain Lake. The cabins where the Holtons spent their vacation in 1952 have been gone for some years, replaced by a discreet resort complex, a haven for wealthy professionals up from the city. Nothing remains of that time, almost half a century ago, when Mom was photographed in her prim blouse and flowery skirt. Indeed, so little exists, outside the memories of Charlie and Rose, of that long ago engagement between Faith Holton and Raymond Petersen. Mom had her engagement ring placed in the breast pocket of the suit in which Ray was buried, along with a locket he had given her the previous Christmas. Then, the day after the funeral, she took the bouquet of flowers he had bought her, their heads wilting, some practically dead, and threw them into the Genesee River at Inspiration Point.

❧

Should I read *Sing All Of Four Seasons*? I keep looking at the book, protected in its Perspex case on top of the low table next to my bureau. The edges of the pages are brown with age and the dark green cover, with its gold and black lettering, has faded over the years. Otherwise, it looks in perfect condition, without a mark or a tear. Obviously Grandpa Holton took good care of it during his lifetime. Whether or not he read the book is unknown.

I think it is around three o'clock, but I have left my watch upstairs, so I cannot be sure. I guess I have had about an hour's slumber since Bobbie and I returned from the Big Tree Inn. I have no idea what woke me, but it brought me round so completely that I had to come downstairs and find a book to read. Hence, I am in my study, trying to decide between one of the drier text books from my days at Columbia, which is usually guaranteed to induce torpor, or maybe my Grandpa's school prize. Meanwhile, Bobbie is upstairs, asleep in my bed.

I got to Bobbie's house this evening just as Jenny Kefnik arrived to collect Becky. She was planning to take Becky and Melissa to McDonald's, then to the video rental store down on Main Street. She had not reckoned with Tim Allen, however. Becky was up in her bedroom watching a re-run of *Home Improvement*. *Tool Time* again.

'Come on, Becky.' Bobbie called up to her. 'Jenny's here. Melissa's waiting in the car for you.'

'In a minute.' came the reply.

'No, Becky.' Bobbie insisted. '*Now.*'

There was a stomp on the floorboards above, then the sound from the TV went dead and Becky emerged on to the landing.

'Come *on.*' Bobbie said, hurrying her along. She handed the child a bag she had packed for her, then thanked Jenny again for agreeing to have Becky stay over.

'It's no problem at all.' Jenny assured her. 'Lissa loves having her for company.'

Bobbie leaned down to kiss Becky goodbye, then opened the front door and released her daughter into the blustery evening. The child ran out to the car and banged on the window for Melissa to let her in. Jenny smiled and shrugged her shoulders. 'You have a good time.' she said to us both.

'Thanks.' I replied.

We walked down to Main Street, the wind thrashing through Bobbie's just-brushed hair. She held on to my arm, her grip tightening with each gust, her hair now and again whipping into my face. By the time we reached the Big Tree Inn, she looked a mess and disappeared immediately into the restrooms. When she came back, I had already ordered a bottle of wine and was sitting in the bar with a glass of Scotch whisky. She was fully re-built, back to the way she had looked when I had arrived at her house: hair straight and shining, lips glossed, cheeks very slightly rouged, eyes thankfully bereft of the enormous round spectacles she has taken to wearing in the last few months. She was dressed as smartly as Bobbie can manage - a black, sleeveless cardigan over her blue blouse and a pair of loose-fitting black pants that cleverly hid the modest bulge of her belly. I asked what she would like as an aperitif. She said that she would wait for the wine.

The waitress sat us at a table by the window, looking out over what was once the garden of Allen and Bethia Ayrault. As well as acting as president of the Livingston County Bank, Ayrault was deeply involved in politics. He was the leader of the local Whig Party and ran unsuccessfully for a state senatorial seat in 1841. After serving as a delegate to the Constitutional Convention, as president of the village and as Town Supervisor, he at last won a place in the state senate, but had to resign after just one session due to ill health. He died in 1861, his widow remaining at the Big Tree Lodge until she too passed away, aged 93, in 1885. James Wolcott Wadsworth then bought the lodge, carried out a program of enlargement, then opened it as a hotel, run by William Nash, who subsequently purchased the building. Charles Baeder bought it after Nash's death and further alterations were made. Since then, it has always operated as an inn, unrivalled locally for the quality of its food and for the ambience created by what was once the Ayraults' mansion.

We studied the menu, or rather I studied the menu while Bobbie donned her spectacles and scanned the room for familiar faces. While I was deciding between chicken satay and crab cakes, Bobbie was observing that three of the realtors from the agency once owned by Jimmy Randolph were sitting diagonally opposite, half a dozen tables away.

'And isn't that the woman from the Letchworth Park Visitor Center?' she asked me.

I turned round to glance swiftly over my shoulder, but Hillary was already gazing in my direction. I nodded in recognition and she smiled in return.

'Bobbie.' I said. 'Can't you focus on what you're going to order?'

'I've chosen.' she replied. 'Shrimp cocktail, followed by the sole. What are you having?'

'I don't know yet. I haven't been able to concentrate.'

She screwed up her face in mock anger, then took off her spectacles and made a big show of placing them back in her purse.

I made my selection and relayed our choices to the waitress. I also ordered another bottle of wine, as the one we had was already half empty and so far we had eaten nothing. Some minutes later the second bottle arrived, immersed in a bucket of ice, and was quickly followed by our first courses – Bobbie's shrimp cocktail and my crab cakes. We talked about how business was at the former gallery, how Becky was doing in school, how much the mauve of my shirt suited me, how the dead leaves had once again this year caused the gutters of Bobbie's house to overflow.

As Bobbie prattled on, my mind drifted back to when my cousin Valerie had gone to the Big Tree Inn with Kelly, my parents and I, in the fall of 1990. We had sat by the window that evening too, although the restaurant had been decorated differently back then and the table arrangements have since gone through a number of permutations. Throughout that meal, I had been almost physically unable to avert my attention away from our visitor, with her sweet, ingenue face and her fabulous dark hair. Kelly had taken me to task over it when we had got back home, hissing accusations in a low voice so as not to alert the rest of my family to our bickering. Unable to deny that I had been staring at my cousin, but equally unable to explain why, I had left myself victim to Kelly's own interpretation – that I found Valerie more attractive than her. For once, she had been completely wrong.

'............ so that's how they left it.' I heard Bobbie say. There was an uneasy silence as she waited for me to comment. 'You weren't listening to me, were you Will?'

'Sorry, Bobbie.' I said.

She eyed me crossly. 'I was thinking about my dad.' I lied, knowing I would be forgiven if I offered that as an explanation.

'Oh Will.' Bobbie smiled sympathetically. 'Here I am yapping on about my car when you've just lost your dad. I'm so sorry.'

'Don't be silly.' I told her. 'It's my fault. I didn't bring you out so that I could sit and meditate.' I reached across the table and touched her hand. 'Come on, tell me again about your car.'

She sighed with a hint of disapproval, but did as I had said and repeated the news that the mechanic at the shop had called to report that her car was ready, but that he had found three more faults that would need fixing in the next six months.

'We'll have to take your car down to Florida at Christmas.' she said. 'I hope you don't mind.'

She was talking as though I had already agreed to go, which was far from the case. 'Fly down.' I quickly suggested, trying to give no indication as to whether or not I would be accompanying her and Becky. 'You can go from Rochester. It's much quicker. You'll save yourself so much time.'

'No Will.' she said. 'Becky won't fly. And, anyway, it's far too expensive.'

'More expensive than having the car fixed?'

'I don't know, but I need the car for more than just going to visit my parents.'

I did not want to pursue this discussion, so I tried to steer us gently in another direction. 'You're right.' I said. 'The car is a better investment. If I were you, I'd ease back on buying so many presents this year. You're too generous, Bobbie. You should spend some of your money on more important things. I certainly don't expect anything from you.'

'I *like* buying you a Christmas present.' she protested. 'Besides, I don't go overboard. It's just a token, really. *You're* the one who spends a lot, Will. This perfume you bought me last year must have cost a fortune.'

'You're wearing it tonight?'

'Can't you tell?'

In truth, I could not. I had bought it because of the shape of the bottle, having smelled the perfume only as the assistant in the shop sprayed a tiny cloud of the golden liquid into the air. I picked up Bobbie's hand and brought it close to my face so that I could smell her wrist. It was a delicate, classy fragrance. I held Bobbie's hand close, breathing in the perfume while wondering whether all the eyes in the restaurant were directed toward us, ranks of Geneseoans at last having their suspicions about my relationship with Bobbie confirmed. I was tempted to kiss her palm, but the thought of weightier concerns than those imagined eyes quickly overpowered that temptation. I released her hand and she returned it to rest on the table.

Our conversation regressed to tittle-tattle, Bobbie sharing with me her encyclopedic knowledge of the lives of the townsfolk. The Kefniks, she told me, are trying for another baby; some guy on Seminole has been arrested for trading in pornography over the Internet; one of the teachers at the High School is going to cycle around Lake Ontario to raise money for African famine relief; a couple from Livonia are moving to the house across the street from where Franklyn and Olive used to live. I nodded in all the right places, asked a few mindless questions, tried to appear interested.

By now, our main courses had been delivered and consumed, the second wine bottle was down to its final third and Bobbie's cheeks, artificially colored at the start of the evening, were glowing warmly. We ordered desserts, which appeared with commendable speed and were eaten with relish. Coffee came next, served in china cups that the waitress returned regularly to refill.

While I paid the check, Bobbie went again to the restroom. As before, I was sitting in the bar when she came back through the door. I was handed my coat by one of the other waitresses, who then helped Bobbie into hers, thoughtfully suggesting she tuck her hair under the collar to prevent it flying wild in the ever stronger wind. Outside, Main Street was still well illuminated, though there were only two other people in sight. Everyone else, it seems, had been sensible enough to either stay at home, or come out, not on foot like us, but by car.

We at last made it back here, windswept and breathless having had to lean into the gale so as simply to remain on our feet. Leaves were flying all over the place, dancing scratchily up the driveway, crunching beneath our feet as we walked up the path to the door. Once inside, I told Bobbie to go through to the front room, while I found yet another bottle of wine, a red one this time.

'Heck, Will.' she said when she saw the bottle and two glasses. 'Are you trying to get me drunk?'

'No.' I replied, truthfully. 'I'd just like us to relax.'

'Can't we relax without alcohol?'

'Sure, if you'd prefer.'

She laughed aloud. 'I didn't say I'd *prefer* it without alcohol. I just wanted to know I have the option.'

I poured her some wine, then sat down next to her on the sofa. I had wanted all evening to talk to her about Dad, but the restaurant had proved to be an impossible location for such a discussion. The atmosphere had been wrong, there had been too many people close by, there had always been the sense that touching upon something so difficult would disturb the pleasant equilibrium of our evening. Even when Dad had cropped up in our chatter, I had deliberately changed the subject. I had envisioned Bobbie becoming upset, blushing with embarrassment, running to the ladies' room and leaving me alone at the table with all those eyes peering at me. Plates left with half-eaten meals are so often the wreckage from an ill-judged topic of conversation. However, now I was at home and there was just the two of us, no prying stares, no dinner to ruin, I still could not bring myself to raise the subject of my dad. Almost as though she was privy to my thoughts, it was Bobbie who took the first steps into the minefield.

'Tell me about the funeral.' she said, looking extremely serious.

'Nothing much to tell, really.' I replied. 'There weren't too many people there. Family and a few friends. These things are so soulless, just a minister who's never even heard of the person who has died going through the motions, sort of like a funeral by numbers.'

'Was your aunt there?'

'Angela you mean? Yeah, she was there. And her daughter. Do you remember Valerie? She came to visit us not long after I got married.'

'She was pretty.'

'Yeah, she was. Now she just looks so sad, propped up in her wheelchair.'

Bobbie frowned. 'It's a dreadful thing, Will.' she said.

I took a mouthful of wine, summoning courage I guess. 'Did you know about Dad?' I wondered.

'Know what?' Bobbie responded, though she was obviously feigning ignorance.

'I don't have to tell you, do I Bob?'

She pursed her lips and shook her head, her eyes fixed on some indeterminate spot beyond my left ear.

'Why didn't you tell me?' I asked.

'What would have been the point? You couldn't have changed anything. Anyway, Will, you know what your dad was like. He didn't exactly make a big deal out of it. He was very discreet.'

'Maybe so, but *you* knew about it.'

Bobbie could not contain her amusement. 'Will.' she smiled. 'You must surely have worked out by now that there isn't much that goes on 'round here that I *don't* know about.'

'How many other people knew, though?'

'Well I certainly didn't go broadcasting it all around town.'

'I'm not suggesting you did, but there must have been other people who had worked it out for themselves. It's a small town, Bobbie. Gossip is the lifeblood.'

She breathed out sharply and shook her head again, this time with an air of frustration about her. 'As far as I'm aware.' she said. 'The only other people who knew were my parents and they definitely didn't tell anyone else.'

'There were no rumors doing the rounds.'

'No.'

There was a clear signal in Bobbie's tone: she did not want to talk about this any more. Unfortunately, *I* absolutely did. I was glad to hear that my dad's clandestine behavior was not and had not been the talk of Geneseo, but that reassurance was merely the part of all this that Bobbie could do for *me*. There was something much greater that *I* could do for *her*, not that I was intending to do anything other than to explore whether she would be receptive to it. As I took a second or two to toss this around in my mind, it all became extraordinarily complicated.

With my thoughts wading through a mire of indecision and cowardice, I had not noticed that Bobbie had taken hold of my hand.

'Don't worry, Will.' she said. 'Everything's fine now.'

It was a comment open to much interpretation.

# Saturday

❁

It started, or maybe *re*started, last October, almost exactly a year ago now.

I returned from the supermarket one morning to find a wedge of letters in the mailbox. There was a credit card bill and a personalized letter offering me inducements to join an historical book club. There was also an envelope embossed with the logo of The Greenleaf Corporation and another with an English postmark. The former was an invitation to a product launch dinner in New York City. The latter was a letter from Aunt Angela, telling me how much she was looking forward to seeing me at Christmas.

I had planned a number of times during the previous year to go to England, but always something had cropped up that prevented me from making the trip. Now I had cleared my schedule from mid December and I had reserved my air tickets. I would be staying almost a month and I was working on my itinerary, hoping to take in London and Cambridge, hoping to trace the elusive Moses Holton of Cirencester.

Knowing that Steve Caspar would also be at the Greenleaf event and that it would be the first time we had seen one another since he had rushed home early from his vacation here the previous August, I accepted the rather pompously worded invitation. This meant that, nine days later, my dinner suit, dress shirt, bow tie and I were in Manhattan. I checked into the Holiday Inn on the day before the launch dinner, then called up some friends and arranged to meet them for drinks that evening. We went to a bar on Lafayette, then to a restaurant way uptown, almost in the Bronx, a Greek Taverna that one of the guys reckoned was the latest just-about-to-happen place, but which I thought was gauche and over priced. I got back to my room just after midnight and crashed out almost immediately, rammed full of vine leaves and mutton and retsina.

The following morning, I awoke at eight o'clock and stepped straight into the shower to wash away the lingering oily aroma of the restaurant. I had made an appointment with a genealogist at the Crafter Institute, who had tracked down Robert McCarthy Sefton for me a few months before and who I thought might now be able to help me with tracing the roots of the

Stafford family. I was also planning to meet Freddie Di Napoli for lunch at Zoë. The appointment at the Crafter was not until ten thirty, so I took my time after showering. I put on just my shorts, then sat on the bed and flicked through the TV channels. I watched the football highlights and the baseball roundup and the nation wide weather forecast, then I found my way to WONM – 24 Seven News, just in time to catch the nine o'clock bulletin. I recognized the polished presentation style of Paul Kohlheimer, who I had met at one of the station's loathsome parties some years before. He was linking with a long-winded State Representative up in Albany and debating the latest moves in what appeared to be a petty zoning dispute that had somehow found itself in a maze of litigation. I was just about to flick again, when Kohlheimer wound up the interview and the camera returned squarely to his aristocratic head, hovering beside which was an inset of an even more familiar face.

'And finally.' Kohlheimer beamed. 'One of our own was making the news last night at the fifth annual Stoltenberg Television News Awards. 24 Seven's Chief Community Affairs Reporter, Kelly Samuels, took the prestigious Gold Circle award for her work on exposing the scandal of Brooklyn's immigrant underclass. She was presented with the award by veteran newsman Laurence Seale.'

Pictures of the ceremony now filled the screen. There was Kelly in a black dress striding to the stage in the glow of a spotlight. She reached out and shook the hand of hoary old Laurence Seale, who bent down and kissed her on the cheek, her response to which was impossible to discern given that she had fixed an implausibly big-mouthed grin on her face. Seale handed her the award and she turned to face the audience, doing her best to appear modest amidst uproarious applause and a firework display of camera flashes. She leaned forward and said 'Thank-you' into the microphone, but her voice was drowned in the torrent of fawning congratulation. Again, she stood and soaked up the adulation, gripping the award as if it were a lifeline. Then I saw the glint. It was only momentary, but it was unmistakable. I lunged forward on the bed to get a closer look and, yes, there it was. She was wearing the eternity ring I had bought her, the one that, fully ten years previously, had cost me almost half of my enormous bonus.

Kohlheimer was talking again now, though I have no idea what he was saying because I was too busy thinking about that ring. I thought about it all morning, throughout my meeting with the genealogist and my lunch with Freddie, when I must have come across as annoyingly inattentive. All afternoon it rattled about my mind as I strolled distractedly in Central Park. When I got back to the Holiday Inn, I took a long soak in the bath, then laid out my clothes for the launch dinner while I listened to WONM for a re-run of the awards story. That was this morning's news, however, superseded now by a whole new stream of events from all around the Big Apple. I sat down agitatedly on the bed. I wanted so much to call her, but every time I looked at the 'phone my head filled with a soup of potential consequences. I had not spoken to Kelly since a couple months after Mom's funeral, when she had called to thank me, politely but coldly, for the photograph I had sent her, a picture of her with Mom posing in front of the Middle Falls in the Letchworth Park.

Eventually, I figured that, if I did call, she was likely to be out, probably working, and that I would be invited to leave a message on her voice mail. I could keep it brief, nothing too familiar, but equally nothing too terse. Kind of neutral. She could return my call if she wished, or she could continue our stand off. It would be up to her.

I picked up the handset and punched in the number.

'Hello?' someone said.

'Hello.' I responded, my heart suddenly pounding audibly. 'Is that WONM's *Chief* Community Affairs Reporter, Kelly Samuels.'

'*Will!*' Kelly shrilled. 'God, it's good to hear your voice.'

This was not quite what I had anticipated.

'Thanks.' I said. 'It's good to hear yours too. I saw you on the news this morning. Congratulations!'

'How did you catch 24 Seven?'

'I'm in town.'

'Where?'

'At the Holiday Inn.'

'Oh, wow. That's great. You know, I've been thinking about you so much recently.'

'You have? Why?'

'Lots of reasons, Will. Lots of reasons I'd like to tell you about.'

'Well fire ahead.'

'No, not over the 'phone. Especially not at Holiday Inn rates.'

She went quiet for a moment. 'I guess you've got plans for tonight.' she said.

'I'm going to a Greenleaf dinner.' I told her. 'Why?'

'Oh, no matter. I'd like to have seen you, that's all. I'm flying down to Miami tomorrow and won't be back for a week or so.'

'Work or vacation?'

'Work. 24 Seven has an exchange arrangement with Metro Scene Miami. I'm swapping jobs with one of their reporters for a few days. Anyway, I guess I'll have to catch up with you when I get back.'

She sounded genuinely disappointed, even a little despondent.

'If you want to get together.' I said. 'I can take a rain check on the Greenleaf jamboree.'

'Don't you have to go?' she asked. 'Won't that jerk Grogan be all upset with you?'

'Who cares? I don't work for him any more. Where shall we meet?'

'Central Park, by the Sherman statue.'

That evening we went to the Italian place on West 42nd, the place I had taken Mom for her birthday. I could not believe how happy Kelly was to see me. She was full of energy, talking constantly, unloading, it seemed to me, like someone who had not spoken to another human being for weeks. She was wearing a red dress, classically cut and patently not from an outlet mall. Her eyes looked like gemstones, twinkling in the candlelight, her hair, that one-time froth of blonde curls, lay tamed and expensively styled. She was exquisite, but there was something going on beneath the abundant chatter and the high-earning-media-figure looks. Gradually, she grew more subdued, her eyes dimmed and her conversation became punctuated with sighs.

'Tell me about it, Kelly.' I said, as she drummed her fingers on the tablecloth. 'Tell me what's wrong.'

She looked up at the ceiling, as though seeking some divine guidance. 'I'm losing it, Will.' she said.

'Losing what?'

'My fire. My desire. I feel burned out, worn down, *let* down, actually.'

'Let down by who? By what?'

'By the very thing I've always wanted. That's what makes it so difficult. I used to love the job I do, I used to get a real buzz. You know what I was like – I threw everything into it. I wanted it so much and I don't just mean the limelight, the fame and fortune. You might think I'm crazy, but I really thought that I could do something for the world, actually make a difference. Now I know I can't. Now I know that I'm just a TV reporter and that's not something I feel too proud about.'

'But you must be good at it, Kelly. You won that award.'

'I know, but what does that mean? I spent six weeks working on that story, six weeks working with the poorest people I have ever seen, people who have come to America to escape deprivation in their own countries, people who were sold the idea of the American Dream, the Land of the Free, only to find themselves even worse off because of crooked landlords and indolent city officials and a system that doesn't give a shit about them. I won an award for that, for telling the world about those people, but what did *they* get out of it. They're still living the same way. If only half the money spent on that awards ceremony last night had been given to those wretched people it would have made a real difference to their lives.' She breathed out heavily, exasperatedly. 'The thing is, Will, I've realized there is nothing I can do, nothing any of us can do. The whole system is corrupt and there are lots of people more powerful than us who like to keep it that way. There'll always be battered women and teenage pregnancies and abuse of minors and child slavery and all the other vile things I've spent the last eleven years reporting. I guess I should be happy – I've got a job for life – but I don't feel happy, I just feel drained, impotent.'

She looked down at the table and picked at some spilled sugar grains. I moved my hand until it was just touching hers, testing her response to this negligible, but, in the context of our past antagonism, daring intimacy. She wrapped her little finger around mine.

'You have such a good life, Will.' she said softly. 'Such an uncomplicated life. You live in a beautiful place surrounded by decent people, a place that's light years away from here. All I get each day is a menu of other people's despair. I used to enjoy it – I know that sounds cruel – I used to believe that what I was doing was worthwhile, that it had value. Now I'm not so sure. I think you did the right thing, Will. You got out while you could.'

'Kelly.' I said. 'You have a great life too. Look at those clothes you're wearing. Think about all that applause last night. You've got money, you've got popularity. You've got your own apartment in Manhattan. There are people who would kill for that.'

'Yeah.' she replied, her face half smile, half sneer. 'There are plenty who'd kill *me* for it.' She gripped my fingers more tightly. 'It's not about money, though, is it Will? It's not about people who pretend to love your work just because you're the latest winner of some stupid award. It's about companionship and respect between people and honesty and integrity and all the things your Mom had. And my parents too. Somehow I've lost that, but you've managed to regain it, to get away from that crazy life we had together. You saw the falseness of it all and you went back to the *real* world.'

'Is that why you've been thinking about me?'

'Yep.'

'And why did you wear that eternity ring last night?'

'You saw it?'

'Yeah, I did. It caught the light really well.'

'I often wear it. It's a beautiful ring, given to me by a man who loved me. The only man who ever loved me.'

We shared the check, then took separate cabs, Kelly back to her apartment, me to the bar of the Holiday Inn, where I sat with a bourbon and tried to work out what had happened. For all my desire to view what Kelly had said as a new beginning for us, I could not help thinking that maybe this was just a phase, a passing disillusionment, brought on perhaps by a particularly heavy workload or the prospect of going down to Miami or the end of some relationship. Perhaps her best girlfriend was out of town and I just happened to call at the right moment, offering a willing ear into which she could unburden herself.

Two days later, she called me from Florida. It was not a long call, but it was pleasant, even light-hearted at times. She promised to call again when she returned to New York City, but still I did not really expect her to do so. I continued to doubt her right up until the afternoon when the call came. We talked for half an hour, exchanging details of what we had been doing, how her trip to Miami had gone, what stories she had been assigned, the sort of things we had talked about when we had first been married. The call set a pattern of weekly conversations, which usually came on Sunday evenings and which gradually stretched in length to over an hour.

At the beginning of December, I went again to New York City, again to the Holiday Inn and again, with Kelly, to 'our' Italian restaurant. Once more, she looked magnificent, in a blue dress this time, a dress with a wide neck and a nipped waist and a bow at the back that reminded me of the clothes she had worn before she transformed herself into a hard-edged television reporter. Her manner was less sour than the previous time we had met, less dispirited, and in place of bitterness and depression was an acerbic, cutting wit mixed with highly agreeable self-deprecation. When once she had taken herself and her career so seriously, now she was mocking, now she was cracking acid little jokes.

This time, I picked up the check. We went and stood out on the sidewalk to wait for a cab, not usually a problem in Manhattan, but on a night dampened by steady drizzle every yellow taxi that passed was already carrying passengers. Kelly held on to my arm as we sheltered under my big Greenleaf umbrella.

'When will you be coming to New York again?' she asked.

'I don't know.' I replied. 'I don't have any plans at the moment.'

She said nothing for a few seconds, then looked up at me, boring into me with those icy eyes. 'Would you like to come for Christmas?' she asked.

Only a few days before, I had collected my flight ticket for England, but I just could not tell her that. I could not tell her that I would prefer to be in England than with her. I could not tell her that because it was not true. I wanted desperately to be with Kelly. I had wanted desperately to be with her ever since she had moved out of our apartment and found herself a lawyer.

That night, I stayed up into the early hours, waiting for dawn to arrive in England. It was seven-thirty in the morning, Greenwich Mean Time, when I 'phoned Dad to tell him that I had changed my plans, that I was going to spend the Christmas holidays with Kelly and not with him. He was, as ever, unruffled by my decision, as though I had simply cried off from a shopping trip. He wished me well, told me to give his love to Kelly, quipped that maybe I would be bringing her with me when I did eventually get to England. He made it easy for me.

I stayed in New York City for most of that day, buying presents that I could send in the mail to Dad and Angela and Valerie. I went into Macy's and bought a jacket and some CDs for Becky and perfume for Bobbie, the perfume she wore last night. Then I searched for a gift for Kelly, wondering what it is a man buys his ex-wife, wondering how expensive it should be, how personal, as opposed to practical, wondering what message it ought to relate.

Just a month after my dad was born, his grandfather, Walter Chapple, died from a heart attack. Still recuperating from what had been a difficult childbirth, Edith Wright traveled with her husband John to the funeral in Madingley. Seven years later, Rose Chapple, Edith's mother, also passed away, also as the result of what we label these days as cardiac arrest.

Edith had visited her widowed mother twice a month, always traveling by train from Letchworth to Cambridge, then taking a bus out to Madingley. Once her mother had died, Edith's visits to the village became less frequent, though rarely did six weeks pass when she did not go to the old churchyard to tend her parents' grave. During school holidays, she would take her children with her. Edward, whose name had already been corrupted into the more familiar Eddie, would ride along with his face pressed against the window, watching the collage of farmlands passing by, the occasional car dawdling along the country roads, the carts and tractors kicking up clouds of white chalk-dust as they trundled across Royston Heath. Angela, meanwhile, would be reading a book or playing I Spy or simply talking quietly with her mother.

England, like the rest of Europe, was at war. John Wright had avoided enlistment by being in what was termed a reserved occupation, though his older brother Percy was seeing active service as a merchant seaman, helping to ferry men and supplies to and from France. In June 1940, he was to command a small freighter that helped men from the Allied armies evacuate from the beaches at Dunkirk. Meanwhile, John continued his deliveries of animal feed and seed grain to the local farms, often surprising the farmers with his ability to haul, apparently with ease, the heavy sacks from his truck and pile them tidily in the corner of a barn or beneath some rickety lean-to. To look at John, one would have thought him incapable of such strenuous work, yet his lack of height and his wiry build concealed an unlikely strength, which was, at that time, undiminished by his proclivity for beer.

Eddie Wright was showing more overt signs of his own physical prowess. At eight years old, it was already evident that he was going to be substantially taller than either of his parents. He had inherited his mother's dark good looks, as well as her calm, unflappable nature. By contrast, his father's influence was due more to John's behavior than to the Wright genes. John's ribald humor seemed, even at an early age, to offend his son's sensibilities; his regular forays to the Two Chimneys left Eddie not envious of such an alluring adult pursuit, but appalled by the damaging potential of its aftermath. Eddie's academic abilities also created problems with his father. Even in the 1940s, the unofficial caste system that had long pervaded English society was still prevalent. Just as the eighteenth century Wrights had known their station and had neither sought nor expected anything better, so too, in their way, did their mid twentieth century descendants. Like so many working class people, they saw only minimal value in education. They were predestined to work in factories and farmyards, so what was the point of learning any more than the basics of reading and writing? Working class kids did not go to university, they did not become managers or businessmen. Thus, John's reaction to his son's interest in science and, especially, in geography, was to order Eddie out of his bedroom, where he would often be pawing over the atlas his uncle Percy had sent him for Christmas, and force him to help with the vegetable patch or with the rabbits and chickens John had acquired soon after the outbreak of war.

As a nation, the British must have felt dreadfully alone after Dunkirk. With the rest of Europe occupied by German forces, Britain was the sole beacon of freedom. While Lüftwaffe raids were smashing its cities, its only lifeline was the convoy route across the Atlantic that brought desperately needed supplies from the United States. In truth, American neutrality was a sham, a political position taken to appease the isolationists on Capitol Hill. FDR knew that the European allies could only succeed in their fight against Hitler if they were aided, directly, by the might of the US military. Yet, as many Presidents have found since, the Chief Executive's hands are often tied by the necessity to mollify the suits on the Hill.

From the outset of hostilities, Letchworth had seen its population enlarged by thousands of evacuees from north London. Production at the town's factories was stepped up, with tanks, submarines and parachutes among the equipment manufactured. This was maybe the time when the pacifist idealism of many of the town's pioneers at last evanesced in the searing light of reality. Back in 1915, two wealthy Belgian brothers, Jacques and Georges Krynn, had escaped to England ahead of the German capture of Antwerp. Along with fellow refugee Raoul Lahy, they had built a huge foundry in Letchworth so as to produce munitions for that earlier World War. This had caused great consternation amongst those anti-war pioneers, yet, by the time Krynn & Lahy began production of armaments for the war against the Third

Reich, such protest had faded into silence. As America was about to discover, communities, whether they are small towns or vast nations, cannot exist in an idealistic bubble.

The USA was finally jolted out of its isolationism by the Japanese bombing of Pearl Harbor in December 1941. Suddenly the country found itself at war with the Axis powers and American troops and airforce personnel were on their way to Britain, among them Philip and Lester Holton.

On an early August Wednesday in 1942, Edith Wright set out with her two children for the railroad station in Letchworth's town center, intending to take the mid morning train to Cambridge. All three of them were equipped with gas masks concealed in boxes hung about their necks on ungainly straps. Eddie was wearing his school blazer, Angela her second best summer dress. Having boarded the train, Edith, she herself attired in a skirt fabricated from an old frock, led her children along the corridor, seeking out vacant seats. There were none. Young men in uniform occupied every compartment. Unperturbed, Edith decided to stand in the corridor and wait for seats to become available, maybe at Baldock, the next station. Hardly had the train begun to pull out of Letchworth, however, when one of the compartment doors slid open and a uniformed young man called across to her.

'Ma'am.' he said, his accent strange and unfamiliar. 'Please don't stand out there. You and your kids are welcome to our seats.'

Two of his companions rose to their feet and presented themselves in the corridor.

'That's very kind.' Edith responded.

'No problem, Ma'am.' the GI smiled.

Thus, Edith, Eddie and Angela Wright found themselves in a compartment with three young Americans, whose buddies had given up their seats and were smoking cigarettes out in the corridor. Already American airmen and soldiers had gained the reputation for being 'over paid, over sexed and over here', a reputation that was not entirely undeserved, though most British people were pleased about the 'over here' aspect. Edith cared little for reputations and judged people on their individual merits, so being surrounded by these peculiar sounding foreigners held no concerns for her. Indeed, she found them to be not brash and condescending, as their image had been portrayed, but courteous and warm. They instantly took to her two children, talking to them about their school, telling them about their own homes back in the USA and, most exotically of all, offering them chocolate and chewing gum. Angela was in awe and remained speechless for most of the journey, but Eddie was enraptured, chatting excitedly with one GI in particular, Joe Meninski, who had been born and raised in Hoboken, New Jersey. By the time they reached Cambridge, the young soldier had taken Eddie's address and had promised to write to him and maybe, when he got back home after the war, send him some postcards to add to the collection Eddie had been slowly accumulating since he was seven years old.

Angela tells me that my dad did not stop talking about America and the Americans for the rest of the day, even when the three of them were tidying the grave of Grandma Wright's parents at Madingley. There were no GIs on the return journey, but that did not matter, for young Eddie had suddenly become an expert on all things American and was able to keep his mother and sister entertained with stories of the great cities and the open prairies, the majestic Rockies and the mellow Mississippi. If Edith thought for one moment that this newfound fascination would soon wear off, she would have been utterly wrong. Nothing, not his return to school that September or the continuing war or the steady approach of his teenage years, could shake Eddie's absorption with that vast country way, way across the Atlantic, an absorption fueled by the arrival, once a month, of a letter from Joe Meninski.

On May 8th 1945, church bells chimed and flags fluttered in the breeze as Letchworth, along with every other community throughout Britain, celebrated V-E Day. Two months later, Harry Truman, who had become US President on FDR's death in April, authorized the use of atomic bombs on Hiroshima and Nagasaki, thereby bringing Japan to surrender and the war to a close. In all, over one hundred sixty Letchworth men had perished, though happily the names of none of my forebears appear on any memorials.

True to caste and despite an intellect that begged to be nurtured by a college education, Eddie Wright took a job, at the age of fifteen, in a factory on Letchworth's industrial estate. His earnings were adequate, though hardly generous, and what money was left over after paying weekly housekeeping to his mother tended to be spent on records and books, all of which were American. He also liked to go to the town's two cinemas, the Palace and the Broadway, where so many of the films would be set in the United States, some, like *New York Confidential*, in the cities, others, maybe *Red River* or *High Noon*, on the wide open ranges of the west. Many times, Angela went along with her brother to see a movie, providing Eddie with a companion when none of his small band of friends was available. He did not easily cultivate friendships, his nature being solitary and reflective in obvious reaction to his father's continual ribbing. Although intended as a joke, John's teasing over his son's bookish tendencies, his parsimonious moderation when it came to cigarettes and beer and, worst of all, his interest in girls, had the effect of driving Eddie into a guarded world of secrets and introspection. It was a world in which his bedroom - its walls covered with maps of the USA, with posters of Humphrey Bogart and Spencer Tracy, with a Stars and Stripes sent over by Joe Meninski - provided a haven, a place to read and learn, a place to dream.

By the time he reached his early twenties, it was surprising that the library in Letchworth had any book about America that Eddie Wright had not read. Yet, most Saturday mornings he would walk into the town center and make his way to the library on the corner of Broadway and Gernon Road. One such morning, in June 1955, he noticed a window display in the adjacent museum. It was a map of a place in the United States, somewhere in western New York called the Letchworth State Park. Eddie could barely believe what he was seeing. He stood at the window transfixed by the blue line of the Genesee River as it cut its way through the middle of the map, through the middle of this park seemingly named for his own home town. He *had* to know more. Unfortunately, the museum had little further information. Neither did the library, where there was not one reference to the Park in any of the books he could find. All he could think of doing was to contact Joe Meninski and ask if he knew anything about this place. After all, New Jersey is not a million miles away from New York, is it?

It was weeks before Joe replied to Eddie's letter. He told Eddie that he had never been to the Park, but had probably traveled nearby when he and his wife had visited Niagara Falls a couple years back. He had found the address of the State Parks Commission in New York, however, and suggested that Eddie write there. By now, though, Eddie had made a monumental decision. He was going to go to America. He was going to fly to New York City on one of the new transatlantic flights, visit Joe in Hoboken, then find his way out to the Letchworth State Park.

It took more than a year for Eddie to save enough money to buy an air ticket, more than a year without new clothes, without new records or books or trips to the cinema. He even took a second job, making weekend deliveries for the same firm as John, his father, had worked since 1930. I wonder whether my dad ever envisaged that his son would be able to pay for the same journey, not from months of hard saving, but from less than a day's pay.

The flight from London Airport landed at Idlewild on a September evening in 1956. Somehow Dad managed to make his way into the center of Manhattan, where he found a perilously cheap hotel and settled down to a full night's sleep. The next morning, he told me some years ago, he walked from the hotel on the Lower West Side all the way down Broadway to the Battery, then up Fifth Avenue, past the Empire State Building and into Central Park. Whilst this is probably no greater distance than a decent hike in the Park, I would never have walked so far in the city. Yet Dad, utterly infatuated by everything he saw, thought nothing of it.

Later that day, he sought out Penn Station, where he took a bus to Hoboken. There, Joe Meninski greeted him at his modest house, so different from the fabulous palace that Dad had imagined all Americans would own. The two of them had not seen each other since that day on the Cambridge bound train in 1942 and Dad found himself shocked not just by Joe's home, but also by his aged appearance. Joe's wife, Dorothy, seemed so young by comparison, though both of them were actually the same age. Dad suddenly realized what the war had done to that young GI he had met fourteen years before.

Dad stayed over in Hoboken for two days, then Joe and Dorothy drove him up to Scranton, where he caught the first of two Greyhound buses that would take him to some place called Geneseo.

The room he took at the Geneseo Hotel on Main Street was scarcely luxurious, but, after the fleapit on the Lower West Side and two nights on the floor of the Meninski's living room, it suited my dad perfectly well. Intrigued at the sudden arrival of an Englishman in town, the hotel manager inquired as to Dad's business. On hearing of Dad's plan to go out to the Park, he said he would talk to one of his friends, a dentist called Franklyn Petersen who he knew had been spending most of his spare time out there for the last twenty years. Maybe Franklyn could give Dad a ride.

Franklyn, naturally, was delighted to take the young English visitor out to the Park, especially one from the town of Letchworth, about which Franklyn knew absolutely nothing. Also along for the ride was Franklyn's old friend Jack Holton and Jack's lovely daughter Faith. Characteristically, Dad told me next to nothing about this first meeting with his future wife, or about the way in which their relationship developed during Dad's ten day stay in Geneseo. Mom, too, was a little reluctant to speak of those first two weeks, almost as though describing them to me would break the spell of their romance. The only person who has told me any real detail is Rose Petersen.

'Oh my gosh.' she said, when I asked her how my mom had fallen so quickly and completely for this absolute stranger. 'He was a *dish*. He had this thick head of dark hair and eyes so sultry and brooding. And he was *so* cool. You know, that sophisticated English cool. Everything on the outside was so calm, but those eyes told you that still waters ran deep with him. He was big and strong and handsome, Will, and he had a voice that made you melt.'

Mom told me that I, too, have that same voice, a rich voice she said, a holy voice according to Kelly. Maybe so, but a voice alone does not create the besotted kind of love that seems to have so instantly flourished between my parents.

'He was a rock.' Rose went on. 'Solid and dependable. People 'round here used to call him 'Steady Eddie'. It was just what your mom needed. Remember, Will, she'd lost poor Ray not so long beforehand and, believe me, she'd carried a whole load of grief ever since. She never once dated another man. Not until your dad came along. I think she felt he was someone she could rely upon, someone who would always be there for her. He had that sort of aura about him.'

I am sure Rose was right. I am also certain that Dad's interest in the Park would have had an impact on Mom. Here was this young Englishman, who had traveled thousands of miles so as to visit a place that she adored. More than that, he seemed so at home there, so much at peace, as though a great weight had been lifted from his shoulders and at last he could stretch and breath and be free. Seeing the positive effect he was having on my mom, the Petersens offered him a room so as to save him staying at the Geneseo Hotel. Some days he would go walking on his own, others Mom would collect him in Grandpa's car and she would treat him to a Holton Tour, a long drive around the nearby towns and villages, through the sunlit countryside and out to Conesus Lake and Silver Lake and the forest down in Ossian.

Dad's return to England meant a return also to his own secret world. He told no-one about Faith Holton and even when her letters arrived, as they often did once a week, he told his parents that they were simply from a friend he had made while on his travels. John and Edith were not fooled, of course, neither was Angela, though she too was keeping quiet about a new friend she had met, Michael Salter. Eddie and Angela shared the same trait of needing to feel entirely secure about a relationship, indeed about anything involving feelings and emotions, before they would broach the subject with their parents, or, perhaps more accurately, their father. They knew just how relentless John's leg-pulling could be.

Angela had met Michael at a dance at the Icknield Halls, a ballroom adjacent to Nott's Café, which John Betjamin had used as his inspiration for *Huxley Hall*. It was one of a number of local venues for young people, which included the nearby Co-Operative Hall and the Hermitage Ballroom in the neighboring town of Hitchin. The Wilbury Hotel had also recently opened. It was roughly the same distance from the Wrights' house as the Two Chimneys and immediately popular with John, who would enjoy his regular pint of mild and bitter in the hotel's public bar. Letchworth, as a whole, was growing, with new housing estates and a thriving industrial zone, though still it remained a Garden City, its modern development kept in tune with its founding principles. Even so, it was rapidly becoming far too suffocating for Eddie Wright, who increasingly saw his future in another place, a place across the Atlantic.

In the fall of 1957, Eddie flew again to America, his fare paid by Jack Holton. Once more, he stayed two weeks, this time rooming with the Holtons on Highland Road. Evidently it was during that fortnight that he proposed to my mom. Jack, Rose told me, was thrilled, but Mary Holton received the news with indifference. She was unimpressed by this quiet, thoughtful man from England, not, it seems, because of anything intrinsic in his character, but because of his upbringing, which she considered to be beneath her daughter.

Now it was impossible for Eddie to keep Faith secret from his parents. Two days after he arrived home, he sat down with his mother and told her about his new fiancée. Like Jack Holton, Edith Wright was overjoyed. To Eddie's surprise, his father, too, was delighted and took his whole family, plus Michael Salter, who had also now materialized as Angela's intended husband, to the Wilbury Hotel for a celebratory drink. Not one of them seemed fazed by the idea of Eddie emigrating to America, even though this must have been the most outlandish action for someone on the Wrights' social stratum. I guess it goes to show the equanimity of the English.

Angela and Michael married in March 1958 and one of the most popular and talked-about guests at the wedding was a young American woman called Faith Holton. It was the first time my mom had met her future parents-in-law and, Angela tells me, they were enchanted.

'She seemed so glamorous.' my aunt explained to me just last week. 'I think a lot of people had met Americans during the war, but somehow they were detached, not really part of every day life. Now, here was this lovely young thing, so slim and pretty, and she was part of our family. He didn't say anything, but I think Eddie was really proud of her. So were my parents. She was everything they could have hoped for.'

In July of that same year, Grandpa and Grandma Wright both left England for the first time. They were met at Idlewild by my dad, who had traveled out some weeks beforehand, and Grandpa Holton, who drove them all across to Geneseo. Jack had wanted to pay for their flights, but the Wrights had absolutely insisted on paying their own way, though how they managed to do so is a mystery to me. At least the Holtons could offer the Wrights a place to stay for the week they would be in town, while Dad stayed over with the Petersens. Already he had a new job, thanks to some string-pulling by Jack Holton, who had convinced the owner of the mill in Nunda, the man who Jack had come to admire so much for investing during the Depression, to take on dad in the lumber yard.

The wedding took place at St. Michael's Church, with the Petersens bolstering the groom's side of the congregation to a grand total of eight – John and Edith, Franklyn and Olive, Charlie and Rose and, up from Hoboken, Joe and Dorothy Meninski. After the ceremony, a reception was held at the Big Tree Inn, from where Mom and Dad departed for a weeklong honeymoon in New Hampshire. They then returned to Geneseo and made their home with Jack and Mary. I guess I must have been conceived in that house, though that is not something one tends to ask one's parents, especially parents like my dad. Whatever; by the time I was born in May 1960, this house which I now call mine was the home of Faith and Eddie Wright.

When Bobbie came down to breakfast this morning she was wearing a silky robe over her bed shirt, the robe reaching just below her knees. She shuffled into the kitchen, still half asleep it seemed to me, and yawned heartily, tucking her chin into her chest and simultaneously stretching her shoulders.

I was cooking eggs, scrambling them in a shallow pan with butter, a little cream and a pinch of cayenne.

'Sleep well?' I asked, taking a side-glance at the toaster, checking that the bread was not burning.

'Like a baby.' Bobbie croaked. 'That wine knocked me out completely. What time is it?'

'Almost ten.' I told her.

'I'd better call Jenny and let her know I'll be late picking up Becky.'

Bobbie went through to my study. I heard her pick up the 'phone, then speak tiredly, presumably to Jenny, though I did not properly hear the conversation. I was too busy finishing off the eggs, then serving them on to plates I had been warming in the oven and taking them through to the back room, where I had already laid out place settings at the table.

'All OK?' I asked when Bobbie came to join me.

'Yeah.' she replied, distractedly, answering my question whilst looking at the eggs and toast, the pot of English tea, the jug of orange juice and the bowl of fresh fruit. 'You didn't need to go to all this trouble.' she said. 'I usually get by with yogurt and an apple.'

'It's no trouble.' I told her. 'When I have guests, I like them to start the day with a good breakfast.'

She smiled and leaned forward to kiss the top of my head. 'You're too kind, Will.' she said.

She sat down opposite me and laid out one of the paper napkins on her lap.

'Any ill effects after last night?' I asked, pouring her a cup of tea.

'No.' Bobbie replied. 'I feel surprisingly clear-headed.'

'Must have been good quality wine.' I quipped, remembering that the bottle we had drunk after getting back here was a rather acidic specimen from one of the wineries out near Cayuga Lake.

'It was certainly good quality food.' said Bobbie. 'Those shrimp were delicious.'

'And how are the eggs?' I inquired, noticing how she had already begun to devour the fluffy yellow mixture. 'Up to Big Tree standards?'

'Right up there.' she smiled.

Once breakfast was over, we cleared the table together then Bobbie went upstairs to get dressed. I followed after her a couple minutes later, intending to retrieve *Sing All Of Four Seasons* from the table in Jackie's room. I pulled up on the landing, however, struck by the sight of Bobbie leaning over the sink as she brushed her teeth, the door of the bathroom wide open. As he bent forward, the back of her robe lifted slightly, exposing her well-developed calves. Her skin appeared so pale, the veins at the back of her knees so blue. I looked at her robust hips, her strong legs and wondered whether I could wake up to Bobbie *every* morning, whether I could watch that long brown hair turn fine and gray and those muscular calves become pulpy and those veins turn through purple almost to black.

I gathered my grandpa's book from the tiny third bedroom, then made my way downstairs again and read for a few minutes in my study while Bobbie was assembling herself, preparing to face the morning air and the people of Geneseo. Presently, I heard her heavy tread on the stair and got up to meet her in the hallway. She stared at me for a few seconds, neither of us saying anything, then she stepped forward and we embraced, holding each other firmly, Bobbie with her head resting on my shoulder.

'Thanks.' she said, kissing me on the cheek.

'My pleasure.' I replied.


Mom's last Christmas was a bleak affair, the effects of her illness compounded by her insistence that she should attend the funeral of her Aunt Clara, who, at ninety-two, had died in a Rochester nursing home. I took time out from Greenleaf to go along to the service at some nondescript chapel in Henrietta, whose empty pews accentuated the shrinking of the Holton family. 'The troops' had all gone and now only Mom and I were left, neither of us still carrying the Holton surname.

Clara was buried on December 23$^{rd}$, so there was little point in me returning to New York City before the holidays. We drove back to Geneseo in the late afternoon, motoring past desolate fields and leafless trees that soon disappeared as darkness fell. In many ways that gloom did not lift throughout my stay. All I remember is grayness, a dour, spiritless atmosphere that so patently portended Mom's imminent passing.

The only chink of light was a visit from Charlie and Rose on the evening of Christmas Day. For maybe two hours, they sat and reminisced with Mom, talking about the days just after the Second World War, when the town's population mushroomed and the businesses on Main Street did a handsome trade. Mom and Rose recalled how they would both run errands for their mothers, fetching groceries from the Red & White Food Store, sometimes stopping off at the Campus Dairy Bar for milk shakes or sodas. Charlie remembered his parents eating at the Spanish Lantern Restaurant and how they had taken Rose and himself there when they had become engaged. He recalled the Park back then, the Mary Jemison Day parades and the building of the Mount Morris Dam. Mom said very little, she just smiled and nodded, her mind engaged, but her body unable to muster the energy to participate, even when Charlie and Rose were laughing aloud at the thought of some of the cheesy films they had all once gone to see at The Riviera.

I wonder now how much Mom's responses were the product of her illness and how much they were influenced by the obvious but unspoken allusions to Raymond Petersen. It would have been around that time, the early 1950s, that Mom and Ray were dating. They would probably have sometimes gone together to the Dairy Bar or The Riviera. Undoubtedly they would also have gone out together to the Park to see the construction work on the dam. Any nostalgia for that period could only have been tinged with sadness and regrets, even if, not so long afterwards, a tall Englishman called Eddie Wright had arrived in town. Despite the outward euphoria at meeting her future husband, Mom's feelings must, at times, have been mixed as she went to the same places with my dad as she once had with Ray.

One certainty about Dad's arrival in Geneseo is that he could not have been around too long before realizing that, almost two centuries since the settlement was founded, it was impossible to keep the Wadsworths out of the headlines. Indeed, throughout the 1950s, members of the Wadsworth dynasty were making news much further afield than Livingston County. Congressman James Wolcott Wadsworth Jr. died in 1952, but his son Jerry continued the family's political involvement as a State Assemblyman. He later joined the diplomatic corps and was appointed by President Eisenhower as chief disarmament negotiator. In 1960, he succeeded Henry Cabot Lodge as US Ambassador to the United Nations. Meanwhile, his brother-in-law, Stuart Symington, who had married Jerry's sister Evelyn, had followed a successful business career by becoming, in 1953, US Senator for the state of Missouri. Just as Jerry was moving to his role with the UN, Stuart was challenging for the Democratic presidential nomination, the exploits of both men tracked avidly by the people of the Genesee Valley.

It was John Kennedy who won the election that year, defeating Richard Nixon by a hairsbreadth. I was six months old at the time, my Christening had passed a few weeks before and my grandparents from England had returned home after witnessing what Mom said were some of the most intense fall colors she had ever seen. The Wrights' second grandchild, Valerie Salter, was born early in 1962. In that same year, down in Hershey, Pennsylvania, Laurel Samuels gave birth to a baby daughter who she and her husband Al named Kelly Maria. By late summer, another baby was on its way, nestled it was thought safely in my Mom's womb.

Jackie's death was the prelude to a dark time for my parents, a time of which I was thankfully way too young to be conscious. In November 1963 came the shooting in Dallas of JFK. I do not remember the event, but I do recall the President's coffin, draped in the Stars and Stripes, presumably when it was lying in state at the Capitol. It was a troubling vision for this three-year-old, who woke up in the middle of many subsequent nights, his dreams haunted by the image of that same coffin resting at the foot of his bed. Roused by my screaming, Mom would come into my room and often sleep with me in my little single bed, comforting me with the warmth of her body and the subtle regularity of her breathing. I had no idea of the anguish she was suffering. Even when her father, Jack Holton, slipped away in a Rochester hospital early the following year, I did not sense her desolation. She must have been some actress.

Franklyn Petersen was the next to go, in the late summer of 1965. He passed away in his sleep, a far better way to go than that endured by Grandpa Wright, who had long been wracked by pain from a cirrhotic liver and ailed by the loss of half his lung capacity to cancer. His only consolation was lingering long enough to see his third grandchild, Anna, who was born in May 1966, two months before John's heart gave up trying to sustain his awfully diseased body.

By this time, I was a little more cognizant of world around me. I remember two or three occasions when I spoke with Grandpa Wright over the telephone, times when he always called me 'boy'.

'How are you, boy?' he would ask. 'You seen any o'them rockets?'

He was referring to the American space shots, which somehow he thought I would be able to see, this despite their being launched from Florida. Nevertheless, I was, even at five or six years old, more than aware of those Gemini missions, by which my Dad seemed completely gripped. They were,

I guess, a supreme example of Americanism, of the excitement and progressiveness that had been so fundamental to his fascination with this country. Unlike my mom, who would soon be using the big map to teach me about this area, Dad was not the sort who would sit me down and talk to me about the space program. Instead, I picked up names and buzzwords more as a by-product of his conversations with Charlie and our neighbor, Dick Wrigley, and Dad's telephone calls to Joe Meninski, who was apparently just as enthralled by it all.

The first time I remember exactly where I was and what I was doing when a major news event occurred was in January 1967. I had been unwell all day and had not been at school, my temperature sky high and my throat raw with infection. I had been lying around on the sofa, oscillating in and out of confused sleep, my mom content to leave me there, within instant reach, even late into the evening. It was, I would say, around ten o'clock that night when the TV show my parents were watching was interrupted by a news flash. There had been a fire at Cape Kennedy; three astronauts had been killed while testing the first of the new Apollo capsules. I heard the names: Gus Grissom, one of my heroes, the second American in space, commander of the first Gemini; Ed White, the first American space-walker, a national hero; Roger Chaffee, a rookie.

'What's a rookie?' I asked my dad, thinking it was a technical term.

Later that year, Robert Kennedy was shot dead in Chicago and once again I remember precisely when I first heard the news – listening to the radio while eating breakfast the following morning. It was also the same day that Grandma Holton received a call from her cousin, Ann Stafford, known, by then, for many years as Mrs. Joseph Lawson. It was an unusual call, the two women having rarely conversed in recent times, their only regular contact being through brief notes in Christmas cards. Unsurprisingly in such circumstances, Ann's call was not for idle chatter. Her son, Scott, just twenty years old, had been killed in Viet Nam.

Scott's body was flown back to the USA and he was buried in his local cemetery in Zanesville, Ohio. Both my parents went to the funeral service, even though they had only met the young man once. I think it was at that time that I realized they both kept special clothes for such somber occasions. My dad had a rather old dark suit and a plain black tie, while Mom had a black dress, with a white collar, and wore this, in winter, with a knee length black coat. None of these clothes ever emerged from their closets except on the days of funerals, which meant they saw plenty more use before the decade was over.

Apart from the apparition of Kennedy's casket in my bedroom, the first coffin I actually saw was that of Olive Petersen. I recall distinctly how the pallbearers almost buckled under its weight as they lifted it from the hearse at St. Michael's Church. I recall, also, the sight of little Bobbie standing by the curbside, holding tightly on to Rose's hand. My mom had thought me too young to attend the funeral, but, after one of the rare overt arguments between my parents, Dad's contrary view had prevailed, so there I was, surrounded and deeply effected by the weight of all that mourning, an emotion I had never directly encountered before. I did not admit to feeling overwhelmed, however. Even if I had not experienced the grief of death, somehow I knew it was something I had to bear, stiff-lipped and impassively robust. I was, indeed, my father's son.

That Christmas, Joe and Dorothy Meninski came to stay with us and we all sat spellbound as we listened to the transmissions from Apollo 8 as it orbited the moon. The three crewmen read the first ten verses from Genesis, the story of the Creation. Joe swallowed hard, both Mom and Dorothy were weeping. 'Goodnight, good luck,' said a distant voice, 'a merry Christmas and God bless all of you – all of you on the good Earth.' In a way, that moment gave us a sense that the coming year would be brighter, better, that the divisions in our nation would be healed, that maybe the war that had claimed Scott Lawson's young life would come to an end. We were, after all, going to the moon and, if America could achieve that, then really it could achieve anything to which it set its collective mind.

Unfortunately, 1969 did not get off to a start as auspicious as we had hoped. First came news of Harriet Weber's death, Aunt Hatty, who had, on a number of occasions during my early childhood, arrived unannounced to create havoc in the Wright household. She had the rudest manner, viewing her visits as an opportunity to criticize everything from the number of weeds in the front lawn to my parents' choice of wallpaper. She would run her finger along the tops of tables, tutting at even the merest hint of dust. She would, if Dad had not concocted some pretext to get both of us out of the house, insist that I sit with her in the front room as she passed on the benefit of her great wisdom to my mom. I was not allowed to speak, of course. I was there to listen. Thus, when news arrived of her demise, I cannot say the Wright family suffered any profound sense of loss. The absolute opposite was true two months later, however, when Aunt Angela called to tell us that

Grandma Wright had fallen down the stairs of her house and was critically ill in hospital. I could tell from the look on my mom's face that the prognosis was not good, though I had not been prepared for the swiftness of Grandma's death. She passed away that same afternoon.

Just as they had when John Wright had died, Mom and Dad flew off to England, leaving me in the care of Charlie and Rose. I was desperately upset, not just at Grandma's passing, but also at being excluded from attending the funeral. It is disturbing now to contrast those feelings with the way I felt, in September of that same year, when Grandma Holton died. Edith Wright, even though she was thousands of miles away and existed only in infrequent telephone calls, had a much warmer presence than ever had Mary Holton, who lived only a five minute walk away. I do not believe I shed a single tear for Grandma Holton. I know for sure that I was indifferent about being at her funeral and that, this time, Dad's insistence was not exactly welcome.

I wish I could look back to a time, just a single instance, when I remember Grandma Holton with a sense of affection. Always, though, her weasel-like face comes to mind, her staid clothes, her lacquered gray hair, everything about her stiff and unapproachable. Just a few months before she died, she sat with us and watched Neil Armstrong and Colonel Buzz take Man's first steps on the moon, perhaps the greatest human achievement since Creation. Yet, Grandma was utterly unmoved, commenting only on the grainy quality of the television pictures. The next day, we held our Moon Landing Party and once again Grandma could not be drawn into the celebratory nature of the occasion, as is evidenced by that home movie Charlie has.

The seventies arrived without fanfare. The Viet Nam War was still far from over and there was every sign that the country's economy was about to go into severe decline. Double-digit inflation was just around the corner and the unemployment rate was about to nudge five percent. In 1970 alone, over sixty-six million working days would be lost to industrial action, with the sixty-seven day long strike at General Motors contributing in no short measure to that number. However, these were statistics about which I would not learn the significance until ten years later. Back then, I was far more interested in *Square One TV* and *3-2-1 Contact*.

One event that did grab my attention, though, was the one that shook and galvanized the country that April of 1970. I was in bed when the story broke on the TV news bulletins, so, in the same way as I had learned of Robert Kennedy's assassination, I discovered over breakfast that the crewmen of Apollo 13 were in mortal peril. This time, I heard the news not from the radio, but from my dad, who had already taken on a countenance of steely determination, as though he were one of those directly responsible for getting the astronauts home alive. The English are at their very best in a crisis, even when their involvement is purely vicarious. Before the explosion aboard the spacecraft, there had been a distinct lack of interest in this third attempt at a moon landing, but now everyone seemed to be following the story, including my teachers, who gave us kids updates throughout that day. Apart from the jubilation of the astronauts' successful return to Earth, the predominant memory I have is of hearing the tired voice of Jim Lovell, the mission commander, as he communicated with the control room in Houston. Here was one of the men who had read from the Bible as he circled the moon on Apollo 8, one of the men who had seemed to instill such hope in us all. Now he was battling for his life aboard a stricken ship and somehow, even to this ten-year-old, that served as some sort of metaphor for the jeopardy that hope was now facing.

I was growing up. School was becoming more serious. The first thoughts of escape were beginning to flit across my mind, escape from what I was starting to see as being a town on the outskirts of nowhere. Soon, I would also have the first inkling of another adolescent characteristic.

When I was twelve, Hurricane Agnes moved up from the Gulf of Mexico, right along the east coast, before turning inland and crossing Pennsylvania and the southern part of New York State. In less than a week, they recorded almost fourteen inches of rain in Wellsville, down near the Pennsylvania border. On the upper Genesee, the floods were devastating, with roads and bridges washed out and the destruction of many buildings. Mercifully, the lower reaches of the river were spared the worst of the flooding thanks to the Mount Morris Dam, which saved a great area to its north from catastrophe. President Nixon declared the entire state of Pennsylvania a disaster area. In all, it was reckoned that seven hundred million dollars' worth of damage was done across twelve states, with one hundred seventeen people losing their lives, twenty-four of them up here in New York.

I went out to the Park with Mom and Dad a week after the storm had abated. Charlie and Rose went too, with Bobbie in tow, nursing a broken wrist. Ten days before, the teeming rain lashing against her window had awoken her in the night. She had climbed out of bed, intending to go to the bathroom, but had stumbled over her big toy bear, Ted, who had somehow fallen to the floor from his usual perch on the wicker chair by Bobbie's dressing table. In trying to break her fall, she had reached out with her hands and fractured her left wrist with a crack so loud that Charlie subsequently swore it had snapped him from a deep sleep. I guess Bobbie was another, admittedly minor victim of Hurricane Agnes and, on that day in the Park, she looked dejected.

I am embarrassed to admit that, on that day, I bored Bobbie to sleep by talking about the Seneca. I believe I told her that the problems the storm had caused us were nothing by comparison with what the Seneca must have suffered when the Genesee flooded, as it was want to do, on average, every seven years. Doubtless I would have related the full history of the tribe, the key dates, the names of the great chiefs and acclaimed warriors, the role they played in the Iroquois Confederacy and in the Revolutionary War. Poor Bobbie, she must have thought I was an appalling swot. No wonder she dozed off. I watched her sleeping for a while, then, oh so carefully, I put my arm around her, the first time I had ever cuddled a girl, the first time I had experienced that special tingling in my loins.

I already knew Linda Danelli, though she was a swarthy girl with a shape that had all the potential of becoming increasingly pudding-like. Certainly I had no great attraction towards her and I think if I had been told, then, that she would be the girl with whom I would lose my virginity, I would have seriously doubted my informant's sanity. Before Linda would transform into the tan beauty of her latter teens, I would find myself immersed in other distractions. At school, I was turning away from Geography and History, a rebellion, I realize now, against what I saw as my mom trying to brainwash me into worshipping Cow Town. I turned, instead, to Math and Science, as well as to what would appear today to be the school's antique computer facilities. Not only were these subjects of interest to me, not only was I pretty good at them, but also they seemed to offer a hint of escape. When merged with some very basic business studies in the senior year, they helped create a door through which I knew I could pass into a different, far more exciting world. The music I liked at that time was all otherworldly, surreal, music by people like David Bowie and Pink Floyd. I watched science fiction TV shows and read books about space exploration and time travel. Even the sports teams I supported – the Knicks, the Giants, and most of all the Yankees – provided me with some sort of conduit into a place I would rather be, into New York City.

We went to the city maybe half a dozen times each year, often combining our visits with a trip out to Hoboken to see Joe Meninski. In early 1978, I made my first trip to Manhattan alone, taking the train from Rochester and spending a whole day at the Columbia Business School, where I was interviewed and tested and given a guided tour. Some time later, I found that I had been accepted. At last escape had come. I was going to the city, not to visit, but to live. I was going to be an Ivy League boy and suddenly I was everyone's flavor of the month, including with the local newspaper, which ran a small story on me, and with the recently slim-line temptress who had once been tubby little Linda Danelli.

In actuality, I never did escape Geneseo, for even when I was consumed in the inferno of New York City, my mom was still ensuring that I received regular reports on events hereabouts, 'phoning me every weekend with updates and analysis, much like my own personal 24 Seven. At first, I found myself switching off to anything other than direct family matters, like dear Great Uncle Hartley's death in 1982. Slowly, though, I realized I was, in fact, quite interested, that news from boring old Livingston County did touch a nerve in me. Even after I met Kelly, I did still come back here alone sometimes, usually when she spent a weekend in Hershey. I would find myself down at The Inbetween, hanging out with some of my old school friends and discussing things that would have once seemed stultifyingly trivial, like W. P. Wadsworth's son Austin inheriting The Homestead or the opening of the National Warplane Museum. In 1989, we even had an astronaut of our own to talk about, James C. Adamson, who had been born over in Warsaw and whose father lived in Groveland. Not that his first Space Shuttle mission caused anywhere near as big a stir as the furore over the building of the Genesee Valley Shopping Center. Week after week, month after month, Mom called to tell me the latest twists and turns in the saga that saw village, town and county authorities embroiled in the most mind-numbing politics, all because Wal-Mart wanted to come to town. I guess it provided me with a counterpoint to the concurrent breakdown of my marriage and offered Mom some distraction from her terrifying illness.

My constant awareness of what was going on back here undoubtedly contributed to me deciding to return when my mom died two-and-a-half years ago. It also eased the transition. Because, in a sense, I had never left, never escaped, I slipped back into life here without any difficulty. It was instantly familiar, not just the buildings and the landscape and the history, but the culture, the way the people think and behave. I never once felt isolated or, to recall again Sally Caspar's word, abandoned. Despite all that, it was a poignant time. I believed Mom had gone too soon, not just because she was only sixty-four, but because there were so many things I wanted to tell her. I wanted to thank her for raising me so well, for loving me so completely, for always supporting me, for never once interfering in my life, even when her good sense would have made such a difference. I wanted also to tell her how sorry I was that I had been unable to sustain my marriage to Kelly, who I know she loved greatly. One Sunday evening, maybe a month after I had moved back to Geneseo, I drove out to the Park and stood alone at Inspiration Point. I knew Mom was there. I stared out across the river and told her all those things I had failed to tell her when she was alive. 'Forgive me.' I said aloud.

I threw myself into redecorating this house not because I wanted to cast out the memory of my mom, but because I wanted to please her, to show her that I was going to take care of the place in which she had lived for so long. Every fabric I chose, every item of furniture I picked, I thought of Mom and tried to ensure she would approve. Now I am studying History, again seeking her approval, rekindling the spirit of those childhood days with the big map.

On Christmas Eve last year, I was back again in Manhattan, arriving by bus from JFK, having flown in from Rochester. I took a cab from Grand Central to Kelly's apartment on the Upper East Side. She greeted me nervously, kissed me on the cheek and took my bag from me, placing it in her second bedroom. We then had coffee and talked about what we should do over the next four days – skating at Rockefeller Plaza, maybe a wander through the Central Park zoo or a ride out to the art shops on Staten Island or a visit to the Guggenheim or MoMA. As we gradually relaxed, I began to take in my surroundings. She still had the Shaker furniture; she had original paintings by two of the trendiest artists around; she had a fine sculpture, another original, of a horse rearing up on its hind legs, nostrils flared, ears pricked, muscles rippling along its flanks. This stuff was all so tasteful, so carefully and thoughtfully collected, yet the apartment had the feel more of a gallery than a home.

We went out that evening, first to a bar in the East Village, then to a restaurant across town, close to Park Avenue. It was a French place, with tricolors intermingled with the Christmas bunting and waiters with unconvincing accents. The food was sensational, each mouthful made even more enjoyable by my being able to look across the table at Kelly. Her blue dress was not substantially dissimilar to the one she had worn the last time we had eaten out together, though this had a broader neck still and revealed tantalizing glimpses of her shoulders. She was wearing, also, her eternity ring, which from time to time she would touch, thinking I was not looking. It was as though she was extracting from it some sense of reassurance, some strength, some confirmation that what she was doing was right.

Another bar followed the meal, which meant that we found ourselves hunting a cab at two o'clock on Christmas morning, which proved to be a prolonged and ultimately expensive exercise. We arrived back at Kelly's apartment some time near three and collapsed on to the sofa, both of us exhausted but buzzing. Kelly slipped off her shoes, then laid her legs across my lap. I rubbed her feet and she closed her eyes, resting her head on the sofa's deep cushions.

'That is *so* good.' she said. 'So soothing.'

'Hay.' I replied. 'I'm glad you like it.'

'I like *you*, Will Wright. I've always liked you. You've got more good sense than anyone else I've known. I must have been crazy to let you go.'

This unaccustomed proximity was driving *me* crazy, the sensuous feel of her skin through the silky smoothness of her stockings. That same tingle I had first felt all those years before, when I had wrapped my arm around Bobbie's young shoulders, was awakening again now.

'I shouldn't have cut you off the way I did.' Kelly continued. 'I shouldn't have been so cold, especially at your mom's funeral. I was just building a shell around myself.'

'Sure.' I said, understandingly. 'You wanted to protect yourself.'

'No.' Kelly shook her head. 'I was trying to protect *you*. Maybe I didn't realize that at the time, but now I do. I still cared about you, still wanted you, but I knew that being with me would hurt you, so I built the shell to repel you, to make myself undesirable.'

'And was buying that Wal-Mart underwear all part of the same plan?'

She laughed. 'Not exactly, but, if you'd seen it, it would have made a *major* contribution.'

I stopped massaging her feet and ran my hand up her leg to her knee. 'You're not wearing it tonight, are you?' I asked, smiling suggestively. Suddenly, her expression hardened into a frown. I took my hand away but just as suddenly as her face had changed, she grabbed hold of my wrist and pulled me towards her.

Her lips were so soft as I kissed them, so amazingly soft. I felt her hand on the back of my neck, drawing me closer. Her breathing became louder, her movements less smooth, more jerky, her grip tighter and tighter. I did not know what to do with my hands, settling for placing them uneasily on her side, just above her hips.

'Dear God, Will, I want you.' she said, disconcertingly frenzied now.

'I want you too, Kelly.' I told her, though how coherently I am unsure, for Kelly was apparently trying to eat my tongue.

Five minutes later we were in her bedroom, scrambling to get our clothes off before we fell onto the bed and began kissing all over again, this time with hands no longer confined to safe areas of each other's bodies. When we made love, Kelly was on top, jiggling up and down, grinding herself against me, grunting and moaning and occasionally squealing, as though I had reached some previously unentered chamber of delight. I stretched up and took hold of her head, tugging it down towards me, my fingers deep in her hair, so deep I could feel the scar on her scalp caused by her falling through that glass door nearly a decade ago. Our mouths met again, wide open, as though each of us wanted to devour the other. With a great guttural groan, Kelly reared up, and threw back her head, rocking on me now. I reached out and took hold of her breasts, her uncannily firm breasts that I quickly concluded had benefited from the discreet work of an undeniably gifted surgeon. Jeez, I thought, he's improved upon perfection. I lay there, letting her use me, my sweating palms cupping those heavenly tits. She whined, she roared, she howled like a dog and when she came she screamed so loudly I feared for the windows.

We woke late the next morning and exchanged Christmas gifts while still in bed. Kelly had bought me a gold pen, with a matching stand that incorporated a small photo frame. I had bought her a fine gold necklace and an elegant crystal vase. We hugged each other, then lay together for a while, saying little, my fingers tracing winding patterns across the smooth skin of her arms. Eventually, she decided to take a shower and slipped out of bed, into a long robe, and headed for the bathroom. I stayed in her bed and listened as the water began to run, imagining it pouring over her soapy body. Well, I reflected, Kelly has moved way beyond *Step By Step To Great Sex*. I guessed she must have been getting some practice, but at no time since we had started seeing one another again had she mentioned a boyfriend.

However, when she returned from the bathroom, I was presented with the opportunity to ask.

'Wow.' she said, a towel wrapped around her head, a glass of grapefruit juice in her hand. 'That feels better. You want to shower too.'

'Sounds good.' I replied and made to get up. Meanwhile, Kelly sat at the dressing table, took a pack of tablets from one of the drawers, popped one of the tiny white pills in her mouth, then swilled it down with the grapefruit juice. She turned, obviously aware that I was watching.

'I never stopped taking them after we split up.' she said. 'Which is just as well, I guess, because I didn't see you offering to take precautions last night.' There was a smile on her face as she said this, a cocky, malapert smile.

'Why'd you carry on taking them?' I asked, surprising myself with my nerve.

'What you mean,' said the psychology major, 'is have I slept with anyone else?'

'Sorry.' I said.

'Don't be sorry.' Kelly told me. 'It's a reasonable question. There's been a couple guys, nothing heavy, a dishy DA and a boring banker. How about you?'

'No guys.' I laughed. 'I never got quite that desperate out in the backwoods.'

'Good.' Kelly said, brushing her wet hair.

'Only one woman. One cute Canadian.' I said, continuing the alliterative motif.

'Mmmm.' Kelly hummed. 'I hope they're more interesting in bed than they are out of it.'

Once I had showered we took a walk down to a diner on 2nd Avenue and ordered the special Christmas Day brunch, which was largely the same as the regular brunch, apart from it being served on plates decorated with holly leaves. The weather was piercingly cold, so we abandoned an idea of going to Central Park and instead made our way back again to Kelly's apartment, where we watched TV and listened to Paul Simon tapes and picked at the finger food with which Kelly had stocked her kitchen cupboards, as though all her life were a buffet. In mid-evening, she fell asleep on the sofa and I sat on the floor, sipping a glass of red wine, nibbling at some Wisconsin cheese, staring at her. I thought about how her face had changed, how she had once done exercises in front of the mirror to tighten her jaw muscles and shed what she considered to be her cherubic, country girl features in favor of a narrow, almost austere metropolitan appearance. I remembered how she had looked when I had watched the videotape of her reports from Times Square, back when I had stayed in Geneseo to be with Mom. She had been smiling, but her face had become so taut that the smile was almost mistakable for a contortion of pain. Now, nine years on, as she dozed happily, I could see that country girl re-emerging.

When I was two and a half years old, in early December 1962, Mom, Grandpa Holton, Franklyn Petersen, Dad and I went to the Park on a glistening Saturday afternoon. The low sun shone through the naked trees, throwing long shadows across the Council Grounds, as the five of us trudged carefully along a half-frozen trail. Mom was heavily pregnant with Jackie, Grandpa was losing the war with his cancer, Franklyn's gangly legs were arthritic and I was riding, for most of the walk, high up on Dad's big shoulders. Our progress must therefore have been slow and no doubt a little erratic. I do not remember. I have no recollection whatsoever of that afternoon. I know about it because my Dad told me ten days before he died.

Wild geese flew in Vs above us as we clambered up to the plateau where the Council House and the old wooden cabin and the bronze statue of Mary Jemison were being slowly enveloped by the steady arrival of evening. Franklyn made for a fallen tree trunk and sat down to relieve the fire in his joints. Meanwhile, Dad lowered me to the ground and, with a zest born of being carried for too long, I dashed off towards Grandpa. He heard the pitter-patter of my approaching footsteps and turned in time to catch me as I ran straight at him, my head low like a bull. He laughed aloud, teasing me by pulling off my little woolen hat and throwing it away, as though I was now a dog practicing its retrieval exercises. I ran to collect the hat, but instead of putting it back on my head, I handed it to Grandpa, who threw it away once again. Wailing with glee at this game, I trundled off to recover it. This time, wise to Grandpa's intentions, I did pull the hat over my head, so far in fact that it almost covered my eyes. It was then, with my vision partially obscured, that I spotted Mom, who was walking away from me, towards the statue. I instantly raced after her, my short legs, clad in thick pants, working furiously to catch up. I was almost there; surely she could have heard me behind her. Grandpa, who had gone to sit with Franklyn, suddenly stood up again, afraid that I would trip or bowl Mom over or something. 'Fay!' he shouted, so as to alert my mom. She turned. She turned right around. She turned and presented me with a target. I lowered by head, reverting again to being a bull, and drove straight into her, straight into the contoured hump that contained my unborn sister.

Mom folded to the ground, all the air knocked out of her, an excruciating pain encircling her abdomen. By now, Grandpa was running towards us, but he was old and frail and breathless after a few strides. It was Dad who reached us first. He threw me aside, causing me to begin crying loudly, though everyone ignored me, including Franklyn, who was rushing as fast as his gnarled knees could manage. Mom's distress was obvious; not only was she gasping, apparently unable to breathe, but she was also writhing with agony. Dad knelt over her, one hand on her stomach, the other cradling her head, protecting it from the cold, damp grass. He looked up at Franklyn, silently soliciting the retired dentist's medical opinion, but Franklyn's only advice was to get her to a doctor. Dad stared again at Mom, helplessness doubled by uncertainty in his mind. At last, he gestured towards Grandpa, who crouched down and took Mom's hand. Dad then sprang to his feet and sprinted off towards the Upper Falls, where he had earlier parked his car.

Having moved the car to the Council Grounds lot, Dad hurried back to Mom. He lifted her gently and carried her to the dirty brown Ford, where he laid her out flat across the back seat. After that, for some reason, he headed home, rather than taking her to a hospital, not that the outcome would have been any different, I suspect. The doctor came immediately, arriving at the house before Grandpa, who had got back to Geneseo in Franklyn's station wagon and who had then collected Grandma. What he found at our house was my Dad pacing fearfully up and down the hallway. Upstairs, the doctor was tending to Mom, who had now begun to bleed. The baby was still alive, he determined, but the heartbeat was both irregular and weak. The bleeding was getting worse, bright red stains beginning to form on the white sheets, though these were soon diluted by the sudden gush of amniotic fluid as Mom's waters broke. Already displaying worryingly fragile life signs, the baby was now unprotected and open to infection.

Mom needed urgent hospitalization, but transporting her would expose her to further danger and cost valuable time. Events were simply unfolding too fast.

The doctor telephoned a local midwife, who rushed to the house and began making preparations for Mom to give birth, almost three months too soon. Dad waited in the back room with Grandpa, while I played on the floor with my toy cars and Grandma, surprisingly, went upstairs to provide assistance. Dad, therefore, could not tell me exactly what happened over the ensuing hour, during which the doctor, the midwife and Grandma tended Mom through steadily intensifying contractions until, at last, my baby sister was born. She did not cry. She never cried. From the moment her tiny body slithered free of Mom, it was plain she would not survive. The doctor tried to give her oxygen, but her breathing was so shallow that she could not properly inhale. Her heart murmured in his stethoscope, its beat, without rhythm, almost undetectable. The midwife wrapped the baby in a shawl and passed it to Mom, who held it close to her distended breasts, as if encouraging it to suckle might arouse some sign of life. That was when Dad walked into the bedroom, his inquiring gaze countered by the doctor's grim face. Mom's expression, he told me, betrayed an obvious lack of understanding as to what was going on – she clearly did not realize that the baby was on the edge of death. Again she tried to nurse it, but the baby was now flaccid, its breathing stopped. Mom's eyes widened, then danced from face to face, desperately seeking reassurance, but finding only blank, unhelpful looks.

Down in the back room with Grandpa, I was still playing, though the game had now changed from whizzing toy cars along the carpet to drawing pictures with my colored crayons. For as long as I can recall, there has been an instant etched into my memory, an instant of shocking lucidity amidst a sea of vagueness, an instant without context until my dad told me about the baby. Now I know what that instant was. It was the very moment when Mom realized her baby was dead. The house suddenly seemed filled with the most shattering scream, a piercing, primeval shriek that made Grandpa leap to his feet and hurtle upstairs, scaring me into wetting my thick pants and sitting frozen with fear in the sodden pool.

Some time later, the doctor took the baby away and left Mom sedated in bed, while Dad sat alone in the back room and I went home with my grandparents. I stayed there for four days, so I missed Mom's first appearance outside her bedroom and the telephone calls from relatives in England and friends in Geneseo. I missed, too, the Christening ceremony they had in the front room, when the undertaker brought the dead baby back to the house and the minister from St. Michael's sprinkled a vile of holy water over its cold, lifeless head. They called her Jackie, for Jacqueline Kennedy, and Mom cut a lock of her hair and framed it with a wild rose picked from the Council Grounds.

My uncle Michael died in 1994, his life ended by an illness to which no-one ever game a name. For eight years, he had carried the anguish of his youngest daughter's death and throughout that time those who knew him had witnessed his slow degeneration. Odd afflictions overcame him, few with any physical symptoms, but all with a miserable weakening effect. Little by little that effect accumulated, forcing him to retire from work, then to become almost completely housebound. There were periods in hospital, times when specialists in almost every field visited his bedside and tried to deduce some cause for his condition. Ultimately, though, their efforts were in vain. Angela believes he had given up the desire to live right from the moment they lost Anna.

The news came of Michael's death one sunny Saturday morning. I was due to view an apartment that day, having found a buyer for the place Kelly and I had shared up on West 61st. It was Valerie who called me, her voice tremulous, but clear. Michael had been taken into hospital the previous afternoon and had, overnight, simply fallen away. I offered the usual words of sympathy, the usual formula, but I cannot say that this was anything more than a reflex. It was not until hours afterwards, when I was being shown around my prospective new home, that emotion finally caught up with me. I have no idea what triggered it, maybe the sublime view of the East River from the living room window, maybe the sound of a Mozart aria percolating from the apartment below. Whatever the reason, I found myself choking on an enormous lump in my throat, my eyes stinging with tears I tried so hard not to let roll down my cheeks. I made some hurried excuse to the letting agent and dashed out to the elevator, riding alone down to the lobby, then bursting out exultantly into the chill February brightness.

Not one of Michael's American family flew to England for his funeral. Mom was too ill and Dad used the excuse of not wanting to leave her alone. I could not go because of Anna.

It was another clear, crisp day, over five and a half years later, when my telephone rang and another unsteady English voice disturbed my morning routine. I had been drying the dishes after breakfast, mulling over in my mind something Gary Lennart had said to me, something about historical revisionism being a luxury of wealth and security. Like much of what he says, it had sounded as though he was composing, out loud, the title for a future essay.

'Hello there.' I said cheerfully as I cupped the telephone receiver in a damp hand. I had anticipated the call being from Bobbie, who had left a sweater behind when she and Becky had stopped by the previous evening.

'Is that William?' the caller asked warily.

'Yes.' I said.

'It's Auntie Angela here. I hope it's not too early to be ringing you.'

'Not at all. It's past nine o'clock. Nice to hear from you.'

There was a brief silence of the kind that steadies the speaker and prepares the listener for dreadful news.

'Look.' she said. 'I'm calling about your dad, William.'

I knew he was dead. That silence, that tone of voice. She did not have to tell me.

'When did it happen?' I asked, jumping ahead in the conversation.

'This morning.' Angela replied, unfazed. 'We found him in his flat.'

'I need to come over there.' I said.

'Yes.' my aunt answered evenly.

We talked a little more, mostly about practical arrangements, not about the manner or circumstances of my dad's death. I told her I needed to make some calls and that I would get back to her within the hour to let her know what I had planned.

That hour began with a call to the airline, then one to Charlie and Rose, who, at first, said they would go to England with me. Eventually, though, I managed to convince them against that idea. Next, I left a message on Kelly's voice mail, knowing she was in DC until the weekend. Steve Caspar followed on my mental list, which meant 'phoning The Greenleaf Corporation and having his PA pull him from a meeting.

'For Chrissakes, Will.' he ranted. 'Couldn't this wait?'

'My dad's dead.' I said in monotone.

'So what's that got to do with me?' he asked. I let him consider his question for a moment. '*Fuck.*' he suddenly shouted. 'What am I saying?'

'It's all right, Steve.' I told him. 'I'm just angling for a drive to JFK on Saturday. Can I leave my car at your place?'

'Sure.' he agreed, still sounding like he had walked into a wall. 'Sure. No problem.'

I did not really have time to let Steve grovel his way out of his self-constructed hole, so I told him we would talk more when I got to Westchester. I still needed to make one more call before getting back to Aunt Angela.

The last time I had seen Joe Meninski was, in passing, at my mom's funeral. I had no idea whether he and Dad had remained in touch, or indeed whether he was still alive. I got his number through Directory Assistance and tapped it into the 'phone with a fair degree of apprehension. I was envisaging an old man with a cracked voice and a confused memory, but Joe Meninski instantly disabused me of that vision. His voice was clear and strong, his memory cogent and complete to an extent that a man half his age would envy. Of course he remembered Eddie Wright. He remembered me too, mostly as a kid when my parents took me to see him as a sort of side-trip during our visits to New York City.

'Dear Lord in heaven.' he said when I told him Dad had died. 'How old was he?'

'Sixty-seven.' I replied.

'No age at all.' Joe snorted. 'Had he been ill?'

'Not that I know of.'

'Sixty-seven.' Joe repeated. 'Sixty-seven. Do you know how old I am, son?'

'No sir.' I said.

'Seventy-eight.' came the rapier-like response. 'I was around when Lindbergh first flew the Atlantic and when Armstrong first walked on the moon. I grew up during the Depression, built roads with the Conservation Corps, took a sniper's bullet in France, watched the Berlin Wall go up and come down. I've seen Presidents shot and resign and have affairs with young girls. I've lived a long time, son. I've lived so long that now I'm going to stand over the grave of that funny little kid I met on a train fifty-some years ago.'

'The funeral will be in England.' I said.

'I know.' he replied. 'I'll be there.'

'You really don't have to come.' I told him, using the same phrase as I had earlier with Charlie and Rose.

'Yes I do.' Joe said with unchallengable finality.

Having closed my conversation with Joe, I called Aunt Angela again and told her I would be arriving early on Sunday morning. Rather than trouble her to meet me, I said I would find my own way to Letchworth, then 'phone her from the railroad station. She seemed relieved that I would be there so soon.

Just as when my uncle had died, I felt no immediate emotion. Instead, my brain seemed to be saying to me: 'OK. So that's that, what next?' It was a strange feeling, one about which I felt simultaneously proud and ashamed. Proud that I had weathered such tragic news in so composed a manner, ashamed that the sudden death of my own father could not evoke even the foretaste of tears. Only when I left the house and drove down to Main Street did that calmness begin to crack. I was about to break the news to someone face-to-face for the first time. I was about to tell Bobbie.

# Sunday

❀

Why did my dad tell me about Jackie?

'Hello Will.' he said, a little hoarsely. 'It's your dad.'

'Hay, Dad. How are you today?'

'Not so bad, I suppose. Had a bit of a cold, but I think the worst of it's over. Are *you* all right?'

'Yeah, fine. I went across to the city for Labor Day weekend.'

'Did you see Kelly?'

'Sure did.'

'How is she?'

'She's good. As busy as ever, but looking well.'

This was all the standard stuff, a sort of housekeeping call, checking on news and welfare. It went on like that for a while, but I could detect something in Dad's voice, something pushing harder and harder to break out.

'William.' he at last said, with a weight and formality that drew a line beneath all that had gone before. 'I want to tell you about Jackie.'

Then it flowed, like a river bursting its banks. Dad's voice remained calm, emotionless, as though he had rehearsed the story over and over in his head, which doubtless he had. To begin with, he kept it factual, maybe a little like Teddy Hewson when he had had to deliver the news of Raymond Petersen's death. I needed more, though; I needed the same embellishment Grandma had sought. I needed more than Dad's equivalent of 'Ray's dead.' I needed more than 'You killed your sister'; not that Dad actually used *those* words. I probed deeper, made him fill in more detail, forced him into descriptions rather than allow him his usual preference for basic essentials. No matter how much he told me, the implication remained clear. I had killed my sister.

'I just thought you should know.' he said, as the conversation came to a horribly uncomfortable end.

'Yeah, Dad.' I said, feeling dazed. 'Thanks.'

I went upstairs to my bedroom, the room in which Jackie had died, and looked at the lock of her hair in that silver frame. I had never known that she was dead when Mom cut it from her head. Somehow I had always imagined a tiny baby fighting for its life in an incubator somewhere, a moment when Mom, realizing her daughter was not going to pull through, had carefully snipped the dark downy hairs from beside a warm, shallowly pulsating fontanel. Now that picture had been brutally corrected.

I had to call Kelly. I had to talk with someone who could offer me some explanations and my ex-wife is never short of those.

'Dear God, Will.' she exclaimed when I told her what Dad had said.

'Why did he do it, Kelly?' I asked. 'Why did he tell me?'

'Maybe he's just a bastard.' Kelly offered, but she could tell I was looking for something more enlightening. 'Sorry, Will.' she said, switching adroitly from Bronx mode to dispassionate Hershey. She took a breath. 'He's obviously been carrying this around inside for years, never talking to anyone about it. Sometimes people get to the stage where they *have* to talk about it, otherwise they feel like it'll consume them, eat them up. He may well have got to that point, especially living alone over in England.

'He might also have been trying to offload or share his own guilt. You say he took your mom home after the accident, rather than taking her to hospital. Maybe he blames himself for the baby dying, maybe he's had to live with the thought that, if he'd taken her to hospital, the baby might have survived. Now he needs someone else to take part of the responsibility.

'Remember too, Will, that he saw his child die, he saw the scene of her death, the circumstances – the doctor, the blood, your poor mom in a terrible, terrible state. That scene would have been harrowing for anyone, but your dad is the sort of guy who keeps it all to himself. Maybe after all these years he needed to blow, like a safety valve. Maybe he wants sympathy or consolation. Maybe he wants other people to realize that *he* went through hell, just like your mom.'

'So you're saying it's a cry for help?'

'It could be. It could be all sorts of things.'

'What I can't understand is why he wanted to tell me now. After so long.'

'Oh, Will. There are so many possible answers to that. He's probably been wanting to tell you for years, but has never found the courage.

Sometimes, though, when that safety valve blows, lack of courage is overcome by sheer desperation. Also, being so far away may have made it easier for him – he didn't have to tell you in person, he could do it by 'phone, protected from your reaction by the distance between you.'

'I think you're right, Kelly. I think he does feel guilt and maybe that guilt has made him feel unworthy of other people's sympathy. He's wanted someone to put an arm around him and comfort him, but he's never felt truly entitled to that.'

Kelly murmured in dubious agreement, as though she was happy that I had found a rationalization that suited me, even if it was not one in which *she* had absolute faith.

'Actually, Will.' she began again after a lengthy pause for thought. 'I don't think what happened that day could have caused your mom to lose the baby. Not *just* that. Women suffer all sorts of injuries without miscarrying, especially that late in pregnancy. I think there was something else, some other reason.'

'Such as?'

I heard Kelly inhale sharply, then breathe out again with a heavy sigh. 'You remember years ago, Will?' she asked. 'When your mom was ill and we weren't sure about going ahead with the wedding and I went out to Geneseo to talk with her?'

'I remember.'

'Well, she told me a lot of things, things about her illnesses. Did you know that she'd suffered from menstrual problems - awful pain and really heavy bleeding?'

'No.'

'Well she had. Ever since she was a teenager, apparently. Sometimes that sort of thing puts itself right after a woman has had a baby, but in your mom's case it never got better.'

'I can't see how that would account for what happened when she lost Jackie?'

'It probably wouldn't. Not directly. When your Mom told me about the symptoms, I had a talk with one of my friends at the Columbia Med. School and she thought that maybe your mom had some sort of malformation of her uterus.'

'And a malformed uterus increases the risk of miscarriage or premature birth?'

'Precisely. Some sort of abdominal injury might possibly exacerbate the situation, but it wouldn't be the root cause of premature labor.'

I wanted to believe what Kelly was saying, but I could not escape the fact that it was based on the diagnosis of an undergraduate who had not even spoken with the patient, let alone conducted an examination.

'If Mom did have some sort of abnormality,' I said, 'why wouldn't her doctors have found it?'

'I don't know, Will.' Kelly conceded. 'All I can think is that it was a long time ago when all this was happening, back in the fifties and sixties, when they didn't have such sophisticated medical technology as we do today'

'That's true. I guess it could have been missed.'

'Yes, it could, particularly as she delivered you quite normally and there was no history of anything similar with other women in the family.'

I suddenly thought of Virginia Holton and the description Thomas Holton had written of her death, a description composed after his meeting with Virginia's sister Rebecca. 'There was.' I said, in a *eureka* tone of voice. 'Way back in the early nineteenth century.'

'Mmmm.' Kelly mumbled doubtfully.

'OK, it's a long shot, but there could be a link.'

'There *could*, but I think there's better contemporary evidence to support the malformation premise.'

'Like what?'

'Well, again according to my friend at the Med. School, *some* abnormalities of the pelvic organs increase, *statistically*, the chances of a woman developing uterine or ovarian cancer.'

'Which is exactly what happened to Mom.'

'That's right.'

I knew she was cherry-picking again, reaching the desired conclusion by dangerously pasting together fragments from God knows what research and third-party diagnosis, evoking the twin terrors of theory and statistics in much the same way as she did when filing her reports on WONM. Even so, and regardless of the scant respect she was showing for science, I was more than willing to be persuaded.

'Maybe I should have told you about this before,' Kelly said, 'but it was so obvious that your mom hadn't discussed the problem with anyone else. I felt as though she was telling me in confidence.'

'It's fine.' I assured her. 'I understand.'

'Thanks.' she said. 'For what it's worth, Will, I still think it sucks that your dad told you about the baby in the way he did.'

'I guess it does, but somehow I don't think he really intended to tell me that I killed Jackie.'

'No. He probably didn't. He probably knew there was some serious medical problem at the source of it.'

I could tell from Kelly's intonation that, once more, her own opinion differed from mine, but that she was content not to argue, not to risk undermining my obviously tenuous conviction.

'You're a good friend to me, Kelly.' I said

'And you are to me.' she replied. 'Let's keep it this way.'

'I agree.'


It was pouring with rain when I woke this morning, the sky outside my bedroom window a washed-out gray through which the sun could barely penetrate. It was seven o'clock. Sleep had once more been a patchy affair, wrecked by the thought of what might happen today.

I went downstairs to the kitchen and revitalized my mouth with fresh orange juice, then shambled back up to the bathroom, where I showered and shaved. I then put on a dark gray suit, white shirt and the most sober tie I possess, a perfect ensemble for going to church. Back down in my study, I checked through the final part of my essay, then sat for a while and read more from *Sing All Of Four Seasons*.

Earlier this year, Kelly and I spent a weekend out at the Hamptons, a break that rekindled memories of our first visit to Martha's Vineyard. I took a photograph of her as she sat on the veranda of our rented cottage, the aquamarine ocean in the background, the sun streaming down from a faultless sky. As I read this morning, I kept flickering glances at that photograph, which I keep in the frame Kelly bought me last Christmas. Ordinarily, the photo is secreted beneath the drop leaf front of my bureau, on view only when I am working in my study. I want no-one in Geneseo to know about

Kelly and I, about the way our relationship has unfolded over the last year. That said, I made the mistake of leaving the bureau open on the evening Becky brought me her painting, 'Fall'. Thankfully, the child was distracted by thoughts of her masterpiece adorning my wall.

By the time I left the house, the rain had miraculously stopped and I was able to walk down to Main Street without fear of a soaking. Indeed, when I reached St. Michael's, the sun had broken through the clouds and was bathing the town in brightness, the wet grass glistening, the white walls of the neighboring houses shining brilliantly. Most of my fellow churchgoers were dressed much as myself, the men in smart suits, the ladies in conservative dresses or skirts with plain blouses. Some carried bibles, others, like me, collected one as they passed through the doorway into the glorious interior. I took a seat in a pew near the back and skimmed through the pages of the worn bible, searching for nothing in particular, just trying to look interested.

The minister spoke in his sermon of tolerance, of the consequences of being judgmental. 'Do not judge, or you too will be judged.' he quoted from Matthew 7:1-2. 'For in the same way as you judge others, you will be judged and with the measure you use, it will be measured to you.' I was looking for inspiration, but what I heard was admonition. We sang *Rejoice The Lord Is King* and *Savior Again To Thy Dear Name*. We listened to the choir. We passed The Peace energetically. We placed money in the collection dish and prayed for God's guidance, seeking joy in his love. Then we left, as politely and deferentially as we had all shuffled in.

I picked up a card on my way back outside at the end of the service. It was one of a number arranged on the table near the bibles, each depicting scenes from Christ's life and offering sage words of advice or veneration. I recognized the words on mine as being an extract from a poem. 'Immortal love for ever full, forever flowing free. For ever shared, for ever whole, a never-ebbing sea!' The words of John Greenleaf Whittier.

'Take more.' one of the attendants told me enthusiastically, as though a complete set might guarantee my slot in heaven.

I smiled civilly and shook my head. 'I only need this one.' I said, slipping the card into the breast pocket of my jacket.

I shook hands with the minister and stood around for a few minutes with the rest of the congregation, aware that to depart immediately would appear improper. However, I soon ran out of small talk so, having lingered for what I thought was a respectably long enough time, I turned away and walked slowly home.

There were two messages on my answering machine, the first from Sally, who sounded frothy, light-hearted.

'Will.' she said. 'You were right. We talked and, well........ Three weeks, two days, but it was worth the wait. Thanks.'

The other message was from Bobbie, asking if she should collect Becky's picture from the framing shop tomorrow. I decided not to return her call until later in the day. Instead, I went to my room and changed out of my suit and into some jeans and a plain, bottle green shirt. I then grabbed an apple from the bowl on Grandma's old sideboard, took *Sing All Of Four Seasons* from the top of my bureau and headed out to my car.

All the way along Route 408, the road was still damp from the morning rain. In places, there were deep puddles beside the verge, some with perceptible palls of steam floating above them. At Nunda, I turned east towards North Dansville. Almost immediately, the asphalt turned dry and dusty, showing how localized that rain must have been, how it must have hugged the line of the river. The farmlands were a picture of quiescence, of sleepy Sunday, of verdant repose laced with autumnal golds and bronzes and vermillions. Through the corner of Steuben County I drove, up to Springwater, Conesus and Livonia and on to Lima, which styles itself as the 'Crossroads of Western New York'. Route 5 took me out to Avon, then across the Genesee to Caledonia, before I hooked up to Route 36, motoring south, to those namesakes of English cities, York and Leicester. I stopped briefly at Silver Lake, where the tranquil waters reflected the pageant of color around the shoreline, in places the image so perfect that the lake seemed more like a looking glass.

From Silver Lake, I drove to Perry. There I took Schenck Road into the Letchworth Park, then drove along Park Road, past the outlook near the Smokey Hollow Trail, past Gardeau and St. Helena, past the Tea Table and round the great loop of the river to the trailhead at the gorge. The whole sweep of the canyon opened up before me as I stood at the viewpoint, my baseball cap shading my eyes from the sun. Pines and firs pointed skywards from the hills across at Big Bend, their greenness at times enveloped by the dazzling deciduous foliage all around them. Below, the river looked so placid, flowing broadly up towards the Mount Morris Dam, having thrillingly negotiated the three falls that caused the Seneca to call the place Seh-ga-hun-da.

I drove next to the Council Grounds, where I parked the car and took a walk along the Mary Jemison Trail, which circles behind the Glen Iris Inn, goes beneath the railroad line and crosses the Deh-ge-wa-nus Creek, before emerging back on the Park Road above the Upper Falls. It is no hike along that trail, just a pleasant stroll, an easy-going way of enjoying the early afternoon. I cut through to the Gorge Trail and walked along the Genesee, its name taken from the Iroquoian language and meaning 'beautiful valley'. The Seneca called the river 'Casconchigon', which translates to 'river of many falls'. I wandered close to the first of those falls within the Letchworth Park, close enough indeed to be sprinkled lightly by water carried on a breath of wind. Half a mile away, the Middle Falls, the most stunning of the three, sang as sweetly as the choir at St. Michael's this morning. Children ran along the riverside path, kicking up the leaves, reaching out to touch the cascading waters, pointing excitedly at the rainbows hanging in the spray. It is that trick of water and sunlight that gave the place its more modern name, Glen Iris, Iris being a Greek goddess, messenger of the gods, who trailed her multicolored cloak in an arc across the sky. Not that those children cared too much for the ancients, just as I had cared little when my mom had first taken me to the Park, when I had hoofed through the crunching fall carpet and hollered at the sight of the rainbows. Still I get that childish thrill, still the magnificence of the place, the sublimity, especially in the fall, makes me feel as excited as those kids.

I sat in the grounds of the Glen Iris Inn and read for a while. I ate my apple, which I had bought last Tuesday at the supermarket on Lakeville Road. It was past its best. The skin had lost its shine and the flesh was a little soft. It left a tart, disagreeable taste in my mouth that I washed away with some water from the drinking fountain at the visitor center. I checked the time again – five past two.

Back at the Council Grounds, the car, which I had left in a shady spot, was now drenched with sunshine and the interior was stuffily hot. I drove the short distance to the parking area down by Inspiration Point, where again I tried to find a space in the shadow of the trees. I left the engine running for a few minutes, allowing the air conditioning to do its work. I began to read again, but the noise of the fan, combined with the sound of cars coming and going, was too distracting. I laid my book on the passenger's seat, switched off the engine, then left the car and walked to the overlook.

I was killing time, waiting nervously for my watch to edge round to exactly three o'clock. I looked at the bronze plaque and scanned the words, words I know by heart.

> *God wrought for us this scene beyond compare,*
> *But one man's loving hand protected it*
> *And gave it to his fellow men to share.*

I leaned on the wall and watched the river come crashing over the Middle Falls, the spray obscuring the view upstream of the iron span that carries the railroad across the Genesee. I surveyed the hillsides, the great slopes still burning with color, a festival of reds and browns, oranges and crimsons, yellows and maroons, colors that science tells us have no function or significance. Way up high, crows flew figures of eight about the now clear blue sky. Grosbeaks warbled in the conifers, squirrels scavenged amongst the fallen leaves, wasps and bees drifted drowsily in search of the year's last pollen. I waited. I watched the people, people taking photographs, people struck dumb by the view, people reading the lines engraved on the plaque. I watched them all, but I was waiting only for one.

'I don't believe that guy.' Kelly said to me, jabbing the erase button on her voice mail recorder having listened to a message from her boss at WONM. We had just returned to her apartment after spending the Saturday of Labor Day weekend up at Coney Island. 'He thinks I'm a piece of meat.' she continued angrily.

She had been informed that ratings increase markedly when she appears on screen in dresses rather than suits, better still red dresses with scooped necklines. 'That guy thinks all the viewers are interested in is my tits.' she said.

'He's right.' I replied.

'Thanks for your support, Will.' Kelly scoffed.

'It's the truth, Kelly. You know it as well as I do. And let's face it, they are amazing tits.'

She managed a grudging smile. 'They should be.' she said. 'They cost me enough.'

Her boss had asked her to change her plans for the following Tuesday. Rather than go to report on some child abuse conference at the Bronx

Borough Hall, he wanted her to go instead to WONM's wardrobe department in the depths of the Garment District, where she would be measured for two new dresses. 'Do you get to keep them?' I wondered.

'What?' she asked, thinking I was still talking about her bust.

'The dresses.' I explained. 'Do you get to keep them, or do they have to go back to the stores or whatever?'

'Anything I don't buy out of my allowance, they offer me at a cut price.' she said, trying to paint a calm façade on a seething interior.

'Well, that's one consolation, isn't it?' I suggested. 'Tailor-made dresses at discount prices.'

'Tailor-made?' she laughed. 'You're kidding. They take my measurements then get some buyer to call around all the wholesale places and have them send over samples. They're off the peg, Will. Nothing special. Someone told me that WONM doesn't even pay for them, that the manufacturers are so pleased to have them on TV that they give them away free. I'm nothing more than a mannequin, a clothes horse, a *dummy*.'

After an hour in the bath, she was more composed, more even-tempered. We went out to eat at a Chinese restaurant, which had been recommended by one of Kelly's colleagues, but which was way over on Staten Island. It required a cab, a ferry, then another cab to get there, a trek that proved worthwhile only because the exquisite main course of steamed fish, subtly enhanced by a curried coriander sauce, redeemed the lamentably plain and unimaginative appetizers and desserts. The journey back was no breeze, particularly on the ferry, which was peopled by a wide array of hustlers, drunks and teenage goons, all of whom stared threateningly or lasciviously at Kelly throughout the short voyage.

Back at her apartment, she made strong coffee and produced, as an accompaniment, a bottle of French brandy.

'I can't carry on like this.' she said, pouring some of the potent liquid into a huge bowl of a glass.

'Like what?' I asked.

'I can't keep doing what I do.' she replied. 'I've can't keep using people. I can't keep letting people use me.' I knew we were entering familiar terrain. I had heard numerous conversations begin this same way over the previous few months, almost all of them oiled by wine or some stronger spirit. 'I go out there and report on miserable people with miserable lives.' Kelly went on, getting into the groove. 'I try to tell the world how those poor people suffer, how their kids get battered, how their women get raped, how the police harass them, how the government ignores them. I try, Will, but no-one listens. All they want to see is a bit more of my cleavage. They don't go to work the next day and talk with their friends about those beaten up kids or those violated women. They go in and talk about my new hairstyle, or the color of my suit, even the length of my fingernails. My bosses use me to boost ratings and attract more advertisers and, in turn, I use those sad, betrayed people as a sort of backdrop, as an excuse for getting my cute ass in front of a camera.'

'Kelly.' I said. 'You've been telling me this since I don't know when.'

'I know, I know.' she sighed. 'I keep telling myself that it'll change, that *I* can change it. Every new story that comes up, I convince myself that my treatment of it will be different. Yet there I am, in front of some wailing woman or a wall covered in abusive graffiti or on the steps of some court building or welfare department, standing under a blinding light, daubing my face with make-up, checking that my earrings are hanging evenly, brushing my hair, smoothing the creases from my jacket. It's so shallow, Will. It's all style, no content. All veneer, no substance.'

'Yes Kelly.' I said, warming my glass of brandy in the palm of my hand. 'We both know it's shallow. We agreed that last Christmas. We've agreed it almost every time we've spoken to one another since.'

'I know what you're saying, Will. You don't have to tell me.'

'Really? What am I saying?'

'You're telling me to stop whining and do something about it.'

I raised my eyebrows, tacitly asking 'So?'

'So.' Kelly said, in her inherited Brooklynese. 'I guess I'd better pee or get off the john.'

Since then, she has done neither. She has continued to vacillate, to shift backwards and forwards between two completely opposite views. One day she will call to say that her job is great, that the latest story she is covering is *so* important, that the station is giving her complete latitude. The next time she calls, she will be once more disaffected, the job stinks, the story is just like all the others that have gone before it, the station has made her re-dub the report a dozen times so as to meet the demands of sponsors. More car chases, she will tell me, that is what they want. More car chases, more tense sieges, more shoot-outs, more cleavage. Now *I* have done something to change all this.

I needed to know where my relationship with Kelly is going. If she stays in Manhattan and continues with her job, then it is going nowhere. We can enjoy the time we spend together, but it will be little different from the way things were with Sarah Weston. The outcome will probably be similar, too. There is now also another dynamic in this scenario – Bobbie, or maybe, if I am being pedantic, Becky. I feel accountable for the child. I feel bound to take care of her. It feels like the right thing to do, yet, however strong that feeling may be, it is overpowered by my longing for Kelly, by my wanting her with me here. On Monday, I sent Kelly a letter. I told her, in, I hope, more elegant language, that *now* is the time to pee or forever get off the john. I told her how deeply I love her, how much I want us to be back together permanently. I told her to think about it, not to 'phone me to discuss it, just to think hard about it, then, if she wanted the same thing as me, to come here today. I told her to meet me at Inspiration Point at three o'clock. It was corny, I know, but somehow it felt natural. I did not tell her about Bobbie, but I did imply that we would probably never get another chance. In my mind, I knew that, if Kelly did not come, then I would ask Bobbie to marry me.


Kelly sent flowers to my dad's funeral, white lilies with delicate ferns. There were flowers, too, from Angela and Valerie, from Charlie and Rose, from the people at the mill in Nunda, from Bobbie and Becky. There were ten of us in the congregation at St. Paul's Church in Letchworth, me, my aunt, my cousin, Joe and Dorothy Meninski and a handful of others, all men, who Angela reckoned were the sum total of Dad's English friends. I knew none of them. In a cortege of just four cars, including the hearse, we made our way to the cemetery, where the minister spoke a few more words then committed Edward William Wright to the earth.

I had arrived at Heathrow Airport just after six o'clock the previous Sunday morning. The flight had been wretched, with turbulence and screaming babies conspiring to keep me awake for all but half an hour's dozing shortly after take-off. The food on board, a macaroni cheese with broccoli, had been kept hot for so long that it had congealed. The white wine was warm, the bread was stale and the cheese had the texture of rubber. I was not impressed. The line at immigration was well up to Newark proportions, though it killed most of the time the baggage handlers required to unload the plane and to dump the luggage on to the carousel for collection. I eventually made it to the outside world at half past seven.

To my surprise, I found there was a coach that ran between the airport and Letchworth, with only three intermediate stops, the entire journey taking around an hour and a half. Rather than catch my first look at the English countryside, I used the time to grab some more sleep. I may not have been entirely refreshed when I reached my destination, but I was feeling slightly more alive than I had when standing in that line at immigration.

I called Aunt Angela from a battered red telephone box and, twenty minutes later, she arrived in her car. Actually, it is more like a van, having been adapted so that Valerie can ride inside whilst still in her wheelchair. We drove along Pixmore Avenue, then into the town center by way of a loop around the John F. Kennedy Gardens. Angela pointed out one or two landmarks, like the Post Office and the railroad station and the old Spirella building, once known as Castle Corset. At Icknield Way, which is part of one of England's most ancient trading routes, she motioned towards Norton Common, that great tract set aside in the manner of Central Park. She then turned to the left and we headed along a street, lined randomly with trees, towards her house, a plain, rectangular semi-detached with whitewashed brick walls and a pale blue front door. It is municipal in design, functional in character, a classic example of 1930s working class housing.

Angela parked the car in the street. I climbed out, then grabbed by suitcase from the back seat and followed by aunt through her gate and along the path through her tidy, unpretentious front garden. Once inside the house, I placed my case in the hallway and walked into the living room. That was when I first saw Valerie. She smiled broadly and reached out for me to take her hand.

'How are you?' I asked cautiously, aware that the wheelchair tended to answer my question.

'One of my good days.' she said, the smile still lighting up her face.

'What's a good day?'

'One when I just have a numb, nagging pain in both legs.'

'Dare I ask what a bad day is?'

'One when it feels like I'm being dismembered by a gorilla.'

'Oh.'

My cousin's good-humored candor shocked me. It was so very different from my mom's way of enduring pain, which had been to pretend, at least in conversation with others, that it did not exist. Kelly is the only person with whom I know Mom discussed the subject.

Angela made us tea and the three of us sat in the little room talking about my flight and the bus ride to Letchworth and, eventually, about my dad. The funeral had already been arranged for the following Thursday. Dad's apartment, or flat, as Angela called it, was paid up until the end of the month. The landlord had given Angela a key, but she had not begun to clear out Dad's belongings. She asked if I would help her. I told her that of course I would, something about which she seemed intensely thankful, even though I personally viewed it as my duty.

I spent the rest of that day in the daze of jet lag, though I was determined not to go to bed until the evening so as to adjust my body as quickly as possible to English time. Just before midday, Angela went to a local church hall, where she serves lunches to old folks each Sunday. This left me with Valerie for a couple hours, a time during which it became obvious how much my cousin had altered since I had last seen her, since she had appeared in New York looking just like her dead younger sister. Now she was a thirty-seven-year-old woman, crippled by multiple sclerosis. Her hair was its natural brown, her face had become gaunt, her skin sallow and wrinkled. Her personality, too, had completely changed, had become, quite understandably, more womanly, more mature. I was so impressed at how phlegmatic she was about her condition, about the fact that it could, over time, only get worse. She was adjusted, philosophical and not at all bitter.

When Angela returned, we took a drive to Norton Common, where I pushed Valerie along the path, down the hill to the shallow valley through which runs the Pix Brook, then back up again to the parking lot. Some trees had already shed all their leaves, others were fully clad and green, while others still were passing through various dried spice tones from paprika to pale saffron. I noticed blackbirds sifting through the fallen leaves, magpies perching in the barren branches, sparrows and robins pecking at the ground for seeds. Children played on the grass, while dogs ran panting in and out of the copses. Elderly couples sat on the benches and said nothing to one another; young mothers wheeled strollers on to the wooden bridge for their infants to see the trickle of the brook. All of a sudden, I realized I was in England, that these were English birds and English dogs, English people. For some reason, though, nothing appeared foreign.

Back at Angela's house, we lit the fire and settled down to watch TV. I was rapidly losing the fight against sleep, but managed to stay conscious long enough to call Joe Meninski and tell him about the date of the funeral. It was Angela's supper that finally did for me. She called it 'tea' and served it around six o'clock, a collection of sandwiches and salad and supermarket cakes. It was hardly a feast, but it induced a state of tiredness that I was simply unable to conquer. I made my apologies and sloped off to bed.

The next morning, Valerie was collected early by a van that takes her to a special center, where she and other disabled people are employed, some assembling electronic components, others, like Valerie, in administrative jobs. This left Angela and I alone to go to Dad's flat, which was on the opposite side of the town. As we drove, Angela explained in detail for the first time what had happened on the day Dad's body had been found. One of his neighbors had become concerned, having not seen Dad for three days and having noticed that his Sunday newspaper had not been removed from his letterbox. At night, there had been no lights in the flat and the curtains had remained drawn throughout the day. The concerned neighbor had contacted the landlord, who had, in turn, contacted Angela, who Dad had named on the rental paperwork as his next of kin. Together with the landlord, Angela had gone into the flat and had found Dad dead in his bed.

'He died in his sleep.' Angela said, repeating what she had told me the previous day. 'I don't think he suffered at all.'

'You didn't tell me the cause.' I said.

'His heart just gave out.' Angela replied, rather vaguely.

The flat was part of an old family home that had been converted into three separate residences some time back in the 1960s. It was not unpleasant, just a little shabby. We had already decided that everything we could remove, like Dad's clothes and his small possessions, such as his kitchen equipment, his radio and his television would be given to a children's charity. Items of furniture would be removed later by a house clearance firm and the proceeds would go to aid cancer research. We would then agree between us who should keep the personal things, though neither of us knew how many of these there would be. As it turned out, there were very few, just a bunch of letters, one of Mom's paintings that Dad had hung above his fireplace, an old atlas, a scrapbook of newspaper clippings from the time of the first moon landing and a battered photograph album.

'Goodness gracious.' Angela exclaimed as I carried the album from Dad's bedroom and into the living room, where she was filling trash bin liners with bundles of clothes. 'I haven't seen that in years. He had it when he was a boy. Uncle Percy sent it to him for his birthday.'

'Did he leave it with you when he moved to America?' I asked, sure that I had never seen it before.

'Oh no.' Angela said. 'He wouldn't have left it. That album was the one thing he had much affection for.'

'He must have kept it hidden.' I told her and she assumed an expression that suggested bewilderment at my surprise.

I sat down and began to leaf through the pages. There were pictures of Grandma and Grandpa Wright and of a winsome Angela with a small, thin young Michael. There were shots from around Letchworth in the 1950s, plus a handful taken at London Zoo and seaside resorts like Great Yarmouth and Brighton and Clacton-On-Sea. I found color photographs, clearly taken when he was living in Geneseo, snaps of Mom and me in our back yard, of Charlie and Rose and even one of Grandpa Holton sitting on his porch. There was no order to the pictures. Color prints were placed side by side with black-and-white images - a fine photo of fall colors in the Park preceded one showing Dad's parents walking through a corn field and was followed by one of Kelly and I taken on our wedding day.

When I reached the final page, I found a small paper bag laid flat against the back cover. Inside were two more pictures that he had obviously decided not to fix into the album. Indeed, they seemed to have been left in the bag so as to protect them. I took them out delicately, sensing their importance and maybe their fragility. One was of Mom, a beautiful shot of her peering towards the Middle Falls at Inspiration Point. The other was of me, Bobbie and Becky, looking for all the world like a happy family group posing by the Wadsworth Fountain at the Genesee Valley Hunt parade in 1996.

It was past two thirty when we left the flat, Angela's car full of black bags stuffed with my dad's clothes and smaller possessions. We also had on board his hi-fi, which Valerie had asked to keep for her bedroom, and a small box containing the letters, the painting, the atlas, the scrapbook and the photograph album. Our first stop on the way home was at a charity shop in the town center where we left the clothes for re-sale. We then called briefly at one of Angela's friends, to whom my aunt had asked my permission to give some of Dad's crockery. This all felt so strange to me, being asked such questions, being made so plainly aware that I had now inherited Dad's belongings and therefore required consultation before they were disposed of or passed on to someone else. It was not a situation with which I was entirely at ease.

Valerie arrived home soon after us. Her bedroom is on the first floor, the ground floor as they call it in England, and was formerly the dining room. This means that meals are taken at a table squeezed into the living room. It also means that there are two spare bedrooms upstairs, the larger of which, the one I had been allocated, was once Valerie's. The smaller room had been Anna's, though I found not a single reminder of her presence when I took a sneaking look while Angela helped her surviving daughter to change out of her day clothes and into a loose-fitting jogging suit. My aunt confines her mementos to the crowded living room. There is a photograph of Uncle Michael on a shelf near the TV; another, on an aging sideboard, is of the whole family, taken when the girls were in their early teens. On the mantelpiece is a photo of my mom and dad, next to which is a small, black and white snap shot of Grandpa and Grandma Wright walking along the promenade at Eastbourne. The most prominent picture, however, is hung on the wall above where the table stands. It is an exquisite shot of Michael and Anna standing on the bridge across the Lower Falls, taken on the day in 1986 when Mom and I had gone with our English visitors first on a Holton Tour, then to the Park.

'I have a copy of that, William.' Angela said, entering the room and catching me spellbound by the photograph. 'Would you like it?'

'I'd love it.' I told her.

'I'll dig it out for you later. Val usually goes to bed about half past eight. I thought maybe you and I could have a chat.'

'That sounds great.'

The three of us ate dinner, which consisted of boiled potatoes, boiled carrots and boiled cabbage served alongside steak and kidney pie. Tinned fruit cocktail followed, accompanied by some sort of synthetic cream prepared by whisking an off-white powder into half a pint of milk. It was evident that, to both Angela and Valerie, eating was a necessity of survival not a route to pleasure. I washed the dishes, despite Angela's protestations, then joined her and Valerie once again in the living room where they were watching some long-running soap opera set in the north of England, where apparently everyone has an accent like that girl in *Frasier*. This was followed by some feeble sit-com that made *Home Improvement* look like a work of comedic genius.

Valerie did indeed go off to bed at eight thirty, astonishing me once again with her ability to do just about everything for herself, including maneuvering from her wheelchair on to her bed, undressing and donning a night-gown, before sliding beneath the sheets and nestling down to sleep. Angela went to check on her after ten minutes or so, but she was soon back, settling herself stiffly in one of the easy chairs. Everything about her body language portended some important announcement.

'There's something odd here, isn't there?' I said, saving her from having to initiate the discussion. 'I've felt something ever since I arrived.'

Angela lowered her head and breathed out heavily through her nose. 'I'm sorry, William.' she said, looking up again. 'It's just so hard to talk about.'

'Shall we try?' I suggested.

'It's just that he told me things. I don't know *why* he told me, but he did.'

'What things?'

'Oh, things about Fay, about how ill she'd been, about how it had effected them both. It was so unlike him. He came here about a week before he died and he sat where you are now and he just told me these things, completely out of the blue. I didn't know what to say.' She paused for a few seconds, twisting her mouth perhaps to accentuate the difficulty she had in articulating all this. 'Do you think he wanted me to tell you?' she asked.

'I don't know.' I replied. 'How could I?'

'Didn't he speak to you at all?'

'He called me a couple weeks back and told me what happened when my sister died. Is that what he told you too?'

'No. He never mentioned it. All he talked about was him and Fay and........'

She stopped and sat silently, twisting her mouth again.

'And what?' I asked.

'Their..... You know, William. Their... their *life* together?'

'Their *sex* life?'

Angela looked both shocked and relieved. 'Yes.' she sighed.

'What about it?'

'Well, he said there really wasn't one. Not after your sister....... He and Fay loved one another, but she couldn't......'

'Have intercourse?'

My English aunt was now red in the face at this directness. 'He didn't say that. He said your mum lost interest. He didn't blame her. He understood. She was ill, William.'

'I know. Kelly seems to think she had some internal deformity. Even before the cancer.'

Angela shook her head. 'These things are terrible, aren't they William? I've never known anyone so in love with someone else than Eddie was with Fay. He wasn't the sort who said anything about it, but you could tell. I think it must have hurt him a lot when the, you know, the bedroom part of the marriage faded. That's why he did what he did, I suppose.'

'And what did he do?'

'He had other women.'

She said it bluntly and with all the force of a millstone cast to the floor from her shoulders. 'When?' I asked.

'After you'd got married. He just said he'd been unfaithful. He seemed terribly upset even at the thought of it, full of regret.'

'Women in Geneseo?'

'Yes. I don't know who, I don't know how many, but I'd guess from the way he spoke that there were maybe a two or three.'

'This is weird.' I said. 'He called me to talk about how Jackie had died, he came to you to admit infidelity. It sounds like he was making a final confession before he died.'

'I think he was.' Angela replied sullenly.

'He killed himself, didn't he?'

Angela visibly shuddered. 'Yes.' she said, as though some great vacuum had sucked all the air from her lungs.

'How?' I asked.

'Sleeping pills. He took a whole bottle.'

My aunt had still not regained her breath and was looking worryingly pale.

'Would you like a drink?' I asked, aware that I was peculiarly calm.

'I've got some brandy in the cabinet.' Angela wheezed. 'Val sometimes takes some when the pain's intolerable.'

'I'll fix us some.' I said.

I went to the cabinet near the table and took out the bottle of cheap brandy. Angela appeared to possess only tumblers and short-stemmed wineglasses, two of the latter being my choice as vessels for the giant shots I poured. The brandy tasted sharp and burned as I swallowed it, but the feeling of it trickling down my insides was entirely pleasing. Angela sipped at her drink, flinching slightly at the sharpness. Neither of us said anything.

After a minute or two, my aunt set her glass down on the hearth and left the room. I heard her footsteps on the stairs, then the door of the bathroom close behind her. When she re-emerged, she went first to her bedroom to collect a box of tissues, then to the room I been had given. Evidently, she found in there Dad's photograph album, which I had left resting on my suitcase.

Returning to the living room, she sat down again in her chair and turned through the pages of the album, not so much studying the pictures as searching for something in particular. At last she came upon the paper bag that contained the photos of Mom at the Middle Falls and Bobbie, Becky and I by the fountain.

'This is Becky, I presume.' she said, seeming to stroke the child's hair with her little finger.

'Yeah. She's a pretty kid.' I replied.

'I can see my mum in her, especially around the eyes.'

This comment did not register with me for a moment, then it abruptly hit me. 'You know who her father is?' I asked.

'Yes, I do.' Angela said somberly.

Before retiring for the night, I needed to take another glass of the discount store brandy. It did little to calm my mind, however. All night my head was filled with images that infiltrated not just my dreams, but also the limbo hours of semi-consciousness in between. I craved the arrival of daylight, though the sun did not rise until past seven o'clock and it was almost an hour after that that the pearl colored sky took on any form of luminescence. I cannot remember a longer night.

That day, Tuesday, equipped with a rather dated street map, I took a long, long walk around the town, heading first along the route of the Icknield Way, then turning to pass Castle Corset and cross the railway bridge so as to arrive at the town center. I took photographs as I went, shots of the tree-lined lower reaches of Broadway, of the out of service fountain in the Kennedy Gardens, of the museum and the library, of the art-deco façade of the Broadway Cinema. Beyond the shops and offices were streets of perfect English houses, all with perfect English gardens, so similar to the one my parents had created at home. In truth, everywhere I went I was reminded of Geneseo, of its streets framed by grass verges and mature trees, of its tranquillity, of its feeling of security, even coziness. By lunchtime, I had circled much of the southern end of the town and had made my way back to the center. I found a pub, bought a sandwich there and drank my first pint of real English beer, a rich, ochre ale that actually gained in flavor as it warmed near the open fire, a picture of Ebenezer Howard staring down at me. It was a revelation.

After leaving the pub, I went to a nearby florist, passing close by the old Icknield Halls and Betjamin's Garden City café. I bought roses, just as I do in Geneseo, then set off again, through the glass-roofed Arcade and down the gentle hill of Station Road. Passing this time *beneath* the railway, I walked for maybe a quarter of a mile before reaching Norton Common, where I plodded through some muddy grass, then along a broad clearing until I arrived at the path down which I had pushed Valerie two days before. This time, I carried on past the Pix Brook and walked all the way to the opposite side of the Common, to the leafy, undulating Wilbury Road.

The house in which my grandparents had lived was a further half hour walk away, a walk that took me again across the brook, through a coppice of aging trees and past homes even more plainly utilitarian than my aunt's. That house where Dad and Angela had been born and raised, the house in which my mom had stayed when she went to Letchworth for Angela's wedding seemed to me strangely mundane. It was smaller than I had imagined, its walls gray with age, its windows tiny, its whole appearance solid and unpretentious. I studied it for a while in complete solitude, save for a bony cat that eyed me suspiciously from the top of a neighboring fence. Nobody came by, apart from an elderly lady in a little Japanese car that disappeared throatily around the bend in the road.

From the house, I walked through the increasingly cold afternoon to the cemetery. Angela had told me roughly where the graves were, but it still took some time to find them, especially my grandparents' which was obscured slightly by a hawthorn bush. I knelt beside it, facing the open book fashioned from marble that is the headstone. 'John Edward Wright' it reads on one side. 'Edith May Wright' it reads on the other. I placed a rose for each of them on the green shingle that fills the marble enclosure, spreading some of the shingle over the stems so as to secure the flowers from the wind. I said a brief prayer, then sat in silent reflection for a few minutes, the birds in the bush twittering noisily, the sound of an aircraft rumbling high overhead.

The next grave I found was that of Uncle Michael and again I laid out a rose, this time at the foot of the black headstone, its gold lettering setting out just his name, his age and date of death. I said a few words to my uncle, then moved away, seeking out the grave of his daughter, my cousin. Her headstone was, in contrast to her father's, almost pure white, flecked and colored only by the elements. 'Anna May Salter' it read. 'Taken from us on November 13th 1986. Darling daughter and beloved sister. Sleeping in the arms of angels.'

I knelt by the headstone and arranged two roses such that their stems intertwined. Then I sat back on the damp ground and silently prayed for her in my usual clumsy way, telling her I how so very sorry I was that I had not visited sooner.

That evening, I could sense Angela trying to make up for what had happened the previous day. Once more we ate a meal that took blandness into a new dimension, but, instead of settling down afterwards to watch TV, Angela asked me to help her retrieve a box from her attic. 'What's in it?' I asked, as I hauled it down the stairs.

'It's all the stuff from my mum and dad's house.' Angela explained. 'All the little bits and pieces. I don't remember exactly what's in there, but I thought I'd get it out so you can see whether there's anything of interest.'

I reached the living room and lowered the box onto the rug by the fireplace. Angela passed me some scissors and I ran one of the blades along the taped seam. The box creaked slightly, then slowly opened. I pulled at the flaps and bent them back, conscious that the box had not been opened for a long time, maybe even since Grandma Wright died in 1969.

Most of its content was ornaments, inexpensive china dogs and souvenir-style gifts brought back by friends from seaside holidays. I found an egg timer and a porcelain butter dish, a rusted alarm clock and a doll in traditional Welsh dress. There were five albums of cards collected from Brooke-Bond tea packets, a book about herbs, a bag full of silver three-penny pieces, a well-thumbed copy of *Lady Chatterly's Lover*. It was all so fascinating, not because of the intrinsic value of these items, but because they had been handled by my grandparents, because they had been part of the Wrights' every day lives. Valerie, leaning forward unsteadily in her wheelchair, found Grandma Wright's pay packet from the Spirella Company, a discovery that struck wonderment into her face. She held it like a holy relic, laid out flat on her palms, the brittle brown paper shaking as she trembled. I looked into her dark eyes, and saw my silhouette reflected in the brilliance of her amazement.

'I thought it was mostly old rubbish in there.' she said. 'I didn't know there were any papers.'

'I don't think there's anything else like that.' I told her, rummaging through more keepsakes and domestic flotsam.

'Eddie told me you were studying history.' Angela commented. 'He said you'd be interested in all this.'

'I am.' I said.

Valerie looked across at me, her eyes still full of excitement. 'Would you like to see the work we've done on our family tree?' she asked.

'Yes *please*.' I replied.

Angela went to her bedroom and brought back a folder of papers, of certificates and wills, of hand-drawn charts with names dating back to the early years of the nineteenth century. She told me about these people, about her elfin grandmother Rose, about her great-great-aunt Emma drinking Hugh Bletchley's disgusting cure-all, about her Uncle Percy, about foul-mouthed Maud West and the Welshman who broke the heart of her father's Aunt Gin. It was wonderful and our conversation that evening capped what had been, surprisingly, a very pleasant day. Somehow, I had managed to deal with Angela's revelations. I had put them in place, filed them away, so to speak. Much as Kelly would undoubtedly disagree, this was not denial. Instead, it was the result of the subconscious reasoning that had been in process throughout the time I had spent walking that day. It was as though some great fog had lifted and the way ahead had suddenly come into the sharpest focus.

The following day, I walked again into the town center, this time catching a train at the station and journeying out to Cambridge. The landscape must have changed greatly since the time when Dad and Angela met the GIs, back in 1942, though still it is mostly rural and still there are vehicles on the chalk heath that kick up clouds of white dust. At Cambridge, I hired a cab that took me out to Madingley. The great hall, where Walter and Rose Wright once worked, stood grandly in fine parkland, a small lake near the gatehouse, the earthwork line of the one-time village street running through the grassland like a long-drained riverbed. In the adjacent churchyard I sought out my great-grandparents' overgrown grave and placed flowers amidst the shamble of weeds. From there, I walked the up-hill mile to the American Military Cemetery, a great panorama of perfectly aligned crosses, intermingled with Stars of David indicating the last resting places of Jewish servicemen. I was, for half an hour, back in America, aware of familiar accents, watched over by a huge Stars and Stripes rippling in the wind. In Section C, I found Philip Holton's grave. I was the first member of his family to visit his burial place and somehow I sensed that he knew I was there, knew who I was.

Unadvisedly, given it was mostly by way of a busy road, I walked back into Cambridge, where I spent the rest of the afternoon being a tourist, visiting the colleges, standing on the Bridge of Sighs, eating an impromptu snack on Jesus Green, strolling across Midsummer Common. Once more, I felt settled, at ease. The way forward seemed clear, clearer than it had seemed for years.

Dad's funeral was the following morning. The flowers, including the lilies from Kelly, began arriving around nine o'clock and were laid out on the lawn to await the arrival of the hearse. By mid-day, it was all over, including the interment. Angela had decided not to prepare food for a wake, but had instead asked all the mourners to join us for a drink at the former Wilbury Hotel, which is just across the road from the cemetery. Only Joe and Dorothy Meninski took up the invitation. We sat in the family area of the bar, which must once have been quite comfortable, but which was now scruffy and defiled by gaming machines and a noisy jukebox. Even so, Angela told us, it was very different from the old days when her father had drunk in there, when there had been a wooden floor strewn with sawdust and spittoons at either end of the room. The Meninskis were heading back to New York the next day, they told us, but they wanted us all to join them for dinner that evening at their hotel. Angela demurred, using Valerie's need for an early night as an excuse, which meant that I went alone, taking a cab out to the oldest part of the town, to the very heart of the ancient manor, Letchworth Hall, which is nowadays a hotel overlooking the golf course. The moment I saw the place, I realized I had seen it before, on the day of my wedding. There is a photograph of it on one of the landings at the Glen Iris Inn.

Poor Joe looked his age. His face was a puzzle of crags and creases; his eyes and his complexion were both jaded. Dorothy, too, looked tired and, although the evening was relaxing and the food made an enjoyable change from the fare served up by my aunt, we all found matters petering out long before ten o'clock. The Meninskis had a plane to catch the next morning and my mind was very much on the same journey that I would be making a day later. I fear now that I may have seemed preoccupied when I was with them, that my yearning to get back home was stronger than my desire for Joe to tell me about his friendship with my dad. I wish now I had taken more time, that I had not, perhaps, used Joe's weariness as a reason not to ask more questions.

That same preoccupation manifested itself the next evening, too, when Valerie and I went to the Two Chimneys pub. The weather was fine, if a little cold, and we decided to go there on foot, or rather I decided to go on foot and to push Valerie along in her wheelchair. It was no more than half a mile, but, by the time we reached the warmth of the smoky bar, I was exhausted. Pushing a wheelchair is not, in itself, too difficult, but the awkwardness of negotiating curbs, of crossing roads and of coping with steps is wearying.

I bought beer for myself, a fragrant East Anglian brew this time, and wine for Valerie, then steered my cousin behind a corner table, where we studied the menu. The food was simple, inexpensive by English standards and far tastier than the staid cuisine I had been served at the hotel the previous evening. Valerie made an entertaining dining companion and more of that superb beer loosened me up to a point of relaxation I had not experienced ever since Angela had called to tell me of Dad's death. Yet, once again, the journey home was on my mind. I felt as though my business in England was done. I had come to bury my father, but I had learned, even before his body had been laid in the cemetery, that my visit had another purpose too. I had reached what Gary Lennart often refers to as a binary moment, a point at which people are confronted with just two options, heads or tails, stay or go, black or white, no gray. I had, of course, been shocked at what Angela had told me, but, by the following morning, it had all assumed its place in the perspective of my life. Somehow it had brought clarity, helped me cut through the gray and see the stark and distinct contrasts of black and white.

As we walked home again, we talked about Anna, the first time we had done so all evening.

'She loved you.' Valerie said with complete lack of compunction.

'I know.' I replied. 'She told me. I think I'd given her some mixed signals.'

'No, Will. She was always like that. It wasn't just you.'

'So she fell in love with lots of people?'

'Quite a few. Almost all of them completely the wrong sort for her. No offence meant, Will.'

'No problem. I understand. I presume the guy she was with on the night she died fell into that same category.'

'Yeah. He was bad news. He'd been in a lot of trouble. Drugs mostly, petty theft, disorderly behavior. He was on probation when the accident happened.'

'What made Anna that way? What made her go for unsuitable men?'

'Rebellion. She wanted to upset our parents, especially our dad. He was really strict with us when we were children. We were scared stiff of him. He used to lock us in our room if we misbehaved, or sometimes even take his slipper to us. I remember once having two great welts on my thighs from where he'd hit me.'

'That's appalling.'

'I know, but the stupid thing was that he really loved us. He was so worried about some harm coming to us that he used those punishments to keep us on the straight and narrow. It mostly worked with me, but Anna was much more bloody-minded. Once she got to about seventeen, she completely flipped. She realized she could get her own back on dad by associating with, as you put it, unsuitable men. What's more, she tended to fall in love with them, to give herself too easily, maybe because, unlike me, she couldn't see dad's love through his strictness, or because she was looking to escape dad by going off with one of those men.'

'You've thought about this a lot, haven't you?'

'When you're stuck in a wheelchair, there's often not too much more you *can* do other than think.'

She reached up to touch my hand, which was turning numb from the cold. 'Did I frighten you when I came over to visit you and Kelly?' she asked, tilting her head to look up at me.

'You terrified me.'

'Sorry. When Anna died, I was really angry. I blamed my parents, which was ridiculous, but I knew she'd behaved as she had because of the way she'd been treated by dad. In the end, it killed her. For a while, all I wanted to do was punish him, even though he was so obviously punishing himself. I used to wear her old clothes sometimes. I tried to look like her and act like her. I suppose I wanted dad to feel haunted. What I did was unforgivable. Now *I'm* being punished.'

'Why? Because of the MS?'

'Yes.'

I thought it was a crazy notion and told her so, but she was adamant. I figured it was her way of explaining her condition. In fact, she seemed thankful that she *could* explain it rather than being left constantly with the question 'Why?' It gave her a strange degree of contentment.

Aunt Angela had gone to bed when we got back to the house. I offered to make coffee, but Valerie was tired and needed to get some sleep. I helped her out of her coat and boots, then crouched down beside her and kissed her on the cheek. Again she touched my hand, then smiled, wished me 'Goodnight' and wheeled herself into her room.

I had already packed my suitcase, which was laying open on the bed. Beside it was an envelope and a tatty old shoebox, both put there since Valerie and I had left for the Two Chimneys. I looked first in the envelope, where my aunt had placed a brand new copy of the photograph of Michael and Anna at the Letchworth Park. Then, I lifted the lid of the box and there, dusty and dog-eared, was Dad's childhood postcard collection.

I shall always remember the look on Bobbie's face when I told her, last Friday night, that I was not going to sleep with her. We had, between us, finished the bottle of red wine I had found. Bobbie was beyond merry and almost all the way to smashed, but she still knew what I was saying. It was not her condition that put me off, or any lack of attraction, or, for that matter, any lack of desire. I wanted to take her to bed, but I knew it would complicate things.

'So what do we do now?' she asked me, her voice like a record played at the wrong speed.

'I guess we hit the hay.' I replied. 'You look beat.'

'I am.' she said, stretching her arms and yawning heartily.

'You can have my bed.' I told her.

She looked at me uncertainly, her alcohol-slowed mind trying to work out my inference.

'You can have my bed.' I repeated, as though to a very dim child. 'I'll sleep in the little room.'

'You're not sleeping with me?' she asked, at last becoming attuned to the turn of events.

'Not tonight, Bobbie.' I said.

Her face was a confusion of indignation and sadness, tinged with resignation. I helped her to her feet, surprised at how heavy she was, a dead weight requiring both my arms to pull her out of her seat. 'Go on.' I ushered her. 'Get up the stairs. I'll come and say goodnight in a few minutes.'

She huffed and walked lead-footed into the hall and then clumped up the stairs. I watched her go, fearful she would lose her balance and tumble back down, but she made it to the landing. I heard her open the door to my bedroom, the shuffle of her footsteps across the floor, then silence. I guessed she had made it to the bed.

I took our glasses through to the kitchen and swilled them under some tepid water, then left them inverted on the draining rack. I took out some plates from the cupboard and placed them on the table in the back room, ready for the following morning's breakfast. I then turned off all the downstairs lights and made my way up to see Bobbie.

The door to my bedroom was open and, in the borrowed light from the landing, I could see her slumped across the bed, fully clothed. I took her shoes from her feet, expecting her to wake as I did so, or at least to stir. She was utterly still, however, her breathing noiseless. She was in the deepest sleep. I moved her up the bed a way, her long hair splaying across the pillows as I tried to make her head as comfortable as I could. I thought about removing her pants, maybe opening her blouse a little, but that seemed too much like taking advantage of her, even though that was not the intention. Instead, I just pulled the quilt over her, taking care to ensure she was on her side, worried that, after the rich meal and all that wine, she might choke on her own vomit. I then left her, leaving the door slightly ajar, and went into Jackie's room.

I slept for an hour or so. Whatever woke me did a thorough job, because nothing I could do would induce further sleep. I lay in that tiny bedroom for a while, but I knew it was futile. Eventually, I went downstairs to get a book from the study.

I know now that I shall probably never tell Bobbie all that I found out from Angela. She clearly had no real desire to talk about my dad beyond a relatively superficial level. She was afraid to go further, but that fear was nothing compared with my own. I knew that telling her everything I had discovered would take our relationship on to another plain, in the same way as sleeping with her would have done. It would have been our Rubicon. Once crossed, we could never go back. We would have to deal with whatever lay on the other side and it was trepidation of that unknown that made me remain on this safe side of the line. The problem is Becky. I have always been minded to take care of her, but that has been solely because of Bobbie's situation, which, whilst never precarious, thanks to Charlie and Rose, has also never been affluent. I have paid for treats mostly, sometimes for schoolbooks, always dressing these as gifts rather than as charity. I try to help out on school assignments whenever I can. I support and I encourage. I guess I take the role of a godfather, although Becky was never christened. In the last week, though, I have sensed a greater obligation upon me. I have felt that I ought to behave less as a godfather does and more as a real father. This is not because Becky is my daughter, but because she is my half-sister.

I have known Bobbie all my life and there have been times, especially when I moved back to Geneseo after Mom's death, when I have felt drawn to her with feelings that are deeper than those of even the closest friendship. Yet, we have never been more than close friends. We have never been lovers, we have never shared the same bed. I know that in recent years my desire for independence, for living alone, has prevented me from considering a cohabiting relationship with anyone, not just Bobbie. I enjoyed my time with Sarah Weston largely *because* she had a home in Toronto – we had not one conversation about my moving in with her or about Sarah coming to live with me in Geneseo. We each had our own lives and that helped make our brief relationship so pleasurable. It was always like two strangers meeting one another for the first time. Finally, of course, distance came between us and that made me realize that, if I wanted to sustain a relationship, it would need to be with someone closer to hand, more accessible. Immediately, that means compromising one's independence, which I know is why I have not pursued such a relationship with anyone, including Bobbie, who would be the closest to hand, the most accessible. Now I believe I am prepared to make that compromise and that is entirely due to what my Aunt Angela had to tell me last week.

There was little detail in her retelling of how Dad had taken Bobbie back home after the Wrights and the Petersens had been to the Hewsons' house on the evening before Christmas Eve in 1989. He had dropped Bobbie at the end of the Petersen's driveway, then had driven home here, where he had helped Mom into bed and sat with her for the short while it had taken her to fall asleep. Then he had driven back to Charlie and Rose's place. He offered no explanation as to why; neither did he mention Bobbie's reaction to his returning to see her. I guess she must have let him inside voluntarily, let him go up to her room, where maybe they sat on that worn old sofa, maybe drinking coffee as I was to do a few days later. All he told Angela was that it was then that it had happened, then when Becky had been conceived. I do not know if this was something he forced upon Bobbie, whether it was something she felt unable to prevent or whether it was something she encouraged, maybe just one episode in a long affair. I wanted to talk with her about it on Friday night, but I found myself unable and unwilling to do so. It matters little, it changes nothing. Becky is my dad's child and now my dad has gone I feel a burden of responsibility, even if Dad never felt this, even if Bobbie has never expected it. The only thing I had to decide was whether I fulfilled that responsibility by becoming Bobbie's husband or by some other means, a decision influenced profoundly by my new relationship with Kelly.

I placed two flowers on Anna's grave last week, one for her and one for her unborn child. She died taking a risk, riding at speed on a motorbike driven by a young guy who had been drinking beer in a pub all evening. I believe she was living out on the edge, tempting fate, goading it perhaps. She did not care. Death was no worse an option than life. She was as messed up as any of those bawling adolescents Kelly is seen interviewing on WONM.

The father of the child Anna was carrying when she died was someone called Rick, a young man, twenty-two years old if I remember correctly, who she had met long before she came to Geneseo in 1986 and who she had seen mainly at parties. The only relationship between them had been sexual and that, she told me, had been infrequent. I am suspicious that she used this Rick to deliberately get herself pregnant after it became apparent that I was not prepared to be unfaithful to Kelly. If this is true, then it only confirms how desperate she was for me, which I find deeply disturbing. Maybe, as Valerie suggested, her desperation was not specifically for me, but simply for love. It is my fault, of course. On that June evening when we went to the Park together, I made an enormous error. I yielded to the most basic of instincts. I allowed physical desire, lust, to overcome good sense.

By the time I had convinced Anna to leave the overlook at Inspiration Point, the sun had disappeared completely behind the hills, leaving the Upper Falls and the railroad trestle obscured by the blanket of night. Once back in the car, I turned on the engine and made to reverse out of the parking space. However, as I turned to look out the rear window, Anna placed a hand on my arm and looked straight at me.

'Thanks.' she said.

'What for?' I asked.

'For bringing me here.' she replied. 'It was beautiful. Thanks for spending so much time with me.'

'I've enjoyed it.' I told her. 'Apart from that nonsense about.......'

'Sorry.' Anna said, though the look on her face was more mischievous than apologetic. She leaned across and kissed my cheek. 'Let's not go straight home.' she continued. 'Let's stay here and talk for a while. I like talking to you.'

'Is that a good idea, Anna?' I asked her.

She kissed me again, more lingeringly. 'I think so.' she purred into my ear. 'I think we've got a lot we can talk about.'

I knew I was about to make an immense mistake, but I did not have the strength of will, or maybe it was the wish, to turn her down. I switched off the ignition, pulled on the brake, then turned to face Anna. In the dimness, the big white dots all over her blue dress glowed luminously, as did the matching white buttons down the front.

'This is crazy.' I said to her. 'I'm engaged to be married. I love Kelly. I shouldn't be here with you like this. Do you have any idea what your parents would say?'

'Will, I love you.' was Anna's response to this.

'Jeez, Anna, will you quit saying that?'

'*No*. It's true.'

Even in the increasing darkness, I could now clearly see tears turning her eyes into moist pools. 'Please, Anna.' I said. 'Please stop crying. You've got to get real here. You've got to -'

She lurched towards me, cutting me off in mid-sentence by attempting to kiss me again, this time full on the lips. I turned my head, but I could hear her whispering something under her breath as she nestled her face against my neck.

'What are you saying?' I asked. 'I can't hear.'

She muttered a few words that were entirely inaudible.

'*What?*' I asked again.

'Kiss me.' she said, with perfect clarity now. 'Kiss me, Will.'

I still remember the instant I succumbed, the absolute instant. I placed my lips against hers, which parted slightly. I felt her tongue probing, coaxing me to open my mouth, which I did. I was holding her awkwardly across the handbrake and the gearshift, rubbing her back to begin with, then stroking her arms. It felt like being seduced by an angel, a dark-haired angel whose tears were now dampening my own face and whose skin was so ethereally silken. I opened one of the big buttons on that polka-dot dress and slid my fingers inside. It was then, right then that I knew for certain that she truly had been made in heaven.

'Dear *God* I want you Anna.' I said.

'I know.' my cousin replied, as she opened another of those buttons, then fiddled crossly with the next. Somehow the sight of her wrestling with the button had an effect upon me similar to an awakening, as though I were suddenly snapped back to my senses. Although Anna claimed to love me, although she may even have believed that claim was true, the way she was behaving did not seem driven by love, or even by passion. It seemed, instead, to be the product of despair, a frantic desire simply to give herself to me.

'No Anna.' I said, placing my hand upon hers, stopping her now frenzied attempts to unthread the recalcitrant button. 'No.' I repeated. 'This is wrong.'

Anna whimpered like a baby as we drove back that night to Geneseo. I do not recall saying anything, even when we arrived at the Petersens' house. She climbed out of the car and walked away, entering the house without once looking back. I did not go straight home afterwards. I drove to Highland Park and pulled the car into an unlit spot near the fence that screens the nearby gardens. I turned off the lights and unfastened my seat belt, then tilted by head back and stared at the ceiling, which was no more than a few inches from my face. I was scared, scared that someone would find out what had happened with Anna, scared, especially, that that someone would be either my mom or Kelly. I was also angry, angry for many different reasons. I was angry with Anna. I was angry with myself for allowing the situation to occur. I was even, in an unacknowledgeable recess of my mind, angry that I had not taken the chance to make love with such a gorgeous young woman who was offering herself to me on a plate.

Anna may have been messed up, but, on that warm June night, she was nowhere nearly as messed up as me.

The sun was passing into its lingering decline, that low afternoon arc across the mid October sky. The air was still for a while, the sun's warmth pleasant against my face. I watched the river flow past, glancing behind constantly, twitchily, like a bird in open country. It was not yet three o'clock and I knew that Kelly was always punctual. I turned to face the far side of the river, across to where I knew the Parade Grounds are hidden beyond the elms and birches, beyond the conical spruces and the maples glowing lava-like in the steadily deepening shadows of the forest. The Genesee hissed and rushed beneath me, Sarah Letchworth's words rhymed inanimately beside me. High above, clouds were beginning to gather where, in around three hours, the sun would set in a blaze of dragon's breath that would fade quickly through cooling embers to total darkness.

I looked back again, but there was no sign of Kelly or of anyone else. I was, for a few moments, completely alone. I turned once more to gaze at the river, whispering to my mom, begging with her to help me. I no longer needed her guidance. I knew what I wanted and now I was beseeching her spirit to make that come to pass.

I thought for a moment about the photographs I had found after Mom's death, the ones she had kept in that Fortnum & Mason biscuit tin. There was one she had taken on my wedding day, an informal version of the picture our official photographer had composed, a shot of Kelly and I at Inspiration Point, standing face to face, each holding the other's hands, the Upper and Middle Falls framed between us. Mom had displayed that official photo on

Grandma's old sideboard and had left it there even after Kelly and I had divorced. I never much liked it. It was so obviously contrived, so stiff, so lacking in feeling or spontaneity. Mom's snapshot was far better, capturing an impudent smile on my new wife's face as we relieved the boredom of endless posing by making cryptic, whispered cracks about the fussily artistic photographer. Forty-eight hours after Mom had been laid to rest on Temple Hill, I removed the photo from the sideboard and replaced it with Mom's more relaxed picture. Two weeks later, Dad left for England and took the snapshot with him. When I moved back to Geneseo for good, I put a photo of Mom and Dad where the wedding snap had stood. It was an act of closure, or so I thought. Now I have that snapshot back in my possession and, as I waited at the Point this afternoon, I tried to recreate the scene in my mind.

Then she was there, as if she had suddenly, magically appeared. She was a few yards away, walking towards me, her eyes wide, betraying the grin she was trying hard to suppress. She was wearing blue jeans, tight blue jeans, and calf skin boots and a white shirt unbuttoned to just above her waist and, beneath the shirt, a white body as tight as her jeans. Her hair was all over the place, blown by the wind through an open car window, but it was held back from her face by a pair of sunglasses balanced stylishly on her head. At last, she was in front of me, within reach.

'You came.' I said.

'I came.' she said.

I saw the eternity ring, not on her left hand, but on her right. I did not comment. Instead, I took her in my arms and held her.

'Thank God you're here.' I sobbed. 'I love you so very much.'

Kelly looked up at me and wiped away a tear that was dribbling down my cheek. 'Don't cry, Will.' she said. 'Be happy.'

'Are you here to stay?' I asked.

'Yes.' she replied.

'Then I'll be happy.' I told her.

We stood at the Point for a while and talked about meaningless things, things like how long it had taken her to drive from the city, things like how the weather had been on her journey, things like the volume of traffic on the roads. What strange banality we speak in times of high emotion. I spotted a hawk skimming the tops of the trees near the Middle Falls and Kelly strained to see it with a look of wonderment on her face that I thought had been forever supplanted by weary cynicism. I put my arm around her shoulders and she cuddled up against me, her haphazard hair blowing softly in the reawakening breeze.

After some time, we walked to her car, which she had parked right next to my own, then each of us drove back along the Park Road, skirting Mount Morris and heading into Geneseo.

'Wow.' Kelly said when she saw the inside of the house. 'You've made this place look so good.'

'Thanks.' I replied. 'It took me a while.'

'You did it all yourself?' Kelly asked.

'Yeah. The decoration anyway. I got someone else to lay the carpets and a guy from Avon to fix the rotten wood around the windows.'

Kelly looked into the kitchen, then the back room, then the front room. She checked out the study, then went again into the kitchen, where she opened drawers and looked inside the oven as though making a health inspection.

'Have you cleaned the place especially for me?' she asked.

'No.' I told her, feigning hurt. 'I live very tidily.'

'So do I.' Kelly said. 'But this is incredible. I'm going to love living here.'

'Is that what's going to happen?'

'Yes it is. That's if you still want me to live here.'

'You know I do. I told you in my letter.'

Kelly walked back into the hall, motioning towards me, indicating that I should follow her. We went into the front room and sat down, Kelly on one of the armchairs, me on the sofa. She assumed a pose of business-like formality.

'I've resigned my job.' she announced. 'I'll need to go back for three weeks, but I want you to come with me, if that's OK with you. I'll look for some work around here, maybe go back to radio or do some freelance reporting for the local newspaper. I could even help you run this film archive you've told me about. I'm going to rent out my apartment. I'll move out all the expensive furniture, maybe bring it here or ask my folks to store it for me down in Hershey –'

'I can organize all that.' I interrupted her.

'I hoped you'd say that.' she smiled.

'Kelly.' I said, trying carefully to pause the gathering momentum. 'There's something I need to tell you before we settle all this.'

She sat up even straighter. 'OK.' she said.

'It's about Bobbie Petersen.' I began. Kelly frowned, evidently wondering what bombshell I was about to drop. 'It's all right.' I continued. 'It's actually more about her daughter, Becky.'

'What about her?' Kelly asked.

'She's my dad's.' I said. 'She's his daughter.'

'You're kidding me.'

'No I'm not. Dad told Aunt Angela about her a few weeks before he died. He confessed a lot of things actually, but the most important was about Becky.'

'A confession?'

'Yeah. Sort of like a verbal suicide note, though Angela didn't know that at the time.'

'He committed *suicide*?'

'That's right.'

Kelly got up from the chair and came to sit with me on the sofa. 'I'm so sorry, Will.' she said, taking hold of my hand, her face a medley of concern and incredulity.

'I'm OK.' I told her. 'I've dealt with it.'

'Are you sure?' she asked with patent skepticism.

'Yeah, I'm sure. I've not told Bobbie that I know. I took her out on Friday night and planned to tell her, but I couldn't. In the end, what does it matter? The important thing is that Becky is my half-sister and I want to make sure she's taken care of. That'll mostly mean financially, but I don't want the two of us being together again to lead to her being shut out of my life.'

'That's not a problem at all. She'll always be welcome here.'

'Good. I'd like to have Bobbie over this evening so that we can tell her what's happening.'

'Fine, but how will you be able to take care of Becky without Bobbie being suspicious of your motives?'

'I don't know. I've wondered that myself.'

'Tell her, Will. Tell her you know about Becky's father. Believe me, it'll be better that way. Secrets kept from people place limits on the relationship you can have with them.'

'From an academic point of view, you're probably right, but this isn't a classroom test, Kelly. This is real life. It's a lot more complicated.'

Kelly squeezed my hand. 'I know, Will.' she said. 'You have to do whatever you think is best. If you don't want to tell Bobbie, then that's fine. If you do, and you want my help, I'll be here for you.'

I tried to envisage the scene, with Kelly and I confronting Bobbie with what we know about her tryst, if that is what it was, with my dad. Much as I love Kelly, I still find it almost impossible to view her as a comforter of distressed women. I know all about her job and about her excellent qualifications, but her demeanor does not lend itself to consoling the injured or soothing the brows of the traumatized. Maybe it is the expensive clothes she wears. Maybe it is those glacial blue eyes.

Nevertheless, I was heartened by Kelly's preparedness to let my judgement overrule the psychology textbooks, a preparedness she had rarely, if ever, shown during our marriage. 'No.' I said, after a few moments' contemplation. 'I won't tell her. I'll sort something out with Charlie. I'll tell him I want to set up some sort of endowment in memory of my parents, which is kind of true. He knows how Bobbie hates taking what she sees as charity. I'm sure he can siphon the money through to Becky without Bobbie knowing where it originated.'

Kelly nodded approvingly and told me it sounded a good idea.

'There is just one thing *I*'d like to know, though, Will.' she said. 'And it doesn't matter what your answer is, I just think it's best to be open with one another now so that *we* don't have secrets come between us.' For an instant I thought of Anna, but there was surely no way Kelly could have discovered the truth of my relationship with my cousin. 'Have you ever slept with Bobbie?' she asked.

'No.' I told her honestly. 'She stayed over on Friday night and she did sleep in my bed, but I spent the night in Jackie's room.'

Kelly closed her eyes in what I was surprised to see was relief. She then leaned towards me and kissed me on the forehead. 'I've got something in my purse.' she said. 'Pass it over.' She had left the purse beside the armchair. I reached down, picked it up and handed it to her, whereupon she took out a small brown envelope no bigger than a couple of postage stamps. She opened out her hand and emptied the contents of the envelope on to her palm. It was the engagement ring I had bought her years ago. I picked it up and gazed at it for the first time in so long I could not remember. I held it up to the light and looked at the inside rim. There was the almost invisible engraving: K and W.

When I looked at Kelly again, she was holding out her left hand. I slipped the ring on to her third finger and she smiled with what appeared to be joyful disbelief.

'Tell me, Will.' she said. 'Is the upstairs of the house as nice as the downstairs?'

'I think so.' I replied.

'Well, take me up there and show me our bedroom.'

We were in bed until half an hour ago, when I left her to take a shower. Meanwhile, I came down here to my study and e-mailed my finished essay to Gary Lennart. I also called Bobbie to ask her over here this evening. I have no idea how she is going to react when she discovers that Kelly and I are reunited, that we have revived something that everyone, including us, thought had died and had been consigned to history.

I believe there is an inviolable bond between the past and the future and that, as Winston Churchill once said, the further we look back, the more we see forward. Like Churchill, my roots lie in the soil of both England and America. They have grown in the loam of East Anglia and in the fertile earth of the Genesee Valley. My Holton forebears have been imprisoned for debt, have indulged in adulterous familial affairs, have died in civil and world wars, have worked as salesmen and bankers and surveyors. While the Holtons' stock rose, the Staffords toiled grimly in the lower social reaches, one of my grandma's brothers starving to death in the Garden City of the Midwest. The Wrights, too, were of low degree, subsisting in London's slums until one of them, my grandfather, found escape in a very different Garden City, raising a family there with his wife, Edith Chapple, whose own line sprang from the Norfolk fens. There will be no more Holtons, no more Staffords, no more Chapples. I am the last of the line. I thought, until two weeks ago, that I would also be the last of the Wrights, my dear cousin being destined, it would seem, never to be a mother. Now there is Becky, though she is only a Wright by blood, not by upbringing. She may carry Wright genes, she may even, as my aunt believes, have echoes of the Chapple looks, but she will, unless and until she discovers who her father was, only ever be a Petersen. My responsibility to her is not just for her financial wellbeing, but also for her identity, for her place in history's eternal chain. Otherwise her bond with the past will be weakened by half and she will only ever be able to look back with one eye closed.

The card I picked up in church this morning is now beneath Becky's paperweight on the top of my bureau. I am going to keep it to remind me of today, the day I regained my own *Immortal Love*. I feel alive, recharged, not burdened by the weight of all those generations, but invigorated by being now at their summit, imbued with their knowledge and experience. I feel I am doing not just what is *right*, but also what my mom, in particular, would want and what she has assisted in bringing about. I feel blessed with a sense of resolve, with certainty. I just hope this is not delusion, for, as I know so well, the biggest fool is the one who only fools himself.

# Afterword

❀

The historical parts of this book stem from a fusion of original research and previously published material. The latter leaves me deeply indebted to various earlier works, in particular those authored by Irene Beale, James Seaver, Lockwood L. Doty, Katherine Barnes, Anna Patchett, Sherman Peer, Nancy O'Dea and Mervyn Miller. Anyone at all familiar with those works will doubtless see their influence on this book. I acknowledge and thank them all.

Reference to numerous Internet web sites has also yielded a mine of information used herein. My gratitude therefore goes to the often anonymous originators of those sites.

Many individuals have helped and guided me. I am especially thankful to Amie Alden, who has patiently answered countless questions. Others deserving of acknowledgement are: Bill Alden and his colleagues at WOKR Channel 13 in Rochester, NY; Dr Graham Hornett for his medical advice; Paul Jarrald and Anna Woodhouse, who, with Amie, formed the 'editorial board'.

My uncle and aunt, Fred and Jean, unknowingly gave much help on the Letchworth sections. My late grandparents – John, Violet, Fred and Ginny – were my constant inspiration, as was my own wonderful Uncle Michael who was taken from us far, far too soon. Like Will Wright, I also have an amazing mom, who may not see herself between these covers, but to whom I owe more than words can possibly say.

Finally, there is Lesley, who has supported and often accompanied me throughout this book's gestation. Wandering around graveyards can be few people's idea of a fun vacation, yet all she asks in return is a Cracker Barrel meal and a teapot to take home.

PB